Goyim

Goyim

Origins

Mitchell M. Loftin

ISBN-13 9781093165562

Txu001855526 Library of congress

Dedicated to my children, Ben, Caleb, Dan, Grace, Hannah, and Noah, and to God whose love strengthens me to face each new day as an adventure in Him

Empress of the Heavens 1
An Unjust Reward 23
The Royal Treatment 43
There's No Place Like Home 48
A New Start 55
A Cherished Moment 62
An Unwanted Calling 68
Trains up in the Sky 82
Three Unannounced Visitors 96
The City of Zion 109
The Path of Least Resistance 127
An Uncommon Man 144
The Remarkable Encounter 162
Forever and A Day 171
An Army of One 193
An Unexpected Confession 208
The Unplanned Trip 221
A Traitor in the Midst 239
A Scandalous Conclusion 254
Unlikely Allies 264
A Very Narrow Door 279
The Beginning of the End 299
A Timely Retribution 308
The Final Battle 326
The Prodigal's Return 342
Epilogue 351
Epi-Prologue 354

Chapter One
Empress of the Heavens

The silence of space is never as deafening as when it stifles the screams of death. This mantra best known by all guardsmen was silently illustrated by the shadowy figure wrestling in the dark and frigid corridor of the USSA Potomac's cargo bay. Hidden within the teeming sea of floating storage towers, the form struggled, its desperate battle aggravated by the constantly convulsing pitch of the giant hallway's floor. A moment later the struggle ceased, signaled by the almost seemingly silent gasp reminiscent of a soul's dying breath.

Frozen fingers now worked, fumbling to check and recheck each airtight seal of the stubborn shield-suit, its shoulder emblazoned with the glowing red, white and blue emblem of the nation's elite. The fingers, occasionally obscured by the trail of frozen condensation floating forward each time the shadow exhaled, performed their meticulous dance. The snapping and re-snapping of the now compliant seals was compulsively repeated to a familiar cadence beneath the shadow's breath. Each frozen canto struggled against being drowned by the rhythmical melody of the storage bay's robotic arms humming in the background.

Wiping the perspiration from his brow, the intruder cautiously stole through the tomb-like bay, ducking and turning to avoid security cameras positioned strategically to prevent exactly what he was attempting. With perfect timing, the fleet-footed shadow ducked past the final camera sweep, and vaulting into one of the dozens of open rectangular cargo boxes, slammed the lid behind him.

"Sssst, Sssst," vented the pressurized suit as his transparent helmet contracted to fit the ruggedly handsome face of the forty-three-year-old stowaway. Three seconds later and the familiar jolt of the ejection tube accelerated both box and cargo into the inky darkness of space.

Approximately three hundred meters below the Potomac lay the stowaway's destination, 'The Empress of the Heavens'. Once the commercial pride of the nation's space industry, she now drifted in a lifeless orbit around Saturn. Her hull shredded and her bridge pulverized, she stood as a monument to the overzealous tourists and inexperienced crew who destroyed her. Frozen and powerless, she was not the first space-liner to be sacrificed to the icy asteroid gods of Saturn's inner rings. Glistening like a million diamonds adorning the neck of the enormous gas planet, the rings of Saturn were a popular tourist trap. 'Empress' was, however, the largest of the frozen victims, weighing over one hundred thousand metric tons. Her enormous size made her almost impossible to protect, but it was also the only reason that any hope of life still remained. This fact alone motivated Jon Logan's insubordination.

Time was the elephant in the room, an enemy which refused to be ignored. Logan knew this better than anyone, having developed the Guard's manual on rescuing crippled tourist ships. That manual, developed in 2086, was now over ten years old. Twenty-five rescues later and a handful of near-death experiences had taught the renowned guardsman that patience was a virtue he could not afford.

Unfortunately, his commanding officer, Admiral Jackson, had a different approach. His orders expressly forbade any premature excursions to the *Empress*. Logan knew better. His external scans of the ship's outer hull told him exactly what he would find. She would be powerless with no more than sixty percent oxygen left, and, with her nuclear nacelles destroyed, the artificial gravity and oxygen scrubbers would begin to fail almost immediately. Thus crippled, *Empress* would become a quagmire of death, with radiation burns and widespread chaos making reconnaissance data critical and Jackson's laborious step-wise approach a recipe for disaster.

So here was Commodore Jon Logan, up to his old tricks again. In his mind, he could already hear Jackson screaming at the top of his gravelly voice. How many times had he been chewed out for disobeying direct orders? Too many times to count, he thought, as a violent lurch and the sound of magnetic locks engaging the liner's hull announced his arrival.

Now came the tricky part. "Empress" had been enveloped for some seventy-two hours in a torrent of miniature moonlets and ice fragments from Saturn's "A" ring shredding everything around her. This was confirmed by the deafening hailstorm of micro-asteroids on the outer skin of his oxygen-filled cocoon.

"What was that prayer?" Logan whispered sarcastically to himself as he cracked the lid of his frozen sarcophagus.

"Sssst." The atmosphere escaped silencing the hailstorm of drums beating in Logan's head.

"Ok, Logan. Open the lid in the wrong direction and you're a dead man. In the right direction you're a hero."

This last maneuver was a gamble on pure chance, with the potential of inviting thousands of supersonic icicles into his coffin or deflecting them away harmlessly.

Touching the release button to crack the lid, it instead flew open, as a wide-eyed Logan lay frozen and crouching staring upwards at the iridescent shower of particles deflected harmlessly into space.

Silently rejoicing over his luck, he resurrected his aching extremities from their former crypt and unfurled his collapsible shield. At the first glimmer of starlight the Head's Up Display (HUD) of his *NanoLens* activated, revealing a three-dimensional schematic of the vessel's landscape before him and directions to the nearest portal. Logan sighed a silent breath of satisfaction at his favorite technology. With the advent of pharmaceutical cures for near, farsightedness and cataracts, contact lenses had evolved to become the personal computers of the masses. While most used them simply to get their weather and access the *Net*, the military's version - the *NanoLens* - allowed them to do much more.

Logan was also an admirer of the collapsible shield, a giant Japanese-Geisha like fan of armor reinforced with nano-fibers which served to deflect the hailstorm of particles. Now properly adorned, shield in hand and magnetic soles to boot, Logan began his race for the nearest portal. Jagged splinters of icy fragments ricocheted from his shield like the spray from a summer hose as he dove for the access key. Immediately the entryway opened as he sailed safely inside with the hatch sealing silently behind him.

The hallway before him was a dark and ominous tunnel, strewn with debris, and thick with the floating entanglement of amputated extremities from both man and machine. Shielded from the distant rays of the sun and devoid of atmosphere, the -120 degree temperature had instantaneously frozen most of the corpses. Logan stiffened as two specters unexpectedly floated past his helmet light, their screams eternally etched across their faces and their arms reaching as if to grasp Logan in an icy death grip. He brushed them hurriedly aside.

"Stupid fools. Why did they have to get so close to the rings? You just had to see what they looked like," Logan muttered bitterly as he picked his way through the dozen or so groping phantoms that drifted towards him.

"Hope it was worth the view."

Making his way down the dark and twisted corridor, Logan followed his HUD to a more intact area of the ship. A golden glow greeted him as he passed the engineering deck and proceeded up the emergency ladder. Looking down through an observation window into the smoldering emergency escape pod bay some three decks below, Logan paused to shake his head.

"Nothing could live in that radiation," he thought as he arrived at one of the higher decks still possessing some semblance of artificial gravity. He now began to move quickly through the ship's many hallways looking for any signs of life.

Ahead, at the end of one darkened hall, he saw the gentle flickering light of a dimly lit portal. As he approached the window he was amazed to see the excited face of a young teenage girl jumping up and down as she emphatically pointed out the window at the approaching guardsman. Inside a dozen jubilant souls, some in tears, some hugging, waved to their guardian.

Their joy made the next two seconds all the more tragic. For as Logan scanned the room, his eye glimpsed the glimmer of an unexpected rainbow reflection through the porthole on the rear wall. The young girl watched as the countenance of her rescuer metamorphosed from joy to terror as instantly Logan threw himself from the doorway and the room exploded into a swirling vortex of people and debris. The cruel and devouring tempest, like some giant serpent coiling and twisting frantically sucked everything not anchored down into space.

Logan sat there in the dark, across from the now half-crumpled hatch, refusing to believe what he had just experienced. Slowly, he pulled himself to his feet wavering towards the fractured pane of the door. Like a child peering through stained glass, Logan could view only sections of the once peaceful shelter. The 'iceteroid' as Logan liked to call them left a gaping hole the size of a small refrigerator in the opposing wall.

The room was now cloaked, lit only by the dim glow of its cerulean emergency lights. Thus illuminated, a steely midnight ambience hung over their suffocated tomb, like that of a moonlit graveyard. In it he could see the remnants of its frozen occupants desperately clinging to the last remaining objects fastened to the wall. Their hands were clinched in an icy death grip, on their faces were screams silenced and frozen in mid-space. A partially clad woman, her clothes ripped, stood huddled against the far wall, entangled in the framework of a corner table. Within her arms lay one tiny frozen baby locked in the immortal embrace of a desperate mother.

Slowly Logan pulled himself away from the surreal scene, staggering backwards into the stifling darkness lit only by the intermittent flashes of twisted electrical systems. Still numb from his latest brush with death, he stumbled a few dozen meters forward towards the frosted portal of an adjacent banquet hall. His gloved hand scrubbed the icy coating from the pane allowing a view of the inner festivities. Like some macabre celebration of the underworld, dozens of richly adorned passengers locked in statuesque dance embraces or reclining at luxurious dinner tables drifted frozen in mid-air. Women in beautiful gowns and men in stately tuxedos, floated through the dimly lit ballroom locked in a final dance of death. Wrapped in an envelope of liquid spirits, succulent cuisine and beautiful music all topped with a toxic gas chaser, they had missed the initial alarms. Logan shivered as he slowly pulled away from the image and turned to make his way to the next hatch separating him from the rest of the ship.

The guardsman carefully scanned the environmental monitor before him. The nano-lens' display read 'Oxygen 12%, Nitrogen 68%, radiation and temperature within normal limits'.

"If you can trust that," Logan whispered as he gazed through the next door's frosty portal. Inside the dimly lit hallway, some five meters ahead, lay the outline of a shrouded figure convulsing violently on the bloodstained floor. The erratic electrical discharges that gave the hall its only hint of illumination outlined the adjacent pool of fresh blood.

Slowly the hatch lurched open, and the airlock cycled as Logan entered cautiously into the darkened hallway. Looking around for a possible assailant, Logan carefully bent over to reach for the linen table cloth covering the quivering victim. As he did so, a blood-soaked woman's shoe slipped from beneath the trembling fabric.

"Ma'am, try to take it easy, I'm here to help." Logan softly spoke as he gingerly reached for the edge of the tremulous cover. The tips of his gloved fingers inched forward until they just barely brushed the covering's fringe.

"YELP!" The creature exploded upward in a rage, lunging like a giant alien serpent towards the crouching guardsman.

Terrified, Logan jumped backwards to escape the violently writhing creature. As he did, he stumbled, tripping as he back-pedaled to safety. Horrified Logan landed on his rear, watching a small black wiry haired terrier, T-bone steak in mouth pop out from beneath the linen cloth. The dog, who was at least as terrified as the experienced guardsman, circled once around its assailant before racing away. Logan laughed with relief the color returning to his perspiring face which seconds before had resembled the bone-white color of his shield-suit.

"What's next?" he mused, noticing the stack of sliced beef medallions and T-bones partially draped by the ruffled linen. Shaking his head Logan rose and proceeded down the sparsely lit hallway, resuming his inspection of each side room for survivors.

"Seems pretty stable in here," Logan spoke as his helmet light revealed another empty room. The words were barely off his lips when, from behind, the sound of groaning metal once again met his ears.

"Not again!" he choked on the words, running as the hallway behind him began to collapse into a newly forming disarray. The incredible vacuum sent him fleeing through a shower of debris outlined by the collapse of heavy bulkheads behind him. Each support fell forward in turn, like a domino shoving its neighbor into the newly formed vortex draining out into space.

Only meters in front of the swirling twister, its vacuous tentacles grasping everything in its path, Logan ran. His wrist computer streamed through dozens of codes, each unsuccessfully attempting to unlock the portal ahead. Seven meters from the sealed hatch, Logan ripped the gun from his holster and fired off an explosive round that blew through the obstinate lock. Flailing through the open airlock and into the hallway beyond, grappling hook in hand, he frantically latched himself onto an adjacent bulkhead. Instantly the hallway behind filled with a torrent of loose debris sucked into the swirling vortex, taking with it one small Yorkshire terrier, still running, bone in mouth, out into the inky vacuum. With that the torrent ended as quickly as it had begun, slamming the interior door behind itself, exiting like an unwelcome guest asked to leave.

As Logan pulled himself into the open vacuum of the hallway, the pressure from his magnetic boots re-engaged around his ankles. The sudden pressure caused him to trip and stumble forward. Cursing, he cautiously approached the sealed hatch separating him from the next section of the ship which instantaneously opened.

"Now you work," he muttered, glaring at the glittering instrument panel.

As the hatch of the revolving cylindrical airlock closed behind him, Logan entered a dimly lit hallway lined on each side with people. Some were passengers, sobbing and clinging to young children, while others were sleeping, curled in fetal positions on the floor. Scattered among the passengers were gaunt looking crew members working feebly to offer what little comfort they could. Amazed at the sudden entrance of the guardsman, they immediately recognized the uniform and began to cheer. Logan raised his arm sheepishly to acknowledge them and removed his contoured fitting helmet, revealing his dark brown hair and charcoal eyes.

"That's Jon Logan," someone half-whispered to others in the crowd. An expression of awe fell over the silent crowd as the guardsman cautiously picked his way through the partially lit, smoke-filled hallway. Further down, some of the injured were still being pulled out of damaged suites by crew members. Oxygen masks were placed over the men, women and children emerging from the smoke-filled rooms. In the background, intermittent sounds of impacting asteroids and groaning bulkheads were heard over distant screams from other areas of the ship. The lights dimmed and flickered as the ship shuddered repeatedly.

Logan recognized some of the explosions as welcome sounds. For outside the ship, the massive hull of the heavily armored *Potomac* was in final alignment over the *Empress*. Bringing to bear the full power of her defensive cannons, she was busy pulverizing anything larger than a breadbox that came within one hundred meters of the ship.

Inside, Logan continued to make his way through the hallways, stopping intermittently to interface his portable computer with the few remaining workstations of the *Empress*. Rapidly scanning through damage report screens from the ship's auxiliary computer, he absorbed each screen line by line analyzing the damage in all areas of the ship. It was precisely at this time, when Logan was intently absorbing each detail from the schematics, that he suddenly jumped grabbing for his right ear implant.

"Logan!" a harsh voice barked in his ear. Logan rubbed his ear attempting to clear the ringing sensation still echoing through his head.

"Yeah, Cap, Logan here... I made it!" Logan replied with an uncomfortable grimace, continuing his work.

"You made it! What do you mean you made it? Logan, you're fired! Do you hear me? F -I - R - E - D!"

Logan by now had grown accustomed to the gruffness of Captain Jackson. A former marine, Jackson was in charge of the largest rescue ship in the United States' national space guard fleet. He commanded a crew of over one hundred of the nation's most experienced astronauts dedicated to exploration, research and rescue. Although his bark was worse than his bite, Logan knew Jackson was angry this time. It had been at least six months since the last time Jackson had threatened to fire him. He knew one day it would no longer be just a threat.

"Sorry, Jack' you're breaking up," Logan tapped on his *earplant* as he quickly resumed picking his way through the passengers and down to the next hall.

"What are you doing on that ship, soldier? You have not been authorized to deploy! How did you get in there?" Jackson was famous for rattling off one question after another like a machine gun pummeling his victim into submission. Crew members used to bet on how long he could spit out abuse without taking a breath. To date the record was two and one-half minutes, and even then he didn't look winded.

"You wanted advanced recon. I got that for you. I just had maintenance fire me over here in one of those old rock collecting buckets we use for asteroid samples."

"If you want to be one with the rocks, Logan, I can work that out for you! This better be good. Real good, did you hear me, soldier?"

"Only the best for you, sir. Well, where do I start? She's a mess. Port side has a grade 3 major blow-out fracture with venting. Deck D casualty estimates look like they could range as high as seventy-five percent. The surrounding pods are uninhabitable too. Radiation from the asteroid belt has penetrated C deck and it has been evacuated."

"Crap!"

"Sixty-five percent of the atmosphere has vented. Gamma radiation levels read lethal on the lower starboard and aft sections of the ship."

"Double crap...Port crap, Starboard crap. Heck she's a crap sandwich! What's in between?" Jackson mused.

"Not much. Only the center of the ship is intact. I estimate 45 minutes of O_2 max."

"Ok Logan. Get them out of there. I don't care how you do it. Just get them out!" Jackson's screaming had receded to a mere yell now, freeing Logan's right hand to manipulate a 3-D schematic of the *Empress* rotating in visual space.

"I'm heading to the center atrium of the ship," he said pointing with his finger to the corresponding location in 3-D space. The majority of the crew is already there with survivors. Mostly radiation burns, oxygen deprivation and minor trauma. I need you to divide the team into three units. One unit will attach O_2 lines to the starboard hull vents at mid deck. The other two units need to converge on the mid-deck promenade and start dis-embarkment procedures."

Logan sighed as he entered the promenade atrium of the *Empress*. Like atriums of the ocean liners in the twentieth century this was an impressive room with a huge vaulted ceiling and a grand central staircase. Despite the destruction rampant in the rest of the ship, this room still reflected her ambiance and beauty. Elaborate trim cast in mahogany and gold accentuated this room which also served as the main ballroom. Large paintings ornately framed reflected the culture of the new aristocracy. The flowing staircase descended to a large open floor carpeted with what appeared to be an exquisite Persian rug. Most of the people were sitting or lying on the floor while what remained of the ship's crew tended to those requiring oxygen or medical attention.

"You better check engineering, Logan."

"Already have, Jack. It's just a hopeless pile of molten slag back there."

In the background, persisting sounds of distant explosions and buckling metal combined with the pulse of flickering lights added to the passenger's confusion. Logan worked quickly, his anxiety partitioning him from the sobs of broken lives drowning around him.

On the outside of the ship, an entirely different battle was taking place. Over a dozen tethered rescue guards were dropping from the Potomac to the battered hull of the *Empress*. Their mission was to drill through the hull and attach emergency airlines while avoiding being skewered by the tiny bullet-like icicles whizzing by at hundreds of meters per second. Working in pairs, one rescuer manned a laser drill while the other angled a large hinged *geisha* shield deflecting projectiles back into space. The system worked well as long as nothing 'unexpected' occurred.

This mission, like most, proved the old adage that Logan loved to quote, 'Expect the unexpected'. For high above the *Empress*, the last guardian, a neophyte rescuer the elders called *mite* was attempting his descent. Mite was a gangly soldier, who stood all of five foot one, not much older than twenty and still suffering from acne. Despite his diminutive stature it was his personality, and not his physical dimensions that had earned his moniker. For *mite*, or as some referred to him as *might*, had the annoying habit of almost never following through on an assigned task.

So it was to be on this day too. Halfway down the tether the unmanageable soldier grinned upward flashing a one finger obscenity to his observers and momentarily took his eye off his high tensile strength guide line. Suddenly *Potomac* shuddered as her cannons fired two large salvos causing the guardian's wire to slacken unexpectedly. Frantically, he tried to swing the wire back into alignment from the twisted position it had suddenly assumed. The maneuver, forbidden in basic training, launched the trainee into a harrowing death spin termed a *twister* by the elders.

Like a fly caught in the death grip of a web, the soldier squirmed as the high tensile wire spun quickly, first entwining his lower limbs and then zipping upward like a cocoon around its helpless victim. It was over almost as soon as it had begun. Unshielded from the barrage of almost microscopic debris, the recruit was struck immediately by three ice fragments in the thigh. The next three struck his abdomen and the last tore through his helmet partially decapitating the frozen cocoon of blood and flesh being hastily retracted to the bay above.

Now fully deployed, the external team set about the precarious assignment of attaching the airlines. Guardsmen, who are adept at the most arduous of tasks under the most impossible of conditions, usually find working in asteroid fields a manageable environment. However, on the final burn of the final connection, a sudden cloudburst of ice particles descended on the group.

The projectiles showered down, each one efficiently deflected harmlessly into space. All except one lone bullet. The errant missile, sent off its normal parallel course by the Potomac's cannons, ricocheted obtusely just off the edge of one guardsman's shield striking his partner in the shoulder. With his penetrated shield suit leaking fast, an alarm immediately sounded in all six helmets of his comrades. In only a moment, like a collapsing deck of cards, the team descended on the wounded guardsman. Surrounding him in a bubble of shields, they sealed the blood-soaked suit and whisked the unconscious guardian to the safety of the Potomac.

Inside the *Empress*, two other teams entered the atrium and joined Logan on the balcony of the great stairway. As the guardsmen looked down onto a sea of collapsed humanity, the welcome sound of fresh air entering from above filled the room. Logan, who had long since removed his helmet, was inspecting the air vents in the ceiling some seven meters above the balcony. He descended the ladder, flashing a 'thumbs-up' to the other guards, who proceeded to remove their helmets. Then pointing back to the ceiling he said, "This is the only way out."

Logan smiled as he pointed to a small circular hatch above the ladder. Lieutenant Miles, the first to reach Logan, looked down at the passengers and then up at the ceiling.

"You've got to be kidding, Commodore!"

Suddenly both men grimaced in pain, as a seemingly incoherent barrage of expletives assaulted their ears.

"Logan! Where the devil are you? What's your status?"

"I'm here Jack, we've got a problem. The entrance hallway is completely compromised. No way are we going to get an air chute through that clutter. I've located an old style terrestrial hatch for escape on emergency landings. There's one problem."

"Oh really, Logan, only one?"

Logan smiled at Miles as he tried to continue.

"Yeah, the passengers will have to climb approximately eight meters to the hatch in artificial gravity."

"Are you insane Logan? Turn it off! Those passengers are elderly and hypoxic. Half of them will probably fall when they get ten feet off the ground."

"Nope, I disagree," Logan countered, "leave it on. You turn it off and we've got chaos. Half of these passengers are nauseated already from oxygen deprivation and toxic gas. Turn it off and we'll have a sea of floating vomit to work in. Not to mention some very smelly, disoriented passengers." There was just enough silence on the other end for Logan to continue.

"Plus, in less than thirty minutes we'll be sucked into '*Pan's*' gravitational field," Logan continued. "We'll have to lift them out, and lift them out now using life belts, if we're to have a chance."

"Commodore's right, Captain," a young male voice with slight Asian overtones echoed over the communication system.

"Our present course brings us into the moonlet '*Pan's*' gravitational field in 23.5 minutes," Lieutenant Breckenridge continued before whispering, "I'd listen to him, Cap'. He's the best in the fleet."

"Hey, Hey, Breck, my man, is that you? Thanks a bunch!" Logan piped in, smiling ear to ear. Jackson switched off his young navigator's Comm. unit.

"See what you did! We'll never be able to live with him now! I know he's good, but the man's a loose cannon." Breckenridge, nodding his head in mock agreement, couldn't help the slight smile that crept across his face. Jackson turned back to the Comm. unit hoping to regain the upper hand as he barked out his orders with even greater verbosity.

"OK, Logan, get to work! Get those people out now!"

"Acknowledged, and tell Breck I want that framed!"

Back on the promenade deck, with the worst of the crying and sobbing having subsided, the emergency hatch suddenly popped open as the security line descended. Thus began the harried process of sorting passengers by priority of age and gender.

Some of the passengers, those blessed with more than their fair share of corpulence, slipped and fell, and being caught by their security line, were hoisted like cattle up through the hatch. As the elderly advanced upwards, the line approached a section containing women and children. Suddenly an attractive woman, some thirty years of age, stepped out making a bee line for Logan.

"Oh, no..." Logan stuttered, having seen this scenario before. He turned attempting to escape.

His maneuver of ducking past junior officers and into a cluster of waiting passengers, having often worked well in the past, instead found him face to face with his pursuer. Now, not only was his escape thwarted by the raven haired beauty, but his efforts rewarded him with an amused audience. With her hand to her mouth in an expression of grief and with tears in her eyes, she began to speak.

"Commander Logan, excuse me, but that man tells me you're the one I need to speak to."

Logan turned to see Miles smiling and waving sheepishly from the ladder as one especially rotund 'trapezean' swung her legs around his torso wildly. Straining and red-faced, Miles struggled to shove her abundant caboose through the bulging air lock.

"Ma'am, I'm very busy. Can't it wait?" Logan asked shaking his fist at the red faced Miles still straining with the oversized extremity like a man squeezing the last drop of juice from an over-ripe orange.

"No, it can't! I'm going to speak to you and you are going to listen! My two children, Tommy and Beci, are not here, but I know they're alive." The unanticipated frontal attack from such an obviously mild-mannered creature threw Logan back defensively.

"Look lady, I'm very sorry, but the only people alive on this ship are right here in this room with us."

Again he attempted to move away, his gaze drifting up at the red-faced Miles attempting to shove an immovable object through an impassable hole. He started to laugh when suddenly he almost tripped over the distraught woman who had maneuvered back into his path. Eyes pleading with tears, she gently grasped the flag emblazoned on his upper right chest. This took Logan aback, as he craned his head sideways looking down at the symbol she so firmly grasped.

"No, you don't understand," she pleaded almost angrily, "I know that they're alive. They were in the engineering department with Chief Engineer Forbes when the first wave of collisions hit and the atomic reactors failed. He placed them in an escape pod to protect them," she continued her hand tugging firmly on the emblem on his chest. He wasn't sure if it was her intensity or the unusual tight hold on his lapel that kept him from turning and walking away.

"Mr. Logan! What would you do if they were your children? I know you have them. I've seen the ring on your hand," she demanded with the adamant conviction of a woman who refused to take no for an answer. At this Logan stopped. Sighing, he looked down at the shining band on his ungloved hand. An eternity seemed to pass as he stared at the ring.

"Please, Mr. Logan, what would you do if they were your children?" Logan lowered his hands and looked away from the woman. Rebecca waited.

"I'll check on it. Now you get in line!" The woman moved silently towards the aerial display above her.

Logan turned back only once to look at the woman.

"Oh well, what can he do? He can only kill me once." Logan mused half silently as he activated the wrist mounted device.

"Uh, yeh, hey, Jack, this is Logan. I've got a lady down here who says her children are in an escape pod in the ship's engineering section. Can you just try to raise those pods?"

Jackson, on the bridge of the Potomac, was neck deep in coordinating the rescue.

"Say, again, you have what?" he shot back.

"A woman……" Logan attempted to repeat.

"I'm not interested in your sordid love affairs, Mister. Quit fraternizing and get back to work."

"I am doing my job. Just scan the pods and see if anyone is in there. This lady swears her two kids are in one," Logan snapped back, knowing he had already pushed well beyond the line, figuring a little more couldn't hurt.

"Already have, there's no response. Everybody in that section is either dead from the collisions or from the radiation leaking out of those nacelles. Like you said 'it's nothing but a heaping pile of slag'".

"Look Jack, maybe they can't communicate because they're kids and don't know how to work the comm. unit."

"Look *Comm-o-dore*, we don't have time to go on any of your famous wild goose chases! We all know what happened last time you tried that. Worry about the living first and let the dead bury their dead! OUT!" with that Logan's Comm. went dead.

To Logan, this was Jackson's way of avoiding the hard decision that violated regulations and yet left open the door to a solution. Logan changed the channel on his Comm. Unit and whispered.

"Hey, Breck, can you hear me?"

"Yes", came back the whispered response.

"When that douchebag gets his head out of his butt tell him where I've gone."

Smiling from his station Breck echoed his response. "10-4. That could be some time. He seems to like it in there and he's in pretty deep this time."

"He's gotta come up for air sometime. Oh, yeah," he said looking up at an exhausted Miles still straining at the burgeoning behind stuck in the escape hatch, "tell Cap to send down a bucket of axle grease."

"Axle grease, what for?"

"Tell him we need to move a caboose."

High above, Breckenridge sat at his station silently mouthing the words "move a caboose?"

Determined, Logan dashed madly forward slipping deftly into his gloves while reactivating his suit's survival systems. Bolting through the first airlock, he donned his helmet as he raced forward into the first of each successively darkening hallways.

"Breck, you still there buddy?" he radioed pensively.

"Still here."

"You and Cap' should start a mutual admiration society. In the meantime, could you rescan those pods for any signs of life"?

"Going on another of your infamous snipe hunts again, huh? Ok, I see, checking the pods now. I'll let you know what I find."

Minutes later Breckenridge responded.

"Alright, I'm tapping in to engineering's remote mini-cameras. First pod, nuttin', now trying pod number two, Ditto. Pod 3, scratch that one." Then as he began to switch away, an almost imperceptible reflection caught his eye.

"Hold everything. I just saw something move. Bingo! Got them! I'm activating life-support and communication link. Yep. They're here and they're alive." Breck's voice came back almost beaming over the Comm. link.

"Great, did I ever tell you that you're smarter than you look"? Logan quipped climbing over the next pile of debris

"Yep! All the time" he answered, "Hold on, we have a problem. Radiation levels in the life pod are normal, but outside the pod Rads measure 22,000. You can't go in there." Logan checked his chronometer; it read nineteen minutes and counting.

"Ok, so, we'll use the manual release override and instruct the auto pilot to direct it into the Potomac."

Breckenridge typed in the command as a look of confusion fell upon his face.

"Attempting now and ……..no can do. The launch mechanism is jammed. Servos work but the launch bay doors won't open," He continued, his typing becoming more vigorous.

"Something's in the way."

As Logan approached the C deck hatch, a tiny yellow light flashed in his NanoLens warning of the excessive radiation ahead.

"Ok Breck, talk to Cap and tell him what you've found. I'm going to get those kids out," Logan commanded, half holding his breath as he stepped forward.

"Are you out of your mind? Didn't you hear what I just told you? If you go into that engine room you are toast!" Logan nodded listening to his friend as the airlock doors began to cycle.

"Look, you worry about your miracles and I'll worry about my own. Find out what's blocking that escape hatch and find me a way to clear it," Logan insisted as he entered the final deck separating him from the engineering bay. Meticulously, he picked his way through a floating sea of razor sharp debris, ducking rapidly as a giant latex serpent suddenly lunged at him from the shadows above. Like one of a dozen other huge paint strips, the creature, peeled from its simmering bulkhead, floated undulating in a cesspool of flowing radiation.

High above in the *Potomac*, Breck searched feverishly on the security screens surrounding the tiny pod.

"Wait until I cross the final bulkhead in engineering before you tell 'Cap. How's the radiation outside of that section?"

Glancing down at his instrument panel, Breck responded "It begins to climb as you go down through C deck and becomes toxic just outside of the launch bay."

Weaving his way down the partially lit hallway, Logan gently nudged aside the frozen corpses blocking his path. At one point, it seemed as if one of the appendages had grasped his suit, attempting to prevent him from reaching the dimly-lit elevator doors. Logan tore himself free nervously, and punching the door's control pad, murmured to the specter, "Wait your turn." The unit lurched, refusing to open, earning it a punch to the mid-section.

With the direct route blocked, Logan was now forced to descend the final level by the emergency escape ladder. Climbing down his foot missed the next step completely. Frantically he searched back and forth with his foot for the last support until frustrated he gazed downward. And there it was.

Nothing.

Only an empty vacuum of darkness stared back. Stunned, Logan clung to the scaffolding scanning millions of kilometers of space where there should have been a massive hallway. Above, beside the access ladder was the truncated elevator shaft, its car ready to descend.

"Watch that next step," Logan whispered as he looked down at the chasm of space that was almost his home. Then, looking out at the entire section of wreckage beside him, he turned to measure the gap between himself and the next hatch. Accessing the rappelling line from his utility belt, he fired it at the doorway ahead. Then with one huge leap, he launched himself over the void sailing through the activated airlock, which miraculously cycled open just as he arrived.

Logan shook his head briskly attempting to dislodge the perspiration hanging heavy on his brow. The faint whirl of the dehumidifier in his oxygen tank alerted him to the increase in respirations as he turned to face the toxic bay before him.

"OK, I'm in, Breck. Are you there? I'm inside of engineering." Silence answered him. "Do you Roger that"?

The voice over his Comm. system sounded mildly stressed as Breck replied.

"I'm here chief and so is ….."

"Logan, what the devil do you think you're doing?" an agitated Jackson interrupted. Exasperated, Logan retorted.

"Just thought I'd do a little sight-seeing, Cap'".

"You are not authorized to perform any other search and rescue procedures, mister! Get out of there now! That's an order"! The voice on the other end was now so frenzied that Logan imagined he heard a little alto in the mix.

"Now-w-w…. you tell me," Logan quipped. "Sorry Cap', no can do. There are kids in there." Jackson hesitated, his voice suddenly softening.

"Jon... I know what you're going through. But getting yourself killed for these kids won't bring your family back. They're dead, Logan. If you don't get out of there you will be too."

"You have no idea what I'm going through!" Logan exploded back, "And this has nothing to do with them! These kids are alive and I'm going in." Constrained by the covering of his helmet Logan was powerless to stop the hot tears now streaming down his face as he tore through the landing bay.

"Besides, you fired me, you big lug head. I'm doing this on my own time."

Jackson sat slumped over his ship's navigation console, the silence connecting the two men as each realized that this was probably their last verbal spar. Jackson finally spoke, his voice gently resigned to the fate Logan had chosen.

"OK, bonehead, be a hero. Get yourself killed, but we can't wait for you. We're going to have to undock in eight minutes. We'll pick the escape pod up, IF you make it out alive". Logan now began to accelerate his pace, continuing to climb over and around the wreckage strewn throughout the main chamber. Toxic gases filtered into the depleted cavity from the cruiser's leaking nacelle's adding to the radiation levels already present.

Climbing through the last cluster of fallen bulkheads, Logan finally arrived at the launch bay entrance. As he did so, he momentarily paused to survey the hallway, when the silence of the chamber was shattered by the radiation klaxon sounding in his helmet. The unfamiliar amber of the flashing caution light shocked Logan almost as much as the sound of Breckenridge's excited voice urging him to accelerate his pace down the clouded hallway.

"You need to move faster! Travel down the bulkhead corridor and enter the starboard Nacelle. Rads are highest at your 11:00 position. The pod is at 2:30," Breck commanded, his voice straining with tension. Logan raced down the long corridor into the glowing hot nacelle chamber.

"I'm in! I'm moving to the pod! Which one is it?"

"Pod 141A, I've activated the internal lights. Do you see it?" Silence was Logan's only reply as Breckenridge hung over his instrument panel.

"Jon, do you see it?"

"Got it!" came back the answer as Logan carefully stepped into the bay littered with small debris surrounding the spherical pod. Quickly, Logan worked his way around to the front of the small craft all the time inspecting the pod's outer hull. There, wedged securely within the channel used to accelerate the pod, was a massive one by three meter steel bulkhead blocking the pod. On earth the girder would have weighed hundreds of pounds. Logan grasped the largest beam he could find and began to pry at the massive obstruction with all his might. The support held fast as again and again he desperately lunged at the compressed truss. His suit alarm now began to loudly beam at him through his helmet. Looking down, he saw the outer layer of his suit begin to peel away as the radiation coursing through the bay began dissolving his suit. Sweating and light headed, he collapsed to his knees.

"It won't budge. Help!" Logan begged as leaning into the beam he felt the room grow dark. In his semi-conscious delirium, Logan suddenly found himself in a familiar labor and delivery room. Still leaning, as if grasping the cold metallic beam, the guardian was now holding the tender hand of a young woman. With his other hand he was stroking her tear stained cheek as a cry of anguished agony fell from her trembling lips. It had been so long since Logan had seen her. Her brow, her eyes, her lips captured his gaze and held him transfixed by the beauty he had almost forgotten. He felt his heart in his throat and the searing heat of tears forcing their way from his eyes as he beheld her.

"God, Help me!" she cried out, her face contorting into a twisted and distorted red mass resembling the Brandywine tomatoes he once picked on his grandmother's farm. Now her frenzy fixated on Logan.

"This is all your fault!" she screamed thumping him with her other tiny fist, "I told you not to let me do this natural! Are you crazy? Why didn't you make me take the nerve block?" she screamed. Logan half smiled, trying to restrain his emotions, as holding fast to her hand he stroked her hair.

"Julie, I'm here. The doctors are here. You wanted a natural birth. I just made sure you got what you wanted. Everything is fine dear, you don't need God." The doctor looked away from his work only briefly to roll his eyes.

"I don't need God? Are you crazy? You get down here and have this baby and tell me I don't need God!" she yelled back. Another contraction started as she reached up, and punching him squarely in the jaw, knocked him flat to the floor. He lay there for some time as the doctors and nurses still working looked down smiling at his now silent form. His wife screamed again as the vision faded and Logan woke to the Pod bay floor.

Shaking his head, Logan struggled to rise from the launch bay's toxic floor. His head spun as the room, a strange mixture of twisted metal and shadows, danced around him. Sparks jumped from damaged electrical elements providing an eerie lighting. It had been years since Logan had felt the icy chill of death, its dark tentacles searching desperately for a break in what was fast becoming a paper-thin suit. At minus twenty-five degrees centigrade, the iciness of space mixing with the toxic heat of radiation was producing a nauseating cold that the shield suit could no longer keep out.

Logan knew that dizziness and its subsequent nausea was an astronaut's death sentence. Desperately, he attempted to rise. Suddenly, to one side in the shadows, something moved. Startled, Logan jumped, adrenaline reinvigorating him.

"What was that?" he whispered to himself, recalling the movement at the edge of his vision.

"Who's there?"

Silence surrounded him, undisturbed except for the faint crackle of electrical discharge reverberating in the wisp of the bay's surrounding atmosphere. Scanning the room with his headlamp, Logan's search yielded nothing but a room full of twisted metal and a bad case of vertigo.

Now fully conscious, the guardian turned once again, reaching for the fallen beam. As he did, he noticed something very strange, for the massive girder that had once been unmovable lay twisted like a pretzel and thrown unceremoniously against the wall.

"What the-!" He exclaimed, now truly bewildered by his environment. It was then that the klaxon warning of a suit perforation shocked him back to reality. His helmet, awash in the red glow of the warning signal and abuzz with the automated voice of his computer, served more to disorient the guardian than to remind him of the proper emergency procedures. From his arm a pin sized perforation was slowly draining the life-giving atmosphere of his shield suit. Shivering at the exposure to the cold of space and the poison of radiation, and too disoriented to locate the perforation, Logan stumbled for the tiny pod's hatch. Multiple alarms in his helmet went off as Logan reached the hatch and attempted to open it.

Desperately he fumbled with the numeric pad, his stiffened hands refusing to respond to his commands. As the room began to spin, and as the icy darkness of unconsciousness returned, he fought to remain on his feet. His aching lungs pumped with all their might for the precious air now venting hopelessly into the vacuum of space. Suffocation was a new sensation for Logan; the very lining of his lungs burned like a raging fire. He had read about its effects on the mind and the steps to take to avoid hypoxia, but weakened by the effects of the radiation, his training failed him.

Suddenly, he began to cough violently, his body desperately attempting to compensate for the hypoxia now unleashing a tidal wave of nausea. He was powerless to stop it as the vomit splattered forward, blocking all but the extremes of his side vision. Now the room began to spin as Logan desperately fought the almost uncontrollable urge to tear off his helmet. His knees buckled and the room began to grow dark again. The last thing he remembered was something brushing up against his arm and then icy cold blackness.

-Whether it was an hour or a day or only a minute, the next thing Logan remembered was waking up in the warmth of the escape pod with the smell of clean fresh air circulating around him. Numbness of both mind and body was fading, as straining, he separated himself from the tattered and vomit stained outer-suit still clinging to his body. Wearing only inner wear, a glorified pair of long johns, he made his way out of the airlock to the pod's cockpit. There, in the shadows of the far corner, huddled miserably were two tiny forms of whimpering humanity, the unwitting recipients of his last *miracle*. Seconds later, the pod's nacelles throttled to full power as the tiny craft exploded forward into space, leaving behind moments later the collapsing sarcophagus consumed by the icy hand of *Pan*.

Exhausted and half frozen, Logan crawled to the corner of the cockpit where the children lay. Reclining into the angle, he cradled them in his muscular arms in an embrace he had not used for a very, very long time. Lying there, content to trust the ship's auto-pilot, and drifting into a deep sleep, his two eyes narrowed to slits transfixed on the blackness of space in the portals above him. As he faded from consciousness, his mind became aware of two very different young children clinging in the warmth of an embrace he had all but forgotten. Logan's sigh, a deep and satisfying breath, was echoed by the two children resting peacefully on their dad's two strong shoulders, while the pod raced silently homeward.

CHAPTER TWO
An Unjust Reward

The discipline and order of the USSA Potomac's crew was a model to every other ship in the fleet. Her immaculate quarters, well designed flight deck, and state of the art technology, were unparalleled in the solar system. Unfortunately, her once pristine decks were now cluttered with 119 more passengers than her design allowed for. The "guests", who judging by their appearance originated from every tribe, nation, people and language, were everywhere. The resulting make-shift hotel on the ship's flight deck was complete with cots, sleeping bags, and emergency port-a-potties. Captain Jackson's strict mantra, "A Place for Everything and Everything In its Place", was taking a beating having been replaced by the crew's spoof, "No space, No space and a dozen runny-nosed kids in your face". So it was that fortune had smiled cancelling all military inspections at this time, for chaos reigned on all twelve decks. A large percentage of the rescued passengers consisted of children whose tendency to invade every nook and cranny of the ship often resulted in the most precarious forms of mischief imaginable.

Sick bay was not to be excluded, where children, forbidden from entering the disinfected bay, were often discovered practicing the skill of artful dodging. Intent on practicing their mischievous sorcery, they made an art of slipping through unnoticed only to awaken their stricken relatives. Mercifully, most of the injured in desperate need of medical care, such as those with radiation burns and exposure to toxic gases, were heavily guarded by the ship's security teams. Many of the beds occupied by men, women and children were also constantly attended by nurses and doctors.

It was in this secure environment, in gurney number seven, that Logan now happily resided. Painfully aware of the chaos reigning throughout the remainder of the ship, he was all too eager to agree to the recommended regimen of sedation and intravenous fluid being fed into his left forearm.

This therapeutic regimen, a derivative of the pharmaceutical agent Plasorbigen, was considered a modern medical breakthrough in the treatment of radiation toxicity. Able to limit the amount of damage received by stem cell DNA, the drug, if administered quickly enough, could significantly prolong the life expectancy of radiation victims. Regrettably, the side effects were severe.

Thus Logan who had been maintained in a drug induced coma began his recovery. The severity of his condition, was undetermined when he agreed to the initial sedation, and of some concern to the guardian. So it should come as no surprise that it was a great relief when his first sight was none other than Nurse Debbie Carrington.

'Debi-K', as Logan liked to refer to her, was a painfully gorgeous, blue-eyed blonde in her mid-twenties whose appearance was only superseded by her professional demeanor. Standing by his bedside, she carefully recorded his vital signs as he dreamily emerged from unconsciousness.

"Doctor Mahdia, Commander Logan is regaining consciousness."

Logan stirred, letting out a low visceral groan.

"Is he responsive yet?" replied the mild-mannered man across the room.

Logan smiled weakly looking up at the fair skinned nurse.

"Oh, an angel," he slurred, "I must have died and gone to heaven."

A wry smile crossed his lips as his hand reached for hers. Debi-K deftly stepped aside as Logan's hand was instead intercepted by the rough muscular grip of a Middle

Eastern man in dark blue scrubs. The man smiled warmly quickly turning the palm upwards and checking the pulse. Logan watched as the middle aged physician worked, his dark brown eyes conveying that curious mixture of compassion and amusement one most often associates with a grandfatherly figure.

"Oh, that's our Logan alright, seems perfectly normal to me. You might want to assume a standard orbit around this one, nurse." Mahdia quipped, gesturing with hugely out-stretched arms.

Logan smiled, attempting to raise himself, hoping for a better view of the *support staff.* This effort was awarded with a second groan as he roughly collapsed back onto his gurney.

"Now let that be a lesson to you, relax. You've been through quite an ordeal," the physician insisted repositioning his patient's pillow. Logan, accustomed to anything but Mahdia's compassion, snatched the cushion away from his hovering physician's hand and unleashed a verbal barrage of his own.

"What the devil's wrong with you?" Logan erupted as he crammed the pillow into its desired place, "What's this sudden ugly streak of compassion? Are you sick"? Logan looked up from the pummeled cushion as Jackson stole into the room. It was obvious from his amused expression that the commanding officer had immediately surmised the demeanor of the exchange taking place between the two men.

"You're home, soldier!" Jackson interrupted in his usual verbose style, "Now lay your butt back down, that's an order." Logan looked up weakly, flashing a momentary relieved smile at Jackson's familiar scowl.

Not everyone is losing their mind around here he thought to himself.

"Well, if it isn't Florence Nightingale. Did anyone ever tell you that you have really hairy legs for a nurse?"

"I'm not here to change your bedpan mister. Now shut up and lay down or I'll put you in leg irons." Jackson fired back as he settled gruffly on to the edge of the bed.

"I am lying down."

"For once in your life you're going to obey one of my orders." Jackson's vibrato continued its volume elevating.

"Yes ma'am." Logan replied saluting weakly.

Mahdia, now silent, but still smiling, walked to the opposite side of the gurney and lifting Logan's wrist proceeded to resume checking his pulse.

"You already did that!" Logan objected, pulling his arm from the physician's grip.

"He's right, Logan, you're not going anywhere," Mahdia pronounced as his patient traced the just noticed elevated ridges running down his forearm. Delicate interlacing varicosities gently traced their way down Logan's forearm to within three centimeters of his wrist. Wide eyed, Logan stared momentarily at the discolored appendage before quickly pulling down his sleeve.

"I'm just a little weak. I'll be fine," Logan stammered incredulously as he stared blankly off into space.

"That's just it, you big lughead, you're not fine," Jackson interjected gently.

Now Logan was really worried.

In more than seven years of working together, *Jack* had never shown an ounce of compassion for neither man nor beast. Logan grimaced at the mild wave of nausea coming over him.

"Why? What's wrong with me?" Logan demanded, his gaze fixed on Mahdia while ignoring a gawping Jackson. Lifting one of Logan's arms the physician gently rotated the wrist once again bringing the tiny network of vessels into view. A slight tap on the bed's monitor screen and a brilliantly colored display popped into view revealing three dimensional images of Logan's damaged DNA.

"You have grade 3 gamma radiation poisoning." Mahdia continued pointing, as Logan strained to see the damaged nucleotides.

"Could I have that in English please?"

"It means you're sick, Logan. You're a very *sick* man."

"Don't mince words Mahdia. Tell me what you really think."

Mahdia took a deep breath, his eyes darting along the ceiling as Jackson intervened.

"You saved those kids Logan, but your suit couldn't handle the Rads. By all accounts you should be dead by now. Thanks to Mahdia's skill, though, you……."

"Just a minute Tom. Now I'm prepared to take a little credit for what we did once he got here, but how he survived before that….," Mahdia's voice trailed off as an awkward silence fell over the three friends clustered around Logan's tiny bed. Finally, Jackson blurted out.

"You'll get the best care available".

"What the heck does that mean"?

Mahdia, who had risen and moved to the end of the bed, spoke deliberately, his gaze countering Logan's incredulous stare.

"Logan, we've made a lot of progress in radiation poison treatment. This kind of thing used to be fatal in hours. Depending on how your system reacts, we can give you a good quality of life for up to fifteen months. That's what you need to focus on now".

"Fifteen months! And then what?"

"Look, we're not God. Your vascular system is breaking down. The DNA in your blood vessels is damaged and degenerating. On Earth you'll receive a full body plasma flush with Plasorbigen. Removing the toxins will slow the degeneration, but we can't fix DNA. We can patch it temporarily using viral genome therapy, but we can't replace it. Nobody can fix DNA," Mahdia gestured, his hands motioning like a mechanic attempting to straighten a pretzel while dejectedly pronouncing Logan's fate. A few moments passed as the truth settled in.

"So that's it? Wow." He hesitated, "… Always wondered how I'd go. Well, at least I'll be able to work".

Jackson stared at Logan, his mouth half agape."Sorry, man, but the admiral has revoked your guard status. You're on permanent disability. Not only that, but it seems you're some kind of a big hero back home. Media's all abuzz. There's talk of a Presidential citation," Jackson begrudged, "and with all the chaos back home, heavens know they need a hero."

"But I don't wanna be a hero. I just want my life back."

"Tough cookies, pardner, time to cowboy up. Oh yeah, one more thing. There's this sealed digital note from one Professor Satorsky at NASA, seems he needs your input." Jackson tossed the sealed note to the bed as he backed his way towards the door.

Rolling his eyes, Logan leaned his head back in frustration.

"My advice, what does he want from me? I'm no PhD. They'll either have me flying a confounded desk in some hole in the wall, or on display in a Washington museum. Tom, you can't do this to me."

"It's not my decision, Jon. It comes from on high. Remember, I told you, *you were fired*."

"Look Logan," Mahdia chimed in, "you saved those kids' lives back there. Because of you, they will grow up, have families, and grow old."

"You did your job, Jon, and you did it better than any of us could have. You gave your life for theirs, and the media's eating that up, "Jackson agreed, "Seems we don't see too much of that these days. Who was that, that said, "There is no greater love, than a man give up his life for a friend"?

"Some very misguided philosopher," Logan muttered with his head hung as he stared off into space.

Jackson looked at Logan, not really knowing what to think or feel. For years he had harbored nothing but frustration at Logan's arrogance and disobedience. Always flaunting his success, Logan had finally come up short. Now Jackson, who had secretly looked forward to this day, felt only regret. Logan had paid a deep price to be a guardsman, first his family, and now with his own life. Jackson stumbled, searching for something meaningful to say. Goodbye just didn't seem to cut it.

"Hey, Logan when you're up to it. I'd really like to know how you moved that girder blocking the pod. That thing was wedged tight. When you're up to it, of course. For now just rest and follow your doctor's orders. Okay? Stay in that bed. Do you understand?"

"Sure thing, Florence", Logan shot back, trying to ignore Jackson's uncharacteristic kindness. Turning back to Mahdia, he asked.

"Oh Mahdia, one thing, what kind of horse shot did you give me, anyway? My rear really hurts," Jackson, having just slipped out of the room, turned catching wind of the query and stuck his head back in to hear Mahdia's shocked response.

"Shots? What do you think this is, 2010? We don't give shots anymore. You know that. I didn't touch your precious rear end. You do have a nice bruise on your tattoo, though."

"Who is she, by the way, this "GB"?" Jackson quipped smiling widely, "Probably, 'Greedy the Bimbo' from Uranus". While the two friends made a mock attempt at suppressing their laughter, the effort only resulted in bit lips and red faces and one very un-amused patient.

"Very funny, you guys. I don't have any tattoos down there," he insisted, turning slightly in his bed to spy under the gown a small bruise and a distinct imprint strategically located on his left cheek. Mahdia, wiping a tear from his eye, handed Logan a small circular mirror with an extended handle. There, framed with an oval border and in a bold Romanic font glowed the letters "GB" on the middle of his derriere. He sat there confused, as Jackson and Mahdia patted each other on the back and walked off. Holding the mirror and turning it at different angles to get a better look, he stared at the bruise on his rear.

"Practical jokers, is nothing sacred anymore?" Logan griped, futilely scrubbing at the crest emblazoned on his wounded pride.

Two nights later Logan awoke from a fitful sleep to the sound of something huge crashing to the crowded bay's floor. The noise emanated from the darkest corner of the now fully occupied suite, and closely resembled that of a glass vase thrown violently to the floor, splintering into a million jagged pieces. Most of the beds close to him had previously been empty, but were now occupied by those most profoundly affected by the radiation poisoning. The influx of occupants was the result of a little-known side effect of Plasorbigen, resulting in Logan sharing his dimly-lit room with five very ill inhabitants.

Silence once again settled upon the shadowy room, disturbed only by the occasional tortured rasp of one of Logan's fellow sleeping sufferers. Logan held his breath as he listened carefully again. Nothing.

"Nerves," he whispered silently as he took a deep breath and rolled over, convincing himself he'd only been dreaming.

The shadowy chamber, lit only by the tale-tale indicator lights of blinking instruments, gave the darkened room an eerie glow. Its radiance, like the ghostly haze of the dead moons of Jupiter, had an iciness to it. Cold and desolate, it hung over the guardian like an oppressive veil, reminding Logan of the *death* chambers he had seen on the *Empress*. A cold shiver ran down his spine.

Logan pulled the covers up higher over his shoulder trying to ignore the feeling of the numinous invading his half-wakened stupor. Just as his eyes closed he heard a rustle, like a bed sheet being roughly jostled. Logan looked up into the dark.

Like a knife tearing out the heart of its victim came the terror-filled shriek that filled the bay. Logan sat up frantically, almost jumping out of bed.

Shriller and more demonic the shriek rang out again. This time the cry's dying note was entombed by a whimpering sob as it lingered in the shadowy crypt. More bone chilling than before, the scream had set Logan's heart racing as he struggled to see the sufferer.

There in the corner of the room, what appeared to be the form of a woman sat motionless on the bed's edge, her back to the guardian. Several of the other occupants were now stirring from their drug enhanced slumbers as Logan rose to his feet.

"Ma'am, ma'am, are you alright?"

Logan struggled to force his wobbly legs to move forward under his weight. Except for the gentle shake of its sob, the figure ignored him, moving not an inch. Slowly, Logan drug himself towards the dimly lit corner of the room. From where he was, he could see that the figure was holding something that vaguely resembled a hand mirror in one hand, while operating a small light with the other. In the background he could hear the sound of voices and running feet from outside the doorway as he approached the patient's bed.

At the edge of the dimly lit bed, Logan paused to steady himself while gently reaching out to touch the woman's shoulder. As his fingers gently brushed the edge of her smock, she turned suddenly on him.

The bloodcurdling shriek exploded again, but to Logan, it was not from a human mouth. For there before the panicked explorer stood a creature of such nightmarish features that the seasoned warrior froze in terror.

The blood-stained monstrosity staring back bore little resemblance to a human, much less a woman. With the exception of its delicate right hand and its two-legged stance, it was almost unrecognizable. Two enormous orbs, barely resembling eyes, protruded like giant turnips from a grossly swollen red and purple cranium. Both were now fixed on Logan. Where there should have been normal facial features, there were instead twisted and distorted vessels clinging to bulbous cheeks and a bulging forehead that alternately throbbed and undulated with the creature's very pulse.

Logan stood paralyzed as the creature turned, reaching for him with a bloody claw-like left hand. In one motion, it both dropped the tiny mirror and lunged forward towards its victim. Horrified, Logan could not move as the creature wrapped itself around him in a bloody embrace. He was all but ready to throw the beast to the floor, when to his very great surprise he realized it was not attacking but clinging to him in terror. He stood motionless as the creature sobbing violently refused to let go.

Suddenly the room burst forth in light as Logan was surrounded by medical personnel. They immediately consoled the poor creature lifting her gently onto a rolling gurney. He stood there, unable to move or speak, the voice of Mahdia echoing as if he were a hundred kilometers away.

"He's in shock," the muffled voice said as they carefully guided him back towards his bed to administer a sedative. Easing back on his pillows Logan surveyed the room. Like a surreal movie playing out in slow motion its frantic occupants raced to restore order. His eyelids grew heavy as he fought the medication, concentrating instead on the four other occupants now sitting upright in their beds beside him. Logan noted how each individual looked different from earlier that day. Drifting off into the fog, he realized that they too were changing into what he had just seen the woman in the corner become. His last image was of her, the writhing creature restrained on a gurney exiting from the room.

"Hello beautiful." Logan announced, his drug induced fog still evident by the cheek to cheek smile he flashed as Nurse Carrington breezed into his room. The unexpected enthusiasm couldn't help but elicit a brief smile from his reluctant attendant.

"Good morning Commander, feeling a little more like your old self again, are we? Back to your womanizing ways?" Debbie K fired back, flashing her steely baby blues in his direction. Encouraged, Logan pressed further.

"What are you talking about, Nurse Carrington? Are you offended every time someone compliments you?" he asked feinting offense. Amused, she glided to his bedside, softly cradling his hand in hers. Logan felt his heart skip a beat, assured that his irresistible charm had finally cracked the ice. Suddenly, she flipped his hand palm up, slapping three red and black capsules into the center, and gently closed his fingers around them. Then bending low and looking directly into his eyes, she spoke coolly.

"Now Commodore Logan, you and I both know your reputation for flattery, especially, when it involves women half your age," she literally purred.

"Half my age! What are you, fifteen? How old do you think I am?"

"It's time for your medication, old man," she smiled, handing him a cup and pointing to the pills still held firmly in his hand, as she proceeded to strip the linens from an adjacent bed. Taking the cup, Logan frowned sitting forcefully back in his bed.

"Give it here," he complained, "I'll take it for all the good it will do. Don't think I didn't notice that you moved me to a new room, *Nurse Perfection*. I know what happened here last night." Choking down the pills, Logan flashed a teethy sarcastic smile at the Nurse.

"Dr. Mahdia has assured me that is not going to happen to you."

There was a pause as Logan looked dejectedly out the doorway. A small commotion seemed to be stirring in the outer hallway.

"What the devil's going on out there?"

"Well, Commodore, the doctor thought you might enjoy some visitors today. Thought it might get your designer label bottom out of that bed you've grown so attached to." Logan crumpled the paper cup, and looking straight into her big beautiful blue eyes, deftly tossed it across the room, banking it into the waste receptacle.

"Visitors? I don't want any visitors. Send them away."

"Sorry, your highness," she replied flashing back her own teethy smile, "doctor's orders."

Then, springing back, like a rodeo gate-keeper doorway, she unleashed two very small creatures into the room. These creatures, vaguely resembling children except for the inexplicably loud screams emanating from their *air holes,* set right to the task of jumping up and down from the guardian's bed.

There on the end of his bed, smiling ear to ear, was one very cute little ragdoll girl and one very squirrely freckle faced boy. Logan froze, his body tensed in a partial *Tae kwon do* defensive posture. The squirrely faced boy tensed, as all young boys do, imitating his hero's stance, and prompting a rousing round of laughter from the two females now looking over the bed.

It was only then that Logan realized that following closely on the two biped's heels was one slightly frustrated raven-haired beauty. Logan stared, his mouth hanging open twice in one day for the first time in many years.

"Good morning, Mr. Logan. Please forgive me, I am so sorry. Children get off of Mr. Logan's bed right now. Now, introduce yourselves properly like we discussed." Rebecca commanded the urchins firmly as they reluctantly descended from the gurney hanging backwards like chimpanzees from a tree limb.

Tommy and Beci Stillwell were six and five years old respectively. Beci had her mothers' beautiful brown eyes and Tommy had been spray painted with freckles. Grinning, they stared adoringly up at the guardsman, bearing very little resemblance to the huddled mass of terrified humanity he had cuddled just a few days before. Alternately, bouncing on and off the chair next to Logan's gurney, they spun on the floor to look up at him flashing huge wide-eyed grins. It was at this time that Logan noticed each child had one irresistible quality necessary for true munchkin attractiveness. Both kids were missing that all important strategically located front tooth. This was especially entertaining when Tommy tried to converse with Logan as each word had its own unique whistle to accompany its pronunciation. Logan could not help but laugh despite his bad mood.

"Now hold on-"Logan tried to speak before Tommy immediately interrupted him.

"Mom says you're a hero, Mr. Logan. Are you a guardian? She says you came and brought us back from the dead." Tommy rattled off one query after another. Almost as fast as he could speak, his sister chimed in with her own line of questioning.

"Are you Jesus, Mr. Logan?" the tiny face innocently asked, her face straining to look over the bars of his gurney's guardrail. Logan befuddled, but pleasantly amused by their inquisitiveness, struggled to respond without laughing.

"Well, I, uh…", he stammered before Beci interrupted. "Mommy says you came back to life from the dead and an angel helped you escape. She says you have a very powerful guardian angel, strong enough to bend steel. What does he look like? Does he look like Superman?"

Logan was still struggling to keep up. "Well Beci I'm afraid your mom has a very vivid imagination…, uh, who's Superman?" Tommy jumped right in.

"Oh, no sir, my mommy doesn't have any imagination," the boy spoke emphatically. "She says the imagination is a silly waste of time. Besides, she's right. I saw him, ten feet tall, on fire with wings and a sword. He used his sword and bent that metal thing on the ground. Then he woke you up. And when you fell to the ground again he put you in the ship and closed the door."

"Tommy, are you saying you were watching through the portal when I passed out?" Logan replied transfixed by the conversation's direction. Tommy nodded his head ferociously. "Yep! The air came on in the room and I woke up. I could see you working and your suit was turning funny colors. You looked sad and then you passed out," the boy finished.

Logan sat back to recline again as an astonished look descended gradually across his face. Rebecca, still motionless, stood across the room, silently observing.

"Obviously, you have no problem with the imagination," Logan quipped shooting a glance up at Rebecca "That's an interesting story, Tommy, but you see, there's no such thing as angels. It was probably just the changing of the air quality. You two had been unconscious for some time, and your mind can play tricks…."

"Oh no! Mr. Logan, Tommy wouldn't say it if it didn't happen. That would be a lie! Everybody knows that it's not right to tell a lie." Beci interrupted, looking innocently over the bars again. Tommy jumped down moving over to the side of the bed and put his hand on Logan's arm.

"Don't you 'member? You woke up off the floor and almost hurt yourself when the angel moved over in the corner," the boy added, snapping the last missing detail of the story into place as his mother moved forward.

"Ok, kids, this has been fascinating for all of us, but let Mr. Logan rest now. I think you guys have worn him out already. Go out in the waiting area with the nice nurse, and I'll be along in a minute. I want to talk to Mr. Logan myself."

The two kids flailed themselves again onto the gurney climbing up to give Logan hugs around the neck.

"Bye, Mr. Logan!" they echoed together as they ran out the door and down the hall. Logan smiled, swallowing hard as he choked back the tears.

"Those are two incredibly cute kids. Thank you for bringing them by. You have no idea." He stopped in mid-sentence and then, struggling to maintain his composure, started again.

"They look like you," he spoke, his mind a million miles away.

Softly and modestly she replied, "Thank you. They're great kids. I love them dearly, and they wouldn't be here if it weren't for you," she continued, resting her hand on top of his. Grateful for the tenderness, he momentarily squeezed hers in response, before releasing it.

"You don't need to go there, Ms. Stillwell. I was just doing my job," Logan replied admiring her eyes, almond in color and set softly above her high cheek bones. The two sat there quietly as Logan traced the gentle contour of her face from her cheeks to her thin but softly rounded nose and down the nape of her gracefully sloping neck. To say that this woman was as perfectly endowed as Nurse Carrington would have been untrue, but to say that she was every bit as beautiful was no exaggeration. Logan found in her a quiet beauty that stemmed from some mysterious inner quality.

"Don't hand me that, we were both there. No one else gave a flip whether my kids were dead or alive," her soft voice was surprisingly blunt.

"They didn't know, that's all."

Rebecca paused as rising from the bed she turned, her disappointment fading into frustration as she shook her head in stubborn defiance.

"They didn't want to know. That was the problem. They couldn't have cared less whether my children lived or died," she pronounced emphatically, "Do you want to know why? I'll tell you why, because no one wanted to go into that Hell-hole and get them out, that's why."

Logan held up his finger to his mouth in a desperate attempt to silence her progressively vocal tirade.

"Hold on, Rebecca. It's more complicated than that. They had their job to do. They also have families to go back to. I don't."

"So you get the dirty jobs," she complained compassionately, "Because you lost your family, you're expendable? Is that how it works?" Logan looked down, arching one eyebrow.

"Mr. Logan, I've heard what happened to your family, and I'm so very sorry," her voice softened, cracking under the guilt, "Please forgive me for making you go down after my children. I didn't know who else to turn to."

Years of military training filled with life and death decisions had failed to immunize Logan from a woman's tears. So despite his better judgment, he reached out his arm and grasping her wrist pulled her gently to the side of the bed. Tenderly wiping the tears from her eyes, he spoke kindly.

"Hey, what are you apologizing for, for me saving your children's lives? Don't you dare say you're sorry. Don't you dare. You fought for your children," he paused, choking on his own words, "Do you know that old saying 'Nobody loves more than he who dies'?"

She smiled through swollen eyes. "Do you mean, 'Greater love hath no man than he who would lay down his life for his brother'?"

He sat back pointing his finger right at her.

"Yeah, that's the one. Who was it who said that?"

"Jesus."

"Yeah, Jesus. Yeah, he's the guy," his eyes rolled trying to convince himself, "Well, that's what I'm kinda' doing. Meeting those kids has kinda' helped me to see that. I'm not looking forward to dying, but at least my death has a purpose. Very few people can claim that, you know?"

"I know."

The two space travelers, now new friends sat alone together for another twenty minutes, the silence occasionally interrupted by the idle chatter of two souls yearning to know one another better. Eventually Rebecca sighed as she summoned her courage.

"You know, Logan, I believe there's a purpose for everything." A strange huffing noise emanating from Logan's side of the bed interrupted her.

"Well, I don't. There is way too much pain in this world to ever make sense of. You just haven't seen enough of it," Logan knowingly objected. Rebecca squeezed his hand, rising as she prepared to head for the door.

"Oh, I've seen my share and I still believe there's a purpose even in those things," she continued, "There are a lot of things that don't make sense in this world Logan. Like how you survived radiation exposure, or how one person may walk away from a plane crash that kills hundreds, or from an earthquake that destroys an entire village. Believing there's a purpose, without yet seeing, that's called faith. Every great leader has had it, and every desperate nation, including ours, is starved for it. We all need it."

"I might have faith in a deity if the universe wasn't such a cold and hostile place. Either he doesn't exist or he's betrayed a lot of innocent people," Logan responded.

"Betrayed," Rebecca sighed, "isn't that a bit harsh?"

"Betrayed, that's exactly what I meant!"

"Look, Mr. Logan, I don't have all the answers. The universe can be a very cold and hostile place, but it is also filled with great beauty and love. If I were in your position, I might feel the same. There would be one thing nagging at me though. If the universe is such a cold and hostile place, how should I have come up with the notion that it ought to be otherwise? I mean, how does one know that a crooked line should be straight unless he has some idea of what a straight line should look like? So where did any of us get this notion that the universe should be good? Where does that come from?"

"Hmph," Logan sat there quietly, leaving Rebecca regretting her debate.

"Look, I've, uh, said too much already. I don't want there to be tension between us. Good Grief. Where are my children now?"

"Try the engineering deck," Logan quipped with a smile on his face. Rebecca laughed as she squeezed his hand before stepping away.

"We'll see you before we depart," she said waving as she turned for the door, "Thank you so much again. Take care, Commander Logan."

And with that she was gone.

Contrary to his doctors' actual predictions, Logan's condition, while guarded at first, changed very little showing no detectable signs of deterioration. One week later, his treatments had decreased allowing him to regain sufficient strength to return to his private dorm and a limited regimen of exercise. Logan's private cabin, a small three by four meter unit resembling more armory than dorm room, bore myriads of antique weapons from over twenty different cultures.

The 'hall of fame', as Logan liked to call it, was his crowning adornment. Consisting of a relatively small illuminated cabinet, containing dozens of awards and trophies of various sizes and designs, it represented the accomplishments of a lifetime. The trophies, some small and gold plated, others large and either bronze or trimmed in silver, together composed a monument to a life of military and guardian heroics.

Logan, however, now lived a life mostly ignoring past victories, instead obsessing on the peculiar mental discipline of driving himself to the point of complete exhaustion.

He was thus engaged in this his favorite activity when Rebecca found him collapsed under the expansive windows of the ship's observation deck. With the enormous panorama of the continents of Earth drifting by, the guardsman lay still, his strength drained from his fourth kilometer around the jogging track.

As he lay there, prone to the world and drenched in sweat, he was suddenly startled by the gentle touch of a woman's hand. Unable to rise, he flinched, and then raising his dripping head, observed Rebecca Stillwell and her two small munchkins standing nearby.

"Excuse me, Mr. Logan, I-- I didn't mean to surprise you," Rebecca spoke softly, "Are you alright? You just looked so pale and when you collapsed the children… well, I'm sorry." Logan smiled to see the munchkins standing side by side with their mother and grinning ear to ear. He slowly righted himself to a sitting position, gently tossing Tommy's unkempt hair and mockingly pinching Beci's rosy cheeks. The children fascinated by the panorama and a place to run took off down the empty track.

"No. No, it's alright, Rebecca," Logan responded. "I'm just a little jumpy, must be the radiation. Look, we're all friends here right? Please call me Jon." Rebecca smiled readily acquiescing.

"Very well, Jon, do you mind if I sit?" she responded, perching herself so far from the guardsman that she all but fell off the end of the bench. Logan stifled a laugh as she struggled to safely reposition herself. Grasping her hand to steady her, he became aware of that which he had so quickly forgotten, how bewitchingly attractive she was.

"How are you feeling?" she began, the concern in her voice like a soothing balm to Logan's beleaguered spirit.

"Is there anything you need?"

Logan cast a quick glance towards the children as the fleeting thought of asking for a hug darted through his mind.

"I'm fine, just winded from my run." Then with a pause, "Look, I'd like to apologize." The two sat there on the bench, facing one another, but still separated by some distance.

"Apologize? Apologize for what?"

"Well you know, for belittling you when you were just trying to be encouraging. I just kinda' threw it back in your face. I don't know why I did that."

"That's ok, Jon. You don't need to apologize for being wrong," she said smiling faintly.

"Wrong, who said anything about being wrong? I just didn't want to hurt your feelings. If you want to go about with 'pie in the sky' beliefs about life that's your business. Don't call my beliefs wrong though."

"What beliefs might those be, Jon?"

"They're personal."

"So, you don't feel comfortable sharing them with me?"

"Nope."

"I thought we were friends."

"We are, and I'd like to keep it that way. That's why I'm not talking to you about it." There was a brief pause as Rebecca mused over the interchange.

"You know, I know how it feels not want to talk to anyone. I was the same way for a while after I lost my husband."

Logan grew suddenly silent.

"He was a good man, patient, kind, a friend to everyone he met. Everybody loved him, especially the children." She hesitated, taking a deep breath.

"Since we lost him, they've never been the same. The doctors said we needed to get away. Take a trip, one of them said, 'Find an adventure'."

"I'd say you found one," Logan agreed with a smile.

"I haven't seen a smile on their faces until that day in your hospital room. I just thought maybe we could be friends. Maybe we could both use another friend," she concluded. A long silence followed with no response. Finally, assuming that there would be none she stood, turning to leave.

"I was on patrol," he started bitterly; "I should have been there. I should have been there." He spoke slowly, head hung, as Rebecca slid back closer in her seat.

"My wife was a beautiful woman. You remind me a lot of her, beautiful on the outside, graceful on the inside. She talked like you, all full of fairy tales about God. How ironic that religious fanatics would be the ones to murder her." Rebecca put her hand to her mouth in silent shock.

Logan heaved a heavy sigh before continuing.

"We met in the military. I was an Air force jockey flying sorties over China and she was an intelligence analyst. She later became an assistant to Senator Hutch who was hated not only for her methods, but her position against religion. I tried to get her to quit, but like you, she felt 'God' had a purpose for her being there. She felt like if she could just talk to Hutch she could dissuade her. How heartless that the very people she was trying to help would murder her and our children."

He hesitated again, staring blankly at the floor as Rebecca gently touched her hand to his shoulder.

"What happened, Jon?"

Logan strained against the stubborn words, his voice cracking with each syllable.

"They call themselves THE REMNANT. It's a 'Christian' terror group, for God's sake! They're trying to stop the banning of religion by killing women and children. How twisted is that?"

"They killed your wife and your children?"

Logan nodded.

"They tried to kill Hutch, wired her armored limo but they'd never built a bomb before. So all they succeeded on doing was setting the car on fire. My wife, my daughter and my son died in that fire before they could get them out. They burned alive. Hutch was so enraged when she became President that she passed the Hutch amendment repealing freedom of religion and you know what happened to her."

"They assassinated her."

"Exactly, and now we have that bozo Masada as *bumbler-in-chief.*"

Rebecca sat there in stunned silence for a moment before she ventured to speak.

"Jon, I don't really know what to say. I am so sorry, but Christianity is a religion of peace," Rebecca replied defensively. "Those people are no more Christians than I'm the President."

"Save it Sista," Logan dismissed her, "My wife and I had this discussion for years, and then it finally cost her life. As far as I'm concerned, your God is dead, because if he were alive, he never would have allowed that to happen."

They sat there in the silent uneasiness of the moment before Rebecca dared to speak again.

"Logan, I know where you're at. I've been there. I've felt that bitterness, felt that anger, that despair, but God can use even the tragedies of our lives for good if we let Him. If we can just trust, during the painful times, He can lead us through them. If we try to get out of them on our own we will only end up failing again."

Logan stood, his patience now having come to an end. He bent to grab his towel, wrapping it around his neck.

"Rebecca, I know you think you've got it all so neatly figured out. It's just that what works for you, may not work for me. We're different. I just can't believe in someone, or something, I can't see or touch and who burns little children alive." Rebecca's eyes began to glisten as she struggled to gently respond.

"You know, Jon when you're right, you're right. We are all different, with our own hopes, dreams and fears. But we're also very much alike in many ways. We all make mistakes. We've all done things or said things we wish we could take back, and we all want to be loved. By the way, love is another one of those things you can't see or touch, and yet most people have no trouble believing in it.

You're hurting now because it, just like God, is real. But he didn't murder your children any more than he killed my Jim. Some very evil men killed your family, and some day they will have to answer to that just God. Give Him a chance, that's all He's asking."

She hugged him for a few seconds as he stood there stiffly, and slowly letting go, she turned and walked away.

CHAPTER THREE
The Royal Treatment

The USSA Potomac, now two days into her scheduled waypoint in low earth orbit, was releasing her space shuttle from the starboard launch bay. Onboard, one very reluctant hero fidgeted as the sleek wedged-shaped vessel touched down gently on Walter Reed's pad number two. The guardian stepped tentatively from the shuttle's exit ramp to the tar mac below, and was immediately immersed in a sea of blue 'Smurf-colored' scrubs worn by adoring nurses and physicians having watched Logan's daring rescue on the net. The astronaut, himself privy to a thousand questions, had himself only two: Where could he get a cheeseburger and fries, and where was the nearest restroom?

Some two hours later, his appetite appeased and his bladder empty, Logan was placed in the capable hands of the world's leading expert in radiation poisoning – David Livingston MD, PhD. Renowned for his discovery of *Plasorbigen* and his ground breaking techniques of DNA repair, Livingston was as famous for his research as for his family moniker.

His tenure at *The New Walter Reed Military Hospital* afforded Livingston two major advantages in his work. First and foremost was an almost constant patient population suffering from the most debilitating cases of radiation exposure. This population consisted mainly of astronauts, guardsmen, tourists and the military. Second was an endless influx of funding from both the military and private enterprise, granting him access to the latest technology available.

His epiphany, *Plasorbigen,* was the powerful radiation absorbing synthetic plasma with properties that flushed and reinvigorated damaged tissues while stimulating the replication of healthy bone marrow cells and eliminating damaged ones. This 'flushing' treatment was administered at potentially toxic concentrations only under Livingston's careful supervision on earth. The *full body flush,* utilized in combination with stem cell DNA repair and vascular grafting, combined to give most victims an extended life span of some twelve to eighteen months.

In addition, the quality of life was near normal for most patients until their last forty-eight to ninety-six hours. It was then that the rapid transformation from a painless, symptom-free existence transformed the sufferer into the writhing tortured creature Logan had observed on the *Potomac*. The terminology commonly employed for this last developmental form was a *GRUB*. The acronym, which stood for *Gamma Radiation Undifferentiated Biogenesis,* was untreatable, *the s*tandard medical treatment being euthanasia.

It was with this knowledge that Logan began his next month of treatment in the radiation unit. Session after session of treatments continued over a period of four weeks. Each hour-long session left Logan exhausted affording him the "luxury" of reclining just long enough to recover before the next. During these periods Logan would closely study the political unrest tearing at the social fabric of his country.

In twelve major cities across the United States, massive demonstrations were paralyzing the populace requiring state officials to call in the National Guard. The protestors, demonstrating in support of religious liberties, included conscientious objectors from all of the major religions. This observation both amused and perplexed Logan, as most of the conflict involved new legislation specifically aimed at restricting the Christian faith. While the vast majority of the protests were peaceful, the sheer size of the crowds amazed Logan. 'How could so many people believe this stuff?' he thought to himself.

Government reports detailed increasing unrest in fifteen of the nation's southern states, with thirteen states actively resisting the newly passed federal legislation requiring a complete and immediate cessation of all religious activities. Religion had been declared a psychological illness according to recent proceedings of the American Medical and American Psychological Associations. For the greater good of the country, all individuals convicted of engaging in religious activities were to be subject to federal prosecution and punishment equaling 5 years in a planetary penal colony. Christianity, in particular, had been targeted as the major offender, due to its vocal opposition to recent legislative efforts. These newly passed bills prohibited public prayer and public demonstrations in support of Biblical values.

State elected officials who were conscientious objectors to the newly enacted legislation called for closed door meetings. Most alarming of all were the recent strong discussions advocating secession of individual states from the union. The federal government's response was a prompt warning that all such meetings were in violation of federal statutes and would bring an immediate military response.

"Religious nuts, they'll get us all killed over some stupid myths and fairy tales," Logan yelled, stabbing a pointed index finger at the monitor on the wall. Frustrated, he turned off his monitor's sound and prepared to launch a missile in the form of a flower vase at his electronic tormentor.

"That's not covered under your health insurance plan," the deep baritone voice of David Livingston announced from behind. "Plus, our maintenance team is way overworked and underpaid, so I'd personally appreciate it if you'd refrain from destroying the accommodations, Commodore."

Logan turned to see a middle-aged man with sandy brown hair and clad in scrubs and a white lab coat enter the room. He was transfixed on the thin semi-transparent recording tablet that contained the sum total of Logan's medical records. Logan immediately replaced the porcelain vase on the night stand beside him. The man walking to the night stand gently transferred the vase to a distant table.

"Dr. Livingston, I presume." Logan quipped, frowning at his empty night stand.

"Precisely, Commander, and I'll be glad to remove all the valuable breakables from your room if you wish."

"Yes, uh, that won't be necessary."

"Great! Now, how are you feeling?"

"Finer than frog hair," Logan replied, flashing a sarcastic smile, "I think I'll go out and run a three minute mile". Livingston looked up momentarily over his black rimmed half eye glasses at Logan. His expression of exasperation spoke volumes betraying his attitude towards Logan.

"Commander Logan, all joking aside, I'm recommending your discharge today. Do you think you're strong enough to carry on normal day to day activities or shall I issue a home caretaker?"

"Nurse Carrington?" Logan asked excitedly.

"I'm afraid Nurse Carrington is literally a million kilometers away by now. I was thinking of a slightly more mature woman, she's say, in her sixties and has hairy legs and a moustache," the doctor continued, working, never cracking a smile. Logan sat up quickly in his bed, pinching both cheeks to enhance the color and flashing that cheeky grin again.

"Now doc, look here. I feel great!" pointing at his cheeks as he spoke. "When have you ever seen such color in a New Yorker? Seriously, come on now, doc, I'm fine, really. Your treatments worked. Even my arms look better," he said holding both forearms in midair, each devoid of the spidery vessels, "So, when can I get out of here?"

"Today, if you like," the physician responded.

"What about future treatments?" Logan asked, hoping there was something the man sitting on the edge of his bed had overlooked. Livingston looked down at his chart again and shook his head.

"They're ineffective after 6 weeks. Most of the degeneration is taking place in your DNA. Plasorbigen can't penetrate the nuclear membrane to remove the toxins. Even if it could, it itself is toxic to DNA. We've spliced replacement parts to patch your stem cell DNA virally, but that won't stop the long-term effects. It will just slow them down. I'm sorry Jon. We've done all we can, no one can replace DNA."

The finality in Livingston's voice precluded any more questioning on Logan's part. The last words that Livingston uttered faded into the drone of medical jargon that Logan had conditioned himself to ignore for years. An hour later, the guardian was packed and on his way home.

CHAPTER FOUR
There's No Place Like Home

As the heavily armored limousine veered from the highway and onto the guardsman's gravel driveway, an oppressive sense of gloom settled across Logan's mind. He knew what was waiting inside as he watched the familiar grey and white portico come into view. Eventually the silent vehicle slid to a stop, leaving Logan momentarily motionless before reaching for the handle. Barely a word of thanks was exchanged as Logan, suitcase in hand, exited the vehicle and walked timidly into the house.

Unlike past homecomings, this was for Logan a mixture of more pain than pleasure. For cocooned within the comfort of the familiar hung the vestiges of a shattered life. Slowly he made his way into the dimly lit hallway, his fingers tracing faded pictures lining the wall. Everywhere Logan turned clung pictures of happiness, no longer to return. Photos of trips to the mountains were peppered with drawings made by a little boy and a little girl, still oh so very dear to Logan. A broken bicycle wheel, long in need of repair, yet never mended by a missing father, lay in the corner of the next room, a reminder of promises not kept. Logan bent near it, tears now tracing their way across his cheeks as he attempted to spin the wobbly orb, its memory tearing at his heart.

In a corner chair sat a doll once carried everywhere, now in need of someone to hold her. Logan picked her up and hugged her tightly, imagining if only for a moment, he was holding his little girl. He shuffled over to the living room desk, doll in hand where a small napkin folded over containing the burned and scarred remains of a wedding ring once adorning a cherished finger. This memento of love was the cruelest, piercing Logan to the heart with a deep regret for having taken so much for granted. He sat on the floor in the dark for what seemed like an hour, unable to move, unwilling to experience this house of torment any longer. Then, the hot stream of tears burning tracks into his inflamed cheeks suddenly felt the cooling release of a liquid balm coming from out of nowhere.

"What the"? Logan squeaked, turning his head and opening his eyes. It was at this moment that he found himself suddenly knocked to the floor, being greeted by a loud bark from a smelly pit hole of a mouth less than three inches from his face.

"Bark" went the huge Labrador, its entire rear quarters wagging in vigorous harmony with the golden tail adorning the end.

"Trigger!" Logan yelped back as the 100 pound golden retriever pinned him firmly to the floor, his long tongue lathering thick mucus laden salivary secretions all over his face. Despite the bath, Logan was thrilled to see the quivering hound, his last remaining family member. Grabbing him by the neck, Logan wrestled him into a choke hold hug that soon sent the mutt scattering in all different directions out of excitement and pent up desire to play.

"Oh good boy! I almost forgot the neighbors were still watching you," Logan praised as he grabbed the mutt by his neck, scratching behind his ears, "Yes, we will play, but first I need to get moved in".

With Trigger's help, Logan decided to stay and the two friends began the laborious task of moving in. No task, no matter how menial, found Logan without his friend at his side. And Logan, to his surprise, would have had it no other way. Some hours later, the two amigos climbed into Logan's sleek red convertible and headed for the ocean.

This respite, while immensely enjoyed by the "two Logans", was ripe with memories of playful family times on the beach. Images flooded back of throwing Frisbees and flying kites with his children, surfing the waves on air-filled floats and hiking the rocky coast to see huge waves splashing violently ashore. Now it was just he and Trigger on these walks, and Logan began to wish his fourteen months over sooner than later.

Trigger, ever faithful, was always at his side. The two were inseparable, and Logan, dogged mercilessly by the media, found this to be of immeasurable value, when more than once, his canine defender chased off unwelcome photographers. On occasion, his long toothed champion demonstrated an uncanny knack for discovering and dispatching uninvited paparazzi attempting to sneak inappropriate photos through an open window. Trigger became so famous that there was even a beach video on the net of him wrestling the pants off of a paparazzi who refused to leave his master alone. The reporter, making the unfortunate choice to cling to his camera instead of his trousers, soon found himself up to his bellybutton in midnight ocean breeze. Attempting to retrieve the stolen pants, the man on the video was next seen dragging a very persistent golden retriever whose jowls were locked securely onto his right buttock. Despite desperately trying to shake the dog loose, the man was only eventually released, sans briefs, by the gentle whistle of a compassionate Logan.

Hours turned to days and days to weeks as Logan, locked in his own prison of guilt, began a slow spiral downward. Binge drinking became more the rule than the exception. Then the terrible dreams began. At first, they were rare, with Logan being visited only once or twice a week at most. Later, they arrived nightly, sometimes coming in waves of two or three episodes per night. Strange dreams, they were filled with haunting images of flaming cars entombing his screaming children, angry conversations with Rebecca Stillwell and flashbacks of the toxic POD bay.

Trigger seemed to be the only friend Logan had left, with the loyal companion often waking Logan from a drunken stupor for walks in the brisk morning air. When Logan would begin with the booze, Trigger would lay, paws over his head and mournfully whine.

In addition to alcohol, there was the other stimulant Logan had come to find acutely difficult to live without. Beginning in the early morning hours, or with Trigger's first inspiration, and escalating throughout the day, Logan submerged his mind in the cascade of electronic media flowing through the net. His favorite topic to follow was naturally, the issue that appalled him most, the impending secession of six or more southern states. Each day seemed to bring new reports about the separatist movement in the south led by the religious right. Two more states had joined the discussion on the issue of secession. The federal government responded by declaring a lock down on several key southern military bases, including NASA and the National Space command, while simultaneously issuing a tersely worded warning with implicit military tones. These apprehensions, working in tandem with the constant reminder of Logan's own personal failures, begat a harvest of depression in Logan's mind.

As this relentless cycle passed, Logan would often awaken lying in his own bloody vomit, like a prize fighter knocked flat by an unseen hand.

This day was no different except for the fact, that for some unexplained reason, his connection to the net was interrupted. After a shower, shave and a hot cup of black coffee, Logan sat at his kitchen table realizing he was watching what little life he had left pass him by. He knew he was down and had no idea how to get up again. Once more the soft warm paw of a close friend found his leg as Logan looked down to see Trigger nuzzling up next to him.

"Sorry ole' boy," Logan started, "seems I've lost my way. I don't know what to do." This response was greeted with a soft gentle whine and the loving gaze of two huge brown eyes. Unable to resist the adoration of his loyal friend, Logan bent down to hug the furry creature's neck. It was at this point, at the lowest point in his life that the phone rang. Trigger whined. Logan sat up, breaking the furry embrace and pointing directly at his four-legged friend.

"And don't think I'm gonna' answer that!"

"Bark!" came Trigger's immediate objection.

"Oh that bothers you, huh? Well, dogs don't have to talk to press correspondents on the phone do they?" Trigger barked again as the phone continued to ring. Placing his coffee cup into the sink, Logan turned to see the dog pointing again at the phone.

"Oh, Yeh! Well you answer it then."

The phone rang for a third time, echoed immediately by a firmer more insistent bark aimed directly at his owner.

"You crazy dog, Ok, OK I'll answer it, but you'll see. You'll see. It will be some telemarketer trying to sell me

EXLAXX doggie treats for my constipated mutt," Logan warned as he waved his finger again at the cowering canine.

"You, buddy. You are eating one". Irritated, Logan picked up the unit barking into the receiver.

"Hello!"

"Hello, hello, is Jon Logan there"? The sweet southern voice came from the other end.

Immediately Logan recognized Rebecca Stillwell. Embarrassed, he desperately tried to collect his wits while Trigger just looked up at him, head cocked and a low whine rumbling from within his throat. Rebecca, speaking on the other end of the phone, was temporarily ignored while Logan covered the receiver and whispered to the pooch. "Don't let it go to your head." The dog, content with his victory, just sat there panting and wagging his tail.

"It's so good to hear your voice again Jon. How are you?" Rebecca continued the concern evident in her voice.

"Me, Oh I'm fine, just great, never better."

"That's great. So the treatments worked and you're OK?" Rebecca asked excitedly. Logan hesitated.

"Uh, yeh, you could say that, just a few minor side effects from the medication. I should be good as new soon."

"Oh, Jon that's wonderful. The children will be so glad to hear that."

'Wow', he thought, 'Somebody who actually cares whether I live or die.' A strained silence followed and then He asked, "How are Tommy and Beci?"

"They're great. They ask about you all the time. As a matter of fact they are the reason I'm calling."

"Really?" Logan responded with genuine surprise.

"Yes, look, I know you're very busy, what with interviews and your career, and all, but everybody needs a break now and then. They just wanted to know if you might have a couple of free days to come down to our farm for some *R & R*. We live on the coast of South Carolina near Charleston and you could spend some time with the kids at the beach."

"Gee, Rebecca, I don't know. I'm really busy." Logan replied, looking at the huge collection of trash and empty vodka bottles on the table. Trigger looked up from where he sat, head still cocked as another low whine escaped the corner of his mouth.

"I understand," came back the genuinely disappointed reply. "I told the children you had become famous, and you probably didn't have time for kids."

Like a dagger the words hit home. Trigger whined, this time a bit louder, causing a suddenly solemn Logan to turn, silently commanding him to be quiet. The dog lay flat covering his ears with both paws, causing Logan, almost on the verge of tears, to suppress a laugh.

"Hang on, uh, Rebecca. Maybe I could squeeze a couple days in between my obligations," Logan struggled clearing the congestion from his throat. Trigger, head still cocked, was now up on all fours and panting. Logan flashed him the thumbs up sign and his furry encourager let out a little yelp of excitement as he started chasing his tail in circles.

"Oh Jon, that would be great. The kids would be so excited. They have done nothing but talk about what they would do if you could come down. I'll send you directions," she replied as Logan looked down with amazement at the crazy four legged friend of his.

"Just one thing, Rebecca. Can I bring my dog?" Logan asked timidly.

"Sure, what's his name?" came back the answer.

"Trigger", Logan said. There was another moment of silence and then a stifled laugh came over the phone.

"Trigger! You're kidding, right?" She snickered.

Logan was confused and a little hurt at first when he answered.

"No, what's so funny? I thought it was a really unique name."

"I'm sorry Jon, it's just that my dad used to make me watch these old *Roy Rogers* videos when I was a kid."

"Roy who?"

"Never mind."

"You did say the beach, didn't you? Where do you live again, Ms. Stillwell?" Logan spoke trying to clear the cobwebs from his brain.

"Please, my friends call me Becky. You can keep us both straight, can't you? We have an old 1800's plantation my family has lived in for 160 years. It's near Charleston, and you can see the ocean from the house. We'd love to have you," Rebecca answered.

"You know, that sounds really nice. I'll change my schedule. And I'll bring my dog?

"Of course, Trigger and any other famous animal you own is always welcome in our home. He can play with Lucky, our collie."

"Lucky! Your dog's name is Lucky? Let me guess. He has one eye and three legs," Logan retorted as Becky laughed.

"Yep, you guessed it. I'm always bringing home stray misfits. So, please come, you'll feel right at home. By the way, your dog does like children, doesn't he?" She fired back. Logan smiled widely, enjoying the banter for the first time in a long time from a female.

"He loves them, especially with ketchup."

"You bring him down here, and we'll spoil him at least as much as we're going to spoil you. We call it Southern hospitality."

"I'm on my way." Logan answered, actually looking forward to something again.

"Fine, we'll see you when we see you. 'Bye Jon, Be safe, God bless."

"I will be, you too, and Becky, thank you." Logan ended as he turned off the monitor and turned to his faithful friend.

"Well, boy, looks like you and I are going on a little vacation," Logan smiled bending low to stroke his best friend's golden brow. Trigger barked, his tail wagging enthusiastically.

"I sure hope you like grits."

CHAPTER FIVE
A New Start

That a man reaps what he sows, later than he sows and more than he sows, was a lesson Logan was gleaning hand over fist at this time in his life. Wading through his bed room was no exception as he began the unenviable task of locating clean articles of clothing to pack into his suitcase. Locating the desired clothing distributed throughout the room was no challenge. The act of extracting them from their various domestic projections was another matter altogether.

Dozens of trophies of every design, purpose and refinement adorned the wall of Logan's room. In one corner alone twenty three brass trophies hung reflecting Logan's martial arts abilities. Each was now uniquely bejeweled with its own pair of boxer shorts. One label read '2087 Air Academy Black Belt of the Year Award'. Every trophy built upon the accomplishment of the previous signaling a prestigious reputation for excellence in the field of military prowess. On the far wall hung two crossed silver plated swords trimmed elegantly in gold and offset by a centrally mounted shield bearing the emblem of Logan's Alma Mata. Below the display hung the brass plate engraved with the mantra 'Northeast Division Conference Champion - Fencing 2081'.

While each of these many accolades made wonderful adornments attesting to the life of a proficient warrior, they made detestable clothing hangers. Just the act of trying to pull one pair of *Hanes* from a low hanging pendant could literally bring the house down.

To say that Logan had experienced an attitude adjustment would be an understatement as he rushed rapidly about washing clothes, drying and ironing before packing his bags and heading out the door towards his car. Like a kid going to summer camp he threw his self-compressing bags into the sleek electric Sportster's back seat, and snapping his fingers for Trigger, bumped the back door closed with his hip. At last the two friends had jumped in behind the controls ready to leave.

Trigger, ever the control freak in Logan's life, naturally jumped in behind the steering wheel before being shoved mercilessly to his navigator position.

"Mind your place," came his rebuke.

Side by side, the two amigos sped southward. Gliding silently and effortlessly down the acceleration lane of the North-South beltway, Logan and Trigger settled back in custom leather seats. The Sportster, piloted by the onboard computer, rocketed down the beltway at 215 kilometers per hour.

Two hours later, the outline of Charleston's metropolitan center could be seen. *Skycars* whizzing in near perfect parallel formation filled the lanes of the virtual skyway overhead. Logan often wondered who the Einstein was that had designed the skyway directly above the beltway. Even though he heard of very few accidents, he could just imagine an errant Skycar careening out of control into the path of his new red Sportster.

It was somewhere around seven pm when Logan arrived at the home of Rebecca Stillwell. Turning the curve of the final highway, Logan could see the entrance to an imposing gate. Its pillars, built entirely of river bedrock, dated from the pre-civil war era and bore on their hinges enormous iron gates beckoning him onward. Silently the Sportster glided down the gravel driveway outlined by dozens of massive Southern oaks each wrapped in a blanket of golden Spanish moss. A quarter mile later, having passed hundreds of acres of patchy white cotton fields, Logan reached the doorway of a capacious Southern plantation. Its main house boasted a huge wrap-around porch with Grecian columns dotting the perimeter. Antique gas lanterns lit the way leading to the front porch steps. As Logan ascended the steps, his school boy enthusiasm began to succumb to an overwhelming feeling of embarrassment and fear.

"What am I doing here?" he asked himself quietly as he gingerly knocked on the huge wooden door.

After knocking a second time and receiving no reply, Logan began to back away from the door. About half way down the steps and almost to his car, Logan heard the huge wooden door suddenly swing open as a middle-aged man, about his own height, emerged. This turn of events surprised Logan, who stammered, eventually finding his voice.

"Is, is, uh, this uh. I mean excuse me, is this the home of Rebecca Stillwell?"

"It is," came the reply from the handsome man at the door, "can I help you? Do we know you sir?"

"Well, uh, no. I don't think you do. And who are you sir?"

"Bill Stillwell," came back the polite reply from the kindhearted looking fellow. "Can I help you?" he continued, seemingly genuinely concerned over Logan's confusion.

Stunned and embarrassed Logan struggled for a way to explain his dilemma.

"Yeh…….. Uh, excuse me I was looking for someone else." His eyes looked down dejectedly as his head bowed and he turned to walk away. Suddenly he heard a familiar voice.

"Who is it Billy... oh my, its Mr. Logan, Jon, come in. Billy this is the man who saved Tommy and Beci. Come in Jonny. Do come in," Rebecca Stillwell said as she almost skipped down the steps and grabbing his arm, practically drug him up the stairs and into the house.

"I'm sorry…..I don't know why I'm here," Logan protested, his face flush with embarrassment.

"Come in here and sit down. You look exhausted. You're so thin. Let me get you something to eat," Rebecca commanded forcing Logan to a seat in the expansive kitchen.

"Look, I'm fine. Please don't bother. I'm just a little tired. I need to be going," Logan demurred, his body hesitating.

"Going, don't be ridiculous, you just got here. You need to rest. You're not going anywhere. Here drink this." Rebecca insisted as she thrust a frost covered glass into his hand. Reluctantly, Logan sat back at the big kitchen table and drank from the still frozen glass.

"That's really good," he proclaimed rolling his eyes, "What is it?"

"You like that, huh? It's a special drink you can only get right here." She smiled as she pointed towards the pitcher. "We call it sweet tea. It's our secret recipe and only real Southerners know how to make it."

Logan laughed weakly, relaxing a little before speaking.

"I'm sorry for being here. I don't really know why I'm here. Now I just feel embarrassed at interrupting you and your husband's weekend."

Perplexed, Rebecca looked at Bill and then back again at Logan, a tiny nervous laugh escaping from her lips. Pointing at Bill and then again at Logan, her mouth ajar and her eyes narrowing, a knowing smile drifted across both the Stillwells.

"My husband?" her tone expressing confusion and amusement, "Oh you mean Billy. He's not my husband. He's Jim's brother."

"I told you what happened to Jim," she added emphatically, "Did you forget?" Then hesitating, she asked smoothly.

"Why is it so important, anyway Jon?"

Now embarrassed in a different way, Logan stammered for a reply. "No reason, I just didn't want to be a bother."

"A bother! How can you be a bother? I invited you down here. You are my guest," she reminded him, laying her hand on his arm and looking straight into his eyes.

"And you are amongst good friends here, Jon. Please make yourself at home," she continued smiling as she sat down by the guardsman.

"Billy, here, has been a life saver. When Jim died, I was at wits end trying to figure out how to run the farm. Billy quit his job and took over. He and his wife and four kids live a couple miles from here. It's helped a lot having the cousins close. Now how have you been? - How's your health?"

With the initial embarrassment dismissed, and reinvigorated by the sudden bolus of sugar and caffeine, Logan relaxed. Leaning back in his chair, he began to speak when suddenly he stiffened, his posture shifting back to the erect position again.

"Oh, my gosh!" he exclaimed getting up and tearing through the hallway out the door to the car in the driveway. Sliding to a stop, he threw open the door, releasing Trigger, who immediately hopped out and raising his hind leg, urinated on Logan's new dress shoe. A startled Rebecca had dashed out of the house on Logan's heels, only to stop, and standing there, began to laugh out loud.

"I suppose I deserved that," Logan admitted, his tone a mixture of fatigued frustration as gently he stroked his relieved friend behind his ears.

"Sorry, fella", he spoke kindly, "I guess I should have listened to you ten miles back. I promise that won't happen again." Trigger just whined, licking Logan's face as Rebecca beamed from behind.

The next morning, the sound of chirping birds drifting through the open bay window of his second story room welcomed Logan. The melody floated in on a cool ocean breeze, settling in like a soothing balm on his frazzled nerves. Its effect was almost hypnotically calming until the familiar barking of his favorite four-legged friend broke the spell. Like a well-timed alarm clock synchronized with the rising sun streaming through his large bay window, the woof beckoned him up and over. Straining he could see two small aliens, masquerading as children, happily playing keep-away with their Frisbee from one frenzied Labrador and an equally excited collie. Trigger looked up at his master before bounding forward, knocking Tommy to the ground, and initiating the tike to a Logan family pasting they had often referred to as "manslobber". This dogged fixation had hounded the canine since puppyhood.

"Yuck! He licked me in the mouth. Get him off. Get him off," Tommy protested as the four-legged fur ball continued his peculiar form of canine water-boarding. Logan amused, finally called down from above.

"Trigger, Yo boy! Here boy. Trigger, let him up," The dog barked stepping back as the two kids jumped up and quickly ran inside the house.

As Logan ducked his head back into the room, his mind was abruptly flooded with the sights, sounds and aromas of a long forgotten sunny springtime beach. Laughter once again intermixed with the playful yapping of an enthusiastic canine. There on the beach were Logan's children, being playfully pounced upon by a hyperactive Trigger establishing his own peculiar canine pecking order. Moments later and Logan was back, the memory leaving a basketball sized lump in the back of his throat.

The antidote for Logan was the delicious aroma wafting its way up the magnificent winding staircase from the chamber below.

"What is that incredible smell?" Logan mused loudly as he tripped over stairway toys almost falling into the entryway of the brick and oak lined kitchen.

"Oh, that? Well that's an old southern plantation remedy for what *ails yee*." Rebecca said in her best southern twang. "We call it red eye gravy and grits. Try it, you'll love it." Logan groaned.

"You're worse than a child. I bet you've never even tried red eye gravy, have you?" she replied, shaking her head knowingly as Logan stepped hesitantly to the table.

An hour later Logan was comfortably downing his third blueberry pancake smothered in syrup and garnished with grits swimming in the red sauce.

"These are great!" Logan mumbled through his stuffed cheeks as the children stared at him through saucer-sized eyes.

"What?" Logan quizzed, his hands raised, as he flashed 'seafood' back at them during one of the rare moments Rebecca turned from the table. This action, completely foreign to the two tikes, had the intended effect of both grossing them out and leaving them giggling uncontrollably. Logan pretended, to Rebecca's bewilderment, to be ignorant of the fickle freckled rug rats' disorder as he continued stuffing his face with both hands.

"Now children, you know it is not nice to laugh at others. I'm sorry Jon. I don't understand," she said genuinely confused and embarrassed. "They're usually much better behaved than this." Logan nodded tolerantly, as he continued to alternately flash his food at the bipeds.

"Hey!" they protested as he began to speak.

“Now, children don’t interrupt. You know it’s not polite,” Rebecca reprimanded taking her seat next to Logan.

“Kid’s these days”, he said with mock derision, “I suppose we have to be forgiving. After all if they have to accept an old burned-out radioactive space jockey in their home, there’s going to be some adjustments.” A moment of awkward silence followed, as Logan gave his best imitation of a sheepish sufferer. Finally, one of the two innocent munchkins, utterly perplexed by the exchange, piped up.

"Mr. Logan, what's your derrière?" Tommy blurted out. Aghast, Rebecca jumped in, almost rising from her chair.

"Tommy Stillwell,” she squeaked, arms raised as if to catch the words and stuff them back into his pint-sized mouth. Logan was as equally amused by her reaction as by the question.

"That's ok,” he reassured her with a tone of false authority, “Well, Tommy, my derrière is my seat. This

part. Why?” he asked pointing to his tush.

"Well, it's just something the man said that day."

"Oh, you mean - G - B - ‘Gabe’?"

"Yeah, Mom says we should call him Gabriel," Tommy insisted as he continued, his mom now suddenly reflective on the impending query. Sensing his host’ solemnity, Logan lowered his fork and fully engaged.

"Well, what did Gabriel say, Tommy?"

The little man hesitated, his mom cajoling him to finish with a motion of her hand.

"He said he enjoyed kicking your derrière, and he'd be glad to do it again if you needed it," Tommy finished innocently, not cracking even the hint of a smile. Dumbfounded, the guardsman sat back in his chair, his mouth agape.

"Tommy Stillwell, you apologize to Mr. Logan right

now!" Rebecca exploded with a horrified expression.

"But he did, Mom. I heard him," Tommy resisted, his protests met with the stern finger of a determined mum.

"You march right up to your room right now, young man.

Jonny, I'm very sorry. I don't know what has gotten in to

him," she protested as she ushered the boy upstairs to his bedroom. Logan sat there thinking deeply, staring off into space and rubbing his still bruised pride.

CHAPTER SIX
A Cherished Moment

The days and weeks after this famous exchange were to be filled with more love and joy than Logan had ever expected to experience again. Love was not the only thing to return to Logan's life. With the beach air and home cooking came back not only his strength, but also the tiny sprigs of red and purple capillaries. Like little varicose veins, the vessels were noticeable only to Logan, their rate of growth all but indiscernible to the human eye.

In the meantime, Logan had zealously taken up chores around the farm. He and Becky worked side by side, gathering the eggs, milking the cows and feeding the pigs. At times they were inseparable, each helping the other, their hands intertwined with the tasks before them. When the animals were finished, there were other chores including plowing and harvesting in the cotton fields. In the event this was insufficient to whet his laborious appetite, there were also the unexpected tasks such as repairing the countless implements, fixtures and appliances continually breaking down. Despite all this, the manual labor was a joy to Logan. Not only did the exercise reinvigorate and restore his stamina, the time spent with Becky was healing something inside Logan he had never thought possible.

Many were the evenings when the two would take long strolls down the Carolina beach, hand in hand, not a word said. In the evenings after the children were down, they would sit swinging on the large open porch, sipping sweet tea and talking.

Some days found Logan dreadfully overwhelmed with chores, only to be side tracked from his countless odd jobs by the earnest pleas for attention by two desperately needy children. This time Logan would not be denied. His priorities realigned, Becky often found herself having the unenviable task of cutting short 'family outings'. Surfing, biking and fishing were common pastimes Logan relished, each experience cementing the bond between their souls.

One infamous weekend found Logan, once again far behind on his list of chores, cleaning the cattle stalls after a 'productive week'. Countless freshly deposited piles of manure surrounded him as he shoveled feverishly attempting to clear a path. The stench, almost nauseating at times, was especially potent given the animal's penchant for some of the wilder oats now growing assertively in the lower fields. Little Tommy and his sister Beci, now well acclimated to Logan's antics, were watching from the stable supports when Tommy observed.

"You missed a spot." Logan, exhausted with pitchfork in hand, was not amused as he paused whispering under his breathe.

"Little brat."

"I heard that, take it back!"

"Make me."

"Oh yeh."

"OH, YEE-," came the bellowing reply interrupted by the wet, slimy mess running down the right side of Logan's face. Pivoting towards his assailant, he was met by a second volley catching him between the eyes.

"Heh...Oomph!" went Logan as the blow caught him off balance, and his feet slid out from beneath him, sending him crashing to the slippery floor. There in a huge pile of cow dung, Logan lie paralyzed, his eyes, ears, nose and mouth filled with the nauseating stench of livestock excrement.

"You realize of course, this means war!" he seethed.

"Bring it on!" The rug rats echoed back as Logan's slippery footing sent him crashing to the floor once more.

"Incoming!" the warning rang out as Logan was splattered again.

"I'll teach you little varmints," he sputtered from a mouth stained with manure as he spat small chunks from the crevices of both cheeks. Back and forth the patties flew hard and fast as screams of glee coupled with feigned protests filled the cavernous stall.

Suddenly, Rebecca entered.

"Stop that! Stop that this instance!"

Terror griped the three combatants as they stood there looking back, covered head to foot in poop.

"Maybe we should stop?" Logan said as the three warriors looked over one another and considered their fate.

"Nah!" all three announced as Rebecca, dressed in her best white apron and work dress, was simultaneously splattered by a torrent of brown oozing muck flying from all sides of the barn.

"Aaah!" Rebecca screamed as she threw herself into the fray on the side of her brood. Moments later, with the battle growing heated, Trigger was drawn into the fray. Retaliating with canine ingenuity, he plowed full speed ahead, grasping each small biped by the seat of their respective pants and dragging them, kicking and screaming into the nearest massive pile of oozy excrement. This tactic delighted Logan, as each child emerged disgusted by their own appalling baptism.

Thus, taking a page from his furry strategist, Logan immediately fell upon the entire group in the biggest man hug he could muster.

'SPLAT' the four fell together, landing unceremoniously in the largest pile and rolling until covered head to toe in the black gooey mess. Laughing hysterically, they collapsed, convinced they would never be clean again.

Despite the joy of such moments, there was one activity Logan could not share with his new found friends.

While Logan enjoyed driving and depositing the Stillwells at Sunday church, no pleading or cajoling from even the smallest and cutest Stillwell could pry his foot past the front door. Impeded by a seemingly invisible barrier, the best he could muster was craning his neck to see the congregation. Eventually, he learned not to attempt even this effort, as it was always met with multiple friendly invitations to come inside.

In contrast, Logan never seemed to have difficulty interacting with Becky's friends outside of the church.

Indeed, he seemed to thrive on activities celebrated on special weekends with church wide country picnics.

It was thus little by little, that Becky, her family and friends drew Logan from his shell, as slowly the painful memories began to heal.

It was a summer evening five weeks after Logan had arrived that brought the conflict to a head. Rebecca's church had organized an old-fashioned square dance for the community. Logan, Rebecca, Billy and the kids had worked for one entire week cleaning, fumigating and disinfecting her huge civil war era barn for the event. The barn, beautifully adorned with a rainbow of streamers and balloons, was lit by the golden glow of dozens of old-fashioned kerosene lanterns.

Inside clusters of linen covered tables lined the walls of the huge makeshift dance hall. Secret family recipes from all over the county, in the form of potluck delicacies, dotted the festively decorated tables. Dozens of platters of golden fried chicken and mounds of fluffy white potatoes, interspersed with every casserole known to man, littered the culinary landscape. Gallons of homemade sweet tea in huge glass pitchers and an abundance of cakes, pies and sundry confectioneries, enough to send the robust into a diabetic coma, completed the spread.

In the center of the vintage edifice, there lay an enormous dance floor. The surface glowed, decorated overhead with streaming banners of red, white and blue draped from the aging rafters above, and descending to the newly disinfected cattle stalls below. Balloons of similar colors floated just below the apex of the old tin ceiling, its ancient metal reflecting the glow of suspended lanterns and their neighboring orbs. The resulting luminosity drenched the room below in a flood of patriotic glow.

The room buzzed with the chatter and laughter of young and old alike, all sharing the gift of chit chat. Men and boys strolled around the room in their best overalls or blue jeans, and the gentler more fair sex paraded in ankle length skirts made for just such a picnic. To Logan this was a picture out of the time and he yearned for the simplicity of such an age.

Contrasting with this nostalgic setting, an oddly shaped circular platform rose dead center of the dance floor. This elevated stage, with its rafter mounted cylindrically shaped projectors, was just large enough for four players perched precariously to stand on. The players, dressed in simple jeans and plaid shirts, mingled affectionately with the crowd surrounding them.

It was this evening, as a fiery red sunset faded, that Logan was lighting the *Tiki* torches surrounding the back deck. Normally utilized to park tractors and farm implements, the old wooden deck had been miraculously transformed into a structure that could double as a second dance floor or romantic escape. For now, with the starry sky above and the flickering glow of lit torches, it seemed fit for the later. As Logan lit the last torch, he was suddenly startled by a gentle touch to the shoulder.

Spinning instinctively to face his imagined assailant, Logan knocked the glass of tea, formerly in Rebecca's hand, crashing to the wooden floor.

"Whoa! Oh man, - I am so sorry."

Flushed, Rebecca tried in vain to speak, her red face and penetrating stare revealing the first flash of anger Logan had ever seen in her eyes.

"I brought you some tea Mr. Logan," she choked out handing him the remaining full glass as the tears slowly formed.

"Becky," Logan swallowed hard. "I'm so sorry. I thought…."

"Logan, I know what you thought. You thought I was a soldier, an enemy. Well I'm not. I'm a woman, but you can't seem to see that, can you?"

"Becky…."

"My name is Rebecca and you just better start calling me that. Do you understand?" she protested as she turned abruptly to walk away. Almost as abruptly Logan caught hold of the infuriated lass and spinning her towards him, caught her in his arms.

"What are you doing? Let me go!"

"I will, I promise, but first you are going to listen to me, ***Becky*** Stillwell. Now, I don't know what you are, but you are definitely not a soldier. I suspect you are a sorceress, or possibly a witch!"

"A witch!" she struggled in vain to break loose.

"Yes, that's it, you're a witch, and you have cast your spell on me." He spoke gently smiling as he held her close.

"That radiation has gone to your brain. Let me go." She struggled vainly.

"Not yet. Not until you tell me how to break the spell." He drew her closer, as she struggled but this time not as much.

"You're insane. I don't know what you're talking about," She replied half-heartedly, her resistance failing.

"Alright, if you won't tell me, I shall be forced to conduct my own experiments and find my own remedy. Let's see, what was it that broke Snow white's spell? I know." His voice trailed off as looking down into her gentle gaze, the two ended the moment in a tender kiss.

"Well, did it work?" she whispered back.

"Not yet," he replied. "I guess I'll have to run some more tests," as he kissed her again tenderly.

Becky was no longer struggling now as she took his hand in hers.

"Come on," she shrugged her head towards the dance floor inside. "I'll let you buy me a drink," she said smiling, and taking his glass from his hand, "and if you're nice I might even teach you to do the 'Charleston'.

Chapter Seven
An Unwanted Calling

Rising slowly from the shadowy depths of the Atlantic Ocean, a drowsy sunrise climbed out of its surf, and crawling across the grassy Carolina beach dunes, beckoned to a sleepy Logan. Dust laden beams of sunlight streamed into the pre-civil war era bedroom as Logan, head buried in the down-filled pillow, reflected on the night before. The gentle singing coming from the kitchen below was a pleasant reminder that life on the farm started early.

Logan rose from his bed, and sometime after he had showered and shaved, the commotion began. Announced by the barking of two dogs who had become fast friends of both the children and each other, the black sedan glided to a stop in front of the house. Logan grimaced watching the arrival of two very muscular looking men dressed in traditional black and blue suits.

"There is only one people group dumb enough to both dress and drive that ugly. PROGS!"

PROG was the modern acronym for progressive reformers of the government. Essentially, they were deemed by many as the mindless pawns of tyranny, the vast majority employed to enforce Federal mandates.

In a moment there was a muffled conversation below, and then the quiet footsteps up the winding wooden staircase, followed by the familiar gentle knock at his door.

"Jonny… Jonny are you in there? There are two men from the government here who…………….

"Tell them to go away!"

"But Jonny, they say it's critical they speak to you. They say it's a matter of national security."

"I said tell them to get lost!"

"...... but Johnny...." her voice sounded scared.

"NOW! Tell them to go away now!" Logan was adamant.

The door opened just as he finished speaking and the men entered behind Rebecca.

"Commodore Logan, we apologize for this intrusion. I'm Johnson. This is Thompson." The first man, a broad-shouldered agent with a shiny bald head, spoke deeply while holding out his identification for all to see. "We're from the office of National Defense, here on the authority of the President of the United States. We'd like to ask you to accompany us."

"Over my dead body! You and steroid man here can tell the President it will be cold in a hot place before you get your hands on me again. Now leave me alone. You guys fired me, don't you remember? I'm retired! R-E-T-I-R-E-D, You guys can spell, can't you?" Logan shot back, his finger stabbing the air in their direction.

"Believe me, sir, we'd like nothing better than to do just that, but we have our orders. I'm afraid we're not allowed to take no for an answer. So please don't make a scene in front of your friends." The second man, a young African American, seemed to be reaching for some type of weapon just under his jacket. "We just need to talk. You have our word that after we talk you will be free to return."

"I wouldn't do that if I were you young man. I'm sure you have a family somewhere who'd like you back tonight."

"Look, Commodore, there are civilians here. Someone else is likely to get hurt, besides you and us. If you don't come now, the President will just send more men."

Logan was prepared to move on the two men, when Tommy and Beci suddenly entered the room. Logan looked their way as they moved sheepishly towards him.

"Logan are they frogs?" Tommy's toothless frown whistled innocently brandishing the common term that he had heard recently. Logan bent low to the ground so he could whisper quietly in their ears.

"They are more like toads, Tommy. Now why don't you two go over to your mom while I talk with the nice men? You don't want to get warts, do you?"

"Are you going tie a knot in their noggins?" Tommy continued, almost causing Logan to laugh as he looked up at the two intruders.

"Think I should give them a tattoo?"

"Yeh, like yours!"

"Well, why don't you go over beside your mom and we'll see if that's necessary," Logan finished as the two children made a mad dash towards their pensive mother. Hesitating, he looked at Rebecca holding her two small children. Then with disgust he replied.

"I'll get my coat, please go outside and wait. I'd like to say goodbye."

"We can count on you to keep your word of course Commodore, can't we?"

Logan returned to the kids, stooping down to their level.

"I said, I'll be there and I'll be there. Now, please just give us a minute."

The first of the two men turned whispering to the second and then both shuffled slowly down the hallway. Concerned, Logan looked as they made their way out before he redirected his attention to the kids.

"Look guys, I've got to go attend to some business for the President. When, I'm through, I'll bring you a surprise and we can do something fun together," Logan spoke gently.

"You promise, you'll come back, right?" said Tommy.

"I promise," said Logan. After kissing their foreheads, he turned to Rebecca.

"You are coming back?" she asked demurely as Logan turned to grab his coat. He winked at her and kissing her too, he was gone.

It was high noon on a hot and humid summer day when the awkward looking silver and black Skycar rotated its nacelles and descended on to the landing pad at NASA's East Coast Research Center. Located in Norfolk, Virginia, this was the country's premier research facility for deep space exploration. Clumsily, Logan extracted himself from the oval shaped pod, nearly tripping over a sign labeled "Pentagon Advanced Space Defense - Ground Terminal 1". This greeting was no colder than its human counterpart which included a full body scan, frisk and abrupt escort to the massive underground auditorium several levels below. Assembled within the brightly lit chamber were dozens upon dozens of professionally dressed men and women milling about and talking, each seemingly as bewildered as Logan. Several flustered individuals looked especially disheveled and partially disrobed. Gathered in angry clusters around bedraggled administrators, the plaintiffs had obviously resisted the "G" men and lost.

As Logan entered the huge metallic auditorium, his attention was immediately drawn to the theater size viewing screens adorning the twenty-foot-high walls. The room was circular, with a single elevated podium in the center of the room. Powerful ceiling lights illuminated the rising circular stage, and from it, the booming voice of a polished announcer filled the chamber.

"Ladies and gentlemen, the President of the United
States of America."

Immediately, polite yet genuinely perplexed applause erupted from the crowd. Raising one of his hands in an almost self-assured swagger, a lean, well groomed man appearing to be in his early sixties rose from his seat to face the crowd. His dark hair streaked like flaming silver across the temples, along with the three-piece pinstriped suit, contrasted boldly with his subtle rose-colored lip gloss and the upper lash-line tattoos now in vogue.

'This man was never a marine,' Logan's smile almost betrayed his thoughts, 'Those guys don't wear lace panties either.'

"Thank you, Thank you ladies and gentlemen, please be seated. First of all, let me offer my most sincere and deepest apologies for the highly unorthodox methods utilized for inviting you here. For reasons that will soon become obvious, absolute secrecy was essential. As you all know this is a top security meeting. Everything, and I do mean everything, discussed here today is classified. Should you find yourself inundated with the uncontrollable urge to repeat these proceedings to the outside world, I'm sure we can enhance your restraint by a nice little Caribbean vacation on Guantanamo. There are some lonely religious zealots down there just dying for a new suitemate." He spoke with a wry smile as a nervous chuckle rumbled through the crowd.

"Let's begin by introducing our esteemed director, Professor Johann Satorsky. Professor Satorsky, if you please."

The President stepped back from the podium as a distinguished looking older, moderately bald man in a flowing white lab coat moved forward under thunderous applause. In his early seventies, the diminutive explorer spoke with a rough gravelly voice most likely due to his fondness for the carved walnut pipe he always carried in his left hand. Logan remembered working briefly with him during his early pilot mission to Saturn. The man, like the planet he had explored, was always encircled by his own rings of smoke, creating an air of both devoted respect and fervent disdain by various members of the scientific community.

"Thank you, Thank you Mr. President, esteemed colleagues and members of the military," the researcher groused over the tiny reading spectacles perched precariously on the end of his nose.

"Over the past thirty five years, I have had the pleasure of getting to know many of you, and I know you are familiar with me. Each of you has been invited here, because you are considered the nation's best at what you do. That's why your decision to work with us on this project may well be the most important of your career.

So without further chit-chat let's get down to the matter at hand. Twenty-three years ago, as director of NASA's Sol Barrier Research Force, I led a team past the 'heliopause', the outer radiation rim of our solar system," he rattled as high definition images appeared on the screens above him.

"It was here, some three years ago, we discovered an amazing and to date unpublished phenomena. Just external to this well-known transition zone of radiation and magnetic fields lay a 'killer'."

Images of several partially crushed spacecraft flashed momentarily above before switching to video.

"As can be seen here, we lost three of our most accomplished researchers before we even knew this killer existed."

The screen showed a small research vessel traversing a relatively nondescript area of space on the screen. Suddenly the ship accelerated disappearing into the center of a starless zone.

"Notice, if you will the velocity reading of the craft one nano-second before her disappearance." A low incoherent rumble ran through the crowd as the digital readout displayed the values.

2.789 X 10^{10}cm / sec.

Satorsky peered down mischievously over the thin rimmed spectacles still perching precariously on his nose.

"Yes, as you can see X-ray photography shows the ship accelerating just before she vanished. It took us two weeks of painstaking analysis before we realized what caused the event." He continued as the screen's starless image transformed to a brilliant three-dimensional multicolored spiral rotating before them.

"We call her **GAMMA X1A**! Categorically she is a subclass "A" rotating black star, less than 3.5 sun masses and no more than 9 km across at her widest diameter. In the later stages of evaporation, she is smaller even than XTE J1650-500. In addition to her incredibly small size, our earliest scans noted two very interesting unexpected features. Number one, the background radiation field and number two, the dark matter distribution grid indicated a space-time rift at area 77 on the outer fringe. This of course was entirely unexpected because it was well outside of the star's event horizon." Images on the screens above flickered through the multicolored photos of the star's outer edge.

"Naturally, we opted to explore closer," he continued as images of the construction of a strange looking vehicle scrolled across the screens above.

"Six months later, our research team devised a novel approach combining the star's own natural gravitational fields with a Cassini slingshot strategy. Using the star's immense energy, we found we could accelerate a vehicle close to the speed of light and safely penetrate the outer fringes. Protected from X-rays by an innovative torsional barium sulphite-argon gas plasma shield, our vehicle was sent on its maiden voyage. Imagine our dismay when only two minutes later it suddenly reappeared, completely intact and unaltered, or so we thought." Satorsky remarked as images of a fertile African plain shot from a low earth orbit rolled by.

"We discovered this imagery quite by accident hours later," he continued.

"But that's earth?" A question rose from the back.

"Exactly, the probe's AI system is designed, if finding no mother ship on its initial exit from the star, to return to earth. This is evidently what it did."

At once a hand raised from the back of the audience was recognized by the professor.

"I'm not sure about those early low orbit shots but these images are spurious: the Nile river basin hasn't followed a course like that for over a thousand years," a Mideastern man in his early twenties observed.

"Astute observations, Dr. Davidson, you know your geography. Continue watching and tell me your thoughts. Gradually the topography gave way to aerial photos of an ancient city, its walled perimeter accentuated by two larger towering structures in its Northeastern corner.

"Clever animation, but we've all seen CGI," Davidson laughed.

"What makes you think it's a forgery?"

"Because of that building in the middle of the city, that's why he thinks it a forgery."

The comment, which arose from within the midst of a tightly clustered crowd of aging men, came from a stunning brunette in her middle thirties. Shapely, with cat-like eyes whose stare could pierce the coldest heart, the woman in her starched white lab coat stepped forward.

"What's so special about that building?" interjected still another participant in the crowd.

"That, Dr. Schafer, is THE temple of Jerusalem, more properly known as *Herod's temple*. It was destroyed by the Romans somewhere around seventy AD when Jerusalem was burned to the ground," the raven haired woman continued.

"Colleagues, allow me to introduce to you the lovely Victoria Strife. Many of you are familiar with her ground breaking work in the area of x-ray archaeology and statistical reconstruction theory."

"Dr. Strife, it's nice to see you again. As usual your statistics are impressive, but I had heard you were...." Dr. Davidson hesitated.

"Retired?" She chuckled slightly. "As they say Dr. Davidson, the reports of my retirement were greatly exaggerated."

"Well I'm glad to see you looking so healthy, Dr. Strife, but you can't possibly expect us to believe that we are seeing live pictures of Herod's actual temple. That was destroyed almost twenty-one hundred years ago."

"Not live, digital recordings of a live event. As for an exact date of the images, well that is impossible to determine, but topographical and infrastructural clues point to the early Herod Antipas era. I'd estimate the spring of 26 AD," Strife responded.

"Why that's absurd! That is approximately the period of the beginning of Christ's ministry," Schafer objected.

"This is preposterous! Are you trying to tell us you have the capability to send probes back in time? Have you been able to replicate this? What proof have you that this isn't some clever hoax?" Davidson clamored.

"Dr. Davidson, Dr. Davidson, please calm yourself. You're much too young to have a coronary, and while there are many doctors here, we don't have anyone from the government to make the referral."

The crowd laughed nervously acknowledging the man's crime being only that he was the first to ask.

"But seriously, our young colleague addresses some very interesting questions. Indeed, we are saying that this," pointing to the images on the screens above, "is the very first Trans temporal transport of a man made vehicle. The AI system plotted its path out of **GAMMA X1A** and then retraced its route back through the star to return to us. We now have a vehicle, a highway and a map to the past."

"This is incredible! What verification do you have this is not some computer hoax," Schafer objected.

"Our sentiments exactly. What are the odds of stumbling over a portal to the past? So, to verify the veracity of our observations, we dropped and later located time capsule markers from our second run over the Mediterranean Sea." Pictures of the naval exercise and the barnacle encrusted marker were shown on the screen above.

"This is remarkable! Man is not even able to approach the speed of light with our current technology," Davidson countered.

"It seems that while we are not able to exceed the speed of light on our own initiative, the star's gravitational field helps us to travel close enough to it to slip miraculously into a bidirectional worm hole located well beyond the event horizon's outer edge. As far as your other questions, I'll leave that topic to our commander and chief. President Masada, if you please," Satorsky answered, stepping to the side.

"Thank you, Professor Satorsky for your brilliant research and another incredible discovery making this historic moment possible. And to you, Dr. Davidson, the answer is an emphatic YES. That is exactly what we're trying to tell you. Not only do we realize the potential for research, we have already been conducting flyovers with unmanned drones for months now, but we are very aware of the potential ramifications on history, especially our nation's future history."

Above, on the viewing screens, the scenes changed. Images of space and exploration vehicles were replaced with images of massive demonstrations in the streets of Atlanta and Charleston. National Guard troops confronted thousands of protestors with water cannons and tear gas. Suddenly the room grew very quiet. No one spoke, nor was there even a hand raised.

"I have therefore authorized NASA to form a coalition of the world's leading scientists," he pointed to the audience, "to design, implement and oversee the most ambitious exploration project ever attempted. This mission will be the first manned trans-temporal transport. Its primary purpose is the scientific authentication of time travel. Its secondary mission, the scientific verification of Earth's most important cultural transition, the phenomena responsible for the Gregorian YEAR ZERO or more colloquially, the ministry of Christ. *GOIEM* will thus operate as a scientific mission within a mission."

A clamor arose as anxious hands went up immediately all over the auditorium.

"I'm sorry, colleagues but we're on a tight schedule. We only have time for one or two more questions", Masada continued, pointing to Dr. Schafer.

"First of all, Mr. President, just what is a GOIEM? Secondly, Mr. President, this mission is liable to be extremely hazardous. Have you considered the mortality risk? Last of all, what about the risk of contamination of history from this team being stuck there and changing something?"

At this point, Dr. Satorsky shifted back to the center stage as the seasoned politician motioned for him.

"Thank you, Mr. President. That's more than one or two questions, Dr. Schafer. But as they seem to sum up the more salient points I'll address them briefly. GOIEM stands for **Gamma star Orbital Insertion and Exploration Mission**. Secondly, as to the mortality risk, we estimate an eighty six point five per cent likelihood of our '*chrononauts*'", he said coining the word, "failing to return." Due to the high mortality risk, we have already made the initial selection of three uniquely affected but highly qualified individuals to lead this expedition."

"That is highly irregular," Davidson objected, "Uniquely affected, how are they 'uniquely affected'?".

"Each team member has a non-communicable and incurable disease. None of their life spans exceed fifteen months from the date of planned departure. Our *Chrononauts* will be very close to death even as they return from their historic voyage. For that reason, their data will be stored in this digital diamond storage crystal, the most durable material known to man," he said holding up a fiery, luminescent diamond shaped crystal floating in a glass incased cylinder. Masada moved forward, standing shoulder to shoulder with the researcher.

"In addition, because their life spans are so short, we feel that even if they are stuck in that time, they will have little time or motivation to do much harm. It will be difficult to 'take over the world' in 6 months even in that time period," Masada interjected half-smiling.

"Won't their health problems affect their performance?" another observer asked.

"Their symptoms, all manageable with current therapeutic agents should be able to be controlled to within one month of their death."

"But why choose this time period? Why not some other?"

"Two reasons, Number one - it works, every time. We know our way in and our way out. Reason number two," he said pointing to the pictures of chaos above, "we hope this will help to defuse the ticking time bomb now threatening to tear at our society's fabric. If we can conclude the true nature of this phenomena at our religion's core, we may neutralize the situation.

"What you mean is you want to decide who Christ is?" A voice rang out from the crowd. Satorsky lowered his glasses.

"Yes!" came the terse reply.

That my esteemed colleagues concludes our first session. Please join us in the banquet hall for lunch, after which we will divide into subspecialty sessions."

If the content of the discussion and the reputation of the delegates wasn't enough, the complexity of the underground research facility alone could have intimidated the most seasoned explorer. Logan followed the crowd through the winding hallways to the elaborate banquet hall where hundreds of hungry delegates from all over the world sat feverishly discussing the information just provided. Making his way in the direction of the buffet table, Logan was suddenly cut off by the diminutive professor and his surrounding entourage. Extending his hand he began.

"Commander Logan I believe? What a pleasure. I've never met a national hero before. Would you have a free moment to talk, in my office, please? Dana please take Commander Logan's plate."

Logan looked around, and then sheepishly nodding handed over his empty plate before accompanying Satorsky down the labyrinth of hallways to the researcher's office.

"Whew! Man, what an ordeal! I'm so glad to be finished with that! Have a seat, Commander Logan. Would you like a drink?" Satorsky asked, reaching for a small decanter.

"No, thanks, I've quit," Logan confessed, prompting an exaggerated expression of raised eyebrows as the researcher reclined slowly into the largest leather chair the guardian had ever seen.

"Well, that's definitely not in our dossier. That Carolina beach air must be doing you some good."

"Nothing ever changes with you guys, does it? What other useless revelations do your pea counters have about me?"

"Everything. As distasteful as you and I both find it, socialism, if nothing more, is very well informed," he responded as he hunched over Logan's electronic file, "They're even bold enough to claim you haven't slept with that woman you live with now."

"Leave her out of this," Logan fired back pointing an intimidating index finger the researcher's way.

"Don't worry Commander, your reputation as a physical specimen will not be tested here. I enthusiastically intend to leave her out of this. That is why I'm pleased to know you have been an honorable man. We don't want to break her heart any more than we have to, now do we?" he stated gently, his voice hesitating only briefly.

"What does that mean?"

"Well, you have told her, haven't you? I mean she does know what you'll become in sixteen months' time?"

"I've told her what she needs to know for now."

"You mean you've led her on? I mean she does know she is falling for someone who in seventeen months will be dead, and well before that a monster, a threat to her and her children's safety?" Logan squirmed in his chair as the elderly man finished.

"Your point being?"

"My point, Commodore, is we need you. This nation needs you. It needs you if it is to survive, and where you're at right now will only result in broken hearts and someone getting hurt."

"My situation might be different."

"No, just delayed," He hesitated, "Shall we have a look at your arms?"

"That won't be necessary."

"Right now in Dr. Livingston's infirmary are three more of your fellow sufferers. Each one more affected than you has *molted* overnight into what I believe is affectionately referred to as a, *GRUB*."

Satorsky turned the monitor towards his guest. Images of the molting victims transformed before Logan's eyes as their faces melted into the hideous swollen forms. Then suddenly there were images of carnage in a family home. Blood splattered walls down a hallway, a bathroom tub and a crib.

"The last one, a father of five, killed three of his youngest before he could be subdued. Is that how you want them to remember you?"

"No," Logan half whispered, his eyes turning towards the floor.

"How do you think those kids will handle losing a second dad?"

"And you have a solution for that?" he replied once again meeting the scientist's gaze.

"I think so."

"How?"

"By giving you a reason bigger than yourself to die for. By sacrificing yourself so that they might live. By letting you leave when they remember you at your best. By giving them a reason for your leaving that someday they will understand."

Logan listened quietly.

"So, what do you think of our little research project?"

Logan crossed his legs and relaxed.

"Impressive, not so little as you'd like to let on, I believe."

"Yes, but much more than that, Commodore Logan, so much more than that. This is THE greatest historical quest the world has ever known. Just imagine, being the first to do what man has only dreamed of for centuries, to travel through time. Not only that, but to answer for mankind a two-thousand-year-old mystery. Who really was Christ? Was he a lunatic, a liar or the unseen author of the universe? It is this very question that is ripping our country apart. Now we have the chance to see what actually happened and to record it. Think about it. What an adventure!"

"You forget one thing professor. I'm dying. What makes you think I want to be your sacrificial lamb and go gallivanting around the universe my last few months?" Satorsky sighed leaning back in his oversized chair.

"I've read your psychological profile Commodore.

You're the kind of guy that needs a purpose for your life, a reason for your existence, and this is your chance to make a difference for Tommy and Beci's world." He hesitated before adding, "Both they and their mother are in the cross hairs of this revolution, you know that. They will be some of the first of the innocent to die, but I can protect them."

"How do I know they'll be safe?" Logan demanded, "I'd need reassurances."

"I can get you whatever you need. The President is behind this. Are you in or out?

Logan sat up straight as he looked intensely into the man's eyes before answering. "If I die on this mission, and you or any of your cronies hurt those kids, I'm coming back to GET you. Do we understand each other?"

"Is that a threat Commander?" Satorsky asked smiling. Again Logan hesitated before he answered. Sitting back in his chair again, he continued to stare at the professor.

“No, it’s a promise,” Logan said calmly, “You keep your end of the bargain and I’ll keep mine.”

“Agreed, besides if you fail, there might not be anybody to come back to GET,” said the Professor. “Now let’s get to work”.

"Oh, yes, one more condition," Logan added.

"Name your price," Satorsky replied, smiling.

"I want the truth, the whole truth reported. Regardless of how it turns out,” Logan demanded.

"We have an entire committee overseeing our intellectual and scientific accuracy."

"I want **your** word." Logan repeated. Satorsky hesitated sitting back in his leather office chair.

"You have it."

Chapter Eight
Trains up in the Sky

Logan spent the next few days trying to explain to Becky why he had to leave. There were tears and hugs and lots of angry words at first. He tried explaining with photos, medical articles and videos the creature he would become. He shared the news articles of *molting* victims who had harmed or killed family members, but nothing seemed to convince her. Then finally there was the discussion of the impending war and the danger to many innocent citizens and believers that might be prevented. Finally, Becky agreed to let him go. There were long evening walks on the Carolina beach until finally the day came that he had to answer to the children.

Logan's voice trailed off as two tear-stained faces sat looking at him from the large wooden swing on their front porch. It was evening and the spring peepers were out in force.

Tommy just sat there silently looking down into his clasped hands, tears rolling down his cheeks.

"Mr. Logan, did you make my mommy cry?" little Beci asked.

"Yes, Beci. I'm afraid I did," Logan replied trying hard to swallow the melon in the back of his throat.

"Why? I thought you liked us. Did we do something wrong?

"Noooo! You were great, Beci. I do like you a lot. That's why I have to go."

"Mommy says you're going to see Jesus, just like Daddy did."

"Yes Beci, something like that."

"Will you ask him to send my daddy back to me? I miss him terribly?" Beci just sat there silently as her eyes began to fill with tears and then silently drip to the ground.

"I'll ask."

"Love you."

With that the little girl jumped down from the swing and ran for the screen door leaving Tommy and a crushed Logan behind. As he sat there staring at the six-year-old boy, he felt the cold wet nuzzle of an old friend.

"Oh, no, not you too," he groaned as the large golden head strained its way over the chair's edge and onto his lap. Two giant brown eyes looked up longingly as a gentle whimper escaped from Trigger's throat.

"Hey, Tommy," Logan started as his large hands began to stroke behind his furry friend's two large ears. Tommy sat there, silent, fingers crossed staring at his hands. His eyes were wet from crying, but for now he was trying to be strong. Logan remembered the stories Tommy told him about his dad's admonition to be brave. So as the boy sat there silently, the man understood all too well. Finally, the boy spoke.

"Mr. Logan are your children with Jesus? Mommy says they are."

"I like to think so Tommy."

"Is that why you're leaving us, so you can be with them?" Logan's lump was back; this time he would have been glad for melon.

"No, Tommy, no, that's not why I'm leaving. I'm only going to visit with Jesus for a little while."

"Then, you'll be back." A long moment of silence followed.

"Tommy, would you do something for me? Would you take care of my family for me?" At this Tommy looked a little puzzled.

"Trigger, he's all the family I have left. He's gonna' need a good friend. I can't think of a better one." Tommy reached across gently stoking the forehead of the silent canine. He nodded his head but said nothing as tears started to fall again.

"Tommy, I'm going to ask you to do something for me I've never asked anyone to do before. Do you think you're up to the task?" Tommy looked up with his swollen eyes, nodding his head.

"Will you, will you pray for me?" Logan asked as Tommy slowly nodded again. "I'm gonna' need some big angels fighting for me where I'm going. Do you think you can call them in just when I need them?" Tommy nodded silently again as he rose to go.

"Take care of your mom and your sister, Ok? I love you all", Logan said as the small boy ran quickly to the door.

"Goodbye."

The conference room aboard the USS Constellation Transport vessel was nothing to brag about, but it was better than the mess hall. Seated around the enormous oval table were Logan, Victoria Strife, Professor Satorsky and one wiry looking middle-aged man. The slightly balding man sat as close as he possibly could to the lovely Strife, and was obviously engaged in getting to know her. His slightly muscular build and bushy mustache reminded Logan of a cartoon character from his childhood videos. While Logan had, until this trip, never met Dr. Nicholas Patel, he was definitely familiar with Victoria Strife. The raven haired beauty was not your stereotypical research archaeologist that Logan had imagined. As a matter of fact she looked more like a fashion model than a scientist, and Logan found it difficult not to stare. For all her beauty, however, she radiated a coldness that Logan deemed altogether different from mere professional sophistication.

The three recruits, having sat dozens of nights under the careful instruction of Satorsky, were reviewing their assignments.

"Now, Dr. Patel as lead biophysical researcher on this mission, your expertise on temporal and trans-geographical bio-scanning technology will allow us to scan any biological systems undergoing metamorphosis. If any phenomena occur you will be able to both monitor and analyze it down to the molecular level."

"Phenomena, what 'phenomena'?" Logan interjected.

"Spontaneous biological transformations," Patel repeated forcefully.

"Miracles, he means miracles, flyboy," Strife interjected impatiently.

"'Miracles', you two geniuses don't believe in that hocus pocus, do you?"

"What we believe,… flyboy, is that over five thousand Hebrew manuscripts and some very well-respected first century Jewish historians recorded that Jesus did miracles."

"Yes, now, Commodore Logan," Satorsky interjected, "if we may continue. Dr. Strife will be our geological and cultural guide. Since she is the only one of the three of you who actually can speak and translate Greek and Hebrew, she will navigate for the two of you."

"Alright baby! I'll follow you anywhere," Patel growled.

"Oh by the way, did I mention she also possesses a black belt in Tae Kwon Do?" At this, Patel sat back staring at the scientist, while Logan smiled approvingly.

"Finally, last but not least, we have the famous, some would say infamous, Commodore Logan. Commodore Logan's reputation precedes him. His accomplishments, while quite different from the academic credentials of our two doctors here, make him the natural choice for our leader. While All-American football and decorated fighter pilot skills won't be needed in Palestine, a nose for getting out of trouble will be. As will a steady hand at the controls and a degree in aeronautical engineering if anything goes wrong. Commander Logan will be in charge of this expedition. It is his job to get you into the culture and get you out without loss of life."

"If that happens we'll have at least one documentable miracle we can bring back," Patel laughed.

"What is that supposed to mean?" Logan shot back.

"It means that this is a scientific expedition. We don't need cowboys screwing it up. That's what it means," Patel fired back. Satorsky held up his hands.

"Gentlemen, gentlemen, and ladies, Commodore Logan has been specifically hand-picked because of his ability to make command decisions under extreme pressure. Besides that his appointment as commander of this expedition comes from no less than the President himself. There will be no debate! Do I make myself clear?"

"I'm sure we'll all be happy to follow the Commander to the end of time, if need be," Strife replied smiling.

"Or the end of our lives," Patel quipped.

"That may be sooner than you think, if you keep that up," Logan countered, as Satorsky jumped back in.

"I'm glad to hear that you feel that way Commander Logan because you may be called upon to do just that," Satorsky began again, "Let's start by laying a basic mission principle. First of all, it is critical that each of you realize that while you are all exquisitely gifted in your own areas, you are each still very expendable. Because of your unique conditions, we expect a high mortality rate on this mission."

"Kind 'a makes you feel all warm and bubbly inside doesn't it?" Patel quipped.

"Each of you is terminal. Dr. Patel here is suffering from terminal brain cancer. A slow growing meningioma, I believe?" Satorsky spoke to the unexpectedly quiet scientist who nodded silently in return.

"Commander Logan is expiring from grade 3 level radiation poisoning and Dr. Strife from an inoperable blood clot growing in the left cerebellar hemisphere. Not an ideal situation for anyone here, but we consider it "acceptable". What is not acceptable is the failure of this mission. Any questions?"

"Thanks for the sentimentality," Patel added.

"Yes. I have one. Which temple do we park our spaceship at?" Logan chimed in.

"Very astute, Mr. Logan, a nuclear propulsion-powered
Direct-drive vessel might draw a little attention in downtown first century Jerusalem..... You'll bury it."

"What?" Logan exclaimed.

"You'll bury it in the Negev desert. There it will remain until the twelve months you have to finish your mission are over. Then you'll get on board and head home. If you're not on it, it will leave without you."

Four days later the Constellation began its docking approach with the USS Lexington. An enormous vessel, measuring some three football fields in length and weighing in at four hundred and fifty metric tons, the Lexington was a beehive of research activity. Small research vessels and exploratory drones formed an almost continuous cycle of bustle as they alternately launched and returned from space.

"Wow!" Patel half whispered as the goliath drew near filling the entire viewing window.

"I heard about this ship but never actually had the privilege of visiting her before now. I can't believe how big she is," Logan remarked. Satorsky joined the conversation.

"Yes, and despite her size, she is the fastest ship in the fleet, outside of our TAV-1. With a crew of 150, she is able to support the full research activities of over 175 of the world's brightest minds."

"I remember hearing of her construction and launch from space dock four years ago. Since then I haven't heard a word of her," Logan replied.

"That's because she's been here since the early days of her shakedown."

"What have you been doing all this time?" Patel asked.

"The research you saw at the conference and some very high tech construction."

"You said something about a 'TAV-1'?" Logan inserted.

"Yes, it's our little 'construction project'. Come with me. I think you will find this very interesting," Satorsky replied as they approached the docking bridge.

The docking bridge itself was a twenty second century adventure to experience. Suspended some fifty meters between parallel vessels, the floating conduit consisted of dozens of transparent concentric rings linked end to end in a fragile chain.

Crossing the gulf between the two ships was an interstellar nightmare, for above and below, as far as the eye could see, lay nothing but an endless blanket of stars. While the others moved slowly, drifting reverently through the sea of stars immersing them, Logan subtly maneuvered well in front. Having previously witnessed the tragic end of a severed bridge, he chose instead to move quickly through the hatch and then into the massive bay before him.

Once inside the cavernous landing bay, the team paused to observe the beehive of activity. The deck was a massive hallway, each side being lined with two rows of smaller research vessels, while centrally an exceptionally awkward looking vehicle rested on its side. The craft consisted of two spiral shaped nacelles attached to a cumbersome central pod. Shrouded by a rotating conical shield consisting of heavy armor, the pod lay frozen in a layer of ice.

On either side of the ship's insignia stood two impressive looking heavily armed guards. Between them lay the ship's name, TAV-1, and the nation's current motto, "USSA, Kind Goodness We Can Trust".

Logan gawked, beaming like a kid on Christmas morning, as slowly he circled the awkward looking craft. Gazing appreciatively, he soaked in each detail, nearly drooling at the workmanship he beheld.

"Exquisitely designed," he whispered, his eyes lingering over the flawless seams adjoining her nacelles. Strife in the meantime was watching from nearby, fascinated by the school-boy reaction in Logan's eyes.

"Look, I think our flyboy has just found a new girlfriend. He's in love," she quipped, "Hey look, Logan, her head is as thick as yours." She sparred knocking her knuckles against one of the four inch frozen plates lining the crew compartment.

"Yeh, I like her because she reminds me of you, cold as ice," Logan fired back as he chipped off a large icicle from one of the exposed refrigeration pipes and tossed it her way. Ducking, Strife turned to see the others leaving them far behind as she and Logan rushed to rejoin their group.

"Come on," she commanded, "the professor and Albert Einstein are getting away."

"Albert, I like that," Logan reflected as the two quickened to a dignified run. "That's gonna stick".

Making their way down the labyrinth of metallic hallways, the four passed laboratory after laboratory of researchers frantically pouring over aeronautical schematics, Palestinian geography or curious black rubber looking suits.

Finally, after what seemed to Logan a dozen turns and twists in the never ending maze, the four entered the dormitory area of the ship. There in the lobby they were greeted by an attractive blond in her early twenties. Patel immediately moved next to the young woman effectively shoving Logan out of his way.

"Everyone, if you will please permit me, may I introduce Yeoman Candice Wilson. She will be your steward for the next four weeks helping you prepare for departure. If you need anything, Yeoman Wilson will be glad to assist you.

"Anything?" Patel repeated, his wide eyes reflecting a moment of rare enthusiasm. Satorsky smiled continuing. "Now, dinner is at 1900 in the captain's quarters, and remember, training will begin promptly at 0600 tomorrow morning, so no alcohol."

"Oh, dad," Logan whined impetuously.

"Absolutely none, early to bed and early to rise," Satorsky chided as walking away, he waved his finger in Logan's direction.

Almost immediately Patel drew himself up close to the yeoman.

"Candy, huh? Well sweetie, I'll follow you anywhere," he smiled broadly; his narrowing gaze meeting the mildest of disdains.

"Of course, Dr. Patel, I'll be glad to show you to the geriatric wing. Then we can move onto the ship's stores where you can pick up your adult diapers. Just follow me please," she quipped, as she turned and tossing back her shoulders, walked briskly away. Patel stood there speechless and unmoving while Logan and Strife followed dutifully, their budding smirks expanding as she turned to fire again.

"Well? Do you need a walker?"

Over the next few weeks work continued rapidly on the TAV-1 while the three *chrononauts* dove heartily into their intensive training. Each day was a smorgasbord of activity with multiple sessions including medical treatments, physical conditioning, and flight training rounding out the daytime. Evenings were filled with courses in ancient Semitic customs, basic Hebrew and Aramaic, intermixed with training sessions in the use of the *Nano Enhanced Research and Defense System. NERDS,* an acronym for the experimental suits tailored to the unique physiology and anatomy of each chrononaut, were the marvels of twenty second century military technology. Consisting of skin-tight uniforms embedded with both strength enhancing fibrils and electronics capable of implementing a myriad of defensive and exploratory procedures, these super-suits could perform incredible feats of strength and research. Their secret lay in the network of nano-fibers and circuitry integrated within the layers of fabric. The microscopic web of stronger than steel fibers and tiny nano sensors served the wearer as both a modern suit of armor and portable laboratory.

Four weeks later, and at the end of the most intensive training of Logan's life, TAV-1 was ready for launch. The three "chronies", as the Lexington's crew had affectionately dubbed them, watched anxiously as the political conditions on earth disintegrated. With the Carolinas edging toward secession, and history on the precipice of repeating itself, the President declared a state of emergency and pressed for immediate launch.

Forty-eight hours later, the hastily arranged final prelaunch session convened in the vessel's dining hall. The large dome-shaped room was brightly lit, its metallic walls packed side by side with grey-haired scientists and technicians all abuzz with excitement. As the three explorers entered with their teacher, they were met with the thunderous roar of a standing ovation. Ascending to the expanse of the elevated dining podium before them, they seated themselves while Satorsky motioned for silence.

In the center of the table was a metallic cylinder, its central core partially transparent. The device measured some eighteen centimeters in length. Floating within the slender tube was a fiery green crystal, its glow casting a luminescent halo onto the surrounding silverware.

Satorsky rose, as his perennial scowl descended, causing him to resemble more third grade school mum than scientist. Impatiently he peered over the dusty half eyes perched precariously on his bridge.

"Come to order, please," he began to speak over the rumble below.

"Here at this final session is our last and most important device to review. This is the Transition cylinder." Logan's face flashed an elfish grin as he immediately raised his hand for a question. Satorsky, agitated, stopped to address his pilot.

"Yes, Commander Logan, you have a question?"

"'Transition cylinder'," Logan smirked, "that's it? No acronym to memorize? No snappy contraction?"

"Sorry, no."

"How about the one who carries it?" he continued turning to eye the diminutive biologist by his side, "Let's see what should we call him? How about a **Transitional Whatchamacallit Escort Research Personnel**? Let's see, what would the acronym for that be?" Logan quipped as all but Patel and the white-haired professor broke out in boisterous laughter. Satorsky smiled weakly, attempting to continue, before Logan interrupted again.

"We could let Patel wrap it in one of his lace hankies and carry it in his purse." At this the auditorium broke out again as a red-faced Patel started to rise before his mentor motioned for calm.

"Thank you, Commander, for reassuring us all that we have certainly chosen the right man to lead this mission. I'm sure we will all rest well knowing if you are captured by the Romans you can paralyze them with laughter and escape," Satorsky fired back.

"Now, as I was *trying* to say. This indestructible fluid-filled casing contains the diamond recording crystal chronicling all the mission's data. Each of your nano-suits will periodically download your telemetry onto the crystal for permanent storage. The data will then be compressed daily and digitally transmitted to the TAV-1 for storage on board. The transition cylinder is the backup for all your data. It will survive time itself, even if you do not! Don't lose it!"

With this the aging scientist lifted his pipe and taking a deep puff, activated a viewing screen above the crowd. The image that appeared was an aerial view of ancient Jerusalem.

"Should you survive the first temporal jump, our calculations put your team arriving on earth in the year AD 29, the year Christ is crucified. This year was a dangerous year in Palestine and of course anything could go wrong."

"Sauce for the goose," Logan ogled, before suddenly his serious attitude returned. "It wouldn't be exploration without some danger. And, as you have so magnanimously pointed out, none of us will have the luxury of getting to suffer for very long." Satorsky puffed again and silently nodded his head in agreement.

"Thank you, Commander. That brings us to our last topic, Survival Protocol. You are expressly prohibited from engaging in mortal combat. You can defend yourself, but the taking of even one life has the potential to unravel all the history we know and threaten our very existence. And while you're remembering how expendable you are, don't forget that the very survival of our nation depends on your return." A large viewing screen snapped to life as a Presidential conference was just about to convene.

"As I speak, the President of the United Socialist States of America has declared a national state of emergency and is announcing to the world your mission."

A screen played in the background showing a silent President Masada speaking from a podium. It flashed to scenes of riots and public protests taking place in the streets of Atlanta and other major southern cities. Other scenes showed military bases coming under the control of cessionary forces. Masada returned to the screen, his voice now booming across the small room.

"This is an historic day. The information you bring back could potentially stop a cataclysmic conflict and save millions of lives."

"I'm glad there's no pressure here," Patel interjected to his two other recruits as the room stared in disbelief at the unfolding scenes of rioting, police in riot gear and national guardsmen that appeared on the wall screen behind the President.

"Good luck to our 'Chronies'," Satorsky said peering over his spectacles, "Gentlemen, this little training exercise is over. We launch in twenty-six hours. Meeting adjourned," Satorsky proclaimed to the sharp tapping of his pipe echoing through the meeting hall.

Logan thought that perhaps the mild nausea churning in the pit of his stomach came from readjusting to military rations after two months of southern cooking. Of course, it could also be that the sensation emanated from the prospect of being cooked himself while traveling through a million Rads of gamma radiation.

"Been there, done that", he chuckled quietly as he and his fellow 'chronies' finished the laborious process of latching on their bulky shield suits. Thirty meters down the hallway engineers in the cavernous docking bay frantically labored on last minute adjustments to the tiny TAV-1. The usually deserted bay was now a beehive of activity as scientists, technicians and newscasters dodged one another orbiting the hazy craft. Perched horizontally on its angled acceleration ramp, the craft's external pressure relief valves snorted forth semi-toxic fumes that veiled the dragon-like ship by submerging it in a blanket of blue gray fog. All of this, the fog, the awkward craft and its bedraggled attendants, served to transfix an anxious world watching from billions of kilometers away.

With the final countdown begun, the massive launch bay doors began to shudder and creak open. Rudely they groaned their half-silenced protest of releasing their precious prey to the vacuum beyond. Brilliant red, white and blue laser torches traced the exit chute boundaries leading to freedom. Like a bird darting from its cage, the funnel shaped craft rose and slipped gracefully into the silent void beyond. Ahead of her lay the radioactive tempest, its invisible tentacles of gravity reaching out perilously towards the tiny lifeboat. The odd shaped vessel, with its conical shield whirling briskly like some possessed windmill, adjusted its course to intercept the dying star's outermost edge.

"All systems report green, TAV-1 is GO for temporal insertion. Initiation sequence begins on your mark, Commander Logan," the bridge instructed.

"All systems initiate on my mark, five-four-three-two-one- initiate," came back Logan's commands.

As TAV-1 neared the fringes of the gravitational fields of the black star, the ship began to shake. Inside the craft's small command cabin, the three explorers were suited and locked in reclined positions. Massive explosions emanated from behind the tiny craft, as its fusion nacelles ignited, accelerating it to incredible sub-light speeds. Traveling over and through massive gravitational waves, like a rock skipping madly over barely submerged barriers, the life boat negotiated the star's outer hem. Heart rate indicators showed Logan's heart rate jumping to one hundred twenty while Strife and Patel's set off emergency alarms on the biometric panels. At this point Patel began to shout over the internal noise of the ship's shaking.

"I'm going to be sick! Who's the wise guy who slipped me that Ex-laxx Mickey in my soup today?"

Suddenly, the ship shuddered violently forward and then back. At this point Logan began to laugh and shout over the deafening noise.

"Sorry, Nick, that would be me. I just thought you were so full of it, you wouldn't miss a pound or two." After a moments' hesitation he added, "But seriously, I'm afraid the fun's just beginning."

Careening down explosively through the outermost gravitational bounds of the star's vortex, the ship vanished from sight, shuddering as it bounced from one wave of gamma radiation to the next.

"Whew! That's better," Strife called out as the shuddering seemed to subside.

"Somebody call Satorsky and have him send my stomach down to me," Patel called out over the decreasing noise to Logan. Logan managed a brief smile as he pointed to the instrument panel in front of them.

"Velocity readings are off the scale, and chronometers have ceased to record lapsed time. Based on these readings we must be traveling at or close to the speed of light, and outside of the space-time continuum. If we are in the wormhole now, we should begin to slow any minute now."

Suddenly the reverberations returned this time even more violently as the ship's infrastructure alarms began to resonate. Strife screamed as a nearby bulkhead suddenly buckled causing a panel to pop open over her head. Then, the rumbles momentarily receded before the final transition.

"How does the Artificial intelligence system know when to decelerate if the chronometers aren't working?" Patel shouted over the partially suppressed noise.

"The sensors feed it observations of our number of orbits and depth of penetration into the star's outer fringe. Believe it or not there are landmarks within the wormhole where variations in gravity and radiation can be measured. These serve as sign posts to the ships sensors and once we've reached a certain point in the star, we'll automatically begin to accelerate as the ship tries to exit. I'm afraid the exit is going to be just as invigorating as the insertion," Logan shouted back.

Almost as soon as he finished, two precisely-timed nuclear fusion events erupted from the ship's stern. Like a child ripped by a tornado from its mother's grasp, the ship sheered violently away from the outer spirals and towards the distant rays of the sun. The blackness of the outer void penetrated the tiny cocoon and with it an unsettling silence. Its motionless inhabitants hurled helplessly towards a destination quite unlike their home.

Chapter Nine
Three Unannounced Visitors

Hurtling effortlessly through space, the silent visitor from another age slipped past the icy rings of Saturn and around the vacant moons of Jupiter. Unnoticed by earth's neighbors, the tiny ship stole behind the dark side of the moon silently gliding back to the small, yet familiar, cerulean orb ahead. Within its cocoon, the shadowy ambience of a single blinking light illuminated the frosty walls of its frozen crypt. Slowly, ice-covered computers began their hazardous thaw as indicators flickered and three faint pulse lights began to glow. Logan was the first to awaken from his frozen slumber and, after checking his comrades' vital signs, he commenced the task of resuscitating the ship's primary power systems.

More than an hour later, Strife and Patel showed the first signs of life. Groggy at first, the two chrononauts awakened to blurred vision and painful extremities.

"What happened?" Strife asked as she removed her helmet, wiping the dripping remnants of frost from her visor.

"I'm not sure, but based on the frost, I'd assume we've had a complete and total shutdown of power," Logan replied. Patel was barely awake fumbling desperately with the latches of his frozen helmet. Finally, with Strife's help, the transparent orb snapped off revealing a wide-eyed Patel with glossy looking corneas. Staring wildly at his surroundings, he began to scream.

"I can't see! I can't see! What's going on? Logan, this is one of your tricks! What did you do to my eyes?"

Smiling from his console, Logan barely looked up from his work as he answered.

"Oh, it's nothing, just a little experiment that Satorsky talked me into before we left. We decided to donate your eyes to science and transplant them into some nice space monkeys. So don't worry. Your eyes are fine, you just can't see."

Strife laughed before intervening. "Good grief, Albert," she quipped sarcastically, "You've just got a mild case of hypothermia. Your corneas are edematous, and your fingers and toes are half frozen. You'll be fine Professor Einstein."

Logan laughed nodding as he continued to reboot the ship's systems. "I told you that would stick. Speaking of stick, we should all be thankful for Satorsky sticking to launch protocol. His forcing us to wear these outdated gorilla suits saved us. If not for them we'd all be bankrupt right now."

"Bankrupt, how's that?" Patel queried.

"Our assets would be frozen," Logan jibed, laughing out loud.

"Very funny flyboy, now how about getting a fix on our time and location?" Strife insisted intent on getting the conversation back on course.

"I'm attempting a star reading now, exact chronological and location readings any second."

Overhead the large screen flickered before illuminating and displaying the critical data.

CHRONOLOGY: 029.1897AD GREGORIAN
LOCUS : 03.856598 AU SOL

A cheer of applause and celebration erupted from the cockpit as the three explorers reveled in their historic feat. Patting each other excitedly, they watched the viewing port as earth came into view.

"Wow. We did it," Patel exclaimed.

"Yeh, now all we have to do is land this thing. That should be simple enough, right?" Logan remarked half kidding as he recalled the mission's bizarre reentry protocol.

Some twenty minutes later, a tiny sliver sparkled as it skirted over the blanket of clouds enshrouding the familiar Mediterranean Sea below. Rolling end over end the conical shaped craft settled into a landing attitude, the heavily armored base kicking up a shower of sparks as the titanium plates dug into the outer atmosphere. Moments later and a fiery TAV plummeted through the earth's fragile veil in a slender arc of blazing gold.

Lost in the furnace now engulfing the small ship, a semi-transparent ripple appeared hovering just over the port hull. Like a gentle breeze barely disturbing a pond's surface, it descended upon the antennae's external access panel. With one motion, the covering exploded outward exposing the sensitive electronic circuits to the searing heat of reentry. Then, just as suddenly as it had appeared, the ripple faded away.

Securely buckled inside the shuddering cockpit, the chrononauts labored to speak over the clatter as the small vessel pressed deeper and deeper into the evening atmosphere.

"Why can't we just land this thing using retros?" Patel shouted over the noise.

"The idea is to arrive unnoticed," Strife shouted sarcastically over the rattle of electronic boards now too hot to handle with bare hands.

"Very clever of them disguising us as a Fourth of July fireworks display! No one will ever notice," Logan shouted over the escalating clatter glaring his agreement as he wrestled with the joystick.

Below them, an ancient Negev desert looked upward. It's crystal canopy of twinkling midnight sky suddenly had erupted with the fiery glow of a falling star. Inside the 'star', Logan was practicing the art of controlled crashing as the small craft careened through the narrow valley of a winding Negev mountain range. Nomads and merchants following ancient trade routes stopped to gaze skyward tracking the scorching celestial display.

The tiny craft crackled as it zigzagged down the serpentine shaped valley. The shadows from its glow danced along the ridges as it shifted first clipping one precipice then another desperately searching for the exit. Moments later it shot out from its stony passageway slamming violently into the distant sands like a volcanic eruption spewing molten sand and rock skyward. Silence followed as the smoke cleared from the nearby cliffs. At their feet sprouted a dazzling red crater adjoined by a rolling sand dune. In the center of the crater the TAV lay half buried by the force of impact. Inside, its precious cargo lay unmoving, shaken again to sleep by the abrupt collision with earth.

It was some time before the chrononauts, having recovered from their fiery entrance, arose to shed their space suits and donned Middle Eastern robes to conceal their skintight armor. Each NERDS was a rubber-like, black suit trimmed in navy and engrained with a fine web of interconnected electronic devices. Over these survival suits, the three wore fine linen tunics and woolen cloaks to protect themselves. The ankle length inner tunics were long-sleeved, allowing better concealment of each traveler's engineering marvel. A leather belt hung from each waist with pouches containing precious valuables such as gold coins, diamonds, extra medicines, mementos from home and the obligatory Swiss army knife. The cloaks were woolen, boasting silk-lined hoods, and wrapped by an outer linen waist sash to further conceal. Strife's cloak was more richly colored denoting the feminine custom of the day, while twisted linen turbans wrapped each forehead shielding it from the desert sun.

"I can't believe logistics couldn't come up with something more comfortable than rubber monkey-suits to wear under these hot robes," Patel complained as he awkwardly attempted to balance the diminutive turban on his head. Logan looked up from his work incredulously.

"You want to stay alive?"

"What are you talking about? These are shepherds.

What are you afraid of? Being nibbled to death by their sheep?"

"Listen, Albert, haven't you ever heard of Roman Centurions? They carried a little sword called a Gladius. It's double edged and about two feet in length. They step into your defensive sphere and with one motion slice you open, spilling your intestines on the ground." As he spoke, Logan demonstrated the vertical incision with his hand on Patel's torso. Patel stared wide eyed as Logan finished and walked away. Strife smiled knowingly before agreeing.

"He's right. The Romans have a garrison in Jerusalem stationed at the Fortress of Antonia. And if the Biblical Herod Antipas is in command, we've got to be doubly careful."

"Ok, so I'm sure we can find some way to reason with this Herod. Right? So what's the big deal?"

"Look Albert, haven't you ever read the Bible?" Strife replied.

"No way, California outlawed that twenty years ago. I'm a law-abiding citizen," Patel announced proudly, as Logan and Strife rolled their eyes.

"Well, this particular Herod is a psychopath. At his command, every child under the age of two was murdered in Bethlehem," Logan explained confidently to Strife's disdain.

"Close but no cigar, flyboy, that was his dad, 'Herod the Great'. Herod Antipas was famous for separating John the Baptist's head from the rest of him. However, in this case, I think it's safe to say 'like father, like son'."

"Funny how you failed to mention all this in class before we left," Patel quipped, "How do you know all this, anyway? Don't tell me you read that in the Bible?"

"Please don't report me," Strife whispered, ducking her head slightly as if she was being recorded, "I did read it in the Bible, and it is historically accurate." She smiled no longer, whispering, "Logan is right; we are unwelcome travelers in a holy land."

"Don't worry, Albert. The technology built into your 'rubber monkey suit' can handle whatever the Romans can dish out. Besides, black is definitely your color," Logan smiled as he flashed him a fake pistol shot to the torso and then blew the smoke from his finger gun.

"My name's not Albert."

"Too much chit chat, let's go," Strife commanded as she finished stuffing her gunny sack.

"Yes sir!" Logan saluted as he shut down power to the electronic components of the ship.

"I've just seen her in leather; she's definitely not a Sir," Patel retorted.

"Remember, speak Aramaic," Strife interrupted ignoring the adolescent chatter. "Use your data link and the translator in your contact lens as well as your cochlear implant to help you communicate. And most important of all……………..Don't kill or maim anyone, agreed?"

"Does that include people from our own century?" Logan asked eyeing Patel ominously. Strife shot back a "do it and die" look to which the two men chimed simultaneously.

"Agreed!"

An hour later, gunny sacks packed and their still smoldering ship buried beneath the desert sand, the robed trio began their long trek to Jerusalem.

"Ok 'Ms. Historian', where do we go from here?" Logan inquired.

"There," she responded pointing ahead at the nearest sand dune. As she did so, a 3-D geographical map hovered in space before each of the traveler's eyes. The image, generated by Strife's suit computer and projected into each chrononaut's nano lens, contained a virtual pointer tracing over the topographical area.

"Our coordinates indicate we are here in the South-Western portion of the Negev," she responded to Logan using her index finger and pointing to a desert-like area to the south. "We're about 100 km north of where Moses wandered for forty years."

"They should have chosen Garmin instead of Moses as their leader," he retorted. Strife rolled her eyes before responding.

"Very funny, can we do the same with you?"

"Well, it won't be funny long if we spend too many days in this desert heat without water," a smirking Patel observed.

"Ok, 'Vicky', based on your map, I suggest we head north," Logan replied adjusting the virtual pointer with his hand.

"I agree, we need to find a water supply and I believe I know just where to find one. Follow me," she directed marching northward, "and if you want to live don't call me 'Vicky' again."

"Well Victoria, I'm behind you all the way." Patel smirked slyly at Logan and slid up so close to Strife that their bodies were virtually touching.

"Fine, walk this way," she commanded turning and swinging her gunny sack over her shoulder striking Patel squarely in the jaw, and knocking him to the ground. For a moment Patel sat there on his pride, unable to move as Logan laughed out loud. Strife in the meantime strutted away, swinging her hips proudly under Patel's watchful gaze.

"I'm afraid Mother Nature will never let me walk quite that way," he mused staring until she stopped and turned.

"Well, do try and keep up," she said smugly as she marched off across the desert sand.

Parched and sunburned, Logan paused to wipe his brow, gazing up briefly at a merciless Negev sun. Casting an exasperated sigh at his shapely guide, he trudged up the next dune and rounding a steep incline halted to look down upon a beautiful sight. Thirty meters below lay a pool of crystal-clear water, surrounded on three sides by a sheer rock cliff. Their path sloped gently down the ridge to a sandy beach bounded by scruffy vegetation. At the apex of the pool flowed a delightful waterfall. Fed by underground springs it exploded over the pond descending in a sun peppered veil of sparkling mist. Stumbling their way down the perimeter of the rocky precipice, the three explorers eventually arrived at the gentle dip of desert lining the water's edge. Logan led the way stepping carefully, followed by Strife and then Patel.

About half way down the shore, Patel could no longer control himself, and pushing clumsily past the others, he caused all three to stumble, rolling face first into the refreshing pool. Thrilled to find the life-giving lake, they splashed each other like children, with Logan and Strife ganging up on Patel. Together they grasped the scientist repeatedly dunking him until it appeared that he might actually drown. Deciding that no matter how tempting that prospect might be, for the sake of the mission, they finally let him up. Laughing, Strife and Logan collapsed with their comrade by the side of the lake. Refreshed and exhausted by their romp, the three made camp and reclined on blankets by a poolside fire preparing for a much needed night's rest.

"How did you know this place was here?" Logan asked Strife as he wrestled with his blanket on the sandy beach.

"I didn't. I made an educated guess based on topographical studies and knowledge of where this pool is in our century."

"Oh, great, she means she got lucky," Patel chimed in.

"This is *Ein Avdat*, Albert. This oasis is on the modern northern edge of the Negev. I simply assumed it was presently in the same location."

"Well, I don't care if it's called *Mein Kampf* and we were led here by the tooth fairy," said Logan, "The important thing is after three days we found water and that's all that matters. Tomorrow we head for Jerusalem."

"Fine, but before we go anywhere, take a couple of these," Patel instructed handing his fellow travelers two tiny green pills.

"What are these?" Logan asked as he squinted to see the tiny specks of medication in the palm of his hand.

"Slow release antibiotics. The cure for 'Montezuma's Revenge' from that cesspool you just drank out of." There was a moment of hesitation as the two exchanged glances.

"You don't have to take them if you don't want to," Patel replied smiling. "What's wrong, don't you trust me?"

Logan looked at Strife, who looking back replied, "Better do it, I think I left the T.P. in the spaceship."

Logan, who was an avid camper and notoriously sound sleeper, was surprised to suddenly awaken at five the next morning from a deep sleep. Rolling over, he turned to see a horrified Strife peering over her pillow towards a nearby thicket. There from behind the overgrowth resonated a horrible noise vaguely resembling a cross between a warthog's snort and grinding metal.

"What's that?" Strife whispered in a half fearful tone.

"I don't know, but whatever it is, it's either in pain or killing something that is.

"Where's Patel?" Strife panicked looking around the camp.

"Oh, no, it's got him," Logan whispered.

"That big lug head, I told him to stay close to camp."

"Listen!" the guardian warned, "I think it's coming from over behind those bushes. Come on, he might need our help." Pulling back his tunic's sleeve, he brandished the small paralyzing weapon attached to his forearm. Crawling on their bellies through the brush and looking over a small dune, they spied the pitiful creature lying motionless in the sand. There, sleeping like a baby in the clearing, was Patel. On his face rested a pink and white lace cosmetic mask, the embroidered type worn for years by woman to firm their sagging necklines and prevent wrinkles. With his head resting on a rock, and a veritable symphony of noises whistling in harmony through cavernous nasal passages, the two intruders lay motionless, transfixed upon the undulating beauty aid.

"What's that on his face?" Logan whispered.

"I think it's what they used to call a face corset," she responded, "My grandma swore they kept your wrinkles at bay."

"Looks like a pair of lace panties to me," he smirked.

Strife did a double take, squinting harder this time. "You've got to be kidding. That is so disgusting," she lamented.

"I'm just glad he slept over here, and not where we were."

"Should we shoot him and put him out of his misery?" Strife asked. Logan smiled shaking his head.

"Nah, why waste a good bullet? Besides we might need some more of those little green pills in the future. I've got a better idea," Logan whispered crawling silently over to the water bag lying by Patel's bedroll. Strife looked at the bag and then at Logan, who wide eyed, was grinning ear to ear.

"Let me, I'd love to cool off our little drag queen," she said as she clutched the leather canteen. Logan gawked as the beauty slowly crept by the wounded creature they called Patel.

The scientist, who was dead to the world, steadfastly had refused to sleep in his tunic, instead choosing to wear his tight-fitting survival suit to bed. It was with this and his feminine accessories that the two chrononauts scanned Patel's adorned figure into the permanent record for the entire world to see.

"That should about do it," Strife pronounced as she uploaded final images and dumped the contents of the canteen over his head.

"Hey, what gives?" Patel sputtered, wiping vigorously the water from his balding head.

Logan and Strife smiled admiring the uploaded images.

"Yep, he's out of the closet now."

"What have you done?" Patel sputtered, standing nearby wrestling with the corset's stubborn latch.

"We 'outed you'," Strife beamed holding high a portable display of the uploaded images.

"We knew you were wrestling with your secret identity by the noise you made at night and your bedtime attire."

"WHAT?" Patel screamed.

"Time to go," the commander smiled, insisting, "Quit your whining and get your little lacy red wagon in gear."

Refreshed by their time at the spring, the three *chronies* broke camp determined to locate the focus of their mission. Some three and a half hours later, they resolutely entered the outskirts of a small thatch and stone village. During this first foray into the heart of a Hebrew settlement, they quickly noticed an unanticipated problem. At almost six foot one, both Logan and Patel easily towered over the less than five-foot-tall Hebrews who stared as they passed by.

"Oh man, I should have anticipated the height difference. Our diets have allowed us to grow much taller than most of the people of this time," Strife confessed.

"Don't sweat it, Strife. What could we have done anyway? Cut ourselves off at the knees?" Logan reassured her. "Just tell them that we're from another country."

"Yeh, good idea. First, we'll need some money. I'll just trade these diamonds for coins. Let me do all the talking," Strife replied.

"That's why we brought a woman along," Logan quipped.

Strife ignored the comment, choosing instead to spend her time observing the market square. Slowly, she drifted over to an elderly man sitting at a makeshift wooden table. A steady stream of customers intermittently surrounded him as he occupied himself buying and trading jewelry and precious stones. Approaching, she noted the stones and coins traded, estimating the exchange rate to be fair. Then speaking to the merchant using her translating computer, which automatically fed responses into her inner ear implant and displayed them on her contact lens, she began to dicker. Moments later, her friends joined her as she pocketed a handful of gold coins.

"Excellent work, now we eat and get out of here," Logan instructed.

"And go where?" Strife enquired.

"Yeh, and go where?" Patel chimed in, sticking his head in between the two from seemingly out of nowhere. Irritated, Logan looked at Patel before returning to Strife.

"You're the historian. You tell me, where do we find Jesus?"

"I haven't the foggiest."

"What do you mean, you 'haven't the foggiest'? You're the expert!"

"Let's see, I seem to, um, yes I seem to have accidentally left 'His Majesty's' itinerary at home. Could I please borrow yours?"

"Ask the old man," Patel piped in out of nowhere.

"What?" Strife said incredulously.

"He said, 'Ask the old man.' I agree," Logan repeated smugly.

"He's not going to know where to find Jesus," argued the adventuress standing next to the gray-haired vendor. At the mention of the name Jesus, he turned to them.

"Oh you seek the Nazarene?" He spoke to them in Aramaic spying the dark spidery veins peeking out from Logan's tunic.

"What do you want with him?"

Logan and Strife both immediately recognized that the elderly man had seen something he shouldn't have.

Strife pushed Logan to the rear as she continued the conversation in Aramaic.

"We've heard he can heal the sick. My two friends here are very sick and they have traveled far for a cure. Can you tell us where to find him?" Strife answered, blocking the view of the aged man who, satisfied with the answer, was leaning still attempting to look at Logan's wrist.

"I have heard he is traveling with his followers north of Jerusalem. He is always moving. It is impossible to know. Even Herod and the Pharisees don't know where he will be next."

"We do have more diamonds," Logan offered, turning to Strife and speaking audibly in broken Aramaic, "I'm sure we can find someone who wants more diamonds." Immediately the merchant turned back towards the group and laying a feeble hand on Logan's arm, spoke.

"There is one," he said hesitantly, "he is a follower of this man you seek. If you wish, I will send my son to ask him to come."

"Please," Logan said, nodding curtly transfixed on studying the morning sun's reflections from a second diamond. The old man himself had caught the glimmer of the new stone and attempting a peak from below motioned for his son to come from the back of his tent. Instead a shapely brown eyed beauty of a young woman stepped out from the opening, catching Logan's eye and almost causing him to drop the precious jewel. The alluring woman, no older than her early twenties, with flawless features and an elegant beauty mark, was adorned in scarlet robes accenting her natural charms. The old man spoke something unrecognizable to the lovely Hebrew and she dispatched the appropriate boy for the task. Then flashing those beautiful brown eyes at Logan she disappeared behind the tent again.

"You have a very beautiful daughter," Logan admired to the feeble elder, as he and Patel continued to gape and stare after the departed enchantress. The old man smiled and mumbled something unintelligible while continuing to count his stack of golden coins. Strife smirked as she eyed her two male companions.

"What? What did he say?" Logan queried, slightly peeved at her ability to understand the old man's murmurs.

Drawing near to him she whispered low enough for both of her two fellow *chronies* and no one else to hear.

"He said, 'She's my wife you loser'. Now can you put your tongues back in your mouths?" Strife requested as she slipped away leaving her two stunned comrades staring at the old man.

"Wife?" they each mouthed silently to one another.

An hour later the dispatched boy had returned with a kindly-looking middle aged man wearing long robes and walking with a cane. As he approached, he and the old man exchanged a greeting.

"Shalom."

"Shalom. My friends, this is the kind and generous Flavius. He is a Roman centurion and can tell you where to find the Nazarene."

"Is that true?" Logan asked stepping so close to his new acquaintance that the man naturally recoiled with discomfort.

"The centurion that once I was is dead. So that is not true. That I know where the Teacher is, is true," the hesitant Flavius replied. At this statement, the aged peddler thrust his withered outstretched hand in between the two men, prompting Logan to surrender for inspection one very small diamond.

"We seek the Nazarene. Can you tell us where to find him?"

"I can.., but it is obvious that you are Gentiles. Why do you seek Him?"

"We are both seekers of truth and of healing. We have heard he has helped others who are Gentiles. Can you tell us where to find him," Patel asked as Flavius eyed the three explorers trying to size them up.

"He should be in Nazareth by now. It is four days from here by beast. You, of course, will have to first go through Jerusalem."

"No biggie. So, we have to go through Jerusalem; what can possibly happen there?" Patel asked emphatically.

At this, Logan, Strife, the old man, Flavius, the old man's son and from behind the tent, his beautiful wife, all turned staring in disbelief at the scientist.

"What? What'd I say?"

Chapter Ten
The City of Zion

Perched at the highest peak of Mount Olive, the three nomads gazed down at the golden beams of sunlight dancing flirtatiously from the ornate buildings dotting the ancient skyline. 'The Holy City', Logan reflected as he stood spellbound by the heavenly scene before him. Looking down on the ancient crag, he began to understand why the title seemed innate to the modern world. Overcome, Logan attempted to analyze the reflective and refractive forces at work creating the illusion of a city made of gold. That stone, spittle, muscle and sweat were more likely the materials before him was an archaeological fact. So, too, the mirage of peacefulness that permeated this glimmering city. This mirage, Logan had already reasoned, was one that could kill.

"It's much more beautiful than I expected," Logan said wistfully as he scanned the city's horizon.

"Yes, isn't it? No smog, no skyscrapers and the buildings look almost brand new," Patel agreed as he continued recording images of the renowned citadel, paying particular attention to Herod's temple and the adjacent fortress. Strife pointed to the northeastern quadrant of the city as she spoke.

"Herod's the Great's paranoia, while pathological, did not stop him from becoming one of the most prolific builders in all of Israel's history. That tall building under construction on the left is Herod's temple. Smaller and less ornate than Solomon's, it will barely be finished before the Romans will burn it to the ground. Just to the right of that is the *Fortress of Antonio* where the garrison is stationed. Needless to say we need to avoid that side of town," she warned through a strained smile.

Moving on, the three descended the elevation's western slope, merging into throngs of people entering the city through the western gate.

"This gate has been sealed in our time for almost two thousand years," Strife pointed out as they passed under the enormous stone arch. "Closed shortly after the time of Christ, it is supposedly the gate through which Christ will return at the resurrection. That is, if you believe in that sort of thing."

"Fascinating," Logan responded as the three dismounted from their newly purchased donkeys and led them through the mass of humanity.

"Whew, what's that smell?" Patel grimaced as he trudged onward.

"The fruit of tainted humanity mixed, I believe with a little donkey and lamb dung", Strife responded as the three continued to make their way through the narrowing streets.

The smell of feces, the sparsely robed figures of starving men and women and the cry of abandoned children assailed the travelers as they stumbled down rock hewn streets to the eastern side of Jerusalem. As they passed through the city's center, biometers, the tiny devices implanted within their survival suits, absorbed the surrounding biological data with electromagnetic efficiency. The digital data recorded included everything from environmental and biological readings to cultural measurements of their entire surroundings.

Passing down one alley to another, immersed within the squalid reality of open-air markets decorated with the flesh of slaughtered lambs hanging on one side and troupes of bleeding lepers crouching on the other, the travelers moved forward. Captivated, they studied the details of every crevice, stone and wrinkle, noting centuries of lost detail. In between their studies, Strife would occasionally stop to converse with some of the locals. These diversions allowed for information regarding potential housing and an opportunity to practice their linguistic skills. Aramaic, even computer assisted, soon proved to be more of a challenge than they anticipated, for they often found themselves taking long detours on poorly understood directions. But continue they did, and as they talked, they learned and so did their computers.

One fact they hadn't yet learned, was just how much attention they had drawn to themselves. This attention, while unbeknownst to them, included the notice of four Roman legionnaires who had begun to follow them at a safe distance. Carefully blending into the crowd, the muscular men in Roman armor made their way through the market some twenty meters behind the wandering foreigners.

It was evening when Logan and his two exhausted friends located near the center of town a very rickety stone and wood two story inn. With no beds, they rolled out their blankets and mats on the rough wooden floor preparing to retire for the night. A single clay oil lamp on a makeshift wooden table cast a golden glow on the small dusty room.

"What I wouldn't give for a nice hot shower and a T-bone steak," Patel yearned aloud.

"You could have taken a dip in that community healing pool we just passed," Strife replied eliciting a grunt from Logan.

"Yeah, I scanned those 'healing' pools with the bio-scanner when we passed by. If you live through a dip in one of those, you deserve to get well."

"That's fine, Albert. Thank you for sharing that with us. Just keep that scanner of yours out of sight. I don't want to have to dig your rear end out of a Roman dungeon."

"Stop calling me Albert," the researcher groused, a slight whine tainting his tone, "Besides, these local peasants are afraid of their own shadow. We don't need to be afraid of them. If any of those guards come near, I'll give them a taste of my paralyzer," Patel boasted pulling his cloak back to reveal his left forearm's spiral shaped weapon.

"Put that thing away. You know the rules. Logan is right. Any use of advanced technology is for research only. Now let's try and get some rest. We've got to find someone here in this city who can lead us to Jesus,"

Strife scolded as lying down she drew the blanket over her shoulders and settled onto her inflatable pillow.

"Why didn't we bring one of those?" Patel hankered staring at the cushy headrest.

"I didn't bring one because I like sleeping on a hard surface. As for your head, I assumed it was already so full of hot air you wouldn't need one." Logan quipped, adding before Patel could respond, "Now shut up and go to sleep."

Strife laughed quietly as the other two settled in, and the glow of the oil lamp gently faded to moonlit darkness. Unnoticed in the alley below, five burly soldiers, steely eyed and battle scarred, watched as the waning glow of the window receded. Silently they waited in the shadows for just such an invitation. Soon the three 'foreigners' were fast asleep with Patel's snorts announcing their slumber to a tortured Mount Zion below.

"Sounds like one of them is in pain. I think I hear a call for help," the Centurion scoffed to his lieutenant who gazed incredulously at the noise emanating from the window above.

"Well, we can't let him just lie up there in such pain. I'd say it's up to us to put him out of his misery," the lieutenant quipped back testing the razor-sharp edge of his Gladius. The centurion nodded and with a quick back and forth flash of his hand sent the company of soldiers moving quietly into the darkened inn.

Inside the tiny room above, Logan was sleeping on his side, his left arm having inadvertently draped over Strife's waist. She, in turn, had unconsciously entwined her hand with Logan's, an act resulting in a remarkably contented nocturnal smile. Drowned by the noise of Patel's animal cruelty were the subtle sounds of a creaky stairway and the scrape of an ancient wooden door as it slid slowly open.

The flickering glow of the hallway lamp was the first vexation to Logan's slumber, but it was not the most acute. That honor fell on the tip of a well-polished sword, which pressing just lateral to his Adam's apple, awakened the wide-eyed chrononaut. The pressure, while not painful, was of sufficient vitality to convince him to lie still.

"Do you wish to continue living? If so, nod your head slowly, but do not make a sound," the thickly accented intruder whispered.

At the sound of the stranger's voice, Strife awakened, stunned almost as much by the sight of the sword as she was by holding Logan's hand. With his arm still around her waist, Logan slowly nodded his head in agreement.

"There is a squadron of five armed legionnaires just below your window. You and your friends must follow me. Do not make a sound. Do you understand?" the intruder commanded.

Logan nodded again and roused himself to cover the mouth of the sleeping Patel, gently wakening him. Patel almost choked on his last snore as his eyes opened widely to the point of the gleaming sword. From the front of the inn, the squadron that had entered followed closely up the stairs on the heels of its Centurion. In the meantime, the trio had almost slipped quietly out the back exit and down the steps. Suddenly, Strife's bag became snagged on the knotty prominence of a protruding pole. Panicking, she yanked the bag free collapsing a fragile shelf and sending several large clay pots crashing untimely to the stony floor.

Immediately reacting to his prey's attempt to escape, the Centurion pursued. The chase was on. Headlong and at full speed, the trio of travelers fled behind their fleet-footed intruder. Racing down narrow alleys lit only by the stray moonlight of a Jerusalem night, the soldiers and travelers tripped and stumbled their way towards the center of the city. Unable to shake their ancient assailants, Logan drifted behind his friends and, utilizing his contact's night vision capabilities, began locating and shifting obstacles into their path. The resulting clamor of armor tripping over armor, and crashing into armor, produced a racket sufficient to rouse a sleeping Jerusalem into the streets, serving to slow the aggressors further.

Logan, now more than one step ahead, ripped from its mooring a corner tent pole and ducking inside a nearby doorway, allowed all but one stalker to pass. Thrusting the support between the feet of the last legionnaire, he sent the soldier rolling head over feet to the ground. Flustered, the legionnaire sprung to his feet, where attempting to draw his sword, he was instead stung by three abrupt blows. The first strike deftly tipped his helmet up and away separating it from the soldier's head. The second and third volleys disabled the warrior rendering him unconscious and allowing him to be bound and drug into the shadows. Pole in hand, Logan fled.

Logan's *nano-lens* immediately displayed the path of his two partners through the town center and out into the outer temple grounds. Racing ahead his survival suit allowed him to quickly close ranks with his comrades, who had unsuccessfully attempted to lose their pursuers in the moon-lit burial grounds of the King's Graveyard. Scaling the surrounding limestone and mortar wall, Logan dashed along its crumbling edge circling the perimeter above his friends. Then jumping to one of the flat tops of a large stone monument, he closed in from behind on the unsuspecting soldiers. Dispersed around the large stone obelisks littering the graveyard's floor, the legionnaires approached slowly cornering Logan's associates.

It was at this time, with each passing obelisk, that the centurion began to notice his squadron mysteriously dwindling in number. Finally, with only he and his lieutenant remaining, he turned back to investigate. It was on this about-face that the lieutenant first discovered the ground littered with his fallen comrades. Suddenly from behind, an attack of lightning speed fell upon the crouching officer in a series of blows aimed precisely between the front and back plates of his armor. Disoriented, the soldier was quickly disarmed and thrown firmly to the ground in one sweeping action.

Logan stood there exhausted, the hot dusty air heaving through his aching lungs. Almost immediately, three sudden and violent blows from behind overcame him.

The force from the centurion's sword clashed violently with the steel-like nano-fibers of the explorer's survival suit sending him tumbling in a heap of arms, legs and various bruised extremities. This was all the opportunity the battle-hardened centurion needed to finish the task. As Logan turned to defend himself, his life literally flashed before his eyes. For there, reflected behind the glimmer of a double edged blade slicing silently through the night air, was the eerie blue and white glow of a paralyzer's arc. The luminescent reflection glanced off the flat surface of the hand polished metal and lingered in the air for only a moment as the Centurion collapsed to the ground. Seconds later, Logan's colleagues were kneeling by the side of their exhausted comrade.

"Indeed, wisdom is not your strong point," their intruder gently observed. "Still, it is not every man who can disable an entire squad of Tiberius' elite foot soldiers. What was that light?" He stood looking around astonished at the bodies strewn at his feet.

"Fire from God," Strife quipped, "Logan are you alright?" Patel removed from his bag a gauze bandage and wiped the blood from Logan's forehead and lip.

"I've been better, yeh," Logan groaned incredulously looking down at the huge gash in his lacerated cloak.

"Just what the heck were you trying to do there?" she asked.

"Just practicing a little old-fashioned non-interference diplomacy."

"Well you can thank Strife here, for not doing the same."

"Thanks." Logan squeaked as he wiped the blood from his lip and struggled to his feet.

"Don't mention it, let's get out of here. The Romans are very disciplined. If this squad does not report back soon there will be others to follow."

"You are just a woman, but you are very bright," the burly stranger interjected emphatically, surveying the graveyard. "She is right. We must go now if we are to escape. The Roman prefect has other patrols out, and he will not let this humiliation go unpunished. Come with me." Rising, he led the three quickly away from the battle zone.

"Whoa! Hold on just one minute. We're not going anywhere with you," Logan protested.

"Logan, are you crazy? He saved our lives," Patel exclaimed.

"Yeah, Logan, what gives?" Strife chimed in.

"We don't even know his name. For all we know he may have been the one who led us into this trap."

"My name is Joseph. My friends call me Barnabas, the name the Master gave me. Flavius tells me you seek the Nazarene and I am here to help you."

"So you know Flavius?" Strife inquired.

Barnabas nodded as he continued, "He is a follower of the Way, yet he still has many powerful friends. They seek you now. The rest will have to wait unless you know how to get through the city gates on your own,"

"He's right, Logan. This place is going to be crawling with Roman legionnaires and they will be all over those gates. How are we going to get by them?" Strife insisted.

"They don't know what we look like."

"As I found you, they too are looking for the tall one with spider veins and arms that glow. Is that you?" The large man smiled kindly as he looked into Logan's eyes.

"He's got you there." Patel quipped. "That would be him. End discussion. We follow Barnabas and answer questions later," Patel pronounced smugly as Logan grudgingly joined the other three and hurried away.

Following Barnabas was a task easier said than done. Furtively they negotiated the narrow alleyways; occasionally observing agitated Roman guards who were patrolling and harassing innocent citizens in their search for the tall foreigners. Everyone, whether big or small, who was leaving the city was being thoroughly searched. Forced to show their arms and submit to a thorough probing of all carts and bundles, the resulting flood of ill sentiment convinced Logan that staying with Barnabas was the prudent thing to do.

Finally, after an hour of slinking and hiding through dark alleyways, they arrived at the tiny thatched covered stone house in eastern Jerusalem. The time was midnight and the tiny house was dark except for the flickering light of several strategically spaced oil lamps.

Barnabas was a marginally stout man in his early thirties with a deep baritone voice and a kindhearted laughter that set all at ease. He rested, reclining on the floor with his new found friends by the family table. On it rested a basket of oven-baked flat bread, an enormous leg of roasted lamb, a wooden bowl filled with figs, a bowl of fried finger food, and a block of cheese.

"Welcome to my home, friends. Eat, eat. You will need your strength on your quest for God's anointed one. By the way, why do you seek our Master?" Barnabas enquired as he poured himself a small cup of wine. Logan and Patel stopped eating as an attractive young slave girl set another plate and poured two more cups of wine. As she momentarily blocked Barnabas' view, they silently struggled for an answer. When she finally moved away, Logan replied.

"Uh... Well it's kind of personal. This meat is delicious! What did you say it was?"

"Roasted lamb. What does this mean, personal?"

Barnabas probed, truly confused. Logan and Patel once again looked at each other awkwardly hesitating only a moment before answering.

"What he means is that he does not wish to lose any honor by discussing it," Patel added gesturing with his hands over his heart. Barnabas stared, confused by the gesture which he attempted to imitate before continuing.

"Oh-you have sinned?" Barnabas declared with a slight smile of understanding, casting a knowing glance at Strife who had silently entered the room from behind. Carrying Logan's cloak, which she has just finished mending, she moved to the corner of the room. Obviously entertained by the line of Barnabas's questioning and his peculiar tendency to imitate each of Patel's gestures, she stood quietly.

"Well, noooo... not exactly," Logan began as he cast a glance towards the smirking historian.

"Not yet! What is this bread? It's really good," Patel jumped in, his hands extended in mock warning as Logan's lids narrowed, his pupils stabbing at Patel from the corner of his eye.

"Oh, you are planning on sinning? ……It is a common bread of wheat with a little barley and honey," Barnabas continued, hands extended in an exact duplication of Patel's meaningless gesture. The two chrononauts lingered over the flawless imitation, their mouths ajar as Barnabas continued.

"Well, whatever it is you must not do it! Ah….. ", he smiled casting an appreciative glance again at Strife, "you have a lustful eye. I could tell at once." Strife, who by now was staring holes in Logan from behind, pinched her lips half restraining the laughter.

"It's not exactly a sin I'm seeking him for," Logan continued, ignoring Strife, as he munched on cheese and fried finger food.

"What is this? It's great!"

"Goat's cheese, then what? …………………….. You are sick! That is it, is it not? You are sick and you seek the Master's healing touch. Here, let me see your arm," Barnabas insisted as he stood up trying to pull up the sleeve of Logan's robe. Alarmed, Logan stood suddenly, and firmly pulling the cloaked appendage from his guest's eager grasp, landed his host firmly on his Cyprian caboose. Stunned, Patel and Strife rushed to their host's rescue helping him from the floor, while Logan looked on in disbelief.

"I'm so sorry, please forgive him. He has had this illness since childhood and he is very ashamed of how he looks," Patel pled as he clumsily attempted to brush the dust from their host's linen-covered hind side. Barnabas, unaffected by the fall, was not amused by this new form of penitence as he politely pushed Patel away.

"Yes, forgive me, please", Logan stammered as he pulled his sleeves lower trying to cover his arms.

"Of course, but there is no need to be ashamed," Barnabas generously explained, as brushing the remaining dust he turned to Logan, "The Teacher knows all and can heal anything if you believe. You do believe?"

"Of, Of course."

"Of course he believes," Patel reiterated with his hands spread.

"Of course," Patel and Strife both chimed in.

This time Strife couldn't resist the urge to imitate Patel. Spreading her own hands and smiling widely in Patel's direction, she bowed respectfully towards her host. Barnabas in return clumsily attempted to imitate her, leaving Patel and Logan silently amused and resuming their meal. Like eating popcorn the two travelers reclined comfortably shoveling more of the fried finger food into their already overflowing mouths. Strife, who had not yet commenced eating, spoke as she continued watching the other two.

"Now, when can we see your Teacher?"

"This is so good! What is it?" Patel garbled stuffing more of the delicacies into his mouth.

"Soon, but he is not just my teacher," Barnabas answered Strife, "He reaches into each life teaching each soul what is needed to live. But enough for now, you must rest tonight for your big swim.

"Swim? We're in the middle of a desert?"

"Yes beloved. Tomorrow, you will swim your way out of the city."

Strife and Logan looked at each other confused silently mouthing the word 'swim', while Barnabas performed an exaggerated swimming hand motion for Patel.

"Fine, be mysterious, just one thing. What is this finger-food? I've just got to know," Logan demanded his cheeks bulging with the delicacies. Strife moved forward from the corner intent on hearing the answer.

"Oh that? It is a common dish. We call it *arbah tigen*," Barnabas replied.

"*Arbah tigen*, what's that?" Logan sputtered chucking in three more, but after noticing Strife's wide-eyed smile began chewing a little slower.

"Fried locust."

"Umph!" Logan wretched as he raced desperately for the door.

"Tasty, but their little legs get stuck in your teeth," Barnabas continued, attempting to pick an extremity from his molars as the sounds of gut-wrenching nausea filtered in from the outer courtyard.

"Humph," Barnabas said tilting his head quizzically "must have choked on a wing. Goodnight all."

Soon the oil lamps of the small cottage were being extinguished as the sounds of gagging still filled the early morning air. Strife and Patel peered out the open window facing the courtyard and then cheerfully exchanging a knuckle bump, yelled out,

"That's disgusting! Hold it down out there, people are trying to sleep." Then blowing out the lamp they reclined for the night.

Tucked against the northern edge in the upper city lay the expansive palace of Herod Antipas. This magnificent structure erected by his father, "Herod the Great," inside Jerusalem proper, stood as a testament to the determination of its most famous despot. His son, Antipas, an obese, balding man in ornate robes outlined in gold and silver trim, sat holding three tiny flawless diamonds in one hand. Surrounded by an army of attendants watching over an elegant table overflowing with dishes of various meats and delicacies, the man was alternately stuffing his face with one hand and guzzling wine with the other. Switching the diamonds from hand to hand he gorged himself, gazing intently at the shimmering stones.

Holding each diamond to the light of a nearby candle and close to his eye, the sweat drenched monarch scrutinized the reflections within. Carefully he studied the smooth contours of each stone running the tip of his index finger down the edges and across the surface. After some time of study, he clapped his hands loudly to summon his two closest attendants. As they entered, he spoke brusquely to the taller of the two who gazed respectfully at one of the stones handed him.

"I've never seen stones of this clarity and design. Even the Egyptians have not the quality I hold in my hand here. I must know their source. What did you find out from the prisoner?"

"He knows nothing your Excellency," the first attendant answered looking downward, careful not to meet the monarch's gaze.

"What! You learned nothing! Imbecil! If he will not talk, torture him more!"

"He is a very old man and feeble, liable to die your Excellency."

"What, you dare to defy me?" the tyrant screamed.

"No, your Excellency!"

"Then he shall have to die if he refuses to talk."

Attempting to speak softly, the attendant approached closer attempting to overcome the despot's imposing body odor.

"But King Herod, he knows nothing more," the attendant protested quietly, half choking from the stench.

"Kill him I said! Or you will die! Do you understand me?" Herod screamed his face flushing red with rage, "Then contact Pilate. I want him to send out two legionaries. Find these so called 'Egyptians' at once! I want them brought here now."

"Yes, your Excellency," the attendant bowed backing slowly away from the throne and turned to leave.

"Wait! One more thing! Have you located the Nazarene as I asked of you two weeks ago?"

"No, my lord, he moves from place to place and ignores your invitations to meet."

"He does what? No one refuses an invitation to dine with Herod! Who is this man?" He protested, his overstuffed cheeks spilling the food it could not hold.

"The people believe him to be a great prophet my lord. Some have even gone so far as to proclaim Him to be the Anointed One, The Christ, for he works many miracles," the attendant answered, continuing to gaze at the ground.

"Miracles, what kind of miracles?"

"There have been reports he makes the blind to see and the lame to walk."

"Indeed," Herod remarked, his eyes squinting at the prospect of such power, "Bring him to me. I don't care how, but convince him to meet with me. If he refuses, this sorcerer will need all of his magic when I am through with him."

Early the next morning, the market streets of Jerusalem, already crowded with travelers, began to flood with the produce and livestock of vendors. Humanity and beast intermingled clogging the arteries of the ancient metropolis. Scattered throughout the chaos, and weaving through the smell of dung and perspiration, legions of Roman guards searched every basket and cart for the tall 'Egyptians'.

Unnoticed by the guards were two heavily cloaked figures accompanying one very tense Barnabas. Darting stealthily from street to street, the trio bore on their shoulders a heavy makeshift stretcher covered in layers of goatskin. Weaving their way southward the threesome finally came to a point where they were forced to pass through the center of the market's multitude. In response to the tidal wave of humanity which pressed upon them, the three lifted the stretcher over their heads in order to move forward.

"Make way for the afflicted! Make way for the afflicted!" Barnabas shouted as he struggled to look around the draping of the stretcher and lead the group through the crowd which reluctantly parted before them. Pleased with his success, the Cyprian momentarily flashed a smile back at his friends only to run his entire party directly into a group of Roman guards.

Barnabas now stood face to face with a very irritated centurion. Immediately he fumbled to hand his end of the stretcher over to Patel, all the while motioning backwards with his leg for the others to move on. The wide eyed Patel, frozen, could see the flailing leg, yet was clueless to its meaning. In the meantime, Barnabas stood face to face with one stern-faced Centurion, explaining about the patient they carried while vainly attempting to signal a still oblivious Patel to move on. The Centurion was only half listening to the explanation, and about to wave the group on, when the disciple's flailing leg accidentally found the edge of Patel's shin.

"Yowl!" Patel yelled as he almost dropped the man on the stretcher. The Centurion cast a glance at the scientist and then suddenly noticed the glint of Patel's blue eyes. He lingered, surprised.

Now wary, the officer moved beside the stretcher and began the task of pulling back the goat skins and slowly removing the linen cloth wrapped tightly around the patient's face. Cautiously, he began unwinding the linen wrap as Barnabas, shaking his head, leaned over and whispered something in his ear. Barnabas motioned wildly with his hands and distorted his face describing the grossly deformed visage hidden beneath the dressing. Eyes flaring, the commander stopped and stared.

Unnerved, the senior officer eased back, wiping his hands on his cape and pointing for one of his junior officers to proceed in his place. Cautiously, the soldier approached and began timidly to uncover the invalid. He too stopped after minimal progress, and wiping his hands, turned pointing to a subordinate. The Optio cautiously moved near and using the tip of his Gladius started to lift the linen. Suddenly the man on the stretcher coughed up the most wretched hacking noise that any poor soul could endure. Finally, the heaving stopped. Sweat trickled down the Optio's face as now shaken, he turned and motioned to a nearby feeble and elderly looking servant. The old gray-haired man with his straggly beard and furrowed face struggle forward, his back bent from years of carrying heavy loads. Grudgingly he grunted acknowledging the command. Gently laying his gunnysack on the ground, he limped slowly forward to the side of the stretcher.

Nervously, the withered hand of the diminutive slave inched over resuming the process of slowly unwrapping the remaining linens. Just as he did so, an ear piercing scream from the other side of the market seized the crowd. Terrified the already nervous examiners spun to see the cause of the disturbance. Thus distracted, Barnabas deftly stepped partially in between the Centurion and the stretcher. With two of his men sent to investigate the commotion, the Centurion now turned back to find Barnabas' turban blocking his view. Acting as if he was helping the slave unwrap the face, Barnabas moved his head to the right and the left, obstructing the Centurion's view with uncanny timing. Frustrated, the soldier moved to shove Barnabas out of the way, but not before the slave had turned around shrieking in horror and running through the crowd.

Unnerved and completely convinced, the Centurion and his guards frantically waved the party onward calling for the crowd before them to make way. Patel and Strife took only a second to exchange astonished glances as they quickly pressed forward raising the covered stretcher over the crowd. As fate would have it, weaving through the crowd, who should they run into some seconds later, but the Centurion's slave? As he stood there, back to the group and cowering against a wooden fence post, the party stumbled directly into his path. Still recovering from his fright he turned to confront the very object of his fear. This time up close and personal, in the very faces of Strife and Patel, he screamed again.

But now our travelers at last comprehended, for as he stood there literally shrieking into their faces, they could see the cloudy scars obstructing the old man' eyes. Terrified, the half blind man stumbled into the crowd again as a highway of the fearful opened allowing the accursed stretcher to swiftly pass through.

The party immediately took advantage of the open pathway, and nearly tripping, ran with their burden through the crowd to the city's water tower. Ducking into the narrow stone doorway, they lowered the stretcher onto the tile floor of a small upper room. The small dimly lit room, crowded with residents intent on drawing precious water, quickly emptied itself.

"Now let's see what frightened our cloudy eyed friend so much," Strife suggested with an anxious smile.

"Do you think that's such a good idea? Maybe we should just leave him like he is. I mean with him being in such pain and all," Patel quipped as Strife began the process.

"You've got a point. He has been refreshingly quiet."

Un-wrapping the outer layers of binding, she finally came to the hideous creature waiting below. There, buried beneath the layers of linen strips lay the impish child, Logan, contorting his face as a boy would to scare his pubescent sister.

"Now there's a mug only a mother could love," Strife commented as she stuffed the dirty rags into Logan's half open maul.

"He's so ugly, I think we should shoot him and put him out of his misery. Don't you?"

"Nah, why waste a perfectly good bullet," Strife replied as they continued the unbinding.

"It is good the old blind man could see he is so ugly, my friends, or we might now be residing in Antonia," Barnabas agreed.

"Hey, I was only making a face," Logan protested to his smirking comrades.

"Fear not my friend. Even this the Master can heal," Barnabas reminded them to Strife and Patel's laughter. "As for now, we have no time for visiting. We must keep moving," he continued as they finished unwrapping Logan.

With torches lit, and packs by their sides, the four proceeded down a narrow stone stairway which spiraled into the inky darkness of the lower levels and opened into a sloping underground tunnel. As the quartet stumbled down the steep tunnel, they soon found themselves hip deep in the flowing water of the tower's half-filled aqueduct. The sudden chill of the black liquid caused Strife to shiver. Immediately the thermal compensators of her survival suit began to activate warming her extremities.

"What is this?" a distraught Patel called out.

"We call it water," a dead serious Barnabas calmly replied.

"No one said anything about having to walk on water to find Jesus. What are we doing?" Patel protested.

"We are escaping, my loud friend. Or at least we are attempting to unless you continue speaking so loudly as to alert the entire Roman guard. This," the Cyprian pointed into the narrow tunnel ahead, "is the only way out of the city which the Romans do not guard."

"Why don't they guard it?" Logan asked.

"Because, they do not feel they need to," Barnabas replied as Logan and Strife exchanged confused looks.

As they descended the narrow tunnel, the golden glow of the traveler's lit torches began to gradually diminish, a fact Patel was the first to notice.

"These torches are beginning to be affected by the thinning air. How much longer until we get through?" he vexed.

"We are almost through now, but you will not need your torch much longer. Do not worry, just follow me," Barnabas replied as the water now suddenly began to deepen.

Patel began to panic as barely able to keep his head above water, his torch light went out.

"My torch it's out. I can't see!"

"Trust me. Swim down to the bottom and follow me towards the light," Barnabas gasped just as the current in the tunnel suddenly surged forward causing the water level to rise dramatically. Now completely submerged in the inky liquid, the travelers followed their deliverer towards the dimmest light near the bottom of the tunnel. Swimming rapidly downward past massive ancient stones forming the city's foundation, they rounded a bend at the bottom of the tunnel and pushed up through an impossibly slender opening to a rusty underwater grating. Barnabas, who grasped three of the iron bars just to the right of the central grate, swung the central section open allowing the travelers to pass carefully through. Patel, the last to pass, snagged his shoulder-mounted gunnysack on the edge of the broken grate. Panicking, he twisted violently kicking against the edifice dislodging a shower of mid-size stones, which collapsing in mass, pinned him to the floor. Lungs bursting, he desperately struggled when the merciful release of two strong arms ripped him from his entombment. Moments later, he and Logan emerged into a sun-washed tepid pool outside the walls of Jerusalem. Exhausted and half drowned, they gasped turning to stare at Barnabas.

"Quite refreshing," the burly disciple declared enthusiastically as he smiled swimming for the stone edge of the pool.

"What just happened there?" Logan panted pulling himself out and onto the edge while helping Strife.

"We almost drowned, that's what happened," Patel injected coughing and choking as he held onto the pool's rocky side.

"Oh, my friends! I forgot to tell you about the *surge*!" Barnabas continued, tapping the water from his ears.

"Three times a day the *Spring of Gihon*, that feeds this *Pool of Siloam*, crests, flooding everything. Many a man has drowned, not knowing the path outward. This is why the Romans do not guard it. They do not need to," he said laughing out loud and slapping Logan on the back. "Now hurry! We must go for the Roman guards patrol this pool every hour."

Wide-eyed, the three travelers sat looking at each other.

"Hurry now beloved. We must go!" the big Cyprian repeated circling his friends as a shepherd would his threatened flock. Slowly rising, the three gathered their packs and stumbled their way through the poolside crowd. Down into the eastern Kidron Valley, and up the *Mount of Olives* towards the morning sun, they followed their new found guide.

Chapter Eleven
The Path of Least Resistance

Having escaped the imprisonment of Roman guards, poisoning by fried locusts and drowning in a Jewish cesspool, the trio and their new found friend tackled the rocky paths to Sychar. It was an especially dusty day, and the path, at times winding and treacherous, narrowed at one particular point. Here, at this narrow pass, Logan's stead momentary brushed against that of a dusty Jerusalem bound mercenary. Agitated at becoming the humorous spectacle of almost losing his turban, the assassin turned on his beast to glare at the traveler who had dared offend him. Perhaps, had the offender not been quite so tall, or had he not borne the strange spidery veins on his forearms, the soldier might have stopped to teach him a lesson. Instead, he seethed and dismissed the encounter with the man headed to Samaria.

It was twilight when the three sojourners gathered around the small campfire sending fiery darts into the heavens. Logan sat alone on the bluff looking up at his own fiery dart, a shooting star arcing just below the big dipper in the northern sky. As he watched, he was suddenly in the backyard of a modern suburb. It was dark and Logan was chasing a giggling little blond headed girl who, falling to the ground, stretched out lazily with her daddy to observe the starry host above.

"Daddy, why can't you always be home with us? Why do you always have to go away for so long?" the little girl asked studying the heavenly stage.

"Honey, you know my work takes me very far away," Logan replied, his face riddled with guilt.

"I know. Mommy says you're up there in heaven protecting people and keeping them safe."

"That's right pearly girl. It's very important that I do what I do."

"But Daddy, aren't I important to you too?"

Logan hesitated at first, surprised at the question.

"Now you listen to me. Nothing is more important to me than you."

"Well Daddy, why don't you let Jesus protect those people up there in heaven and you stay here and protect me?"

Logan smiled, stymied by the simple logic of a six-year-old.

"Oh, I see. Your momma's been filling your head with that religious stuff again. Besides, who would ever want to hurt a sweet little girl like you?"

The gentle sound of padded footsteps from behind stirred him as he quickly wiped a tear from his eye.

"Oh, there you are, my friend. Are you well? You seem a long way off," Barnabas said gently placing a warm hand on Logan's shoulder and stooping to sit beside him.

"You have no idea just how far," Logan laughed staring at the lights above.

"Your eyes are wet, my friend," the big man noticed as he handed Logan a small cup of diluted wine.

"Thanks, it must be the dim light," Logan replied, trying to ignore the remark.

"Perhaps the dimness is in your heart and not in your eyes."

"You see better than you let on."

"To see with the heart does not require good eyes, it requires faith. If you would believe, all things are possible, but you must have faith."

"I have faith. I believe in myself."

"Faith is more than saying you believe. You must be willing to trust. In life we all face many obstacles. Most men will eventually face one that they cannot move by themselves. Do you face such an obstacle today?"

Logan's silence answered the big man's query.

"I see. Well, if you do, to what will you look for help, if you will not look to something bigger than yourself? Come, I have something to show you."

Barnabas led him over to a small sandy area peppered with brush. At the edge they came to a camel-hair hammock that Barnabas had tied uncomfortably close to the fire between two very fragile looking shrub-like trees.

"How do you like my bed?"

"Nice," Logan said looking hesitantly at the slender shrubs.

"Do you trust that it will hold me?"

"Uh! Yeh, sure."

"Excellent. Please?" Barnabas smiled pointing with both hands to the outstretched hammock.

"Please what?" Logan asked, wide eyed and staring at the fragile looking structure hanging precariously close to the flickering flames. Strife approached from a distance, a bent finger once more covering her smile.

"Please, lie down."

"But, I'm not tired," Logan protested, eyeing the fragile structure and wondering how he had been maneuvered into his current predicament.

"But remember, your eyes are tired my friend. Please lie down," said Barnabas as he gently placed his hand on Logan's shoulder.

Very gingerly, Logan inched himself onto the hammock, his eyes widening with the sound of straining twines. As his legs swung ever so slowly over the edge, he marveled at how far the small trees could bend. The hammock stretched and stretched and stretched, but did not fall. Logan looked up to see two gentle brown eyes beaming at him from behind the smile of a thick dust covered beard.

"Excellent, beloved, now you know what it means to trust. When you have as much faith in God's anointed as you have in this hammock, you will begin to live," Barnabas said looking kindly into his new friend's eyes.

Logan stared back momentarily. Embarrassed by the gentle compassion, he looked away fighting stubbornly to rebury his feelings.

"I'm afraid to tell you this, but I'm already alive."

"Logan, if that were true your eyes could meet mine. Perfect love casts out all fear," Barnabas said softly as Logan continued to stare at the ground.

"Like many, until now, you have lived to eat and breathe and to possess. But in here," he spoke, gently patting Logan's chest, "you are dead." Continuing, he pointed upwards. "He wants to give you life." Touching the shrub that supported the hammock, he said, "Trust him who will not break the tender reed".

Inside the eastern edge of Jerusalem's wall stood the imposing citadel of the Fortress Antonio. Illuminated harshly with the glow of flickering torches, the imposing edifice was awash with nocturnal activity. It was late, and from a second story window a shadowy figure looked down at the murky square below. Turning back to the room behind him, the smarmy form stared into the eyes of Jerusalem's Roman Prefect. Pontius Pilate, the praefectus, was a muscular middle-aged man with slightly graying temples and a small scar across an otherwise handsome face. Decorated with the trappings of a Roman hero, his persona exuded the authority of an experienced warrior.

"Forgive me, Herod, I have been detained questioning a very interesting visitor to our city," Pilate announced bowing respectfully to the swarthy ruler. Herod approached, his countenance brightened by the anticipation of good news.

"And, you have learned, what?"

"It seems our visitor has a financial proposition to offer us. He believes he has seen the one with spider arms heading towards Sychar. For a modest fee, he has offered to lead us to him and his friends."

"Kill him," Herod insisted.

"My lord?" the commander replied unintimidated.

"How dare he try to extort me?"

"If you please your highness," the Praefectus continued, "If we kill him, we won't be able to locate the Egyptians. We need him to identify our visitors."

"Very well, take him with you. Promise him what you must, but after you have the strangers, kill the traitor," the monarch smiled thinly popping a grape into his mouth.

Pilate bowed and replied tersely, "I shall consider your request." Then slowly he backed away and exited the royal chambers. Closing the door behind him, he made his way down the stone stairway to the quad below. Descending into the dimly lit courtyard, he was immediately greeted by a tall soldier who was overseeing an assemblage of foot soldiers. The young man draped with the crimson cape of Centurion authority and adorned with the steely eyes of combat, saluted his commander. Despite the authority that both figures commanded, a hint of an unexpected kindness was seen in the young officer's eyes.

"So, what did his highness say about our visitor, here?" the tall soldier asked sarcastically pointing over at the mercenary.

"We're to follow his lead, with a detachment, to Sychar," the Praefectus responded with a vertical roll of his eyes.

"Huh," the young centurion chuckled, "Well that sounds reasonable. So he's willing to use this mercenary. And then what?" "Once we locate and detain the three Egyptians, we are to kill him," the Praefectus nodded towards their guide as he walked away. "Issue the order and move out."

Disgusted, the young leader shook his head and with one motion of his hand summoned his squadron.

The Judean sun struggled skyward as four weary beasts of burden labored down the dusty road near Sychar. Making their way towards the small village in the northern kingdom of Samaria, they passed through lumbering mountainsides dotted with craggy slopes that spawned large grassy hillsides. On these gentle hillsides flourished flocks of sheep as they had for more than four thousand years. Ahead of them leaned an insignificant looking stone and wooden gate which welcomed the four travelers as they entered the tiny walled village. Making their way down the rutted alleyways the tiny entourage arrived at a small cottage with stone walls. Greeted by a modest-looking Jewess robed in a long traditional woolen mantle, they were soon smothered with strong warm hugs and revived with cool spring water.

Inside the modest home, the small group gathered by a fire kindled in the family's bread oven. Reclining on rugs scattered on the stone floor, the three travelers spoke in hushed tones. Their two hosts and Barnabas, temporarily distracted by the preparation of food, were sharing a lighthearted moment in the other room.

"Ok, my best guess is that we are headed north to the town of Capernaum. It's a small village that Jesus called headquarters. Located on the major North-South trade route of King's Highway, it affords easy access to all parts of the country. Have you checked your equipment lately?" Strife pointed to Patel.

"I was just getting ready to do that. We'll need some place private to test the telemetry link."

"I'll ask our hosts," Logan volunteered rising to make his way across the room to the small kitchen where the Jewess, her husband and Barnabas stood chatting around the table. The close friends grew silent as he entered the room, approaching slowly, and attempting not to interrupt.

"Thank you, dear friends, for your kindness and your generosity. My comrades and I seek a time of - solitude - before we meet the Master tomorrow. Is there some place quiet where we may meditate?" Logan inquired eliciting a slightly confused look from his hosts.

"You may use the stable out back. No one will disturb you there," the diminutive Jewess offered casting a suspicious glance Logan's way.

"Thank you so much. We won't be long," he assured her returning quickly to his friends.

"Follow me," he whispered.

Once in the stable the three visitors pulled three small rectangular devices from their suits. The devices, approximately the size of a modern cell phone and glistening with an illuminated screen, held the entire content of each chrononaut's recorded data. Kneeling in a tight circle on the hay strewn floor the three began their adjustments. Strife, the keeper of the transition cylinder, pulled the small component from a pocket in her suit.

"Begin linking and loading your individual data to the cylinder and I will upload it to the ship," Strife instructed as she adjusted her instrument's keypad.

"That's funny. There's no response on the ship's channel," Strife responded in a confused tone. Patel reached over taking the device from her and inspecting it for damage. Finding none, he then tried to reset the instrument's components.

"This is not good," he said and a moment later, "She's right, the signal's dead. We can't transmit to the ship. The data antennae must've been damaged during that insane re-entry."

"What'll we do now?" Strife replied tensely to Patel.

"There's nothing to do. We'll just have to record everything onto the cylinder and make sure it gets back to the ship."

"That means one of us will have to survive long enough to get back," Logan appended.

"Whew! I'm glad we got that settled. Now we have to survive," Patel quipped and then in anger, "For a minute there I thought it was going to be optional!"

Patel looked down continuing to check the recording cylinder for defects.

"In your case we'll make an exception," Strife fired back, flashing Patel a subtle smile as quickly the three gathered their equipment and scrambled back into the tiny stone abode.

Emerging from the stable's coarse atmosphere of hay and excrement, they gasped as they plunged headlong into the incredible aroma of freshly baked bread. A few moments later and the three were reclining by a small wooden table, breaking the steaming bread in the restrained lamp light of the tiny rock hewn den. Flanked by their three hosts, the travelers eagerly plotted the next day's agenda.

Night had long since fallen when the young Centurion led his unit under the shadow of the town's precarious gate. The midnight moon draped its zenith glow on the twelve soldiers, who dismounting, fanned out over the entrance of the sleepy village. A half hour later, with nothing to show for their efforts, the exhausted and famished legionnaires made their way to the local inn. While the mercenary and two soldiers guarded the village's main gate, the tiny squadron bedded down on one side of the town, completely unaware that their quarry slept soundly on the other.

Perhaps it was morning's first light or the cool summer breeze that stirred Logan awake from a restful sleep. Staring upward at the tapestry of the crude thatch and mud ceiling hanging above him, he was struck by the complexity in its simple design. Something in it reminded him of the life he now lived.

The crackle of a warm oven fire coupled with the smell of fresh bread baking summoned him upward. Slowly he rose from his padded bedroll, stretching and yawning as he approached the open window before him. Within its boundary lie the form of a new rising sun, its golden rays promising an eventful day. As he bent down to pack his roll away, he became suddenly aware of an inexplicable sensation of vulnerability. Standing and looking out, he shook the sand from his roll and gazed anxiously through the open portal, unable to ignore the troubling sensation.

"Too much cheap wine last night," he assured himself as he nudged the other two awake with the edge of his sandaled foot. A few minutes later and the entire house was abuzz with activity preparing to face the coming day.

On the other side of town, the legionnaires had long before arisen and begun to scour the village. Moving methodically like a well-oiled machine, the small squadron started at one end and advanced in a series of parallel sweeps towards the other. Fortunately for Logan and his friends, this house to house technique commenced on exactly the wrong side of town and took quite some time. The result was that despite their best efforts, no one seemed to be aware of the arrival of the three 'Egyptians'.

Back at Deborah's home the three visitors now fully packed, nourished and medicated prepared to depart. Completely unaware of the commotion going on in the village around them, they made their way to the kitchen area.

"Wow that smells wonderful," Logan exclaimed, cleaning his sullied dish and placing it with the others.

"Thank you, Joseph says you have traveled far. Is that true?" she asked, pouring him a glass of wine.

"Why, yes, but who is Joseph?"

"Your friend who brought you here, of course."

"I thought his name was Barnabas," Logan said shaking his head in bewilderment.

"It is, the Master gave him the name Barnabas, after he believed. The name means "son of encouragement" and you have benefited from its fruit."

"Now I wonder what kind of name the Master will give to you," she conjectured, her finger to her forehead. Strife leaned against the kitchen wall helping herself to another healthy portion of the warm bread, while Patel reclined silently.

"Oh, I've got some ideas," she said enthusiastically raising the bread to her mouth and drawing a disdainful look from Deborah.

"As head of this house, I a woman, have the right to speak. As an unmarried woman, and a guest, you would be wise to learn some discretion," the perceptive Jewess censured. With Strife now silenced, Deborah turned back to pour Logan a second cup of wine allowing the chrononaut just the opportunity to stick his tongue out at Strife.

"He's not likely to be what you expect him to be," the middle-aged woman warned Logan.

"We're counting on that," Patel intruded, rudely stuffing his face with another generous slice of the warm crust as Barnabas entered the room. The big man cast a knowing look at Patel and turned to speak to Logan.

"Yes, to each man he is different."

"By that you mean?" Logan asked, sipping on his wine.

Deborah turned to Logan and spoke directly to him as if ignoring the other two altogether.

"He knows you, Jon of Logan, even before you speak. He knows who you are and why you seek him better than you do".

"More importantly, he knows what it is you really need," Barnabas interjected. Turning towards Strife, Patel whispered, waving an imaginary wand over his imaginary top hat.

"Sounds like telepathy to me, probably some kind of Hocus Pocus or a brain wave scan."

"What was that?" the Jewess asked.

"Nothing, he just said we need to leave when we can. Where is the Master now?" Logan interrupted, casting Patel an evil eye.

"In Capernaum, you will find him there. Go in peace, but be careful of the Romans. They search for you even now," Deborah cautioned.

"Romans! Here, in the village? When did they arrive?" Patel blurted out as his comrades rose.

"They arrived late last night while you were sleeping, fragile one," the diminutive woman advised, "Do not worry little one. The brothers have been watching them carefully. They are asking about Barnabas and his companions. You must be very careful. Now I would advise you to make haste".

Patel turned to Strife, his face distorted, and whispered.

"Who's she calling fragile?"

"Shush," came the reply from their host as the *chronies* and their guide quickly moved to the stable and began to saddle the donkeys to leave Deborah's home. Peppered with many hugs from their host, the travelers made for the door led by the big burly Cyprian.

"Capernaum is a three-day ride from here. Are you sure you're up to it, my pale companions?" Barnabas asked laughing while slapping Logan firmly on the back. Logan, rattled from the blow, grimaced at his smiling companions who nodded vigorously in affirmation.

"Lead on, ole' dusty one," Logan groaned thumping his friend in return. The slap, firm but friendly, erupted a veritable cloud of dust which rising, hovered briefly in the morning air. Logan watched amused as the aberration floated and then descended on the transfixed members of his team. A brief cough, gag and dusting of the hands had the three smiling and running for the door. Logan as well was on his way out when suddenly his path was blocked by the pint-sized Jewish woman in what resembled a twenty-second century martial arts stance. Logan tensed as the elderly woman approached, hugged his neck and whispered in his ear.

"Be careful, my brother. The Spirit has told me to advise you 'beware the deceiver'."

"What does that mean?"

"I don't know," came the tearful reply, "but Jehovah has his hand on your life. Go in peace, and remember we love you, even if you are Goyim." She spoke kindly before hugging his neck again and kissing his cheek. Stunned by her mysterious compassion, Logan stared hard at the small elderly woman as the three travelers exited quickly falling in line behind their leader. Stealthily negotiating the broken streets of the tiny village, the group resumed its travel through a break in the village wall. Just as they approached the narrow crevice a very large Roman soldier stepped from an adjacent alleyway to block their path. The rugged soldier, adorned in polished armor and brandishing an equally shiny Gladius, approached the quartet, thus prompting Barnabas to step forward.

"Friend, friend, *Shalom* to you, is there something we can do for you?" Barnabas spoke as Logan deftly pulled from his donkey's saddle one of the stolen swords plucked from his last Roman encounter.

"Yes, Samaritan, you and your Egyptian spies can surrender and march yourselves to the center of town. The Praefectus has orders from King Herod to detain you. Now come along and perhaps we will not harm you." The large scar tracing its way down the warrior's left cheek convinced Logan that perhaps Barnabas' diplomacy might find better use another day. Gently, he nudged the reluctant Cyprian aside as he stepped forward.

"My dear man, your conditions for surrender are most generous; however, I'm afraid that we have a previous engagement. Please send our regrets to King Herod and thank him for his most magnanimous invitation. Now if you'll please be so kind as to lower your weapon and let us pass…"

"You're not going anywhere."

"Did I not say please," Logan reminded Barnabas as he turned back towards the soldier, "I did say please."

"If you try to resist, I will have the pleasure of slitting your throats and gutting you like pigs," the soldier bellowed while raising his sword ominously.

"I was afraid you'd say that," Logan replied disgustedly, then rapidly whipping his sword into the air, and settling into a perfect 'engarde' position. Logan waited for his armor-clad assailant's first violent lunge forward. His momentum, more a product of his sheer size and fearlessness than his fencing skill, hurled him rapidly past the smaller and more evasive guardsman. As he passed, Logan deftly snipped the shoulder bindings attaching the breastplate to the soldier's torso.

The soldier's next volley, sans breastplate, was only slightly more successful. Ceaselessly, the brute force of the Optio's lunges met awkwardly against centuries of avant-garde technique as Logan easily deflected each of the massive blows. Two minutes later, the soldier's reflexes had rapidly slowed, and now Logan was on the offensive.

In lightning quick motions, almost mechanical in efficiency, Logan left the bewildered soldier retreating rapidly. Mercilessly, the barrage became a blur as the two swords struck sending up a cloud of sparks almost obscuring the combatants. Finally, in one vicious circular motion, the explorer ended the battle by sweeping the soldier's sword from his hand and onto the roof of a nearby hut.

"Amateur," Logan pronounced to the wheezing warrior now pinned with a sword to his sweat drenched neck. Moments later with the soldier tied to a nearby post, Logan smiled.

"Tell Herod, we're sorry to decline his kind invitation," he seethed tightening the man's bindings, "but we have a more important appointment. WITH A CARPENTER!" Then he and his three duly impressed companions slipped through the break in the village wall and disappeared down the road through the Judean hills.

The Galilean lake shimmered with the last slivers of light seeping from the slowly drowning sun. As the scarlet orb sank slowly into its watery grave, an exhausted trio and their guide rounded the sea entering the small village of Khersa. A mere three hours southeast of Capernaum, the tiny community, famous for the legend of '*Legion*', was a welcome sight to four exhausted and starving sojourners. Confident that by taking the less traveled eastern route, they had thrown off the armored band, the travelers converged on the village inn to rest and stable their donkeys. Dust covered and in need of a solid meal, the four travelers followed Barnabas' lead and dismounted entering the inn. Two hours later, on the other side of town, a very different set of instructions was being issued.

"Take these three men and go search the eastern side of the village; we will take the Western side. Remember, do not kill the Egyptians," the Centurion announced pointedly.

"Fan out in pairs! Cover the village. They must be herc somewhere," his second in command directed.

In the meantime, Barnabas had located the stable and commenced to feed and water all four of the animals. Halfway through his chore he turned inadvertently, and spying the legionnaires through an open window, ducked out immediately and shuffled out the back door to warn his friends.

"Logan! We must leave now," Barnabas spoke in hushed tones as he burst in upon Logan, who seated, was finishing off a meal of roast lamb and bread.

"Why? We just got here," Logan protested.

"Legionnaires, everywhere," an animated Barnabas exclaimed quietly. Alarmed, Logan pulled his friend over behind a dividing door.

"What? How did they find us so fast? How many are there?"

"I'm not sure, six, eight, maybe more. We must go." Patel and Strife, having noticed the sudden commotion, lay down their plates and crossed over to join their friends.

"What gives?" Strife demanded as Logan held a finger to her lips for quiet.

"Shhh…Be quiet. The legionnaires are here."

"What? How did they find us so fast?" Patel demanded. Wide-eyed he crouched quickly behind his comrades, his rear almost touching the floor. Logan and Strife, already having learned to ignore their associate, peered from the doorway into the village streets.

"Let's go. Let's get out of here." Patel exclaimed as he launched from his crouching position into the solid wooden door suddenly swung shut by Logan's leg.

"Umph! Ouch!" Patel yelled as he slammed head first into the unexpected obstacle and ricocheted backwards onto his seat in the dirt floor.

"No, I don't think so," Logan replied as if he'd seen nothing happen. "If they have spears, we'll have one in our backs before we get 10 yards out of town. Besides, they're most likely on horseback. There's no way we're going to be able to out run them on donkeys."

"So what do you propose we do?" Strife probed as Patel rubbed his head picking himself up off of the dirt floor.

"We'll have to slow them down. Throw them off our trail or we'll be running from them forever. Look, I've got an idea."

"I am very sorry my friend, but I can not help you. I cannot be part of doing real harm to my fellow man," Barnabas interjected.

"What?" Logan reacted, "is this coming from 'Mister Sword to my throat'?"

"I'm sorry, my friend, but you can rest assured I would have never hurt you that night. That was just to keep you quiet and get you moving," the burly Levite smiled.

"Ok-k-kay…," Logan said, "apology accepted. I think. You just watch our backs, Barney. I'll take care of the tin cans."

The four stole their way out of the back of the inn and over to the stable. Logan then slid back out through an open window as Patel followed while Strife and Barnabas saddled the donkeys for travel.

"What do you want me to do?" Patel whispered.

"Just get them over here. I'll think of something," Logan replied spying the tethered donkey in the alleyway.

Using his suit-enhanced strength, Logan leaped from the creature's back to reach the adjacent roof. There from above, he watched two legionnaires pursue Patel into the alley below.

"Logan!" Patel yelled as the soldiers closed in. Just as they reached for the diminutive scientist, they were knocked forcefully, head first, into an intervening wall. Patel stopped turning to see the downed men and Logan dropping from a thick rope of hemp used to lift barrels.

"You, you knocked them out cold!" Patel marveled.

"That was easy. Quick, get some rope! Tie them up!" Logan instructed the others who had joined them from the stable.

Strife and Patel, quickly locating some twisted hemp, fashioned the cord into a rope and bound the unconscious guards. In minutes they were gagged, tied and lowered feet first into an abandoned cistern.

"Fun," Patel said excitedly like a kid with a new toy.

"Just stay close."

"Logan, one of those two was just a boy. His skin was cold and clammy and he wasn't moving, even after we lowered him into the dry well." Strife commented, an air of concern reflecting in her voice. Logan looked down and sighed heavily.

"Ok, now not only do we have to stay alive without killing one of them, we have to worry about fighting kids," Logan complained. "We'll check him again before we leave. For now, we've got to keep moving."

A few minutes later and two additional pursuers were drawn into the fray chasing Patel as he raced down the narrow alleys separating the two-story mud and stone buildings. In another part of the village, Strife had acquired a third adversary who was chasing her down a narrow alley in the direction of the market square.

Logan, who had strategically placed himself in a side alley along Patel's path, was following his associate's flight using the head's up display of his nano-lens. As Patel raced by Logan's position, the Commodore deftly placed a borrowed shepherd's hook into the slower legionnaire's path, sending the soldier head over heels to the ground, Logan finished the job with the opposite end of the hook rendering the fallen soldier unconscious.

A moment later and he was again in hot pursuit of a fatiguing Patel who, chased by a foot soldier, was stumbling through the market square and into a different alley. Tipping several pots, Patel caused the soldier to fall and roll into the alley, thus affording Logan time to catch up. Then with the borrowed staff in his hand, the guardian once again snagged, as one would trap a wild hare, and disarmed the stunned pursuer. Moments later he was bound and carefully stored away in a large woven basket only to later join the ranks of his immobilized comrades.

Meanwhile, Strife fled through the alleys furiously pursued by one exceptionally well-conditioned Centurion. Despite the technological advantage of her survival suit, the close pursuit narrowed. With her assailant literally on her heels, Strife emerged from the alley to discover her path partially blocked by an enormous brown camel. Quickly ducking she passed under the animal creating a momentary natural barrier between herself and her adversary. Now facing the animal and temporarily obscured,

Strife was treated to a flushing maneuver consisting of a succession of three quick thrusts of the warrior's sword underneath the camel. She leaped up and out of the way, catching one foot in the animal's stirrup and the on the hump its back. Whether it was from the fleeting glimpse of the shadow sailing over his head or the sudden thud of crunching gravel behind him, the soldier froze, his fruitless lunges abandoned.

Wheeling around quickly, the Centurion was immediately greeted with a tremendous blow to his exposed forehead. There stood Strife with her spare bra, holding it as the shepherd David had held his sling, strap in one hand and stones in the other. Logan and Patel emerged from the alley just in time to see the strapping young soldier come crashing backwards to the ground. Lying there with a huge knot on his forehead and his crown half submerged in a fly infested camel paddy, the Centurion slept soundly. The two male explorers stood there stunned looking at Strife and her 'missile launcher'.

"Don't say it!" Logan smiled pointing emphatically at the victor.

"You guessed it!" Strife quipped as they joined in unison.

"The bigger the bra, the harder they fall!" Logan and Strife declared together.

"I feel great!" Strife announced, back straight, with an air of satisfaction as she marched off towards the stable.

"I thought I noticed an extra little bounce in her step," Patel quipped. Logan nodded his head as they watched Strife saunter down the dusty alleyway.

"I told you that girl was a knock out," Logan added, not to be outdone. Patel looked at Logan, smiling in agreement as the two followed her down the alleyway, dragging their unconscious adversary behind them.

The next morning, the four weary travelers rose early gathering to perform a brief check on their quarry. Looking over the edge into the dry well, they saw the soldiers still struggling with their bonds. Gagged they were making various grunting and groaning noises of protest. One young man, was however, mysteriously quiet. Logan had a look of concern as he reflected on his inactivity. Speaking briefly with Patel, Logan instructed the diminutive scientist to scan the young man and after doing so he injected him with a medication from his medical kit. This resulted in the young man seeming to stir giving the trio relief as to his condition.

Standing nearby, but out of sight of the Romans, was a scruffy looking teenage boy, skinny as a rail, wearing a makeshift turban and grinning ear to ear at the soldiers' plight. Logan approached the boy and after a few short words, held up two fingers. The boy nodded and Logan set two shiny gold coins in the boy's hand. Slowly the three explorers lowered a loose-fitting wooden cover over the opening of the broken cistern. Pointing to the now covered well from which the sounds of muffled cries emanated, Logan patted the boy on his back. Moments later the three explorers and their guide were racing on horseback towards Capernaum.

"These are fine animals," Logan shouted back to Barnabas as they rounded the next curve.

"Yes, I wonder if Herod will be more upset that you have them, or that he is missing that shiny new collection from his armory?" The big man bellowed back casting a glance at Logan's gurney sack brimming with six shimmering new swords.

"They make great clothes hangers," Logan replied.

CHAPTER TWELVE
An Uncommon Man

A yellow sun hovered high above the little town of Capernaum, its heat wilting both man and beast as the four travelers wound their way down the last stretch of dusty road. Dismounting, our heroes paused to look down at the village before turning to confer with Barnabas.

"Welcome to Capernaum, beloved," Barnabas spoke as he gazed at the seaside community surrounded by plush green meadows growing right up to the surrounding walls.

"It is here you will find the Son of man," he continued wistfully, his eyes transfixed on the tiny village; "the people who live here have walked in darkness for centuries. In this, the land of death's shadow, they have seen a great light. On them it has dawned. The prophecies are fulfilled."

Logan exchanged a confused look with his friends and then towards the tiny village situated on the western shore of the Lake of Gennesaret. Wiping the sweat from his brow, he thought how darkness would be the last word he would use to describe this tiny borough. It seemed no more or less imposing than any other he had observed in his short first century tenure. The tear in his ancient friend's eye said differently. Hesitating, the Cyprian continued, his voice insistent for the first time,

"I will find us a place to stay tonight. You stable the beasts."

Intimidated by Barnabas' new found authority, Logan nodded an affirmative, almost bowing at the waist. A few moments later, with Barnabas gone, the guardian turned and looking at his fellow travelers, began to gather his gear. Patel looked up from his seated position.

"Where are you going?"

"I'm going to follow him and have a look around. You two stable the animals. And don't go near any legionnaires," Logan commanded as he walked off leaving the other two to reluctantly tend the horses.

The sweat dotted Logan's brow as he made his way down the hill and into the alleys and streets of the small village below. Logan, still growing accustomed to the effects of the sweltering heat, gagged as he encountered his first whiff of discarded maritime remains. He had forgotten the Levite's warning that this was a fishing village renowned for its tilapia, carp and sardine production. Every alley Logan explored was sprinkled with wooden carts filled with mounds of drying fish and accented with the obligatory fly-covered mounds of refuse. The stench was accentuated by the aroma emanating from several large stone-walled buildings producing a popular fish sauce widely consumed by the Jewish nation. Logan found it sobering that the most illustrious figure of the human race would choose this for his home.

The scanning devices built into his survival suit had been activated for some time before Logan thought to consult his wrist mounted display. Studying the device for any unusual readings in the environment, he continued his foray deeper into the heart of the village.

Meanwhile, Strife and Patel finished stabling the horses and began their own search for the Nazarene. Making their way down the thoroughfares of the eastern side of the town, Patel and Strife worked opposite sides of each street. After a few minutes of meaningless readings Patel stopped, and pulling out a small screwdriver-like device, inserted it into the back of his scanner unit. A few minor adjustments later and he rebooted the system tuning the scanner to a new wavelength. The device immediately began to flash a bright green color from the small wrist mounted display.

"What are you doing?" Strife asked after crossing the street to observe his adjustments.

"Come on!" he yelled tearing off in the direction indicated by the display unit. Following its signal they raced first down one alley and then back again in a new direction.

"It's moving, faster!" Patel insisted as frustrated, they stumbled knocking over baskets and vendor carts.

On the other side of Capernaum, Logan had given up.

"This is a dead end and a stinky one at that," he said almost choking as he headed back down the next village street. Frustrated, he shook the wearisome device cursing the blank display attached to his left wrist. At one point he grew so agitated that he almost tripped over and into one of the low-lying fish filled carts strewn carefully along the narrow alleys.

Thus, he continued stumbling down the alley, all the while thrashing the stubborn device, man and machine blinded to the commotion ahead. For there, in the center of town, and temporarily blocked from his view by the glare from above, stood a crowd of some one hundred villagers. Congregating in one corner of the market square, the mass consisted of those normally lining the narrow streets plus dozens of a special class. These privileged, the lame, the blind and the deaf were scattered amongst the villagers. The spectacle of the train of afflicted, crippled borne on homemade stretchers and blind led by hand, led to the savior, clamoring desperately for his attention.

Initially, Logan dismissed the crowd as political in nature, until straining to see more clearly the figure in their midst, he suddenly noticed Patel and Strife converging on the crowd from the other side of the *agora*. Patel, animated and pointing emphatically at the man above the crowd, was followed by an equally mesmerized Strife. As Logan neared the group's outer fringe, he realized this was the one they had traveled immeasurable distances and eons of time to see.

Logan hesitated to absorb the irony. He had imagined the Nazarene as always surrounded by the huge throngs that accompany the famous. Here instead, he was confronted by the reality that the most celebrated figure in history was not always welcomed by the rich and powerful.

Little Capernaum, with its small population in rags and its dirt roads, was the chosen beachhead for the Christian invasion. For here in the donkey and mule paddy-covered streets stood the central figure of the human race. As Logan pondered this irony, the veteran sentinel temporarily froze, pressed down by an almost irrational sense of insane curiosity mixed with an incredible fear of what he might find.

While Logan hesitated, Patel and Strife closed in from behind on the spellbound crowd. The people stood silently, hanging intently on every sacred syllable. Strife was transfixed, her mouth forming strange silent syllables as she echoed the famous scriptures being uttered for the very first time in history. With their eyes fixed on the one clothed in the seamless tunic, and the crowd gathered tightly at his feet, the figure seemed to float in midair. This illusion only added to Logan's sense of awe, which persisted, even after he realized the presence of the supporting marble platform.

Slowly the three time travelers drifted together converging at the edge of the assembly. As they did so, Strife silently whispered to her comrades.

"Of all the armies that have marched, all the ships that have sailed, all the rulers that have ruled, no other has changed history more this one solitary life. Gentlemen, I give you - Jesus of Nazareth."

The moment seemed an eternity as the three stood transfixed by the object of their expedition.

"Are you sure this is the one?" Logan asked staring at the young rabbi.

"Yeah, and he's lighting up my spectrometer like a freakin' beacon," Patel exclaimed as he glanced at his flashing wrist display. Stunned Logan grabbed Patel's left arm and pulled the glowing screen into view.

"What! Let me see that! My unit didn't register anything," Logan protested quietly examining the readings on Patel's arm scanner.

"Ow, that's my arm!" Patel responded wrenching his arm away from Logan's grip.

"Mine either," chimed in Strife.

"Is that coming from him? Logan demanded.

"It's either him or his cologne", Patel retorted, massaging his sore wrist, "I adjusted my scanner to scan for radiation." Logan, still disbelieving looked again at Patel's wrist scanner.

"Let's get a closer look," Logan replied skeptically. Moving to the right hand side of the crowd, only several rows from Jesus, they could easily hear and observe the young Hebrew speaker. Dressed in traditional cloak and possessing the characteristic beard, tanned skin and facial features common to his Jewish heritage, there was nothing exceptional about his appearance. Possessing broad shoulders and muscular arms, the physique of a carpenter, he spoke as much with his large gentle hands and compassionate gaze as with his voice. The universal translators built into each traveler's earpiece and nano-lens translated each word he spoke to English. His voice was soft and halting, his words piercing. As he spoke, those who listened smiled, as if for only a moment they looked at peace. Life's fog had dissipated, its meaning illuminated. To Logan they looked free, free of worry, free of fear.

".......and so it is with you my friends," Jesus continued.

Stepping down to the ground and walking over to a wooden cart piled high with bread, Jesus reached for one of the many loaves. His hand wavered as he sought just the perfect loaf and picking it up he held it high while he spoke. The spiral pastry was misshapen having been inadvertently mixed with an excessive amount of yeast resulting in a large air-filled mass. Like some cartoon character's nose, its bulbous appearance was so inflated as to be comical triggering the crowd's laughter. Logan and his friends used the distraction to move to the front.

"The Pharisees... have fed you, with the yeast of pride, religious pride that separates you from your Father in heaven. Beware the 'yeast' that permeates the soul and puffs it up." Peter stepped forward from behind the other disciples, his nose in the air, strutting about and almost tripping. The crowd laughed. While mildly amused Jesus largely ignored the fisherman and continued to hold high the cake. A seething group of richly robed Pharisees clustered at the crowd's edge.

"They burden your lives with man's rules and traditions; works of pride, like *yeast,* working its way into the soul, nullifying God's grace. Your Father in heaven seeks an unleavened life," he continued holding up a perfectly round and flat unleavened loaf.

"True faith does not consist of rules, it abounds in love. Indeed there is only one foundation you truly need. It is 'Love the Lord your God with all your heart and all your soul and all your mind. And love your neighbor as much as you love yourself'. Do this and you will find that you are not only keeping, but surpassing all of **their** rules." He nodded towards the Pharisees.

"And so I give you a new command. Love one another from the heart. Love as God loves, without thought to yourself, always placing the other's good before your own. In so doing you usher in the kingdom of God and catch a glimpse of the One from whom all love flows."

Suddenly, an entire regiment of Roman soldiers, sans swords, burst in on the meeting and rode briskly up to Jesus. Jesus unflinchingly turned to face the regiment as, casting a glance at the mules they rode, a faint smile fleetingly crossed his countenance. The unarmed soldiers parted, their younger members allowing their leader to walk boldly forward. In three brief steps the Centurion had closed ranks with Jesus. Stunned, Logan and his companions tried to fall back, but wedged in by the crowd, the three braced for conflict. Instead, with only a momentary glance in their direction, the Centurion in all his armor, and before his fellow soldiers, bowed his bruised head and bent his knee to the ground.

"Forgive me Teacher", the young leader began.

"What can I do for you Julius?" Jesus replied gently encouraging the commander to stand. Meanwhile, Logan and his friends, still trapped by the crowd, watched in amazement.

"It's my servant, Teacher. He was injured in a recent conflict in Khersa. It's my fault. He should not have been involved. His neck was injured and he can neither move nor scarcely breathe... He's just a boy," the warrior's face was taut and his voice edgy as he fought to hold back the tears.

"He and his family have been with me his entire life. We were undermanned so I allowed him to help us.....It is my fault."

"Your fault?" Jesus asked with almost surprise, his eyes glancing briefly in Logan's direction.

"Yes, mine," the Centurion replied with his head bowed in shame. Jesus turned laying the loaf back on the bread cart behind him, his gaze half falling on Logan again as he turned back. This second look was to Logan different, more deliberate than the first, its effect flushing his face and sending an unexpected wave of guilt trickling down the guardian's back.

"I see. I will go and heal your servant," Jesus said, nodding. Head still bowed, Julius moved to block the rabbi's path. Haltingly, the warrior spoke with anguish, unable to look Jesus in the eye.

"Master, forgive me but... I...I am a sinner! I do not even deserve to have you come under my roof. But just say the word and I **know** that my servant will be healed. For I myself am a man under authority, with soldiers under me. I tell this one 'Go', and he goes; and that one 'Come', and he comes. I say to my servant 'Do this' and he does it," Julius continued, his head still bowed.

"Julius," Jesus said softly and emphatically as the soldier slowly raised his head. Jesus looked deeply into the Centurion's eyes and smiling winsomely, he turned to the crowd.

"I tell you the truth……… I have found not a single one in all of Israel with this much faith. Many will come from the east and the west and take their places with the prophets," Jesus sadly pronounced to the silent crowd, and then casting only a glance towards the Pharisees, he continued, "And many of the children, stumbling over the cornerstone, will fall away."

"You may go. It is done….Just as you believed." Placing his hand on the Centurion's shoulder he stepped down from the wooden *bema*. Julius bowed, and eyeing Logan, turned to leave the village, his second in command pointing at Logan and questioning as they made their way out.

"Seems we have some limited time before we see our friends again," Logan smiled weakly watching the last of the soldiers reclaim their weapons and horses and ride quickly away.

"They didn't look too friendly to me," Patel quipped.

"I told you to check that young boy Logan, what's wrong with you," Strife protested, her index finger waving vigorously in Logan's face. Logan just stared, his face draped with concern. Finally, the finger retracted allowing him the opportunity to speak.

"I did. I mean we checked his vitals before we left. Patel gave him an injection. What can I say? I feel terrible about it but he was trying to kill me, you know."

"Yeh, well if you keep screwing up, he might have some help," she said as they gathered their bags and donkeys.

Turning back to the platform, they noticed that the crowd had mostly dispersed and Jesus was nowhere in sight.

"Oh, great! We lost Him again, and it's getting dark. We better find him before we can't see anything," Logan barked.

"Yeh, and don't forget we're going to need some place to stay for the night."

"And something to eat," Patel chimed in.

"Ok, Ok, what do I look like, a short order cook? Let's find Barnabas," Logan suggested as turning around he almost tripped over the smiling Levite.

"Where did you come from?"

"I am from Cyprus, beloved, but enough about me. It seems the Master is expecting you. As a matter of fact, he's specifically invited you to come and stay at Peter's house tonight." Barnabas spoke rubbing his two hands together with excited anticipation.

"Ahhhhh, he specifically invited us, and after I…?" Logan exclaimed rolling his eyes as he and his friends struggled with their response still flabbergasted at the big man's sudden appearance.

"Yes, now, let's see, we will need to get the beasts and then there's the………," the Cyprian's voice trailed off as he led the way. Logan followed silently holding his hands up as if to ask 'How?' Patel and Strife shadowed behind both holding their hands up in an equally confused response. Barnabas turned just as they lowered their hands to see them following.

"Splendid! You accept. Follow me," Barnabas replied, a huge smile adorning his face as the others trailed silently through the dusty streets.

Halfway through the town, Logan and Strife were strolling shoulder to shoulder with Barnabas as Patel followed kicking and dragging the four stubborn mules which sometimes chose to follow and sometimes not. In time, they arrived at a moderately-sized limestone and basalt house that boasted a large open courtyard and a half-dozen outdoor ovens. The base of each stone oven had been stoked to a gentle amber glow, its rack roasting some choice morsel not yet served.

Entering, the travelers found dozens of Jesus' disciples scattered about. Some reclined on woven mats arranged in wide circles on the grassy surface of the spacious courtyard. Other stood in small clusters thoughtfully recounting the events of the day. Patel and Strife mingled through the large crowd searching for Jesus, while Logan was content to visit quietly with various groups of men clustered on the cushy turf. Several casual conversations later and he was eventually directed to the back corner room of the modest L-shaped home.

"They say he's in that back room with Peter's mother-in-law," Logan shared quietly.

"What! What is he doing in there with her? Come on!" Strife said, her sudden agitation leaving a befuddled Logan behind.

"Hold on Victoria."

Oblivious, Strife forged ahead, dragging Logan by the arm to the dimly lit back room. The house was dark and tainted with a musty smell; its dingy walls cracked and plastered over in a spoiled attempt to seal out the mildew. Adding to the shadowy dimness, cast from the sparsely scattered collection of oil lamps, was just the softest mist of light trickling through embroidered drapes dancing over the open windows. As they entered the room, their eyes strained adjusting to the flickering light. There in the corner was Jesus with his back to them sitting on the edge of a modest wood frame bed.

Initially, he appeared to be holding the woman as a mother would a cherished suffering child. Supporting her on the crudely fashioned cot, Jesus cradled her seemingly lifeless, pale body. Gently he smoothed her sweat covered hair, and closing her half open eyes, he laid her down again. Her breathing had become labored and her wheezing and coughing so profuse as to suggest she was drowning in her own fluids. Logan stepped forward only to be firmly forced back by a very large and sturdy fisherman.

"Sit down and watch," Peter gently insisted his tone hushed yet intimidating. Logan settled back against the wall with Strife.

"Watch what? Her suffocate to death?" Logan whispered.

Softly Jesus kneeled by the bedside and taking the woman's hand in his, began to pray silently. Logan watched searching for the slightest hint of deception. To enhance his powers of observation, Logan reasoned that activating the night vision capabilities of his *nano-lens* might prove beneficial in the low illumination. It was then that Logan saw what no one else could, for there on the cheeks of the kneeling carpenter were the almost imperceptibly subtle trails of two tears.

"For Pete's sake……..." Logan almost whispered out loud before the deep voice behind him interrupted.

"Yesss….." the deep baritone of the gentle fisherman softly responded. Except for a suddenly enlightened nervous chuckle that barely escaped Logan's mouth, the interaction silenced the guardian.

Logan's temporary amusement at the potential origin of colloquial phrases was soon broken as Patel, with his usual sensitivity to etiquette, forced himself roughly through the others and into the room. Then as if oblivious to the disturbance he had just created, he maneuvered silently behind Logan deftly activating his biometric scanner. Looking over the guardian's right shoulder, Patel began the scan. The device was silent, and unnoticed by anyone in the room, yet Jesus turned and pausing, looked the scientist directly in the eye. At once he returned to praying over the elderly woman's sweat-drenched form, pale and unmoving.

"BP 135 over 105….. and falling, Core temperature 104.5 F…… and falling. Respirations normal, Heart rate 95…… also falling," Patel whispered in English to his comrades. The recitation drew barely a glimpse from the Hebrew and Aramaic speaking occupants of the room as slowly the woman's choking subsided and her breathing grew calmer. Eventually her coughing and groaning also stopped as she slowly began to come around. Finally, the frail elderly woman opened her eyes, and a true blush of embarrassment flushed her once pale cheeks as she beheld the crowd surrounding her.

"Where am I? Oh my, why are all these people here?" she said sitting upright. Peter and his wife at once rushed to her side helping to steady her as she turned to sit on the bed's edge. Jesus stood slowly and backing away from the bed he gently spoke.

"You are in your home, Mary, and these people are here because they love you."

One by one the crowd slowly backed out of the room, each eye fixed on Mary as she began to rise. In the corner of the room, Logan slowly moved over with Patel and Strife at his side.

"Did you get that?" Logan whispered to Patel. Patel, annoyed by the question, remembered Jesus' piercing gaze moments earlier.

"Yes, we'll look at it later. I'm going to get close enough to scan him," he whispered emphatically, joining the crowd and exiting the room with Jesus.

Outside, a cool breeze drifted up from the lake announcing the approach of evening as the glowing ovens and a half-dozen sparkling fires threw dueling shadows over the crowded courtyard. Here dozens of Jesus' disciples gathered in small groups of four or five scattered about the enclosed terrace. Reclining on the traditional mats padded with woolen blankets the men sat in circles around each fire. In the middle of the courtyard Jesus and his inner circle of disciples chatted around the flickering flames.

Peter joined the other eleven all eagerly anticipating the meal being prepared by several middle-aged women in the kitchen area. Soon Mary joined them, looking healthy and happy, giving and receiving many hugs. The large outdoor tannur ovens radiated their golden glow offering a refreshing buttress to the increasingly cooler draft blowing in from the tiny beach. Amber coals now well-seasoned from hours of smoldering disuse stoked the huge beehive shaped ovens pouring out a flood of mouth-watering aromas.

By now, more than two dozen men had gathered around the outer perimeter of the carpenter's tribe, all seemingly talking and laughing in one continuous chorus of confusion. Peter and the other apostles, forming the inner ring near Jesus' feet, were engaged in a jovial discussion which at times seemed to border on chaos. Intrigued by the laughter coming from the group, Logan and the other two slowly approached the circle from different positions. From the outskirts of the group, Patel switched on his scanning unit directing it to lock in on Jesus. This time,

Jesus oblivious to the effort, was steadfastly engaged in the discussion taking place around him. Strife attempted to be discrete by helping to serve with the other women, while approaching Patel from behind.

"Rabbi, I have a question?" spoke one of the deepest voices Logan had ever heard. The voice belonged to one of two tremendous disciples reclining against the trunk of a nearby tree. The young men, who were almost identical, appeared to be no more than teenagers, each possessing an enormous stature and size for their era. Logan began to understand Jesus' reputation for escaping unscathed from disgruntled crowds.

"Speak, O Son of Thunder, for who can ignore your call?" Jesus pronounced affectionately as he broke off a morsel from the warm roll just handed to him. The comment drew a chuckle from the group as the mildly embarrassed disciple struggled to speak. Before he could, the man sitting beside him interrupted.

"What my brother wanted to ask you teacher was this. Today in the square, you said many would come from the east and west and join with the prophets. Did you mean that Our Lord's chosen will include Goyim?" The young man's question was asked with such politeness that none dared jeer at its inquirer. The mention of *Goyim* drew an immediate reaction from Patel, who wide eyed and pale, almost tripped backwards over the stump by which he stood.

"GOIEM, did he say GOIEM?" Patel whispered excitedly to Strife who stood nearby.

"Not GOIEM, you big dummy," she whispered, "*Goyim*, it's the Jewish colloquial term for gentiles. You know, anyone who's not a Hebrew. Now be quiet!"

"I tell you the truth, my young friend, many will come from the east and west and take their seats at the marriage feast… but many, many more will not…," Jesus answered his voice trailing off. Silence hung in the air for a moment before the vibrato of an equally blessed voice echoed.

"And Master, what my brother would really like to ask the Rabbi is this. What of our good leaders the Pharisees?" At this Jesus' demeanor shifted, his gaze falling as he sighed deeply, before speaking gently.

"Who is good, James? Is not only *One* truly good? Parading in flowing robes and sitting in seats of honor at banquets, is this what your heavenly Father calls 'good'?

Or is it to always act with justice, to love mercy and to walk humbly through life with God? Is it to follow the rules of men, or to forever love the Lord your God with all your heart and mind and soul and the person sitting next to you as much as you do your very self? By this truth which of the Pharisees, or for that matter which of you, has been 'good'?"

Logan stared intently at the simple carpenter before him.

On the far edge of the group stood Patel, shaking his head, and recording every word Jesus uttered. A tone of disgust too low to be audible leaked from the scientist's mouth.

"Truth, what is truth?" Patel whispered. Immediately Jesus, some three meters away, turned looking directly at Patel and with a weak smile he asked kindly but distinctly.

"I'm sorry, friend, what did you say?" Jesus waited as Patel's belated answer gave Strife an opening to move quickly away. Stunned, Patel stammered to answer.

"I…I… I said there's no such thing as truth."

"Really?" Jesus smiled weakly, responding with a tone that suggested he hadn't considered that, "Let me ask you, do you believe that to be true?"

"Why, yes!" the scientist emphatically announced. Jesus smiled as he leaned back upon the tree behind him, taking a bite of the apple he had held for some time now.

"So what you are saying is that it is *true* that there is no such thing as truth? Jesus responded after swallowing the first bite. The crowd laughed. Patel now trapped by his own impetuousness tried to respond.

"Well, I guess what I mean to say is there's no way you can be certain."

"Really, are you quite certain of that?" Jesus retorted, smiling again and taking another bite. Everyone in the court chuckled including Logan and Strife.

"I think you have a problem, friend." James intervened as Patel shrunk back into the shadows and Jesus resumed his teaching. Logan made his way slowly over to Patel as the scientist began to talk quietly.

"I got close enough to scan him directly."

"Looks like he got a pretty good idea about you too."

By this time Strife had made her way around the crowd to her two comrades. Carrying a tray with two cups of wine she pretended to be serving the two men as the three talked.

"Yeah, what's the big idea getting into a head match with him? He just ate you for lunch and spit you out again."

"Look doctor, historically I need to find out as much about the big guy as I can. That includes not just using a scanner. So, I made a little tactical error." Logan rolled his eyes at Patel's defiance, as he turned to lean imposingly over his fellow traveler.

"Yes, Albert, but you piss him off and we're out of here. Don't get us thrown out!" Logan's finger stabbed the air directly in front of Patel's face.

"Look, I keep telling you, my names not Albert. Besides, you forget. He's all forgiving."

"He might be, but I'm not. Don't screw it up!" Logan whispered firmly sending Patel sulking back into the crowd.

The evening passed without further disruptions as the crowd feasted on fire roasted tilapia, diluted wine, and a delicious olive oil stew made with lentils and beans. Sopping it all down with an oven fresh loaf of soft chametz bread, the three satiated their appetites for food. Now revived, they made their way quietly to the flat rooftop of the house in order to appease their curiosity. The disciples and Jesus, led by Peter, and a handful of instrumentalists had begun their nightly practice of singing hymns and songs of worship. The earthy chorus, accented by the playful melody rising from the combined resonance of the lyre and flute, provided the ideal acoustic concealment for the anxious travelers.

Huddled high on the packed surface of straw and dried mud above, the three explorers began their analysis.

"You realize, of course this is *the* first canonical miracle ever recorded by modern man," Patel warned them. Both of his observers nervously nodded their heads.

In the courtyard, the rhythm of ancient Jewish praise songs, passed down from the time of Moses, resonated pulsating to the sounds of joyful dancing. With the crowd distracted and celebrating the miracles of their faith, three of the unconvinced plied their traitorous art. Silently they labored between their ancient friends below and an inky black sea of stars sweeping over them to the water's distant edge.

Faintly illuminated by the reflected torch light dancing like a child fancifully to and fro from the nearby waves, they silently knelt over the small holographic device. Mesmerized they watched the eerie sapphire glow rise and hover before them.

"First let's look at the electromagnetic scan," Patel announced opening the first level data like a kid opening a present on Christmas morning.

"Wow! Look he's off the Richter scale. He is channeling some kind of mega radioactivity. No wonder he's called the "Son of Light," he quipped his sarcastic smile briefly imitated by his irritated comrades.

"Wow," was all Strife could manage as she refocused, her glance reflecting the shared astonishment of her friends over the historical significance of what they beheld.

"Ok, that's impressive. Let's prioritize. First of all, what type of radiation are we talking about and how does he control it?" Logan redirected.

"It must be some kind of a device," Patel assured them, "but what? He doesn't carry anything at all. The only thing he owns is that silly seamless tunic he wears. It looks just like ours."

Silenced by the moment, they all stopped and looking at each other, they all but sang out in unison.

"A seamless tunic!"

"Eureka, that must be it." Logan proclaimed, his finger to his lips to silence the others. Strife nodded her head enthusiastically as she spoke.

"That would explain a lot. The Bible itself places special significance on that tunic! For instance, in the story of the healing of the bleeding woman, it states he felt "power" go out as soon as she touched the edge of his garment."

"Yeah, I remember Bible stories my wife read to our kids; people just wanted a touch of his cloak and they would be healed."

"Exactly, which to this day, explains why many in the Catholic religion, just want to touch the Pope's robes to be healed. It must flow from what the people learned from their experiences with Jesus."

"Well, there's one way to find out for sure. I'll just reprogram our biometric scanners to scan for embedded nano-fiber devices. Here, hand 'em here." Patel instructed.

Strife pushed Patel's hand away as he tried to reach for her scanner.

"Wait just a second. Let's look at his biometric DNA scan first," Strife interrupted as she pulled up the data on her scanner. Patel shook his head knowingly as he synced his scanner to hers.

"Are you wondering what I'm wondering?" Patel asked as the two worked to pull up the three dimensional images. Logan sat back on his haunches cocking his head, clearly aggravated by what he considered a waste of time.

"Oh no, you two aren't serious, are you?"

"You got it," Strife quipped back. She and Patel looked at each other smiling as the data began to display. Then even before looking at the data, turning to Logan they chimed in.

"ET!" they exclaimed. The huge smiles adorning each face lasted only long enough for Logan to appreciate the let-down as the results displayed. It read, Genetic DNA origin: HUMAN 99.9% probability. Smugly, Logan folded his arms and leaned back rebuking them.

"Ok Captain Kirk and Mr. Spock, he's not alien. He's human. What do you say now?"

"There's only one alternative," Strife persevered.

"Oh, no, here we go again," Logan rolled his eyes as Patel nodded his head in unison with Strife.

"Yep, only one alternative," Patel agreed confidently shaking his head, "Uh? What alternative?"

"He's one of us."

"Yeah, he's one of us," Patel turned repeating it to Logan before turning back to Strife, "One of us? What do you mean one of us what?"

"As in time traveler, one of us?" Logan nodded towards Strife.

"Undoubtedly, I estimate from his technology, he's at least fifty years ahead of us chronologically. That would be the only way He could do the things he does."

"More like one hundred years," Patel chimed in nodding in agreement.

"Here, Logan, give me your scanner. Let Patel adjust them all to look for nano-devices," Strife insisted, holding out her hand in his direction. Hesitantly, Logan retrieved and held out the tiny unit, handing it by way of Strife to Patel. Strife collected all three units and handed them to Patel who began to pry the back cover off of each scanner. Fumbling, he struggled before a frustrated Strife shoved in grabbing the device.

"Here, let me help you, Professor," she insisted. Quickly slipping a screwdriver-like device into a tiny notch, she easily popped the back off each unit. Logan and Patel, duly impressed, watched silently.

"How did you know how to do that?" Patel asked amazed. "That's my own design".

"Women's intuition, I guess. I had to repair our electronics on archaeological digs as a research assistant," she quipped with a smile and a shrug.

"Wow! Can you cook and iron too?" Logan responded, immediately drawing "the evil eye" from his antagonist, as she and Patel worked quickly together. After a few moments and some minor adjustments later, Patel was handing them back to Strife to re-install the covers. This procedure posed more difficulty than removing them, but by now Strife was more determined to do it herself than ever. Waving them off, Strife sat, legs crossed, leaning intently over the instruments as Patel and Logan stood at the edge of the roof surveying the courtyard's lively worship service. The singing, the dancing, even the distant flickering of torchlight reflections dancing on the water's surface reminded Logan of Becky. Eventually he grew impatient.

"What's wrong? Did your women's intuition go shopping?"

If looks could kill, then and there he would have died a thousand deaths. Three minutes later, the scanners were back in each traveler's wrist socket and Patel was holding up his wrist unit.

"Voila, one zuit-suit scanner! If he's got nano-particles embedded in that garment, we'll find them."

"Ok, let's see if they work. Reprocess the scan of Peter's mother-in-law," Logan instructed as the three resumed their huddle over the floating sapphire display. Tapping the instructions into his wrist unit, Patel waited as the data recycled and the floating sphere's display changed.

INITIAL DIAGNOSIS: PROBABILITY
STREPTOCOCCUS PNEUMONIA 99%

X-ray photometry demonstrates exponential lung clearance of bacterial load. Electromagnetic radiation scan shows a

loading dose emission of a Ka - band microwaves from proximal entity. Source unknown.

A sub-cellular display of the bacterial involution appeared on the three-dimensional orb before them.

"That Ka-band electromagnetic radiation must be coming from Him; it's got to be his tunic."

"I agree, professor. That's how the initial data appears, but we need evidence of the embedded particles first. We also need proof that the radiation is coming from him. Tomorrow we start looking for a way to get a direct scan of that tunic of his," Logan observed.

"That will be very difficult, if not impossible," Patel remarked, "We'll need to come in direct contact with his garment to run a comprehensive scan."

"Precisely, which is why I suggest we sleep on it," Logan answered with a quick smile, "For now, Strife needs to store these findings on the Transition cylinder. While she does that, you and I are going to rejoin the party. Come on, Albert, let's go get some food."

"Great, I think I saw some freshly fried locust," Patel replied, rubbing his hands before a grimacing Logan.

Strife laughed as she opened her cloak, unzipping the special pocket containing the precious glowing cylinder. In the dimness of the rooftop, the radioactive diamond glowed brilliantly filling the air with a greenish-golden hue as the raw unprocessed data was permanently burned into the crystal.

CHAPTER THIRTEEN
The Remarkable Encounter

The early morning's first few rays peered timidly through the sparsely adorned trees lining the courtyard wall. Mingling with the gleaming waves of sunshine washing upward from the Sea of Galilee, the radiance beckoned two very different types of fishermen from their sleepy abodes. Throughout the town, men from all corners of life converged with the disciples on the modest limestone and basalt synagogue located at its northern most edge. Their simple purpose: to hear the carpenter from Nazareth speak a word from God. Unfortunately, they were not alone.

The sacred house, accustomed to the familiar faces of Galileans, welcomed a new audience to her vestibules this morning. In the milling crowd drifted not just the faithful, but the skeptics, not only the downtrodden but the blessed, not simply the contemporary but also the alien; diverse in every other way, their only conformity was their curiosity.

With the ripening Sabbath morn, the small crowd soon grew to a small mob, as Capernaum reluctantly welcomed travelers from throughout the civilized world. Throngs of visitors, people of another other kind, interested only in being astounded, had arrived to hear the gentle carpenter speak.

Within this rabble dwelled as many diverse cultures as there were motivations for being there. From the water's edge gathered the citizens of Capernaum, fishermen, their wives and children, simple folk dressed in common linen tunics, their faces wearing suspicion towards the strangers flooding their town. From the King's Highway descended Greeks from the Decapolis, Gentile Phoenicians from the sea villages and Pharisees in long flowing robes. This last group with their painstakingly tied gold and purple sashes, dismounted from their donkeys, and dusting their phylacteries, strolled forward shoving their way through the crowds into the overcrowded tabernacle.

Finally, scattered on the edge of the crowd were the unclean, the outcasts from society, branded by the obvious mishaps of nature disfiguring their bodies and their lives. Some came seeking to save life, gladly bearing the load of a loved one; others came searching for answers to questions still asked today. Lastly, came the powerful desperate to hang on to position and willing to destroy any who stood in their way.

Into this environment entered Jesus, surrounded by a wall of disciples, and led into the overflowing synagogue. Like a statesman immersed within a cocoon of secret service, he moved forward through the surging mob, which parting before him, affording many of the afflicted a fruitless attempt to rise and touch Him. Logan and Strife, having entered well before the Nazarene, positioned themselves carefully observing his every move. From Logan's perspective, he could watch Jesus' gaze as he paused in the entry way to linger over each member of the suffering humanity.

His countenance, unlike the Pharisee's indifference, was solemn, tainted by grief as he gazed upon the blind, crippled and diseased souls before him. Pausing, he reached out to, even embraced some of the most disfigured, his large hands shaking as in turn he was released from each clasp. Pulling away, he entered the ancient edifice and, moving past the three explorers, entered the main vestibule with its black basalt walls and cobblestone floor.

The sanctuary face southward, its portico kneeling humbly towards the temple it resembled in Jerusalem. Inside, the dingy black walls were covered with layer upon layer of plaster, intricately adorned with delicate artwork symbolizing the *menorah* and the *shofar.* Past these walls and several large storage rooms, Jesus strode into the well-lit heart of the synagogue. Here in the crowded chaos of the sanctuary he headed for a lesser seat of honor at the back. Intent on sitting according to age, he was no sooner in his chair before being quickly interrupted by the leader of the synagogue. Bowing his head, the leader respectfully handed Jesus the scroll of the day and slowly backed away. Immediately the room grew still. Like a blanket of silence descending upon and suffocating the room's noise, not a syllable was spoken.

Thus, Jesus rose, effectively appointed the speaker, he moved to The Most Holy Place at the front of the congregation. Clasping his hands tightly, he closed his eyes in a moment of silent prayer, and then began with a whisper, the *Shema*, the opening prayer of all Jews. His voice began kind, almost pleading, speaking like a mother begging mercy for a wayward son.

"Let all of Israel hear me, the Lord, your God, is One." Jesus paused as a low rumble of amens quickly rose and subsided from the crowd. "With all of our hearts, with all of our souls and with every fiber of our strength, we love you. Thank you for your truth chiseled on our hearts. We will teach them to the children. In our rest, in our homes, let them ever be on our hearts, on our lips and in our minds. When we work, when we travel, in our sleep and when we rise they will never leave our minds. Hidden in our eyes and written in our features, guiding our hands they lead us. On every door and through every gate we walk let them adorn our paths."

The crowd sat at peace, listening to the inflections and dialect of an ancient language of origin, once thought lost, now alive. Logan followed the discourse intently, his attention so enwrapped that he almost failed to overhear the exchange between two young Pharisees standing right next to him.

"I have never heard the *Shema* spoken so tenderly. Are you sure this is the man they wish to kill?"

His compatriot nodded, motioning for silence, as the plea for mercy, the prayer of Amidah, and then the reading of the Torah preceded the words of Isaiah. Unlike other rabbis, Jesus spoke if he had walked side by side with the courageous prophet.

“Blessed are the merciful, for they shall be shown mercy,” he said slowly running his hands gently over the mercy seat. “Do you remember David’s search for the undeserving? This story, a demonstration of God’s mercy to mankind, shows David pouring out mercy upon the only remaining son of Jonathan, Mephibosheth.” After repeating the story, he asked.

“Is it right to by doing good, to save life…?”

“Yes,” a voice from the crowd rang out.

“….On the Sabbath?” came the close.

Silence filled the room.

It was with this and the closing benediction that the miracle man took his seat leaving the impatience of the thrill seekers to permeate the crowd. Gradually at first, and then more rapidly they fell away cursing and muttering under their breaths for coming. Another quarter hour and the crowds had thinned extensively, leaving only the faithful and the crippled to struggle to their feet, and in the corner, two young Pharisees diligently observing.

Their counterparts, a handful of several angry men, gathered around three of Jesus’ disciples demanding their rights. With voices loud and faces red they appeared close to violence. Logan, noticing their behavior, moved closer to help Jesus, who seemingly oblivious to the threats was instead intent on concluding some instruction with his inner circle of disciples. The violent men, however, had not gone unnoticed by the young Pharisees who rose from their seats, content to leave Jesus at the mercy of the mob.

In the midst of all this confusion, a timid middle-aged man sitting unnoticed in a shadowy corner of the hall struggled to stand. Forced outward at the start of the service, the quiet man and his family had slipped in after the thrill seekers had begun to leave. Silent tears of pain traced their way down his tan and furrowed face as struggling to rise he stumbled towards the door. Suddenly, in mid conversation, Jesus looked up.

"Excuse me! You there!” He said pointing. “Please, don’t leave……… come forward.” The man, at first disbelieving, froze and then turning, slowly moved forward.

"Stand here." Jesus motioned continuing to talk with his disciples as the man began to limp forward.

"Remove your bandages please."

Jesus stepped back and, separating from the disciples, pointed directly at the startled man moving from the corner of the room. At once the chamber grew completely still and silent.

"Who me, Sir?"

The man stumbled and quite nearly fell being steadied by an astute family member, who reaching out at just the right moment, grasped him by his good arm. Steadied now, he stood there trembling, his face growing paler by the minute as the blood drained quickly to his feet.

Jesus nodded silently, almost obsessed on not disturbing the silence of the room.

It was then, in the stillness of the moment, that every eye now became fixed on the timid man's odd-shaped bundle he so carefully cradled. For there, slung close and tied neatly to his chest was the man's crippled left arm. Atrophied and drawn upward tightly, once revealed it more closely resembled a bird's broken wing than a man's arm.

Logan who stood near Moses' seat moved closer to the eastern wall where the trembling man now stood. Patel, who had been recording from the front corner of the western wall moved towards the rear, careful to stay behind Jesus' line of sight. Strife, once recording from across the partially draped western wall, also moved closer to observe. The three travelers, now repositioned, were not the only ones interested to see the drama unfold. A remnant of the fledgling Pharisees, most of whom had departed, trickled hastily back to their positions at the back of the crowd. Dozens of the committed and uncommitted mingled quickly in, standing or sitting near the rear.

"What does it mean to be Holy?" Jesus asked pacing before the small crowd which, bolstered by the influx of the curious, had slowly begun to grow again. Except for the dirt and gravel quietly crunching beneath the weight of his sandaled feet, the room echoed back only silence.

"What does it mean to live a Holy life?" he repeated, his gaze scanning the room intently for any willing soul.

Logan smiled thinking to himself he had heard more noise in the vacuum of space than he heard now. Jesus continued to pace, the stone-faced crowd unwilling to meet his gaze much less venture an answer. Some in the room turned unashamedly staring at the reticent Pharisees, who usually quite willing to venture their opinion, smiled primly.

"Is it *Holy* to 'observe the Sabbath' or to '*live* the Sabbath'?" Again, no answer followed the Rabbi's query

"Beware the yeast of the Pharisees who do so well to *observe* the Sabbath, yet offer you no rest, no Sabbath, for your soul."

"What does it mean to 'live a *Sabbath filled life'*?" Jesus asked once more, scanning the crowd for even one willing to venture where angels feared to tread.

"Aaah, This generation…," he breathed despondently, his eyes closing, a curious mixture of fatigue and sadness intermingling with his words. Even Logan grew a bit frustrated at the silence.

The crowd, now partially encircled the room as Jesus and the crippled man stood within their midst. Late-morning beams of sunlight, swimming with motes of dust, filtered through the open windows highlighting the open space in which the two men stood.

"Among the faithful are many of the 'broken' of this world. Like Mephibosheth, my Father delights in refreshing their souls and welcoming them to Sabbath - a place to rest and be made whole." Jesus hesitated, stepping back a moment to catch every eye.

"In the same way the Sabbath was made *for* man, not man for the Sabbath!" he said forcefully.

"So I ask you once again, is it lawful to do good on the Sabbath? To save life, or by doing nothing," nodding to the Pharisees, "destroy it?"

Jesus half raised his hands in a gesture of frustration. Again silence was his only companion as he circled past the Pharisees and the crowd, his hands reaching for any inclined. No one spoke as he gingerly moved to the front of the crowd and gently gripped the back edge and raised side arms of the *mercy seat*. Then sighing, and shaking his bowed head in disgust, he lifted his arm stretching it out towards the crippled man.

"Stretch out your hand," Jesus commanded softly, his voice half choking with grief.

In response, the man strained to raise the exposed twisted limb back in Jesus' direction. Sweat mixed with tears poured from the timid peasant's brow and flowed down his taut crimson face. The strain was so wrenching that many missed the first subtle ripple under the forearm's twisted flesh. The subcutaneous spasm was quickly followed by others as the bones and sinews of the twisted hand began to straighten and relax, transforming the crippled appendage to a healthy, functional one, pointing back in the Nazarene's direction.

The crowd, the man and even Logan and the other two chrononauts gasped as a flurry of amazement filled the room. Immediately the man's friends and family rushed to touch the man now made whole and complete.

"Amazing," Strife declared, having moved beside Logan.

"If, I had not seen it with my own eyes…."

"He didn't even touch that one," Patel chuckled as he joined his two reflective companions.

With the crowd thinning the three explorers slowly made their way out of the ornate building. Dozens of wide-eyed witnesses stood in groups of five or ten repeating the astonishing events they had just witnessed. In one large group, stood six young Pharisees adamantly discussing with four older comrades what had just transpired.

"I'd like to see how they're going to try and explain that one away," Logan chuckled to an equally perplexed pair of antagonists.

"Oh, I'm sure they'll come up with something," Strife responded, her usual confidence betrayed by the cracking of her voice.

"Puberty?"

"Nah, that guy was at least thirty," came Patel's half-engaged response.

"Thanks for the in-depth analysis, Professor."

"Well we better come up with something. That was pretty impossible, It… doesn't... make… any... sense! How does radiation restore a crippled deformed hand? I can understand it killing bacteria, or even dispensing with cancer, but how does it cause spontaneous regeneration of living tissue?" Patel probed.

"Well if you don't know...Oh, never mind. Let's wait to see what the scanners show tonight," Logan responded as they passed through the buzzing crowd and past the small group of still fuming Pharisees.

Late that night, in a small lamp-lit stall, the three chronies gathered to view the collective data. As the holographic display hovered silently in three-dimensional space, the analysis terminated yielding identical results from previous miracles. The biometers identified Ka radiation emissions at the time of the healing. Spontaneous regeneration was seen on the cellular level of all tissue types with regression of glial cysts in the nerves of the left hand. When asked for an explanation of the regeneration, the computer simply responded *insufficient data.*

"Well, that answers that," Patel crowed. "The hand simply relaxed after the neuromas regressed."

"Not so fast Albert, I'm no doctor, but even I can read. Your scanners indicate unexplainable regeneration of dead tissue. You yourself said what you saw was impossible," Logan countered, his finger waving in the air at the blank expression on his Chronie's face.

"Yeh Albert, are you trying to tell us that was all soft tissue disease? Don't try and tell me that chicken wing he was carrying was really a healthy radius," Strife echoed.

"A severe contraction of two or more major muscle groups can give the gross appearance of broken bones. As for the computer's analysis, we're not dealing with a supercomputer here. This is most likely just a glitch in the system, the contracted tissue was mildly atrophic but not dead. The software is not programmed to discern the difference between the two. *'Insufficient data'* is simply the catch all term for inability to analyze," Patel argued, "I say we head home. We have what we came for."

Logan stood there, his disdain for Patel's cowardice fueling his imagination, which running wild, reveled in the immeasurable pleasure he would feel in punching his comrade's highbrow nose.

"It's all about you, isn't it Patel? We are staying. Insufficient data is insufficient data! I want to know how he's doing that, and until we understand, we don't have the full picture for our friends back home!"

"But that could take weeks or months!"

"Let it!"

"Are you crazy?"

"Maybe, a little anyway, but our orders say we're to stay here until he is crucified. I'm in command, and we're staying until that Jew is dead."

Like two bulls, their horns locked in mortal combat, the red-faced chronies stood nose to nose, their eyes firing silent bullets into each other's head. Finally, Patel turned and walked away.

CHAPTER FOURTEEN
Forever and A Day

Logan's steadfast resolve for following any assigned mission to its natural conclusion did not come without a price. The animosity with Patel, despite Strife's best efforts to smooth over the conflict, continued to simmer over the next few weeks. This resulted in difficulties which had the inconvenient tendency of expressing themselves at just the wrong moment. Added to these troubles were the persistent hardships inherent in dealing with chronic health problems in a hostile environment. The resulting dialogues were quite amusing until it was discovered that most of what was being observed was not only recorded by the chrononauts, but also by others.

In almost every case, the recorded dialogue between the disciples and Jesus was nearly identical to that represented in the New Testament. This remarkable tendency troubled Logan for weeks on end, until on one occasion, he happened to be dining by an open campfire with a little known diminutive disciple. The tiny balding somewhat reclusive fellow often could be seen speaking to himself and scribbling on parchments. Rumor had it that he had been abused by the Romans, who having pressed him into service as an accountant, were responsible for using him to collect taxes and remember just who owed what to whom.

This chap, given as Levi, but affectionately nicknamed Matthew by Jesus, possessed one very unique ability. Logan discovered it when he sat down to chat with the oft-ignored man while they dined on lentil stew and pita bread. It was then that the discussion came up about Judas and the funds acquired and dispersed for the meal. There seemed to be a question as to the existence of a recent discrepancy. The shy fellow, after being bantered about by the group, had finally suffered through enough abuse when he proceeded to rattle off all of the names of every contributor in the last three months, as well as the amount given, without so much as consulting a single scroll.

Logan was amazed, so much so that he spent the remainder of that night reviewing the digital log. This curious aptitude demonstrated why Jesus had been so adamant to insure this particular fellow's attributes were brought into the fold, and the mystery of scriptural accuracy also became clear.

It followed that one after another opportunity was presented to the travelers for recording Jesus' preaching and ministering, but none for coming in contact with the presumed source of his power. As opposed to the Pharisees, who preferred speaking to the people from ornate marble platforms, Jesus preferred to walk amongst the people who sat in groups at his feet. This allowed for a disquietingly humble interchange between the teacher and any of a multitude of his adherents whom he spontaneously chose to 'interview' at any given moment.

This troubled Logan little, for most of the disciples were forever nearby, being fishermen whose Navy SEAL-like physiques could easily manage the large unruly crowds. 'Desperate humanity' was the common term Logan preferred to describe the masses which dogged the Nazarene. Constantly, they begged. With outstretched hands, for food or for just a touch of the carpenter's tunic, they pled as Jesus walked amongst them.

Jesus traveled throughout Galilee, for the most part, with impunity. Despite his great popularity and the even greater need for his touch, the deeply engrained Jewish traditions protected him by restraining the crowds from clinging to his feet or grasping his tunic. This cultural barrier presented a substantial dilemma to the explorers also, for they too feared offending their host and losing position within the group. They, of course, desired the touch of his robe for an altogether different reason.

Healings, often abrupt, as with the man lowered through the torn asunder roof, came just as often from silent sufferers handpicked by Jesus. Then, after six weeks of watching the miraculous, day after day, the healings suddenly stopped. For three weeks no one among the crowds was healed. Everyone, including Barnabas and those closest to Jesus began to wonder.

That evening, on the Galilean beach, beside a crackling fire sending glowing ashes into a crystal clear sky, Logan and Strife reclined on blankets staring at the tracers fading into a starry host.

"Where's Patel?" Logan whispered, his irritation evident as he craned his head to survey the entire camp.

"Who knows? I don't think he's feeling very well lately. It may be all the travel or it may be his symptoms recurring."

"Maybe Patel can ask our host for some help in that area. After all, he's not healed anyone in a couple of weeks. He must be rested by now."

"Yes, most curious, he seems content just teaching the people. Have you seen the way he interacts with them?" Strife responded.

The chronies rolled over, spying their target, as he sat with two disciples on a log by the fire eating fish and laughing. Suddenly, a small boy some four to five years of age with curly black hair ran straight to Jesus jumping abruptly into his lap. Logan almost laughed as Jesus tipped backwards, almost spilling his food, before catching the boy and himself just in time. Laughing he lifted the small boy upward by his ankles, swinging the inverted tyke gently in the seaside breeze, before finally bringing him to rest upon his lap. Horrified, the boy's mother arrived too late, begging for forgiveness and attempting to extract the child from the carpenters grasp. Jesus laughed, reassuring the disheveled woman and waving her off as he shared his meal with the hungry child.

The spectacle unknowingly observed, seemed singlehandedly to venerate, by the mere act of patient humility and generosity, the man they deemed a liar. As the innocence of the two talking and giggling played out before him, Logan felt an incredible rush of confusion wash over him again. Suddenly, the little boy was off like a shot with Jesus watching, leaning backwards and laughing, before resuming his meal.

"Yeah, not at all what I expected." Logan ran his hands through his hair.

"For a narcissistic ego-maniac with delusions of godhood, he seems like a regular Joe," Strife agreed straining a half smile as she spoke.

"Darn peculiar, that's what it is. I expected someone like a preacher, you know, but like -on steroids. Fire and brimstone, that sort of thing - not someone kind, who lets a little runny nose kid eat off his plate. Good grief," Logan said crossing his arms and leaning backwards. Strife simply stared at the ground nodding as she spoke.

"Yeah, I know what you mean, if he's not crazy, he must be lying. And if he's lying, he's lied and misled billions and he's anything but the good guy we think we see here."

"So how can such a bad guy come up with such good stuff?"

The silence returned once again as the two studied the man now settling in to sleep against the tree. Logan finally stood, momentarily preparing to leave. "Or maybe he's not lying," Logan smiled staring at a blank faced Strife, "Good night."

She looked up at him as he walked away to bunk down for the night. On her face crept a very real expression of concern and confusion.

"Now what the devil did he mean by that?"

Further down the beach, Logan approached the fire by which his bed roll was located. Unrolling his blanket and settling in for the night, he stared into the smoldering coals as he drifted slowly off to sleep. As he did, his mind wandered to a distant memory of another familiar campfire. There, he and a small boy, missed greatly for two years, were riding piggy back and running around the campfire screaming and laughing. The little boy giggled as Logan swung him around briskly by his ankles, settling him gently onto his lap, just as the carpenter had only minutes before. There at the base of a tree, he reluctantly released the pint-sized boy into his mother's loving arms. As she sat there, hugging the little boy by the fire, and smiling sweetly back at Logan, the scene stole away. A shooting star streamed overhead as the widowed guardian silently drifted off, clinging tightly to a tear stained bag.

The gentle salt breeze, combined with the smoky aroma of roasting lamb, served as an effective stimulant to rouse Logan from a restless sleep. Shaking the sand from his hair and sitting up weakly, he recognized the clamor of activity consistent with a move to the next village. Most members of the group were loading up, preparing donkeys for another trip and dousing their fires. Patel and Strife having already loaded their donkeys with supplies, were talking as Logan approached. Jesus could be seen giving instructions to His disciples in the background. Logan watched him from the corner of his eye as Barnabas walked over.

"Good morning Goyim!" Barnabas bellowed, his thunderous voice nearly causing a stunned Patel to trip and fall over backwards.

"How did you sleep? Are you now ready?" He smiled, neck extended as if part turtle, looking excitedly at Logan.

"Ready for what?" a still groggy Logan asked while strapping his possessions to his donkey.

"Why, to be healed of course, is that not why we are here?"

"Well, uh, I'm not sure…," Logan replied, thrown off guard by the sudden prospect.

"Remember Logan, all you need is faith. Remember the acacia tree? Surely, by now with all you have seen, you believe!"

"Yeah, sure, but I don't think I'm quite ready." Logan stuttered. Barnabas approached him putting a big burly arm around the suddenly awkward Commander and tried to lead him away. Rattled, Logan clung to his donkey's bindings, stopping Barnabas dead in his tracks.

"I'm not ready!" Logan protested loudly as the big man, surprised at first, responded by smiling with compassion and released his grip.

"Ok beloved, you are shy. I understand. You stay here. I will bring him to you." Barnabas smiled as he forcefully slapped Logan on the shoulder and happily strutted towards Jesus.

"I tell you, I'm not ready!" This time Logan shouted his protest to the burly Levite, who was apparently oblivious, continuing his proud strut to the feet of the Master. From where Logan stood, he could see Barnabas talking with and gesturing to Jesus. A moment later, the two friends began to walk over towards the freaked out Commander. Logan tried to think quickly, but all he could do was continue to mutter underneath his breath, "I'm not ready, not ready". Unable to control the unfolding situation, Logan returned to loading his donkey taking the opportunity to activate his scanner. His mind raced frantically, a dozen possible scenarios each ending futilely played out in his imagination, as Jesus and Barnabas approached. Seconds later and the two were standing at his side.

"Logan, Barnabas tells me you have a need. Are you well?" Jesus asked softly, his concerned gaze unmet by the explorer.

"I am sick. It is as you say. I had hoped just the touch of your hand might heal me," Logan replied as he stared at the ground feigning humility. Transfixed, Strife and Patel watched silently as Jesus, motionless except for the slightest wisp of a smile crossing his lips, spoke.

"Might? Have you been with us all these weeks and have you seen the miracles and still you doubt?"

Hesitating, half from embarrassment and half from fear, Logan felt almost as if the penetrating gaze was looking into him.

"Logan, you do believe I can make you well?" The moment was followed again by silence.

"Or is it just a touch of my cloak you seek?"

This time it wasn't reluctance keeping Logan from speaking, it was genuine astonishment.

"Go ahead, touch it Logan. For it is what you seek."

Once again flustered, Logan looked up and fumbled eventually grasping the linen tunic as his wide-eyed comrades stood nearby, their mouths literally hanging open. The biometer scanned the ancient linen instantly as Logan stood frozen, staring anxiously into Jesus' eyes.

"As long as you keep seeking, you will eventually find the truth, and until you believe, you can not be born again. You have traveled very far seeking truth. Be sure you have it when you leave. Much depends on you."

Jesus finished at precisely the exact moment the scan completed. Turning he walked away leaving a stunned looking Barnabas.

"What does he mean by that?"

Logan stopped to look at his arms, his eyes tracing the spidery veins still reaching towards his elbows.

"I think that means I'm not healed," Logan answered bluntly.

"Let me see your hands," Barnabas insisted, gaping as he gently turned the arms to view the swollen vessels. Logan stared downward, clenching and unclenching his fists as if the action would slow the insidious transformation.

"Hmm blessed," Barnabas quipped, "I do not think you are yet ready." Logan rolled his eyes.

"Oh really?"

That afternoon as the sun rose high behind the tiny troupe, Jesus and his disciples made their way down the eastern side of Lake Gennesaret. Already large crowds, having heard of the teacher's arrival, had begun forming on the shorefront. As usual, the worship began with singing led by the baritone brothers of thunder, also known as the Zebedees, and orchestrated by Peter. The lively singing consisted of the same mixture of ancient praise songs and hymns dating as far back as Moses, the favorites of Jesus.

With prayer offered and the singing concluded, the time for the carpenter from Nazareth to speak had arrived. The large crowds that had begun to assemble on the shorefront presented difficulty. Pressing in more and more on the small group of disciples surrounding Jesus, the crowd began to grow restless. Gradually there was more and more shoving as those sick and their friends seeking to out-maneuver one another pushed within Jesus' reach.

In the surf behind, Jesus noticed a small fishing boat manned only by a single occupant. There in the middle seat sat Peter who, alternating between battling the waves and waving, struggled to get the rabbi's attention. Jesus was at first unaware until, alerted by the rhythmic sound of the oars, he happened to turn discovering his attentive disciple within wading position. This was fortuitous for the crowd pressing further in, sought desperately to touch Jesus, thus forcing the teacher to turn and wade quickly to the small boat. Climbing in he turned to face the burgeoning crowd, while instructing Peter to push out into deeper water. This action had the double advantage of effectively limiting most of the crowd from pursuing him and creating a virtual sound system with his voice reverberating over the waves and onto the shore.

Pharisees, Roman soldiers, peasants and town officials were all among those who sat focusing on the natural echo of the Nazarene's voice. Hidden easily within this plethora of observers were the three 'Egyptians' sought earnestly by the Romans, recording nature's magnificent cooperation. For two hours Jesus spoke words of exhortation and encouragement, his teaching pointing to God but declining to heal.

As the aging sun began to set, and with the still hungry crowds dispersing; a somber Jesus motioned for the disciples to prepare for crossing the lake. Peter and four other disciples began the work of loading the larger boat which would carry Jesus and the twelve across.

Meanwhile, Logan and his friends paired with Barnabas to both arrange care for their animals and to secure their own boats for the trip. The crowd had now mostly dispersed as Jesus made his way through the camp. The smell of grilling fish still lingered as the flickering embers of a dozen small fires cast a golden ambience around Jesus feet.

At the far southern end of the camp Patel, Strife and Logan verified that Jesus was walking amongst his disciples before they prepared to review their latest data. Secluded in tall grass on a quiet dune back from the beach they huddled and set up their projector. In a moment the hologram popped up in 3-D space illuminating a miniature tunic rotating on its vertical axis. Dispersed within the matrix of the virtual weave was a geometric lattice of interconnected green and red nano-threads.

"Wow! Well, that does it. He's a fake. Look at those fibrils. He's projecting some kind of massive energy field from that garment he's wearing." Patel traced the alternating threads outlining a lattice of alternating octagon and pentagon shapes within the fabric.

"No matter how sophisticated his technology is, he must have to recharge it. The question is where and how?" Logan observed still staring at the rotating image.

"Perhaps that explains the recent dearth of healings," Patel interjected.

"Yes, that could explain a lot in his recent behavior," Strife heartily agreed. Logan nodded as they shut down the projector, and storing it away, made their way down the grassy knoll to the beach.

"Hmm, perhaps, or perhaps he's just sick of being treated like a side show freak. Look, let's stick close to him tonight. He getting rid of His disciples so maybe there's something he doesn't want anyone to see. He must have a way to recharge his batteries even out here." Then looking around Logan finished, "By the way where is he?"

Unbeknownst to anyone, the solitary shadow slipped its way swiftly and silently up into and beyond the darkening meadows overlooking the beach. Heading in the direction of a series of large bluffs hanging over the meadows, the figure moved effortlessly. It was some time later before the observers learned of the Nazarene's getaway as he ascended the path through the dark clouds gathering over the distant hills.

A brief fireside chat with Barnabas and moments later they had located the trail. Using the tracking capabilities built into his scanning system, Logan set the pace. The night vision display of their nano-lens guided the travelers who moved rapidly aided by what Logan called, their 'electric underwear'.

Straining, they ascended the slight incline of the meadow ahead, following the well-worn path to the shadowy base of the bluffs. Each turn through the rolling hills was littered with scattered shrubs and ankle-height rocks, seemingly set at exactly the perfect height to slow pursuers down. In the distance, the faint outline of Jesus' shadow could be traced as he weaved through the rocky cliffs overhanging the knolls. Initially, the three travelers seemed to be converging rapidly on Jesus' location. But just as quickly as they closed in, they would suddenly seem to be strangely far behind as the carpenter moved away with increasing fleet-footedness. At times, he appeared to be just ahead and within their reach and then suddenly they would be far behind. Logan, quite winded by now, was somewhat amused at the erratic nature of their pursuit. He swore, if he had not known better, that Jesus was toying with them, quite able to outdistance them at any time, but wishing them to continue the pursuit.

"I remember him saying something about taking up your cross if anyone would come after him." Patel gasped. "Nobody said anything about dragging it through mountains."

Another major obstacle to their quest, in addition to the increasingly immense boulders, was the changing atmosphere around them. In contrast to the calm, warm climate next to the sea, foreboding towers of storm clouds draped the rocky cliffs were foreboding. Each turn of the tortuous mountain path became increasingly dark and windy. Angry looking skies raining down a torrent of wind and dust exploded as the expedition climbed higher.

Despite the ominous conditions, the travelers persisted through the blowing dust which worsened by the moment. Looking upward at the imposing ledge of rock looming above them, they briefly spied the tunic draped figure appear, lit brightly against the flashing sky. Lightning swirled majestically above the hillside, its interconnecting blue lacy discharges dancing over the landscape before them. Patel took one look at the exhilarating display of electromagnetic radiation above them and began immediately to yell over the wind to his two companions.

"Come on! I know what he's up to," he demanded as he now led the posse' which struggled to keep up.

"Well, would you mind telling us?" Strife shouted attempting to shield her face from the rising swirl of the abrasive sand. Patel ignored her, climbing higher at a still faster rate, as Logan and Strife paused for only a second. A moment later, and a perturbed Logan had accelerated and was holding Patel by his tunic, pointing into the storm above.

"Are you crazy? We can't go up there. Look at those arcs. We'll be fried. Leave Him be," Logan insisted loudly.

"That's just what He wants. He's gone up there to recharge his batteries and he's counting on no one else to follow. Come on! We'll catch Him in the act," Patel yelled back.

Letting go, and staring as his comrade climbed higher, Logan reflected on this the latest in "one of the professor's many wild goose chases'. Unfortunately, he had to admit that Jesus' trek high into the mountains under such extreme conditions was suspect at best. For this reason, he was content to continue the pursuit, letting Patel lead the way. Patel, on the other hand, was ripe with anticipation, convinced they would soon trap Jesus in the very act of conspiracy.

This anticipation was soon to turn quickly back on the trio, as rounding the hill where Jesus was believed to be, they squeezed single file through a pair of towering boulders onto an expansive mountain ledge before them. The ledge, a flat grassy covered plateau some ten meters at its widest, hung precipitously over the beach dunes below. A natural outlook over the open sea, it would have been relaxing had it not been for the aerial light show that now surrounded the three.

Deeply immersed in the rapidly changing currents of the descending thunder cloud, the travelers hesitated as the blue-white glow of electrical discharge lit the sky around them. Their first sensation that something was amiss was the instantaneous tingle of statically supercharged air causing their hair to stand on end. Patel, who had little hair to bother with, was the most amused as suddenly Strife's long flowing mane and Logan's modest outcropping took on virtual lives of their own. Momentarily mesmerized by their appearance, they reflexively shivered as their skin began to prickle and burn.

"Move!" Logan yelled suddenly realizing the natural phenomena they were about to experience.

It was too late. The full force of the arc hit like a trail of lit gunpowder ripping open the well-worn path some four meters ahead of them, cornering them against imposing boulders. The force of the bolt's shock wave struck violently, reminding Logan of a pounding he took from a three-hundred-and-twenty-pound linebacker in college.

In the moment it took for the smoke to clear, two of the three explorers lay unmoving some five meters beyond their original point of collision. Shielded by their nano-suits, Logan and Strife were able to struggle to rise and shake the cobwebs from their head. Logan was the first to his feet, making his way to Strife who sat unmoving near the foot of a small acacia tree.

"Are you alright," the commander choked as he steadied the woman helping her to stand upright.

"Yeh, I think so. Did anybody get the number of that bus?" she quipped leaning on Logan in a feeble attempt to walk. Eventually with some effort she was upright and moving gingerly. Patel was nowhere in sight.

"Where's the Professor?" Logan asked apprehensively. Immediately they both turned in opposite directions scanning the scorched ledge for their missing member.

"I don't know. He was right here with us before the blast. He couldn't have disappeared, there's nowhere to go but…." Strife froze unable to finish her sentence as she stared dreadfully at the cliff's narrow edge.

Slowly, Logan crept forward testing each step carefully as he approached the foreboding abyss. Crouching down, with Strife at his heels, he leaned gently over the stone and vine covered precipice to view the landscape below. Some seventy meters down lay the rock and sandy bottom of a shallow depression tracing the jagged edge of the mountainside. The two *chronies*, hanging halfway over the stony edge, suddenly became aware of a not so subtle rustling in the nettles of a large prickly bush. The oval shaped scrub resembled more a bird's nest than a plant as it grew within the natural net of a precariously suspended vine. Cocooned within the suspended confines of the large thorn-riddled plant, a wide-eyed Patel struggled grunting and groaning desperately.

Each movement upward by the scientist resulted in an equal and opposite reaction of soil and stone raining down to the valley below. The resulting pitter-patter of gravel against boulder echoed through the small valley serving to terrify the net's occupant and perpetuate the unnerving cycle. For their part, Logan and his supine companion remained frozen observing their suspended friend in disbelief. Fearful that any word they might say could make the situation worse, they silently watched as the chilling drama unfolded before them. As Logan lay there immobilized, one tiny bead of sweat trickled from the tip of his nose dropping to his index finger below. This almost imperceptible sensation compelled him to speak out.

"Don't move! You're bringing the entire cliff down on top of you!"

Patel's reaction to this advice was to panic even more as he struggled to climb the vines entwining him. The two would be rescuers sat back up on the ledge staring wide eyed at one another. After a moment's thought, Logan smiled half-heartedly as a thought came to mind.

"Let's leave him there. With all that grunting and snorting, maybe someone will think he's a pig and put him out of his misery."

Strife forced a smile as she bent back down again to watch Patel becoming more psychotic with each movement. Sitting back to face Logan again she smiled.

"You forget, Jews don't eat swine. They think they're nasty and unclean." Logan looked back down to survey.

"Yea, I guess you're right. I suppose we'll have to get him out or all his grunting and snorting will give us away," he retorted before bending back down and calling out to Patel.

"Hey, Albert, did you happen to notice that the more you struggle, the more you're loosening those vines? I bet if you just give it one good thrash you could bring the whole mountain down. Why don't you give it a try?"

At this bit of sarcastic wisdom, Patel ceased to struggle and attempted to relax in the bark and thorn sarcophagus encasing him.

"Or - on the other hand you could relax and let us throw you a line and haul you out of there. I on the one hand am rooting for a good thrash and a climatic ending, but Strife here doesn't like the sight of blood. So what's it gonna' be? You want to chill and let us get you out, or shall I order up some chips and dip and just enjoy the show?"

"Logan, get me out of here!" Patel screamed at the top of his lungs.

"Ok, Ok, don't get your panties in a wad. We're going to lower you a vine. Just grab it and we'll pull you up.

"Are you crazy? Grab a vine. I'm not a Neanderthal like you. I'll lose my grip and fall before you pull me half way up.

"Well, I guess the other option is we could just leave you there professor. I know you probably thought of this already, but if you activate your 'defend' mode and wrap your arms around the vine you won't have to hang on. The suit will do it for you. So what do you say?"

"Alright, alright, just do it and quit gabbing!" Patel agreed disgustedly as he activated the defend mode. Slowly, the two chronies lowered the largest vine they could find directly into the suspended nettles.

"Use your arms to tear open a portion of the bush not suspended by the supporting vines and grab hold of this," Logan instructed the terrified but desperately obedient chrononaut. Slowly the scientist pulled himself from his swinging position and shifted all his weight to bear upon the rescue vine. As he did, the shift in weight suddenly tore the bulk of the nettled bush free sending it pummeling to the valley floor below. Patel watched as his botanical parachute drifted down.

"Pull!" He commanded frantically as slowly he ascended from beneath the rocky ledge to almost parallel with its lowest edge. As he did, he suddenly became aware of a tugging sensation on his left ankle. The tension, slight at first, became uncomfortable then excruciating, as suddenly he slipped backwards, and an incredible weight came to bear on his lower extremity.

"What are you doing?" he could hear Logan screaming from the top of the hillside, Patel's leg feeling as if it was ripping from the hip. Fortunately for him his survival suit, already active in the 'defend' mode, was contracting with full force attempting to counter the sudden weight pulling him downward. With that he finally ventured enough courage to spy his nemesis, a moderately sized boulder ripped from the hillside and entangled in a residual vine wrapped tightly around his left ankle. Both he and the boulder hung from the straining vine whipping violently in the stormy winds.

"I'm caught!" he screamed as his arms slipped slightly from their grip on the heavy vine. Logan and Strife, up above on the ledge, were pulling with all their might but losing ground to the enormous load. With their feet unable to gain any traction in the sparsely grass-covered sandy earth, the two slid dangerously towards the edge.

"We're gonna' have to let him go!" Strife pleaded fearfully as they fought violently against the pull.

"We're not letting go! He's the only one who knows how to analyze this information. We need him to get it back. If he dies the whole mission dies!"

"I'm not dying for that idiot!" Strife shrieked as Logan's footing began to slip even faster nearing the edge of the cliff, "Let go or I will!"

At this Logan's right foot slipped over the edge, his body straining such that the veins on his temples protruded like large tributaries on a three-dimensional map.

"Help me! I'm slipping!" Patel yelled louder as Logan's expression progressed from frustration to anger and finally to despair. It was then that Patel saw something dart past him in the air below. Exactly what it was he could not tell, for it moved faster than anything he had ever seen. He noticed only a shadow of movement, like a wrinkle in the dusty air, and then suddenly, miraculously, the enormous weight was gone followed by a tremendous crash below.

The effect above was immediate as the enormous resistance to the survival suits' backwards tension snapped like a rubber band. Immediately, the suspended explorer came exploding up to the rocky ledge, his ascent propelled by the combined contractile force of his comrades' suits. The resulting collision was so vigorous that Patel almost lost his grip at the edge of the cliff.

In a moment, he was up and over. Exhausted and emotionally drained, he just lay there sobbing and mumbling something unintelligible.

"Did you see it?"

"See what, the rock? No we were up here. How could we see it?" Logan complained, exasperated and a bit frazzled himself.

"Not the rock, you idiot, the shadow. Did you see it?" This sounded vaguely familiar to Logan and he hesitated to respond.

"No-o-o, did you see something down there Patel."

"Yes, it was fast," the exhausted explorer proclaimed emphatically, "It moved past me through the air like a ripple in the breeze and then on to the rock below. A second later and I was free.

"Look Patel, you're in shock, you almost died. The mind plays tricks on us sometimes. There was nothing there. The vine just broke under the weight," Strife responded in her most reasonable tone. As she spoke Logan sat in the sand rapidly pulling the end of the vine from the abyss below.

"What are you doing?" the other two said finally turning to watch their comrade retract the fibrous band.

"Just testing a little scientific theory," Logan responded as the end of the vine suddenly popped over the edge and into his hands. All three sat there completely still as the severed end lay before them in the sandy loam.

Grasping the neatly sliced cable with its end still smoldering from the scorching laceration, Logan examined the cut that had set Patel free.

"Now what kind of a thing could do that?" Patel wondered out loud as the three silently studied the burned fibers before him.

"I'm not sure," Logan said hesitantly his eyes still scanning the neatly sliced vine. Then suddenly turning his head, he put his finger to his mouth.

"Shush!" he exclaimed, freezing the other two in mid-sentence as the distant but very distinct sound of three disciples approaching from below could be heard. The wind, having subsided somewhat, allowed the familiar echo of Peter's boisterous laughter to resonate through the narrow stone passages leading to the ledge above. With a hobbled Patel in tow, Logan and Strife arose quickly resuming their original pursuit up the mountain trail. The visibility was now temporally improved, as the winds from the passing front, having cleared the highland, moved out to sea.

The three, moving rapidly up the final ascent to the peak, approached the plateau through another series of boulders forming a natural partition. As they neared the final turn in their destination, Patel fainted under the combined stress of fatigue and pain. The ascent, a climb of some one hundred meters, had been too much and now they risked detection by the disciples who were closing on their location.

"Quick, help me pick him up and follow me this way," Logan instructed as the two sojourners frantically darted down a narrow crevice that ascended to a quiet elevation atop one of the adjacent boulders. Climbing to the top of the natural lookout, Logan and Strife laid flat observing the approach of three familiar figures below. There on the trail beneath them ascended Peter, James and John calling out Jesus' name above the gentle winds now tainted with rain.

"Jesus, Jesus, are you up here? We've finished with the boats and we came as you asked…" Peter's voice trailed off as they completed their ascent. From their elevated position on the overhanging rock, Logan and Strife observed the reunion below.

The peak of the mountain, a plateau resembling a large sandy ledge overhanging the water below, served as an ideal location for private prayer. It was into this private sanctuary that the three disciples blundered, emerging from the crevice to join Jesus. The plateau was surrounded on three sides by a rock partition towering some eight to ten meters above the surface. The surface itself was similar to the earlier ledge only larger, being dotted sparingly with scattered shrubs and smaller rock formations. From the rock partition above, the three explorers looked down upon Jesus, who standing two to three meters from the drop-off, seemed oblivious to the three men joining him.

"Well, what do you make of that?" Strife whispered pointing below as they struggled for a better position to record. Logan hesitated, some three to four meters apart from Strife, seemingly mesmerized on the scene below him.

"Ugh…," a groggy Patel groaned.

"Shush him! Come 'er Strife, you gotta' see this!"

Strife shifted attempting to see over the edge, but the angle was wrong and a still woozy Patel rolled over emitting another raspy moan. Immediately her hand firmly smacked the dazed scientist's mouth, muzzling him back to consciousness. With her hand still firmly in place, the attractive explorer peaked slowly over the edge to view the event below.

There in a glowing eddy of wind and dust stood Jesus. The disciples, having arrived only seconds earlier, stood mesmerized as they beheld the wonder before them. Bathed in a glowing blanket of light, which neither contracted nor enlarged, and which flowed like a giant whirlwind stood the carpenter. Enveloped with him stood two translucent specters, their forms resembling middle-aged Jewish men. The *spirits* appeared to be reaching through a veil-like membrane which separated them from the surrounding world. This character gave them the illusion of floating in midair despite the fact that, whenever they changed position, some unseen limb would come briefly into view. Anyone not noticing this subtlety would assume they were without legs or substance, merely floating as a ghost.

Another quality Logan was careful to note was the manner in which the apparitions spoke. Their words indiscernible yet quietly and reverently expressed to the man before them. Their gestures were seemingly of deep compassion and anguish, as when one has to tell a loved one of the passing of one so dear to both. The effect to Jesus was disheartening, leaving an observable discouragement as when a message of bad news finally 'sinks in'. The Nazarene, positioned precariously on the edge of the translucent veil appeared at times to linger somewhere between a state of being in both worlds.

"For this you came into the world," the one resembling Moses could barely be heard to say.

"Is there no other way?"

"Oh Lord, if there only were."

Jesus hung his head, nodding dejectedly as the two specters, through forced smiles, appeared about to cry.

Somewhere near the end of this ethereal exchange came the unwelcome interruption of two intruders. The first impetuous trespasser was the weather. Once again, arcs of blue white lightning cascaded over the horizon. This in turn coinciding with the reappearance of a rain streaked breeze incited the second interloper.

"Master, uh, Lord," Peter stammered his half wave aimed timidly at Jesus who, turning his head, stared back blankly at the steadfast disciple.

"Glad we could be here, umm, shall we build the three of you shelters?" he continued pointing meekly at the worsening skies, "I mean one for each of you. Like one for you and then one for Moses and one for Elijah."

"Logan smiled as Jesus just stood there staring silently at the big fisherman. On the overhang behind the disciples, an additional observer now quietly watched as well. Patel who had recovered more than slightly from his ordeal was attempting to analyze the data pouring in from the fading apparitions.

"Well, professor, how was your nap?"

"Thanks a lot."

"What do your readings make of that? What are those? Are they projections, ghosts, how about zombies? And by the way, where's that lightning rod you were so excited about?"

"Very funny. Look this is strange. The life indicators say they are human but they're off the chart. Every category, except for reproduction, is not only normal, it's *Arch-normal* - mind-boggling. There's just one fly-in-the-ointment: as physical entities, they don't register."

"What, that's not possible. How can they have life readings then?"

"Beats me, it's like they're living disembodied souls."

"Now you're starting to sound like him." Logan pointed below to Jesus.

"They must be from another universe. How else could they be alive and yet not exist?" Strife interjected.

"Possibly, but if they are mere projections from the multiverse, how could Albert's scanners register them?"

"The multiverse! Give me a break. That lame theory died out with Al Gore and global warming," Patel responded.

"I think Albert means that's highly improbable," Logan retorted.

"Why?" Strife responded incredulously.

"Other life supporting universes most likely don't exist. The one we live in now is a statistical enigma itself. The initial conditions present at the big bang were so statistically impossible……."

Quiet! Look, they're praying with him," Logan interrupted.

Patel and Strife exchanged confused glances as they turned their attention to the scene below.

Jesus extended each of his arms and clasped the two apparitions' hands through the enveloping barrier. As he did so the three began to glow brilliantly, becoming so blindingly bright that no one could watch, until the two specters faded leaving no one but the Nazarene. A golden image, translucent and shimmering, adorned the royal robes of the warrior king. In the background returned the violent flashes of lightning and the howling of the wind, its pitch oscillating wildly. Amidst the swirling vocals of the wind came the subtle baritone of a still small voice.

"Listen to my son."

Moments later the light faded leaving the familiar Jesus alone as gently grabbing his astonished disciples by the arm, he encouraged them to begin making their way down the hill. As they passed through the crevice, Logan observed Jesus giving instructions and pointing towards the sea to an obstinate Peter, who initially objecting, finally bowed his head and nodded. Descending ahead of Jesus, they made their way back down the stony path to the sea as their leader returned to the flat area to pray. Kneeling, he looked out over the sea at the swirling turbulence of dark clouds.

"Well, that was pretty darn peculiar," Logan whispered.

"I'm not sure, but I believe we just witnessed what the Bible refers to as the transfiguration. Most likely it's some type of multi-dimensional projection, most impressive technology," Strife responded quietly.

"Multi-dimensional my foot, you've been drinking too much of that water to wine Kool-Aid. Those things, whatever they were, were alive. Their individual biological responses were measurable in *this* universe. Instruments in this dimension cannot measure and eyes cannot see creatures in another dimension or a projection," Patel insisted, prompting Logan to respond.

"Ok, Albert, you're the professor, how can something be alive and not have physical substance? Most people would agree you can't think without a brain. However, in your case I am willing to listen to other possibilities."

"That begs the question. What is life? Is it our bodies or our souls, or are we dualistic? Who says we can't think without a brain? How much does a thought weigh? Where is it located? After all, we don't say the brain is sad, we say we are," Patel fired back.

"The problem I have with the miraculous is simply that it defies the laws of the natural universe and physics. There must be a rational explanation," Strife argued.

"Rational? Define rational. We ourselves are self-contradictions to that statement."

"How so?"

"Well, here we are right now in the middle of the first century AD. How did we get here? By the fact that the laws of physics *break down* right at the *'event horizon'* of a big black hole in the fabric of space. So don't tell me that the laws of physics, while universal, can't break down. We're living proof that they do." Patel replied.

"Ok you two, let's let the experts back home figure this one out, Logan instructed, "Now before we leave I want to canvas this entire area. Look for anything unusual such as a device or a projection once unit Jesus leaves."

Forty-five minutes later, Jesus headed down the mountain path to the beaches. The skies above, having gone through a cycle of meteorological fluctuations, were now especially dark. Intermittently laced with lightning and wind gusts, this squall had been exceptional for its paucity of rain. Logan and his two companions now decided the coast was clear, and descending from their rocky fortress, they slipped through the narrow crevice and onto the flat sandy ledge before them.

"Stay away from that edge!" Logan commanded brusquely, pointing directly at a startled Patel who, jumping back from his position, looked frantically around for the dreaded rim. Moments later they had fanned out on the grounds before them commencing a thorough sweeping search, for anything that might clue them to the suspected technology. Gradually the wind and rain began to resume, and despite their best efforts there was nothing to be found. Logan, having scoured every square centimeter of the rocky protuberance, crouched over the edge with an air of frustration.

"There's nothing here," Strife fretted as she finished working her fingers through the stubbly grass dotting the terrain at her knees, "Forget this. If we don't get back to the others below we're going to be left behind."

Logan sighed in agreement as he rose to his feet. "I guess you're right. There's nothing to see here. We better go."

It was at that moment, left alone on the ledge, that a barely perceptible movement in the far distance caught Logan's eye. Zooming in on the water below, the telephoto function of his nano-lens spied the shadow of a solitary figure walking on the waves. Through the wind the form moved effortlessly as if composed of a substance much stronger than the physical world around him. Only momentarily did he stop, hesitating just long enough to turn so Logan could see the face of the Nazarene.

The waves surrounding him were of sufficient height to mercilessly toss about the nearby fishing boat filled with terrified disciples. Yet even this did not dissuade Jesus as the waves, cowering like a trained pet, shifted laterally to the left and right, clearing an almost level path for the rabbi to pass.

Fascinated by the frothy almost animated dance of the sea, Logan hesitated as he watched the historic scene unfolding below him. A few moments later and Peter, true to the narrative and impetuous as ever, launched himself over the life boat's edge, toddling like an infant on the briny surface towards his master. As the burly fisherman closed within seven meters of the carpenter, he suddenly lost focus, his vision shifting to the intimidating creature -like wave towering ominously beside him. The wave had risen like a miniature obelisk, suddenly transforming its foamy surface into the very countenance of evil. Terrified and transfixed Peter immediately began to sink.

Logan, impressed at the big man's courage, could not help but laugh out loud at the predictability of his audacious attempt and his characteristic failure. The last thing Logan saw, as the enormous stone of a man went down for the third time, was that of Jesus' hand stabbing beneath the surf and grasping the large fisherman, hoisting him from his watery grave.

Moments later and Logan was racing to catch his friends who, already having started their descent, listened intently to the scene they had just missed. On the tiny sea below, a small wooden boat bobbed effortlessly under clearing skies as Jesus slept, drifting silently towards the shores of Gergesa and home to *Legion*.

CHAPTER FIFTEEN
An Army of One

The small wooden boat creaked as it glided silently through the murky surge of the windswept sea. Its timbers were laden by the burden of four weary and bedraggled disciples along with their modest belongings. Only the lacy haze of a damp and gloomy morning fog remained from the torrent which had tortured their sister boat bearing the carpenter and his twelve apostles an hour before. Now Logan and his friends, led by Barnabas, followed in their wake to the shores of Gergesa. Above them the black and gray scalloped canopy of the waning tempest still tortured the skies, its web of blue arcs dancing just above the hilltops lining the beach ahead. Logan studied the menacing skyline.

"Are you sure this is where they were headed?"

"Yes, beloved. They set out for Khersa no more than an hour before you returned to camp. What I can't understand is why they would leave the master behind."

"If my intuition serves me, I think we'll see him there."

"I would like to agree with you, my friend, but unless he has his own boat, he will have a long swim."

Logan smiled at his burly friend before responding.

"Perhaps… now it is you who underestimate him. At any rate we shall see. Come along, we're close enough to pull into shore." At this the two friends jumped into the water, and grabbing the main line, pulled the craft to shore, tying it securely to a fallen timber.

The beach the four followers arrived on was anything but a welcome respite from their past adventures. Its midnight sky, at times partially lit by the mysterious glow of a shrouded moon, and at times luminescent from the distant display of celestial fireworks, grumbled with thunder. The remnants of the passing storm welcomed the explorers as they, together with an occasional swirling dust devil, explored the small dunes abutting the rocky beachside.

Down the beach leaned the oversized schooner that Jesus and the twelve had commandeered to cross the lake. A quick inspection of the craft left no doubt of the disciple's successful crossing nor of their departure into the hillsides above.

"Well, they were here. Look, there are footsteps heading up that narrow pass." Logan stooped, studying the chaos of imprints tracing their way into the shadowy crags above them.

The hillside, like the weather surrounding them, was itself dark and imposing. Dozens of jagged and obtusely shaped rock formations protruded forward as if suspended in mid-air, their appendages casting a myriad of shadowy illusions.

"We're not going to follow them - in there - are we?" Patel protested, pointing to the narrow pass where the footsteps led.

"Of course. What's wrong, professor, afraid of the boogey man?" Strife responded feigning claw-like hands while shifting her pack onto her back.

"Well no, but…."

"No buts. They went there, so will we. Now grab those torches from the skiff so we can proceed," Logan commanded as turning he pointed to the boat, only to be grappled by the arm and turned around briskly.

"What the…?"

"One moment, my friend, we need to talk," the burly Levite interrupted.

"Talk? No talking, we need to go," Logan protested struggling to wrench free, before again being hoisted backwards. Logan looked at the big hand that held him fast and the knowing expression that guided it.

"O-kay… so talk."

At once the whining of the wind whistled down through the shadowy slopes.

"Shhh...., did you hear that?" the big man whispered.

The three explorers froze, listening hard for the almost imperceptible moan creeping through the slender crevices of the stone cavities and descending eerily upon them.

"It's just the wind."

Barnabas hesitated looking around the cliff side before continuing. His voice was quiet and cautious.

"Perhaps, but these cursed hills are dreadful not only in their appearance, but also in their inhabitants. The caves in these hilltops hold the tombs of the dead. In these undisturbed sanctuaries rest the damned, the murdered and the betrayed. In addition to the dead who rest here peacefully, there dwell the living dead, those who still seeking have not yet found rest. Legend says they roam these hills seeking release, and not finding it, inflict their anguish on all who dare enter."

"Oh, come on, Barney you don't believe that voodoo stuff, do you?"

"In these hills it matters little what I believe, yet very much what *they* do."

"Sounds like the man knows what he's talking about, Logan. I'll, I'll just stay here and protect the boat," Patel stammered.

"Well, that's ridiculous! I never heard such foolishness. So this is a burial ground, BIG deal. Look, we're - here - to- find - Jesus and he went in there, so it must be ok. Now come on, we're going," Logan insisted as the three reluctantly fell in line behind their torch-bearing commander, with Patel bringing up the rear.

Slowly they moved through the damp and narrow crevices that ascended the hillside to the terraced cave sites above. The walls of the narrow passageway towered some seven meters above on every side, their shadows brought to life by the torchlight, whipped mercilessly by the whirling winds cascading down the maze-like trail.

Three terrible apparitions suddenly appeared above and moved swiftly along the canyon's edge. Parading in sequence with the storm's own brand of flickering stalkers, they menaced the explorers around every curve.

"What's that?" Patel exclaimed.

"Shadows, your highness," Logan retorted, "nothing but shadows. Now keep moving."

Slowly the tiny pathway rose, its sandy surface expanding, littered here and there with the footprints of the twelve devotees following their leader. Logan pursued it meticulously, like a pit-bull whose iron-like jowls locked steadfast on its quarry's tail.

"So professor, something you said on the cliff back there has been bothering me," Logan admitted.

"Yeh, what?" Patel responded nervously looking over his shoulder at the shadows pursuing him.

"You know, that bit about our universe being an enigma, casting doubt on others existing."

"Yeh, what about it?"

"Well I just find that hard to believe. I've always heard just the opposite."

"Kool-Aid"

"What?"

"You've been watching too much science fiction. I did a graduate research project in statistics on the likelihood of life sustaining universes. The fact is, ours should not exist."

"That's a pretty bold statement. Why would you say that?"

"Because I'm a scientist and I deal in facts. Physicists as far back as the late 1900's have studied the big bang. They found that the initial conditions present at the universe's start were incalculably slim. Do you remember reading about the physicist Stephen Hawkings?"

"Yes, he was a brilliant atheist."

"Well, he said that if the rate of the universe's expansion one second after formation had been less by even one part in a hundred thousand million millionths, it would have collapsed into a big fire ball. Just to have conditions favorable for star and planet formation has a chance of only one out of one followed by a thousand billion, billion zeroes. There are around fifty of these impossible constants that had to be fine-tuned at the very beginning for life to exist. In addition each of these constants had to be exquisitely fine-tuned in ratio to one another to permit life. Taken together improbability multiplied by improbability leaves us with numbers that exceed human comprehension. This universe should not exist; I'm sure there are no more."

"Wow, that's amazing. So if some type of intellect obviously monkeyed with the universe, why was Hawking an atheist?"

Patel shrugged before answering. "Science only allows for the natural. It has no interest in the supernatural."

Well, that hardly seems tolerant. Cancel my subscription to the *New Republic*. I've got to stop reading those science fiction stories they publish each month," Logan quipped.

"That's all very interesting, you two space cadets," Strife intervened, "But it doesn't explain what those three apparitions were we saw up on the cliff."

"Shadows." Logan dismissed to the increasingly quiet crowd.

It was ten minutes into their climb when they heard the first scream. Logan and the others froze as the eerie cry echoed, like an animal in pain, piercing the rocky hillside surrounding them. They hesitated only slightly before Logan drove them to continue their climb.

Then a minute later.

"L-e-e-a-v-e…!"

The wail echoed off the surrounding cliffs and reverberated back at them from all directions. A moment later it repeated. This time its pitch was higher, yet more discernible. Patel, who was carrying a torch, shoved his way to the front.

"We better go," he said nervously.

"Give me one good reason." Logan retorted incredulously looking back at the scientist and then up at the surrounding walls.

"Because he is *Legion* and you are not," came back the unexpected Cyprian voice. Logan turned to face his husky advisor.

"You don't mean to tell me those are Romans?"

"I don't."

"But you just said it was a legion."

"Not it, *he* is *Legion*."

"Now you're not making good sense."

"Some things in life are inexplicable, my friend. This is one."

"Hold on, fly-boy," Strife intervened. "I've got this one. Barnabas, who is *Legion*?"

"His true name has long since been forgotten, but not his story. Legend says that ages ago a wealthy family was betrayed to marauders by the people of Khersa. Only one survived, a young man who ransomed his soul for revenge. With the strength of ten men he attacked the marauders and destroyed them. Now he lives among the dead, unable to be restrained.

"You mean these caves?" Strife asked.

Barnabas nodded in return.

"Possessed by demons, he became violent, uncontrollable to the point of breaking even chains."

Logan smiled listening impatiently until he could listen no more. "Ok, so we've got an unarmed man who's a little schizoid. I say we keep pressing ahead. These types usually won't bother you if you don't bother them." He turned pressing ahead, only to have his path blocked by Barnabas.

"No Logan, you do not understand. This man is not all man, he is part creature."

"Creature! Look Barney if he's a dog we'll throw him a bone, but we're moving forward. Do I make myself clear?"

Barnabas grew quiet, his eyes refusing to meet the guardian's as Logan turned and marched past him. The others passed the Cyprian giving an affectionate pat on his shoulder as they too pressed ahead.

Twenty minutes later and the quartet had emerged onto a flat sandy plain, below the first and lowest level of caves carved naturally into the rocky hillside. These depressions, some branching into the subterranean realm for a mile or more, formed dark menacing expressions on the overhangs. Above each opening clung the gnarled and twisted roots of dozens of shabby bushes and scruffy acacia trees, each entangled with a myriad of misshapen vines interwoven and hanging down forming a natural curtain to the individual openings. Taken together with the shards of broken burial pots and shattered coffins garnishing each opening, the elements created a daunting natural impression. Foreboding mausoleums, lined successively on the desolate hillsides and shrouded in a web of vines, also unnerved the small band. Logan paused to get his bearings and decide which path to follow next. As he crouched low to the ground studying the chaos of footsteps in the torchlight, he suddenly became aware of a new shadow moving behind him. Standing he turned and scanned to his left at the ledge above him. As he did so, he caught a fleeting glimpse of what appeared to be a man moving towards him on all fours.

"There!" he yelled, pointing above at the shadow which, moving abruptly in the afterglow of the lightning, seemed to disappear. Suddenly, an ear-piercing cry rang out again, its pitch so high as to resemble more animal than man.

"L-e-e-a-v-e…!" the shrill warning rang out again, echoing off the stony walls surrounding them on all sides. Logan activated his suit's defend mode with the subtle flip of a switch, signaling his comrades to follow his lead.

"I'd say we're not welcome," Strife advised as she picked up her pack and motioned for the four to move on. Logan turned to lift his pack and lead the group forward when the first blow hit. The force, quite unlike anything Logan had prepared for, hurled him forward into the sand leaving him breathless. Instinctively, he rolled forward bouncing defensively to his feet.

It was then that he saw it.

The creature or man was moderate in size. His dark hair, unkempt to the point of entanglement, and interspersed with the leaves, branches and vines he obviously called home, descended to his waist and danced wickedly around him in the wind. In one hand he lifted a club, fashioned from the remains of a human thigh, and adorned with jewelry apparently stolen from one of the tombs. It was with this club that he pounced down upon and proceeded to attack Barnabas.

For his part Barnabas, a full six inches taller than the rag cloistered assailant, was attempting to serve as a barrier separating his friends from the mad man. The creature attacked, his blows viciously well placed. In seconds the Cyprian was down, lying some two meters from where he had initially taken his stand.

At this Logan retrieved the remaining Roman sword from his pack and charged the fiend. The guardian aimed sharply, his blows intending to disable swiftly, and not kill. His first blow was effective in severing the brute's weapon. His second was harmless. It was then that Logan realized the tyrant was adorned, wrist and ankle, in iron shackles long ago broken from their chains. The rusty bracelets were flawlessly employed as wrist armor, easily deflecting the hammering blows of Logan's sword in a shower of sparks.

In only a moment the sword lay harmless, swept from its warrior's grip and cast several meters away. Suddenly the creature was upon him, teeth bared. Its mouth thrashed wildly, held only at bay by the guardian's strength enhanced forearm. Horrified, Logan stared at the face that lashed out towards him. Illuminated by a single flash of lightning, the monster's face changed. The charcoal eyes grew narrow and slit like, their appearance made less imposing only by the dingy yellowed fangs emerging from the protruding jowls. Another flash of lightning and the beast's teeth had latched onto the edge of Logan's tunic, ripping a small seam wide open.

Unable to draw blood, it screamed like a wounded dog and spun, slinging the guardian across the small plateau near the place where Barnabas lay ominously still. A second scream followed as the sky was lit twice with the gentle blue arcs of two simultaneously fired paralyzers. Logan rolled expecting to see their attacker down and unconscious at his partner's feet.

Instead the creature stood upright uninjured. The head was writhing in anger at Logan's cowering associates while the strange metamorphosis began again. This time the brute's grotesque countenance turned pale and hairless. The cheeks and forehead bulged projecting the nearly flawless features of a human skull covered with the thin veneer of a translucent skin protecting a sea of lacy blue veins. The jagged teeth dripped with mucous and the pointed ears lay back, painting the portrait of a living nightmare.

Logan reacted quickly, throwing himself at the creature like a linebacker, locking his arms and legs around the heaving beast.

"Run!" he yelled at his stunned companions.

"I said Run!" he screamed as the wild man thrashed violently spinning this way and that to dislodge the guardian. At this the other two fled, stopping only briefly to lift the fallen Levite and drag him away.

The beast now fully enraged was transforming at will to a myriad of specters, each identity more terrible than the last. Logan clung with as much strength as he could muster, until he suddenly found himself clinging to something so horrible his imagination had never dreamed it could exist. The creature smelled like the stench of rotting flesh. Every hair gone from its head, the crown covered in large multi-lobulated vessels, it throbbed as if alive. At this, the beast's head turned almost completely backwards on its neck to look at Logan.

In panic, the guardian suddenly relaxed his grip and was flung in terror from the writhing fiend. On his back some three meters from the creature, Logan stared up into the face of his worst nightmare, himself. For the ogre that stood now laughing before him was the thing he would soon become.

The GRUB, his head swollen as was the woman's in the recovery bay, with large pulsating purple and blue vessels and enormous eyes bulging from their sockets, closed on the terror-stricken explorer.

Then.

"Come!"

The strong voice rang out, its command echoing around the plateau and penetrating through the crevices of the rocky crags like the first rays of the rising sun.

The beast froze, then immediately transformed to the rag covered man Logan had first met only minutes before.

"Come here, I said!"

The voice rang out again to the man-creature, suddenly cowering like a scolded family pet, who whimpered and ran crouching to the feet of its master.

Logan rolled over and looked up.

There in the distance stood Jesus alone except for the terrified monstrosity shaking at his feet. Strife and Patel cautiously emerged from the rocks behind the carpenter followed by Peter and the other eleven. Silent, they watched in awe as the kneeling man, hands clasped and eyes closed, shook violently with fear.

"Jesus," he stuttered, "Son of the Most High, please don't hurt me."

Jesus said nothing, only staring at the man.

"What do you want with me?" the man screamed, "Please don't hurt me!"

"Come out of him," Jesus said calmly. The man-creature cowered closer to the ground, whimpering and shaking its head.

"What is your name?" Jesus spoke gently. The creature battled as if trying to speak his earthly name, his mouth unable, seemingly overpowered within. Instead what emerged was the deep echo of a half-choked hiss.

"My name is *Legion*, for we are many; please don't cast us into the outermost. Please!"

Jesus looked around. There was not much to work with, only rocks, sand, beach and a large herd of pigs some distance away being driven to new feeding grounds.

"Alright, you choose," he said pointing to the herd being driven past a grassy knoll that ascended to a sheer cliff overlooking the sea.

Immediately the man was thrown to the ground thrashing wildly as if locked in the throes of a severe seizure.

"Hold him!" Jesus yelled at Logan who along with Peter and a very sorely missed Barnabas pinned the thrashing man to the ground. Finally the flailing stopped as his breathing grew calm again.

"He'll be fine now," Jesus assured, walking away.

Immediately, a sudden shrill noise came from the hillside as a thunderous rumble broke out. The herdsman was screaming at the top of his lungs as the animals began tearing one another like ravenous wolves. The chaos quickly became a stampede that rumbled past the mortified owner and over the cliffs to split open on the rocky shoreline below.

Some moments later Jesus and his disciples, with their unconscious patient in tow, ascended the hillside and looked down at the carnage. Many of the animals were torn to shreds upon the rocks, their remains floating aimlessly in the gentle bloodstained water off shore. Everyone else moved away from the edge now, except for Barnabas and Logan, who with arms wrapped around each other's shoulders, continued to stare.

"Wonder what's eating them?"

"Demons, they never could resist a good pork dinner," Barnabas replied with a huge grin across his face. The two men laughed loudly as they turned to join the others down the hill. As they descended, Logan slapped his big friend on the back sending an enormous cloud of dust upward. The two men laughed pointing to the rising swirl. Barnabas, who appeared especially amused, laughed loudest before repaying the favor, almost sending Logan rolling down the grassy hill.

The worldly saying that *'no good deed goes unpunished'* soon proved prophetic to Jesus and his disciples. Forced to leave in the wee hours of the next morning by an influential delegation from the terrified city of Khersa, the camp was in disarray. The delegation, accompanied by armed escort, was polite to the point of being diplomatic in their insistence that the small band leave immediately. In their haste Logan, Barnabas and the other two explorers had the inestimable honor of crossing the Sea of Galilee with Jesus and his twelve in the larger boat. Logan and his friends sat in the middle of the craft, while Jesus, John and Peter, buried under a small mountain of cloaks, napped towards the aft. Logan and Barnabas sat across from one another, talking quietly and sharing a bowl of figs.

"So you believe the man on the bluffs was possessed by demons?"

Strife and Patel slept silently, each still exhausted from the early morning rise and the previous day's adventure.

"What else?" the big Cyprian asked, spitting a pit into the water behind him.

"Perhaps they were just what we wanted to see? What our people like to call hallucinations."

Barnabas scratched the back of his head for a moment.

"And so you wanted to see this lump on my head and that thing with the big bulgy eyes?"

"Point taken," Logan acknowledged, "but what happened to the apparitions after the pigs went into the water?"

Barnabas spit another seed into his hand before chucking it into the brine.

"If you speak of the demons, I assume they are in hell."

"Hell, did you say hell?"

"Yes, you know the lake of fire, prepared for Lucifer and his angels."

"You don't really believe in that sort of thing, do you, Barney?"

"Oh yes, my friend, hell is a very real place, where the condemned spend eternity."

"I don't - know - Barney."

"You do believe in hell, don't you?"

"It's not the place itself I have a problem with, and I couldn't care less where those demons went. But why, Barney, would a loving God send souls to eternal punishment for crimes committed in such a relatively short life. I mean think about it, the crime doesn't fit the punishment."

"Hmmm, those are excellent questions, my friend. Perhaps we should ask the master." Barnabas rose intent on stumbling his way towards the aft where Jesus lay sleeping. Logan, embarrassed, immediately stood endeavoring to block his friend's path.

"No, no wait. Barnabas! Don't bother him! He's asleep!" Logan barely spoke the words when the sudden shift in weight sent the boat lurching. The pitch, mild yet unexpected, sent both men toppling over a stationary oar and into the aft of the boat, falling in an embrace at Jesus feet. Peter and John stirred while Jesus woke and looked down at the two entangled men.

"Uh, am I interrupting something?" he asked smiling.

The two men looked up and then just as abruptly pushed quickly from each other into a sitting position.

"The boat lurched and we fell...," Logan babbled.

"Of course, must be leviathan up to his old tricks again. Now if you don't mind I'll just finish my nap." Jesus smiled as he slowly leaned back again. Meanwhile, the disturbance, which forced Peter to shift and resume his snoring, caused John to stir and open his eyes.

"Teacher, Logan has a question," Barnabas blurted out despite Logan's best efforts to silently hush him. Jesus's gaze froze Logan who stared back in alarm, stuttering for something to say.

"No, no, I mean we were just talking. You know, guy talk. Light stuff, fluff, nothing important. Go back to sleep."

"About hell," Barnabas interjected.

"Would you be quiet?"

"What about it?" Jesus sat back seriously, shaking off his grogginess.

"Nothing really, we were just chatting."

"He doesn't believe in it."

"P-l-ease, be quiet," Logan chided him, sheepishly explaining, "It's not that I don't believe in it. It's just ……It just doesn't make sense. I mean why would a God who loves us, punish us eternally for sins committed in such a short life time?"

Jesus hung his head, a deep sigh escaping. Eventually he spoke.

"Your error lies in your assuming you are more compassionate than God. A student is not above his teacher, nor a servant above his master."

Logan nodded slowly contemplating the response.

"Granted… which again begs the question why would such a compassionate God send people to an eternity in hell?"

"I myself was not sent to condemn anyone, but to save them. When a man hears my words, but does not keep them, I do not judge him. The problem is that men love darkness and will not come into the light. God is not willing that any should perish, but that all should be saved." Logan nodded his head as if he understood, but his expression betrayed his ignorance.

"Or said another way, if I were to quote one of your fellow *Egyptians*," Barnabas added with a smile, "The gates of hell are locked from the inside?"

"I don't understand."

At this John, who had listened from a sleep induced stupor, stirred and sitting upright interjected.

"The lost separate from God, they *depart*," John added.

"Departing, the cursed go into the fire, prepared not for man, but for the devil and his angels," Jesus continued.

"So by rejecting God's love…," Logan rephrased to the nodding disciples, "man chooses separation from God."

"Despising his birthright man chooses, as Esau did, to live for the moment, to pursue his immediate desires, rejecting the One who holds his eternal destiny. But beloved, we were meant for so much more," Barnabas agreed.

"Such as?"

"Trusting in the light," John said nodding towards Jesus, "we become what we were meant to be, *sons of light*."

"What is a Son of light?"

"You have already met three… on the cliff-side," Jesus smiled knowingly.

Logan thought again for a moment.

"And if we do not, what do we finally become?"

"Pharisees," Barnabas quipped, as he and John jostled each other laughing out loud.

"Woe to the Pharisees," Jesus replied shaking his head, "who winning one convert, turn him into twice a *son of hell* as they are."

"Sons of hell, now there's a term. I've heard you use that before. What does that mean?" Logan observed, "Are those the occupants of hell?"

Jesus smiled.

"O-K, soo….what happens to these sons of hell?" Logan pressed.

"I am the true vine, you are the branches. If you do not remain in me, you wither, fit only to be burned."

Logan shook his head in frustration.

"There you go again answering a question with some obtuse image. Can't you just answer the question?"

"Perhaps you are receiving the answer to the question you should be asking," Barnabas observed.

Logan smiled before taking another breath and venturing further.

"So these branches, what does it mean that they wither? Are they still human?"

"Everyone who has will be given more, and he will have an *abundance*. Whoever does not have, even what he has will be taken away from him."

Logan stared for a long moment.

"Forever?"

"Hell only lasts as long as those who hate God refuse to repent and accept forgiveness," John added.

"Forgiveness must be received to be of value," Barnabas agreed.

"So these *sons of hell*, these withered creatures, are trapped by their own continued selfishness and hatred for God," Logan mused.

Staring out toward the dawn's first light, Jesus hesitated before reclining again and pulling his cloak back over him.

"For whoever wants to save his life will lose it, but whoever loses his life for my sake will find it."

CHAPTER SIXTEEN
An Unexpected Confession

Winter in Israel was fraught with its own set of challenges for even the hardiest of souls. While mild by North American standards, the cooler temperatures of the rainy season had taken its toll on Patel. Weakened by a combination of poor health, the scarcity of proper nutrition and his near-death experience on the mountain, Patel had developed a noticeable pallor and emaciation that worried his comrades. Perhaps this was why he often asserted to Logan that the group had completed its mission almost four months early. Logan suspected that this was only one of Patel's reasons for wishing to leave Palestine. The almost continual struggle to find food and the constant presence of human suffering had taken a toll on them all. At times, they had given in to bickering and fighting amongst themselves over the smallest of things. These conflicts, rare as they were, made them stand out like sore thumbs within the close nit group of Jesus quiet followers. Traveling by beast of burden or on foot, the small band of devoted followers was constantly on the move.

During this first month of winter, Strife joined in with her own discontent over the delay. Conflicts once never a problem between Logan and the beautiful explorer now intruded at some of the most inappropriate times.

While he sensed this darkness that had settled over the mood of his two companions, Logan was unable to address it, having his own difficulties with increasingly occurring flashbacks. It was during these times, when Logan felt propelled into periods of deep depression, that Jesus paid special attention to the explorer, often striking up spontaneous conversations. For all of Logan's skepticism, he found himself experiencing great difficulty getting past the genuine compassion that Jesus displayed for anyone who hurt. Thus persisted the terrible mental dilemma of imposter versus friend.

Logan sat by the campfire trying hard not to stare at the increasingly gaunt Patel, who emitting a huge sigh from the fire's other side, was preparing to once again engage.

"Logan, how much longer are we going to keep dragging this out? We've got what we've come for. I'm almost out of medication and time is running out."

"Time for what, time to get home and die?"

"Time to get this data back to the ship, and get back to our own century, while we still have the strength."

Strife hesitated only briefly before beginning her own assault.

"He's right, Logan. As much as I have enjoyed my last few weeks with dust between my teeth, I have no desire to die here. The transponders have been damaged and we've got to get this info back. The longer we wait, the weaker we grow, and the more we actually endanger the mission."

"Not you too. Look, I'm not satisfied yet. I'd like to die in my own bed too, but our directive was to observe Jesus' death. The pivotal claim of the Christian faith is his *resurrection*. If we were to leave now the argument would be that we hadn't stayed the course and disproven that claim. The entire mission could be compromised. You knew what you were getting into when you signed on. We all knew."

"Our directive was to determine if he was a fraud or not. We now know that! The cloak is the source of his power. What more do you need to see? What can we possibly gain from staying?" Patel argued, the strain of catching his breath between sentences becoming more obvious when he grew excited. Logan hesitated before answering, partly because he knew his response would be met with derision, and partly out of reluctance to see Patel grow more agitated.

"A confession," Logan let the words roll out slowly, bracing for the response. For a moment there was nothing but silence as Patel sat there with a disbelieving smirk, his sentiment echoed by Strife's own bewildered stare.

"A what?" Strife exclaimed incredulously.

"A confession," Logan smiled quickly answering again.

"You think that con man of con men is going to come clean and admit he's not their messiah? You're as deceived as he is," Patel blustered stabbing the air with his index finger in some random direction back toward camp.

"Possibly, but I believe that if confronted with our proof, he will have to confess. When he does, we shall have him for all posterity to see. No one will be able to argue with that."

"It could also get us all killed."

"Albert is right, Logan. You've seen the power He wields. What if that tunic could be used as a weapon?"

"Oh great! Now she's calling me Albert. My name is Nicholas. Look, I'm feeling generous! You guys can call me Nick."

"I think not. Look, don't you remember what he said when I touched his tunic? He knows why we're here. If he were going to harm us, he would have done it by now. What about the way he treats children? I guarantee you no Hitler would let these dirty children sit on his lap and eat from his plate," Logan continued almost without taking a breath.

"Look guys, which of you has ever seen Him ever show a hint of anger, much less violence? The man is in perfect control of his emotions. He's not evil, so he must really believe he is the Son of God. If I confront him and get him to admit any part of what we suspect, then his delusion of being an all-loving savior will keep him from killing me."

"That's a flimsy theory and bad logic if you ask me, Strife reasoned, "He seems very lucid to me, and if he is he'll attack. If he's not lucid, and you force him to see the truth of his own delusion, he may become unstable and attack. Either way, if you're wrong, you're dead and we have no pilot to take us home."

"She's right Logan. He has too keen a mind to be delusional. No crazy man could come up with those quick responses that humiliate those Pharisees. This is all a charade. I for one want you at the helm when we go home." Patel added.

"Ok, Ok, let's for the sake of argument assume He is dangerous. I disagree. I have never heard him utter an unkind word. Have either of you?" Logan asked as the others shook their heads quietly, "Ok, everything he preaches is the opposite of the evil deceit you're claiming him to practice. I think you're wrong, and he's just a little crazy. You know in a good way. You know like actors or some of those men in Washington. But just in case, I'll confront him alone. If something happens to me, you and Albert here can escape with the truth. The ship can fly by autopilot better than I can fly it, so you really don't need me. Plus, I just want to see the look on his face when he realizes someone is on to his little game.

"I don't know," Patel grimaced shaking his head.

"Look, if we go home with what we have now someone may say we doctored the data. If we get a confession, we have him cold for all to see. Nothing will be more convincing."

At this Strife surprisingly intervened.

"You're right. I'll agree as long as we have your word that we'll leave."

"As soon as he's alone I'll talk with him. Then we can go home. Agreed?" Logan finished as his reluctant partners nodded, and weary from the fight, prepared to settle in for the night.

Two days later, on a Judean hillside, Jesus slipped out of camp for one of his frequent prayer hikes. The sun was just now beginning to release her rays over the hillside. In the lingering shadows a second figure, unnoticed by a still sleeping camp, stole out to follow the Nazarene. As the two hiked well into the wilderness, Logan began inching closer to his target.

Jesus strode briskly ahead apparently unaware of his silent stalker, whose years of military training enabled him to minimize all but the tiniest sounds of broken branches and shifting gravel. Self-assured by his experience, Logan thought nothing of following Jesus who disappeared into the rocky ravine ahead of them. Halfway through the network of massive stones, Logan was stopped by the sound of a gentle cough from behind him. Turning he stood stupefied to find Jesus smiling. Finally Logan spoke.

"You know, you're brighter than you look."

"Infinitely preferable, I would say, to looking brighter than you are."

"Touché," Logan responded hesitantly.

"Only now do you begin to follow me?" Jesus asked smiling.

"Uh, yes, I mean no," Logan stuttered a response while shaking his head, "I've been following you for some time now."

"You have pursued, but only now do you follow."

"I'm not sure I know what you mean."

"I think you do. What is it you would have me do for you, my son?"

"Look I'm forty-five years old; I'm not your son," Logan responded sarcastically.

"Not yet," Jesus whispered kindly. At Jesus response, Logan felt the first conflicting twinges of anger and admiration rising up within him.

"Look! I've just got one question. Who do you think you are?" Logan blurted out. Jesus walking closer, looked deeply into the guardian's eyes.

"I am whom I have always claimed to be. I think the really important question is who do you say that I am?" Jesus stepped back still looking intently at Logan. Unable to maintain the stare Logan looked towards the ground, shaking his head as they walked out from the maze and onto a grassy meadow.

"An imposter! You're either a time traveler with a God-fixation or you're from another dimension or, I don't know! You tell me." Jesus smiled at this last suggestion looking away as he spoke.

"Logan, the eyes of this world, no matter how piercing," he hesitated briefly looking at Logan's eyes, "see only what they choose to see. Each soul sees the other's blind spot, but is curiously unable to see its own. Then the man, believing he sees yet blind to his misplaced priorities, leads himself and the ones he loves to ruin. The blind lead the blind into a ditch. Do you know anyone like that?"

"Ok, Ok, what's your point?" Logan responded beginning to feel frustrated.

"Often a man's only hope is the people who love him most, helping him to see through his own self-deception. So before I answer your question, you must first answer mine. Who did Julie say that I am?"

Stunned, Logan could feel the hair on the back of his neck stiffen, his heart racing and his blood pressure rising in sync.

"Look, I don't know what kind of mind game you're playing here or how you know her name, but you are not the Son of God. We've mapped you, scanned you and recorded you for six months now. Our readings show your 'miracles' are anything but. Our devices……" Logan held up his index finger preparing to launch further into his tirade when he was interrupted again by the almost whisper of a voice.

"Lie."

Jesus' expression was one of pity as he nodded slowly. Logan now fought to control the emotions boiling up within him. The revelation that his own blindness may have somehow contributed to his family's demise was a fear Logan had wrestled with for some time now. That regret itself was almost too much to control, but now this new assertion seemed ludicrous.

"What, - What did you say?" Logan stuttered unsure if the gentleness with which the sentence had been spoken actually distorted its meaning.

"Your sand-based implements are shifting," Jesus smiled.

"What?" Logan said still angry.

"Your devices lie," Jesus said plainly.

"Give me a break. What do you mean they lie? Machines can't lie. You know that."

"They tell you what the deceiver wants you to see and hear," Jesus replied, "and ignoring your own heart, you remain in your deception. Claiming that you see, your sin remains all the greater."

"What deceiver? I'm here for the truth, that's all."

"There are three of you," Jesus observed. Logan listened intently, his mind grappling for a rational explanation for Jesus' insight.

"Yes," he admitted.

"One of you has a demon."

"What? A demon, I'm sorry, I don't believe in demons." Logan grunted his disbelief.

"Unfortunate, because they by now certainly believe in you."

"Like me, Logan, you have a traitor in your midst," Jesus continued, "Let me ask you, have you ever met a person who lies as easily as he talks? A person who's every word you questioned?"

"Yes, once. How do I know you're not such a liar?" Logan responded with a note of harshness that surprised even him. Jesus smiled.

"A house divided amongst itself cannot stand."

"What is that supposed to mean?"

"What is hidden will be revealed. Not every one of your group seeks truth. There is one among you who follows the father of all lies. They lie so naturally that it is almost impossible to tell. But you will find a way, you will find a way."

"You really expect me to believe that all of our technology..."

"Lies"

"I saw the radiation come out of your tunic. I know IT is the source of your power."

"God is the source of my power. Without Him I can do nothing. You do not see it, but the same is true for you."

"Without your tunic you're nothing!"

"Do you remember your first date with Julie? What happened? At the game...?" Jesus asked. Logan's eyes narrowed.

"How do you know this stuff? You must have got it from some database?" Logan replied. Jesus just smiled again.

"Do you remember?" He asked gently and more emphatically.

"Ok, yeah. We went to the Giants game and it rained. So?" Logan responded curious as to where this line of questioning was heading. Jesus continued.

"You won her heart that day. Do you remember what it was you did?" Jesus prodded further as Logan hesitated, shaking his head and thinking.

"It was pouring rain and you gave her your cloak". Logan's mind now flashed back to the day. The scene now formed clearly, of he and Julie laughing in the rain and Logan lifting his coat over her shoulder.

"You walked a mile in the pouring rain, and you were soaked. You were soaked to the bone. Do you remember how cold you were when you got to her dorm?" Logan laughed nodding his head as the bittersweet memories came flooding back.

"Before that she was ambivalent to you. After that selfless act of love, she blossomed," Jesus continued with Logan nodding silently. "Did you ever tell anyone that story?"

Logan thought hard for moment before answering. "Why, no, no one, how could you know that? I barely remembered it myself," Logan asked meekly.

Jesus pulled his tunic over his head and held it extended towards Logan. As he stood there, naked except for his loincloth, he continued.

"I know it because I was there. Here, this is my 'coat'. I give it to you," Jesus spoke gently. Stunned, Logan hesitated.

"Look, it is cold here. At least you have something underneath to keep you warm. Give me your tunic," Jesus repeated. As Logan slowly removed his tunic revealing his survival suit underneath, he spoke.

"How could you have been there?" Logan spoke slowly as he handed it to Jesus. The Nazarene was silent as he quickly slipped on the traded tunic.

"Did you know Julie believed in me when you married her?"

"Yes. Look, I don't know how you know these things." Logan responded as he meekly pulled the seamless tunic over his own head.

"I know them because I was there," Jesus repeated smiling at Logan as he helped straighten Logan's newly acquired tunic.

"There, you now have my 'power'. May it bring you good health. Now would you care to join me in prayer? That is why I came here." Jesus moved to a nearby grassy knoll and sank to his knees. Logan sat nearby, perched on a nearby rock, staring down at the roughly woven fabric now draping his form. Two hours passed, and Jesus was still praying as Logan slept quietly against his limestone edifice. The next thing he recalled was the not so gentle sound of one clearing his throat in a manner sufficient to raise the dead.

"I'm returning to town now. Would you care to walk?" Jesus offered his hand helping Logan to slowly rise to his feet.

"Oh, my aching back, Sure, let's walk," Logan said as he rubbed the kinks from his neck and lower back. The late morning sun, positioned well over the Judean hills, set the stage for a beautiful day. Walking briskly the two men crossed through the hills making their way to the valley below.

"You are unusually quiet, my friend."

"So you expect me to believe all of those healings, and the wind, and all that were not the result of some sort of technology? Well, how was all that possible?"

"Their faith healed them."

"Faith, you've got to be kidding me! Look, I saw the howling wind calmed. I've seen the blind see. I, me with my own two eyes, I have seen a paralyzed man walk. This is not some nursery school kid here Jesus. I've traveled all……

"All across the heavens, yes I know, and only now, do you just begin to see," Jesus stopped walking as Logan grabbed his arm and turning him looked directly in his eyes.

"See, like that! How do you know that?"

"You've seen so much and yet you remain blind. Yet you *will* see, and when you do, Logan, remember, I am with you, always, to the end."

They walked for several more minutes in silence before Jesus began to speak again.

"When you were a boy, do you know what your favorite thing to do was?" Logan's eyes widened as a moment of silence passed while he continued walking and looking at the ground.

"Why do I get the funny feeling you're going to tell me?"

"Playing catch with your dad", Jesus replied followed by another long silence, "Sometimes you and your dad would go with your friends and their dads to a large grassy area with many trees. Do you remember that place?

"Central Park, yes, who could forget Central Park."

"There was this one dad, slightly balding and a little taller than your dad. He had a nickname for you,

'Parrot' -- because you repeated everything your dad said. Do you remember him?"

"Yes."

"He was your dad's best friend."

"Ok, so you know who my dad hung with. So what?"

"And when your dad died, he was the one who called you and broke the news to you?"

Logan looked up through narrow lids. Tight lipped, he said not a word. He looked away from Jesus as if looking out over the horizon, trying to avoid the questioning. Finally, through gritted teeth and on the verge of tears he answered.

"Yes."

"There was another call from this man? A call about your wife and children."

A single tear traced its way down the guardian's bearded face as he struggled to answer.

"Yes," he whispered.

Jesus paused for only a second before he gently asked the final question.

"Do you remember…? " Logan turned suddenly grasping Jesus' tunic by the shoulders.

"YES! YES! A thousand times yes, I remember! How do you know these things? No one knows these things! I've never told anyone about that. How could you?" he said releasing his hold and turning away again.

"I know them, Logan. I know them because I was there. Don't you see? Every pain you've ever felt, I have experienced too, then and now. Don't you understand? Some people just want God to leave them alone. Someday he will, but when he does ….'" His voice drifted off momentarily, "But while they live I can't. Every heart that breaks mine breaks with it. Every tear that falls sears the cheeks of God. So you see, there's a very real reason God is the one injured in each offense. Your life flows from mine. I am the vine, you are the branch. When you hurt or you hurt someone else, you are hurting me."

"And lo, I am with you always until the end of the age," Logan whispered reciting a distant memory from his childhood Sunday school.

"A friend that sticks closer than a brother," Jesus echoed.

Logan tensed his hands clinching them over his head as if to keep the words from penetrating his mind.

"No! This is some kind of trickery! If I thought you really were God, I'd punch you in the nose right now! No loving God would allow those monsters to do what they did! You betrayed me!"

"Julie understood. She tried to tell you. Freedom comes with a terrible price, Logan. Each man chooses to do good or evil. Each man's life affects someone else. And so, unless a choice is made not to pay back evil for evil, the destruction spreads. The evil and the anger, like yeast, works its way through the whole. One man's freedom costs another man everything."

"Well, then someone needs to step in and stop it! Get rid of the ones who hurt others. Break the cycle," Logan insisted. At this, Jesus smiled again.

"What would you have me do, drown them? Wipe the whole face of the earth clean and start from scratch?"

Logan scratched the back of his head.

"Yeh, I guess you've been there, done that."

"The disease still rages. Don't you see Logan; everyone's life is entangled with and thus damaged by some many others'. If I destroy an evil man, I kill a good boy's father."

Logan bristled with frustration, his finger stabbing at Jesus. "Then why didn't you make us good to start with?"

"You were… but you rebelled and pulling away from me you released my hand and slipped into darkness."

"Then why didn't you make us so we wouldn't go astray?"

"Logan, how could I make you free and at the same time not free? If you were to truly be free to do good, you must truly be free to do bad. What you are asking is impossible even for God."

"OK! So, you're supposed to be God. Then do something! Send us someone new who's not affected, someone to break the cycle, someone to be a role model. Send us a doctor, an advisor, someone to a…"

"You mean like a rescuer?

"Yes."

"Like a guardian."

"Yes."

"Someone who's immune, unaffected?"

"Yes."

"You mean like a Savior?"

Logan became suddenly silent again, the angry tears having dissipated.

"I have," Jesus said smiling.

Then cocking his head to meet Logan's gaze, "but even with that, each man must be strong and choose to break the cycle, even if it costs him everything he holds dear."

"That's impossible."

"With man, yes, but with God's help all things are possible." Silently they walked on as Logan thought about what had been said. Twenty minutes later, the two men rounded the last hill and stopped before their decline to the beachside village. Logan stared off at the distant sea before him. This time his tone was bitter.

"You betrayed me."

"I thought you didn't believe in me?"

"I don't know what I believe," Logan continued more angrily, "You betrayed my wife who loved you and my children who never hurt anyone. How can you stand there and ask me to believe in a God who so cruelly betrays those who love him?" Jesus looked down nodding his head.

"All who walk this earthly sod will feel betrayed, each life in its own way, but not one of those given me will be lost."

"Is that supposed to be some consolation?"

"There is none greater. What is it you want me to do for you, Jon Logan?" Logan leaned back, both shocked and momentarily stymied by the question.

"Well, for one thing, if nothing else to mend the rift."

"For this reason, I came into the world."

"How?"

"My Father will reveal this to you, when the time is right." Logan stood there staring at the Nazarene before continuing his descent to the beach.

"Just one more question"

Jesus smiled.

"Only one?"

"Who is the devil you spoke of?"

"Ask, seek, knock."

"What is that supposed to mean?"

"You will find a way. Be of good cheer," Jesus finished as the two separated walking briskly into the bustling camp.

CHAPTER SEVENTEEN
The Unplanned Trip

The small beachside village ahead of Logan was bustling with frenetic preparations for the day ahead. This activity was made even more apparent by the effect of the delicious waves of roasting tilapia and carp fanned from courtyard ovens by the cool morning breeze ascending from the nearby lake shore. The beach bristled with fishermen busily repairing the enormous nets used in their daily hauls. In town, the various operations involved in the cleaning and distillation of a cherished fish sauce operated in one corner of the community. These aromas, coupled with those of the very active industry of smoke and salt preservation occurring on the opposite end of town, resulted in a most curious mixture of fragrances to a twenty second century nose.

All the time Logan, oblivious to this activity, undulated between a state of deep thought and a new found admiration for his present attire. It was only when his appetite rebelled, no longer content to remain subordinate to his mind, that he was forced back to reality. Awakened by the proximate aroma of baking bread and roasted lamb, Logan finally looked up as he approached the edge of camp. Martha and Mary, cooking over an open fire, quietly watched as the guardian made his way towards the trio's campsite. As he passed through the gate and into the open courtyard a robed hand stretching from behind a nearby tree grabbed and pulled the newly adorned explorer aside. Logan reacted instinctively, immediately twisting the arm backwards into a painful chokehold that left Patel gasping for air.

"Hey, hold on. It's me, let go. Let go I said"

"You idiot, don't ever do that again," Logan protested quietly as he retracted his clenched fist.

"What did you find out?" Patel gasped attempting to clear his airway. Logan shook his head, struggling to control himself.

"He's not quite what I expected." As he turned his back to Patel and straightened his robe, the two made their way down to the village streets below.

"I take it he didn't confess."

"Not exactly," Logan answered scratching the back of his head, still trying to process his conversation with Jesus.

"Well, did he say anything when you confronted him?"

"Oh yeah, he said a lot. It wasn't quite so much what
he said as what he did."

"Well………………..! What did he do, some more of His magic tricks? Don't tell me you fell for that?" The two passed into a narrow alley which led through town and towards camp.

"I can't tell you."

Suddenly an arm reached out of the shadows grabbing the nape of Patel's neck. Panicking, the explorer spun quickly around tripping and falling gracelessly to the ground. Strife, emerging from a side alley, held one finger to her lips.

"Quiet, you bonehead, I could hear you ten yards away. Do you want the entire village to know what we're doing here?"

Patel stood, dusting himself off and picking up his wounded pride from the ground. Strife in the meantime had turned to face Logan and resume the pointed questioning.

"So, what happened? Do we need to fear for our lives? Did he confess?"

"No…" Logan responded irritated. Patel, now fully recovered, joined the conversation.

"He brainwashed him."

"Logan, just what did you two talk about?"

"I can't tell you."

"What do you mean, you can't tell us? Don't tell me Albert is right. You don't believe anything this man told you, do you? Look Logan, this man has been deceiving multitudes for generations!"

"Look, I'm just keeping an open mind right now. I talked with him and now I'm going to watch what happens. Our protocol has us here for at least another month anyway. I'm giving him the benefit of the doubt."

"The benefit of the doubt! You mean you're going to ignore the science right in front of you? What happened to 'I'll talk to him and then we'll go'?"

"Let's just see what happens."

"See what happens, are all of those readings we took going to suddenly change their findings?"

Logan stopped, and looking at the two, realized his position.

"We're staying! That's the last of it! Consider it an order."

Patel and Strife stopped, mouths ajar, staring at one another in disgust, as their colleague walked away towards camp.

Sometime later the two gathered to talk alone in the shadows.

"Well, what are we going to do about our two-hundred-pound problem?" Patel despaired.

"I think he'll be alright. He just needs some time to figure out he's been brainwashed. Let's scan a few more events and analyze them for him. That should bring him around."

"And if it doesn't?"

"Drop it. It's not going to be a problem. He's just going through a phase."

Patel, frustrated as much by Strife's rebuff as by Logan's stubbornness, pushed the issue.

"I can't just drop it. I don't think I have to remind you that nothing is more important than this mission. Millions, maybe billions, of lives are hanging on what this mission finds or fails to find. Every moment we delay could bring our nation that much closer to war. You know what we have to do."

The newfound determination in Patel's' voice, and the implication of his questioning, struck a nerve with Strife.

"Are you insane? Do you know what you're proposing?"

"If it comes to that, any one of us is expendable. Those are our orders. You know it as well as I do."

The words echoed with Strife as she watched the diminutive scientist turn and walk off through the village. Moments later, Patel paused briefly to inspect the settings on his wrist paralyzer. For only a second he switched the device to the 'kill' setting. Then steeling himself he quickly reset it to 'stun' and shaking his head pulled his sleeve back over the device.

Logan awakened at dawn to the now familiar aroma of baked bread roasting over an open fire. Wiping the sleep from his eyes he struggled to focus, his mist and fog tainted lenses gradually distinguishing the familiar figure crossing the crowded courtyard. Straining to rouse himself from his bedroll, Logan watched with amusement as the robust figure of the Cyprian stepped gingerly over the scattered sleeping forms on the courtyard lawn. The urge to laugh out loud was almost more than Logan could stand as he watched the two-hundred-pound man dance like a ballerina around the corpse-like disciples. Logan had seen this performance before, usually at breakfast while he and his fellow travelers busied themselves with secretly stuffing their pills into fig skins and hurriedly downing the concoctions. Washed down with a goat's milk chaser, the Chronies' medications had never been detected. Perhaps, Logan thought to himself, it was partially due to the ignominious performance he now witnessed being a regular source of distraction for the camp. This feat, as well as countless others, had endeared the affectionate Levite to Logan for life.

A few seconds later, with Logan hard at work packing his gunny sack and attempting to ignore the banter from his groggy comrades, he heard the familiar laughter. This giant of a man, whom they had come to regard with such a true measure of trust and affection, having once again successfully negotiated the minefield of souls, approached the trio. With a huge grin draped across the corners of his face, he approached slapping his hands on his chest, and leaning back he breathed deeply to take in the crisp winter air.

"Good morning, beloved. Ah, what a beautiful day the heavenly Father has made for us today."

Logan, still a little groggy from an unsettled sleep the night before, looked up in mock disgust.

"Please, Barnabas it's way too early to be so pleasant."

"It is never too early or too late, my friend, to be grateful to the One who gives us new mercies each day. Now rise, beloved, and eat, for we are moving at daybreak."

"Moving, where are we going?" Strife responded.

"Why, to the city of King David, of course. Many believe for the Master's coronation," Barnabas replied with such happiness that even Logan could sense the raw anticipation coursing through proud veins. The three travelers sat there silently looking at their friend in disbelief.

"To Jerusalem?" Patel asked incredulously.

"Yes, dear friends, to Mount Zion, the Holy City of God," the big man repeated almost singing the words, and patting his chest again he continued to soak in the morning air.

"There is no other place on earth quite like it. Now quickly, get ready. You do not want to be left behind."

Barnabas smiled and turning from his stunned friends, walked away. He was barely out of ear shot when Patel began his tirade.

"Oh, yeah, there's no place on earth like it. I almost drowned trying to get out of there last time, and what about that maniac who is trying to kill us? "Logan shook his head in agreement, this time taking a moment to respond.

"I think we all agree that returning to Jerusalem is dangerous."

"Very dangerous," Strife chimed in.

"However, we don't know the exact date of the crucifixion," Logan continued.

"And if we want to go home as soon as possible, we better be there when it happens," Strife reluctantly concluded.

An hour later the three were packed joining their donkeys with Jesus' caravan as it headed down the road via Bethany to Jerusalem. The crowd consisting of Jesus, his twelve disciples and several dozen devoted followers included Logan and his colleagues. The individuals who followed Jesus were a diverse group as evidenced by the variety of dress and customs each displayed. The one thing they held in common was a dogged devotion to their master and a steadfast tendency towards selflessness. No better example was evident to Logan than that set by Jesus' inner circle, who could regularly be observed sharing their meals, their cloaks and their animals with others in need. Sometimes spontaneously, and sometimes with a mere whisper by their leader, the disciples excelled at locating the weakest member of any group and responding. The silent practice hit a tender nerve when Patel, faint from the rigors of travel, was hoisted suddenly and unceremoniously onto the very beast Jesus rode. No disciple regretted following, or even suffering, in the footsteps of such a leader, a point not wasted on Logan.

These times of travel bestowed a second precious reward to weary travelers. For in the silence of the Judean hills, Logan found a new love for solitude. There, left to the peace and quiet of his own thoughts, he was forced to confront two haunting realities. The first was his own eminent demise with the subsequent ravages of disease upon his body, and the second the simple pleasure of lives lived by the common men surrounding him. Only in one other place had he seen such contentedness, Rebecca's farm.

Now, perched high upon the narrow outcropping of a massive limestone crag, the explorer stared into an infinite heaven. To Logan, peering into the depth of firmamental darkness was like drowning in a weightless current of the deepest ocean. The surrounding inky void weighed him down like the welcome arm of an old friend. The suffocation of this awareness he knew to be illusory, for within this darkest of voids, the sky literally dripped with stars he had once called home.

What an odd impression, he thought absorbing what seemed an almost infinite vastness surrounding him. Perhaps it was this feeling of total solitude that led Logan to risk at that moment what had before been unthinkable. In one quick motion, he reached into the security pocket releasing the latch and unzipping the torso unit of his survival suit. His intention was to check that which had been troubling him most for the past few weeks, the status of his disease. As slowly he peeled the shirt from his chest, sheets of dead skin swirled up and into the night air like chaff, revealing hundreds of tiny red and purple branching vessels enveloping both forearms and chest. The moment served to reveal the exoskeleton's Achilles' heel. Its second skin nature meant it provided ultimate protection, but at the cost of being extremely cumbersome to remove. Unable to monitor the disease's course, Logan viewed his chest for the first time since his arrival. Appalled, he stared at the throbbing snakelike vessels undulating just beneath his skin like some alien invader.

Logan felt the first true twinge of despair quietly escape his lips as a deep sigh. The sound foreign to the guardian surprised even himself as he labored to replace the skintight garment. With one last bewildered glance to the heavens, he snapped the final seam shut and turning made his way slowly to the camp below.

Early the next morning the tiny caravan finally reached the hillside of Gethsemane. Perched upon the gentle rise littered with olive trees, the tiny troupe paused to gaze down over Jerusalem's walls. There stood the temple, glimmering like a shining jewel in the morning sunrise; it towered over the city's second quarter. Just adjacent to it stood the fortress of Antonia, which housed thousands of soldiers, some seen marching in formation across the huge courtyard.

Dozens of soldiers trained in swordplay, while others participated in mock hand to hand combat. Still more could be seen mounting horses to join scouting parties being regularly dispatched from the city. Watching silently, Logan's mind played out a dozen different scenarios in which those excursions were desperately looking for him. A gentle squeeze to the shoulder and Logan looked up to meet the brief but knowing smile of Jesus. Slowly the carpenter released his grip before turning to lead the disciples to a higher view of the city.

The narrow trail, a winding steep boulder strewn sandbox of an ascent, was at its widest only passable by one individual at a time. The resulting chaos that followed when Jesus began his climb, amused Logan as disciples and followers alike gave way to a humorous yet polite *divine pecking order.* This afforded Jesus the opportunity to leave the main group behind. Logan, who had no qualms about climbing over any obstruction, animated or otherwise, arrived at the perch just behind the teacher.

There leaning against a bent and twisted olive tree at the very edge of the precipice, Jesus stared wistfully over the city below Him. His first attempts at speaking faltered.

Approaching from behind, Logan could see that Jesus was now leaning much heavier on the gnarled and twisted stump. His head hung in anguish, silently distraught, eyes focused on some nightmare of a distant image.

"Oh Jerusalem… Jerusalem….. My little ones, my children. How I wanted to protect you. How I would have gladly gathered you, sheltered you under my wings but you would not. How I wished I could have been there for you, but you would not..." Jesus wept. A few moments later, a pensive Logan shuffled his feet and cleared his throat.

"Ahem."

"Logan?" Jesus hesitated as Logan moved up just next to him. "A question for you", Jesus added, eyes still wet and with a slight stammer in his speech. Logan looked out over the valley before him, his eyes darting back and forth over the ancient community below.

"Ok..."

"What do you think? Can God be hurt?" Jesus asked. Logan hesitated, thinking a moment before he answered, expecting a trap.

"How could God be hurt? He's all powerful."

"He would have to choose to make himself vulnerable."

"Why? Why would anyone choose to feel pain?"

"For love's sake, Logan, for love's sake. Love anything in this life and your heart will mostly likely be wrung or possibly broken."

"Then why risk that rejection, why even create something that you might later regret." There was only a moment's pause.

"Do you regret your children?"

"No," he replied wistfully.

Logan shook his head, hesitating before speaking again.

"And since no one can love as deeply as God."

This time it was Jesus who looked down, unable to speak or meet Logan's gaze.

"Huh? Infinite love begets infinite rejection, and in so doing self-inflicts infinite pain. What must that feel like?"

"It hurts, like Hell," came the soft reply.

Jesus now moved away from Logan and the rest of the crowd as he kneeled to pray silently for Jerusalem, his head bowed and hands clenched, the tiny trail of tears lost in the fullness of his beard to all but Logan. After twenty minutes, he rose brushing the sand from his borrowed tunic and shrugging a silent apology for dirtying the fabric. Turning from the guardian he addressed his followers.

"We must go into the city for a short while. Some of you may wish to stay outside the city walls. There may be some danger." Confused faces exchanged anxious glances as Jesus led the way back to the narrow trail.

Slowly, the crowd made its way down and over the Mount of Olives passing through the Kidron valley. Within its cocoon the three explorers remained immersed following Jesus past the water gate just outside the outskirts of the lower quarter.

"I can't believe we came back here. We were lucky to get out with our necks last time," Strife complained to her companions carefully out of ear shot of the disciples.

"What I want to know is what was all that about back there? Was he crying? Why is he crying? Maybe He's coming unglued," Patel asked Logan who nodded.

"That *was* unexpected."

"You're doggone right it was unexpected. What's this misdirection game he's playing? He sounds more like a jilted lover than a preacher," Strife responded.

"Look, I'm going with Him." Logan said, "I should be safe as long as I'm with Him. You guys stay out here." The other two looked briefly at their comrade and then at the Roman guards at the city gate. Nodding their heads in agreement, they quickly allowed for the guardian's decision.

"I wouldn't count on Him protecting you, though. Remember, they eventually hang him on a tree," Strife said with a nod towards a nearby group of the soldiers.

"I'll be fine. Somebody has to record this stuff and besides, which one of us is better in a tussle?"

Strife's glaring response flashed back a dagger-like expression.

'*Hmmph! Silent but deadly*' Logan mused to himself as Patel jumped in to break the tension.

"He's got you there.........OK, Logan," he said patting the guardian on the back and walking quickly away, "We'll just wait up there on the hill."

"Be careful!" Strife added.

"Ok mom, I will," Logan responded as smiling he raised his hood and turning re-immersed himself in the large group following Jesus through the open gate. Seconds later and the entourage surrounding the teacher was engulfed by throngs of Jerusalemites rushing to meet the 'rabbi who heals'. With a wall of twelve disciples surrounding the teacher, and a second layer of devoted followers spearheading their way through the mass of humanity, Jesus' delay was only momentary.

The pause, albeit brief, was just long enough for Logan to catch the carpenter's sudden glance westward. Turning, Logan saw nothing at first. Then out of the corner of his eye he glimpsed four roughly hewn crosses on a distant hill. Lifeless shadows hung upon each of the framed structures, their unmoving forms being slowly removed by Roman guards surrounding the plateau. The moment passed as quickly as it came, yet Logan was convinced he was not the only one to have noticed the event.

As Jesus continued his move northward, the disciples stayed close pushing slowly through the crowd. Near his feet lay the blind, the crippled and the diseased, their hands stretching out for even the slightest touch. As he walked Jesus brooded, pausing at times to reach through his disciple's arms to comfort the hand of even the most afflicted.

Ten minutes later, the swollen crowd rounded the next bend in the street. The imposing sight of the nearly completed temple came into Logan's view. Its massive columns splitting the common ground from the divine were surrounded by hundreds of pilgrims of every size, shape and color. Logan turned back to catch Jesus' reaction. The steely eyed expression that greeted him, with its gaze sternly focused on the gleaming tower, was faintly reminiscent of the expressions he recalled of soldiers inserted behind enemy lines.

Fifteen minutes more and they had breached the outer wall of the court of the Gentiles. They briskly penetrated beyond the massive whitewashed colonnades, ignoring the seated classes of young Pharisees in training, and emerged on the other side into a virtual ocean ebbing and flowing with livestock and humanity. Merchants in their turbans and peasants shouted at one another as they argued over sacrificial exchange rates. At two different tables the conflicts erupted into a violent fight. One struggle resulted in the bloody bludgeoning of a fellow Israelite. As they watched, Logan walked up to Jesus standing there spellbound by the chaos around him.

"Do you remember, after your children died?" Jesus spoke, his gaze still transfixed on the bedlam before him. Logan grimaced before nodding, interrupting his attentiveness only long enough to see if any Roman soldiers were following them.

"…….where did you go to mourn?"

Logan's eyes narrowed as he scanned the crowd the two began to pick their way through.

"Home, To my parent's house, Why?"

"Why? Why did you go there?"

"I don't know. It just seems like that's where you go when life falls apart."

"Hmm, home, the one place in this world where we feel safe, a place of rest. Do you know what this is?" Jesus asked pointing to the temple and its surrounding courtyards.

"This? This is Herod's temple, constructed to replace the most religious building in all history, Solomon's temple, one of the foremost archaeological wonders of the ancient world," Logan recited with an air of satisfaction.

"No," He said with a deep sigh. "Logan, this is home - My Father's house. It is where the children of God come to feel safe, to rest. It is a picture of heaven. Everybody wants to feel safe, everybody wants to go home, Logan, because everybody in this life is afraid. E*verybody*."

"What are you afraid of?" Logan shot back. A moment of silence fell on the two as Jesus continued to look away.

"Separation," Jesus answered glancing over at Golgotha and then refocusing on the money changers before him. Logan nodded looking out over the mayhem.

"Don't look now, but your home has become a three ring circus," Logan said pointing at the menagerie.

"An unholy circus, the thief does not want anyone to rest. He came to kill, steal and destroy. He would steal even mankind's rest," Jesus remarked hesitantly, "if we'd allow him to." The determination returned to his gaze.

For only a moment, Logan was distracted looking away at the crowded courtyard littered with proliferating conflicts. The situation seemed to be worsening by the moment and looked for all the world destined to end in a riot. When,

WHACK!

The loud crack of a bull whip rang out with such intensity that Logan literally jumped around prepared for battle.

WHACK! WHACK!

The air split violently as the snap of the whip rang out creating the sensation of static electricity filling the courtyard. At first Logan was confused as to the source of the disruption, until turning he saw standing on the lower rail of a makeshift corral, Jesus swinging a massive whip over his head.

The whip lashed forward again cracking the air loudly as its recoil completed its serpentine over the crowd's head and back to its handler. The effect was an immediate rush of the crowd away from the corral whose gate had now been opened releasing dozens of sheep and oxen. Driven by the relentless assault of the crop the animals began a slow stampede driving their human obstacles from the courtyard. Jesus moved forward, knocking over the few remaining tables not already decimated by the stampede. Eyes glazed with anger, he pursued the money changers, the whizzing whip popping just short of their feet.

"GET OUT!"

Shouting above the uproar of the fleeing crowd, he continued as both man and beast filtered through the stately colonnades lining the courtyard.

"DID YOU HEAR ME? I SAID GET OUT... I SAID GET OUT!"

One especially reluctant exchanger, having raised his tunic, was hurriedly stuffing both it and his loincloth with handfuls of coins. As he turned to run, Jesus caught sight of the greedy merchant and unleashed the twisting serpent onto the offender's bountiful booty. The resulting explosion of coins and linen echoed through the courtyard as the terrified swindler escaped with his treasures exposed for all the world to see. Logan's amusement was echoed by the crowd surrounding the plaza as hundreds filling the colonnades beheld the emboldened Nazarene cleaning house. They were not alone. From high atop the colonnade walls the High Priest, surrounded by a wall of Pharisees and Sadducees, stared steely eyed at the solitary figure below.

"IT IS WRITTEN, THIS IS A HOUSE OF PRAYER, BUT YOU HAVE MADE IT A DEN OF THIEVES!" Jesus shouted his voice echoing from one corner of the courtyard to the other. The silent stood there, some terrified and others mesmerized.

Having cleared from the courtyard, the worshippers watched as a new disturbance unexpectedly erupted. For far on the courtyard's southern wing, roughly a dozen well-armed and brutish appearing temple guards had rudely shoved their way through the crowded colonnades into the now deserted enclosure. The enormous men were adorned ominously in white robes stained crimson from previous temple intrusions, and brandishing gleaming double-edged swords, surged forward. Logan moved instinctively forward as if to protect Jesus, his hand reaching to activate the weapon on his wrist. Surprisingly it was Jesus, who raising his hand, warned Logan off, the guards freezing suddenly at the sight of the Nazarene.

Their commander, a burly, one-eyed mountain of a man sporting an open cavity above his left cheek, was the first to stop short. The sword he bore in his right hand froze in its upright position, as looking upward he sought direction from the high priest. Logan watched, his hand still hovering over the futuristic weapon on his wrist, as he carefully scanned the courtyard trying to determine what would happen next. Hundreds of eyes stared back, each one locked on the tussle playing out between the man in the plaza and the figure on the balcony.

The intimidating hush oppressing the plaza weakened and a middle-aged priest stepped proudly from the shadows. The richly ornate robes, intricately woven around his torso and thighs, highlighted his chiseled jaw bone and deep-set eyes, features that could easily have branded him a politician in Logan's century.

And then the whip dropped. Falling from the carpenter's hand to the ground, it stirred the dust as it coiled itself in a settled heap.

"Caiaphas, do something with those guards!" a somewhat younger yet similarly adorned Pharisee whispered through clenched teeth. Caiaphas stood there, eyeing the young antagonist through suspicious eyes. He hesitated as if deep in thought.

"No… I think not," he spoke haltingly. "He has offended the people and driven them from their worship, disrupted their routine and interfered with their celebrations. They will remember this. Someday….. we will use this against him. We just need to wait, be patient, and restrain the guards. Leave Him to the Romans for now."

At this, a new clamor arose at the edge of the colonnades. A squadron of Roman foot soldiers, dispatched by Herod, to break up what he assumed to be a potential political uprising, arrived to force their way into the courtyard. The temple guards immediately reacted to this new threat, rushing from Jesus and his followers to confront the force and prevent a desecration of the temple. As they blocked the entrance of the pagan force, the tiny band of Jesus and his followers slipped silently out the opposite entrance blending quickly into the chaotic crowd.

Logan, who recorded the entire event, was the last to leave. Walking over he stooped to retrieve the leather serpent still coiled on the sand covered tiles. As he studied its intricate design, admiring each beautifully woven lace, he marveled at the expert precision with which it had been wielded. Seconds later, whip tied to his waist, he was running to catch up with the others.

On the one side of the temple grounds, Roman foot soldiers were engaged in a shouting match with the temple guards. Unaccustomed to retreating, the Centurion finally acquiesced, thus allowing his squad to reluctantly side step the horde of people led by Caiaphas exiting the holy ground. The frustrating encounter left no captive to take to Herod, and sent the now diverted squadron circumventing the outer temple walls and out into the swollen marketplace. They found, as they turned to pursue their prey, a sea of humanity which had completely swallowed the elusive 'Egyptians'. In Roman eyes they were spies, masquerading as Jesus' followers, set on destabilizing the normally peaceful sect.

While the soldiers searched the grounds bordering the temple, Jesus and his small band of followers were making their way down the streets of Jerusalem. Unnoticed by the packed crowds pushing and shoving into the holy city, the dedicated troupe formed a human chain weaving through the chaos. As Logan struggled to keep pace with the rest of the group, he suddenly noticed that the crowds were dissipating.

Two narrow alleyways later, they emerged upon an unfamiliar section of the city where Jesus was making a beeline for a somewhat dilapidated city gate. The crumbling edifice, with its beams rotting on the very hinges that hung the doors, bore no resemblance to the grandeur of its neighbors. In addition, the size of the crowds at this “Sheep Gate”’ was by comparison to others non-existent.

Led by the teacher, the small band entered the opening which bordered one corner of the courtyard surrounding the expansive pool of Bethesda. As they entered, a sudden wave of nausea, resulting from unexpected exposure to the reek of oozing blood and body fluids, the very scent of suffering humanity, caught Logan off guard. There in the courtyard, huddled miserably under the surrounding porticos, lay hundreds of the crippled and diseased. Only a few of the younger Pharisees, having spied Jesus’ entrance, dared to follow. Adding to this stench was the ritual rinsing in the first pool of the entrails of sheep once sacrificed at the temple. Carefully, Jesus and His disciples picked their way to the edge of the pool. The stench from rotting flesh, excrement and entrails competed with the groans which filled the air surrounding this side of the first pool. Sullied by pockets of drifting algae and excrement, the turbid fluid, with its crimson stained water, was originally a naturally occurring crystal clear spring.

Halfway down the descending steps of the ancient pool, an elderly man sat. Fully clothed, he had attempted to bathe his body and clean his open sores when he had fallen unable to get up. Logan watched with compassion as a handful of healthy, yet harried Jerusalemites skirted the pool stifling the instinct to respond to the old man’s pleas for help. The noon heat, like a propane stove, cooked the reddish stew until a rancid odor wafted effortlessly from the water, its nauseating effect sending Logan and two other disciples vomiting to their knees.

Now rid of their lunch, the three looked up to find Jesus shedding his outer cloak and tunic, handing them over to the recovering guardian.

"Here, hold this would you? I wouldn't trust it to anyone else," he smiled as he stepped forward clothed only in his loin cloth.

"What are you doing? The Romans could show up any minute now? No-o-o! You are not going to go down into that!" Logan protested stuffing the garment into his bag. Jesus stepped gingerly into the pool towards the helpless man. Moved to help, but repulsed by the odor, the guardian could only look on helplessly as Jesus extended his hand. Immediately, as the first of his two feet touched the putrid liquid, the wake left by Jesus' legs turned stunningly clear. As the Nazarene moved deeper into the pool, an entire path of transparency followed each step. Moments later, Jesus was squatting by the man on the stone tiles lining the pool's edge. Logan however was oblivious to this, his mind's eye locked instead onto the current of transparency wafting slowly through the turbid media.

He was not alone, as a low murmur gradually spread throughout the disabled mob gathered around the water's edge. A commotion arose as dozens of the diseased and crippled dragged themselves into the clearing pond.

"The pool is stirred, the angels…! The angels…!" a voice from the crowd cried out.

Soon dozens lined the pool's edge as Jesus, his lower half dripping wet, approached another man feebly attempting to drag himself to join the crowd. The man was obviously crippled his legs folded to one side and atrophied from decades of disuse. Standing near the man, Jesus quickly draped himself in the unblemished dryness of his outer cloak and cleared his throat. The man at his feet froze, too fearful to look up at the cloaked figure whose shadow enveloped him. Seeing this, Logan tossed his bag aside and approached the man intending to help. Immediately the surprisingly strong arm of the teacher brushed him aside. Dumbfounded, he wobbled back as Jesus, looking out over the crowded pool, spoke.

"Well?"

Straining to block the noon day's glare, the invalid looked up at the cloaked shadow lost in the contrast of the burning rays.

"Uh? Uh? What, 'er, are you speaking to me, sir?" the paralyzed man stammered. Gently Jesus spoke again pointing at the rest of the crowd making their way to the pool.

"Do you really wish to get well?"

The young disciples assigned by the Pharisees to follow Jesus only now located him in the corner of the courtyard. Out of breath form running, they looked on with a strange mixture of wonder and indignation. Jesus suppressed the urge to glance their way, casting instead a half glance in Logan's direction eliciting a silent smirk.

"Sir, I have - no - one…" The man looked away, a lifetime of despair written across his face.

"I see." Jesus reflected.

"When the water stirs, I can't get in. Always someone enters the water ahead of me and is set free." Growing silent, he began again to slowly drag himself towards the pool. Jesus stooped, stopping the man's efforts with a gentle hand upon his shoulder. Standing now, he spoke where all could hear Him.

"Do you wish to get well?"

The man sat there, propped up by his arms with his head hanging. He nodded silently.

"Take up your mat," Jesus said, this time not hesitating to look directly at the Pharisees…"and walk!"

For thirty-eight years the legs, which had run only as a boy, had not moved. Now, the barely perceptible but undeniable twitch of a muscle spasm caused the man to gasp. Buried down within the dark entangled catacombs of his soul, a tiny spark of hope flickered escaping as the feeblest of whimpers.

And then it happened. His legs moved for the first time in thirty-eight years. At first, it was only a twitch, an uncontrollable tremble of both limbs as the unaccustomed muscles reacted to the sudden flood of neurological input. Then the feeble man began shaking uncontrollably, tears flooding his eyes and rolling silently down swollen astonished cheeks. Fixed in an expression of astonishment, he sat fully upright for the first time in almost forty years.

"What? What...! WHAT - HAS - HAPPENED - TO - ME?" the man thundered to all around him as he looked up at the teacher. Slowly, leaning on Jesus' arm the man stood, half shaking from lack of balance and half from trepidation at the one who held him. Now others approached helping to steady him, but he pushed them away.

"PRAISE GOD...! PRAISE GOD...! I CAN STAND! I CAN STAND!" Immediately he took his first shuffling footstep.

"I CAN WALK! I CAN WALK!"

Turning he looked for Jesus, who with his disciples had melted away into the crowd leaving behind yet another mesmerized group of young Pharisees.

"Where is he?" the man squeaked through sobs. Crying violently, he picked up his mat and rolled it up under his arm. Desperately he looked around.

"WHERE IS HE...? WHERE IS THAT MAN?" the elderly man shouted as he stumbled on shaky limbs through the portico's crowd.

Beginning with those nearest to him, he scoured the crowd, all eyes transfixed on him, including those standing in the pool; but none seemed to know the whereabouts of the man from Galilee.

Just beyond the Essene Gate, Jesus and his disciples walked away from Jerusalem. Patel, Strife and the others joined the group which drifted off heading across the Kidron valley.

CHAPTER EIGHTEEN
A Traitor in the Midst

Someone once reflected the more complicated your mind, the simpler your recreation needed to be. This axiom was being increasing proved true in the present life of Logan. Constantly reclined under the endless sea of lights perforating the Judean canopy of darkness, he reflected upon the contrast between the boundless display of majesty above him and the chaos of his own inner turmoil. Fortunately, Galilean magic was breaking through this spell, forcing Logan to consider a universal reality he had previously not. 'After all *Nothing comes from nothing*', he mused staring at the expanse above and recalling his conversations with Patel. Years of scientific, engineering and military training had taught Logan to think rationally. Logic dictated that if the universe had begun to exist, there must have been a cause, and if that cause had started the universe at a unique point in time, it must have been intentional. Intent implied purpose, and if there was a purpose, it only made sense that it would be revealed. But Christianity just seemed so odd to him, so unpredictable. How could something so quirky possibly be true?

On the other hand, so many things in nature seemed odd to him when he had first learned of them. He remembered his reaction the first time in sixth grade that

Johnny Adams told him about the birds and the bees. "No way!" he'd said. "That's disgusting."

And what about the first time he studied the solar system and began as a boy to dream of going to space. It too had all seemed so odd, when he discovered that the planets were not all the same size, nor made the same, nor orbiting at equal distances from the sun. He had expected they would all increase in size or have the same number of moons. Instead one had none, another four and one had a ring. So if the created order was in some very interesting ways so quirky, so odd, why did he have such great difficulty with the Christian faith being so unconventional? In his more honest moments, he had to admit that this peculiarity might actually work in its favor.

As he stared upward, disturbed only by the feathery light touch of a gentle winter breeze, his senses gradually began to entice him from his contemplation. Slowly the crisp evening air, tinged by the aroma of roasting lamb, garnished by the loving hands of the women who followed Jesus, awoke his hunger. For the most part the small group had grown silent, the night air disturbed only by the crackle and pop of the enormous fire in the center of the camp. Perched nearby on an adjacent boulder and looking down over the roaring fire, the *Egyptians* reclined to eat. As was their custom, they drank wine from lambskin canteens carried all day and warmed on the flanks of their donkeys. The brooding silence, which had hung over the trio for most of the afternoon, now broke as they stared into the distant fire.

"You haven't said two words since you left Jerusalem.

What happened back there?" Strife insisted.

"Oh nothing, other than our man here threw a temper-tantrum, stripped down almost naked and waded into a cesspool, all-the-while making a paralyzed man walk and throwing the Pharisees and Romans into complete confusion. Just a typical walk in the park with Jesus," Logan smiled tersely, not looking up from his meal.

"He was naked?" Patel choked.

"Except for a loin cloth, for only a second," Logan nodded.

"Wonder what the convent nuns would say about that?" Strife mused, a smirk on her face. Logan smiled, and Patel laughed out loud.

"Interesting, are you saying our hero was disrobed when he healed the paralytic?" Patel observed.

"He was wearing only his outer cloak."

"Was he wearing his tunic?" Patel reiterated.

"Look, Strife, will you tell Albert here to stop repeating the same stupid questions?"

"Gladly, shut up, Albert. Now, where was it?" She repeated.

"What?" Logan jested, shoving more food in his mouth.

"The tunic, you doofus," Strife responded giving him a mock punch to the upper arm.

"Ow! That hurt! It was in my bag."

"By the way," Patel quipped, "my name is Nick. Well then, that tunic couldn't be his power source,"

"Why not? Logan, how close were you to him?"

"I'd say I was standing less than two meters from him and the bag was on the ground one meter behind him. Why?" Logan responded, trying to disguise the intense curiosity this line of reasoning was inciting.

"That's simple enough. He just has to stand close to it."

"Yeah, I suppose it might be possible for him to use some type of brainwave pattern connectivity like the technology we use to control artificial limbs," Patel commented.

"Perhaps…" Logan said nodding slowly, "but I'm really curious to look at the biometry. I'll bet we see how he does it."

"I agree. If there is some type of connectivity, the EEG function of the biometer will show it."

"Ok, Logan, let's set up the display," Strife agreed removing the equipment from her survival suit.

Withdrawing further from the main crowd, they relocated behind a secluded cluster of boulders while the rest of the disciples were preparing to bed down. Logan engaged the hologram display as the three explorers lay back on their sides in a tightly knit circle. Seconds later and the entire scene was being replayed accompanied by a detailed analysis of the electromagnetic energy employed. Logan watched with incredulous fascination as the scene unfolded, transitioning from the clearing of the pool to the channeling of energy from Logan's shoulder bag, through to Jesus and into the paralyzed man's body.

"Fascinating. Well, I'm satisfied," Strife exclaimed as she rolled over to go to sleep. "He's a fraud."

"Pretty slick technology," Patel chuckled sitting up to watch a replay of the images before him. Logan stared at his companions and then lying back quietly, a wave of deep frustration slowly began to descend over him. He spread his hands behind his head. Gazing intently once again at the stars above him, he whispered tersely.

"Once I was blind… but now I see."

In the early pre-dawn hours of the following morning, Logan rose from his bedroll and silently stole off up the hillside alone. Under a moonlit sky, perched high on a rocky precipice, Logan popped the back off of his biometry wrist unit and unplugged the circuit Patel and Strife had inserted months earlier. Holding the tiny circuit board up, he compared it to an identical circuit from a repair kit in his suit pocket. The number on the repair kit circuit read

Model ID **HA1SCU1.415.01C.**

The circuit he removed from his scanner read

Model ID **HA1SCU1.415.01E D.O.D.** .

"*D.O.D.*, what the heck is that?"

A number of theoretical combinations flashed across Logan's mind. Most of them had something or another to do with digital data output, or some other technical jargon dealing with nano-circuitry. Then suddenly it hit him.

"*Department of Defense*," he mused, his eyes rolling back in his head at his own naiveté.

Reassembling the unit using the repair circuit, Logan activated the scanner and began to systematically reanalyze some of the data collected to date.

There before his eyes, two dimensional images of the miracles performed by Jesus over the past six months and their analysis appeared on his *Nano-lens*. The predawn hour passed quickly as Logan methodically scanned and reanalyzed as many of the events recorded as time would allow. Finally, with his mind filled with images and data whizzing by, he sat there, arms and legs folded, staring into space.

In the briefest of moments a new reality with all its far-fetched and preposterous implications began to take root in Logan's mind. Instinctively his mind's first reflex was to struggle violently against what he was beginning to believe. As the first rays of the morning sun sliced their way through the crevices of a distant Judean hillside, Logan sat transfixed on the computer-generated scene of the pool of Bethesda.

The screen flashed a warning Logan had never seen before until this last hour, and despite having seen it a dozen times since then, he still found it hard to accept.

DATA INCONSISTENT WITH KNOWN PHYSICAL LAWS

Gradually, the sunlight seeped over the horizon in an ever-increasing flood of light, descending like an overflowing waterfall, it splashed down upon the bewildered explorer waking him from his stupor.

"I've seen quite enough. 'There's more than one Judas in this troupe'……, but which one?"

Hurriedly he rose to join the early morning routine.

It was noon on the dusty road to Capernaum as Jesus and his disciples made their way towards home. The winter sun had reached its familiar peak in the sky over Palestine stirring a bevy of 'dirt devils' and a minor dust storm announcing the impending arrival of Jesus' caravan. The small group of followers, shrouded head to toe in their dark woolen cloaks, resembled more a funeral dirge as haggard and hungry they trudged their way slowly through the city gates. There amongst the outermost fringe of the troupe entered the three 'beasts of burden' bearing their weary explorers.

"Well, we're almost back to home base." Patel proclaimed solidifying his reputation for announcing the obvious and eliciting the customary obligatory eye rolls from his two companions.

"Yeah, he's as predictable as clockwork. Back to recharge his batteries before going out again," Strife responded with an uncharacteristic tone of agreement.

For a moment, Logan said nothing musing at her new found sensitivity to Patel while stifling the sudden twinge of anger pricking his consciousness. Surprised by his own growing sense of defensiveness at the verbal barb thrown by at least one who knew it to be false, Logan couldn't help responding.

"Hey, whatever happened to your lightning bolt theory?"

"That was Albert's idea here."

"He must have a hidden source that he can access when they're not looking. I bet if we monitor Him here in Capernaum, we can catch him recharging red-handed," Patel predicted.

"Yes, we both think it's an excellent idea," Strife echoed looking to Logan for a reaction. Logan just smiled.

"Ok. I'll go along with it on one condition."

"Only one?" Strife retorted.

"You agree that we will all review the data together before you upload it to the cylinder."

"Standard operating procedure," Patel piped in with a grin. "That's the way we're supposed to be doing it anyway.".

"Seems a bit formal all the sudden, but ok, agreed," Strife complied.

Logan nodded and moved away to join the rest of the group leaving Patel and Strife alone again.

"I'm still worried about him," the diminutive scientist whispered as he watched the guardian walk away.

"And why would that be," Strife quizzed, looking down her nose like a third grade teacher at her unruly pupil.

"Because my dear, he has been hanging out with our narcissistic carpenter. They've taken a dozen private strolls in the early morning hours. God knows what kind of ideas he's planted in our good man's head."

Strife hesitated before responding.

"Logan's a big boy. He can take care of himself."

"And if he can't?"

"You're overreacting again."

"Look, Strife, we have got to be on the same page about this! If he's been compromised then our data is in danger. Too many lives hang in the balance here to leave it up to a post-traumatized soldier."

Strife hesitated.

"What are you saying? Are you implying Logan's not fit?"

“I’m not saying anything. He’s vulnerable, though. He’s lost his family and he’ll do anything and believe anything if thinks he’ll get them back.”

“So, what do you want me to do? Shoot him? Are you insane? That’s the only way you or I are going to stop him,” she replied incredulously.

“I’m just saying we’ve got to be prepared to do whatever it takes to finish this mission. Whatever it takes! I for one have no intention of dying in this God forsaken place. I need to go home.”

“Just calm yourself. We’ll figure it out.” Strife stepped back waving off the explorer. She turned heading back towards the main group, struggling to hide the concern on her face.

Later that evening the group settled in again at the warmly lit stone house of Simon Peter. The twelve disciples had positioned themselves into small groups, each group reclining by a dimly lit oil lamp. Jesus himself sat on a small woven floor mat, reclining by the main dinner table, picking at the remains of a humble yet lovingly prepared meal. Peter, John and James, still covered in their dusty robes, reclined nearby. Strife was one of several women who were diligently hovering over the four men seated by the teacher. Jesus smiled winsomely at the women, amused at the reaction of the other three men who seemed agitated by all the fussing going on around them. Peter tried to wave off one especially attentive female.

"Ok, ok, that’s quite enough. I’m not a baby that you have to wipe my mouth and burp me too." His thundering baritone provoked a collective outburst of laughter which emanated from all corners of the room.

"No, No, my boisterous friend, we all know you need no help, for you are very talented in many areas," Jesus quipped causing everyone in the room to laugh.

"But Lord, you know we’re all made but from dust." John retorted, patting his robe creating a small dust cloud.

"Except for our friend Peter here. He was made from the dust of a camel’s seat, thus explaining his almost endless supply of ‘hot air’," James interjected as more laughter filled the room.

Suddenly, Jesus who had been enjoying the moment of levity began to choke, as if a date or some other obstruction were blocking his throat. Rushing to his side, John gently supported his friend helping him to sit in an upright position. The sudden concern for their friend and teacher was amplified by Jesus pallor and obvious weakness. The travelers took special notice of the change.

"Master, are you all right? Can I get you some water?

Are you ill?" John stammered with concern deeply etched in the corners of his face. By now everyone in the room had grown silent.

"No, thank you, my good friend, I'm fine."

Again, he coughed, almost choking.

"I just need a little rest. It must be the dust." Jesus wheezed as he struggled to his feet.

"Oh Rabbi, I am so sorry. I knew the lamb was too rare," Martha replied, her tone reflecting the concern on her face. Jesus looked pale as he steadied himself struggling to flash a brief smile.

"Martha, dear Martha, the food was wonderful. I am just very tired."

The cough returned.

"Here Rabbi, come to the guest room. There are blankets on the floor. You need to rest," Martha whispered gently as John escorted their unsteady leader to the back room.

Strife watched intently from the opposite side of the room. Gently laying her serving tray to the side, she carefully made her way through the crowd ignoring the beckoning of more than one empty cup. Then, unnoticed by the disciples, she slipped silently into the darkened hallway just outside the back room. Ducking into the shadows to avoid detection, she quietly waited for Martha and John to leave the chamber. Then with all the others once again engaged in conversation, she slipped down the hall hovering just outside the doorway hesitating briefly to report her observations.

"Something's happening".

"What's going on?" Logan replied.

"He's sick!"

"Yeah, that's what you've been telling me all along, so?"

"No, doofus, He's become ill. They've taken him to the guest room. I'm going to peek in."

"Be careful." Logan insisted. Patel who was listening also piped in.

"I didn't think gods ever got sick?"

"Evidently this one does."

Strife slipped past the simple linen curtain separating the small dimly lit bedroom from the outer hall. A moment later and her eyes had adjusted to the almost complete darkness. A chill ran up her spine as the cool breeze blowing through the portico's large open windows brushed against the exposed skin of her face and hands.

Unintelligible, muffled sounds like the low guttural moan of a man in the last throes of death greeted her as she settled into the shadows of one corner of the room. At first she saw nothing. But soon, there in the dimness of one corner, a man came into view. He was crouched against the limestone wall. His head was in his hands, and he sat unmoving and sobbing quietly. Frozen half from fear and half from disbelief, Strife strained to hear each anguished whisper.

"Abba", the words drifted on the wisp of a breath barely discernible even to Strife's enhanced hearing.

"Father in heaven, please, help me," the voice pleaded cracking with sorrow.

"What can I do with you, Ephraim? I have never known such sorrow. They are - ***so*** - blind. No matter what I try, no matter what I do, they ignore me, believing only lies against me."

Seemingly oblivious to the presence of an intruder, Jesus turned and straining, pulled himself to his feet. Leaning against the large open window, he stared upward at the star filled sky. Strife moved silently for a better angle, her efforts rewarding her with only a momentary glance of the Nazarene's renowned tear stained countenance.

"Oh, my child, I have loved you as my own son. Yet the more I love you, the further you run. Can't you see it is I who have led you all the way? Holding you with my own hands, I - have taught you to walk. I - have healed your wounds. I have fed you?"

"You have eyes and yet you cannot see!"

"How can I give you up, my bride?" At this the discourse broke down into unbridled sobbing again.

"How can I hand you over to the one you have chosen? How can I give you over to be destroyed? Oh, my heart breaks within me."

Bewildered, Strife could watch no more. Visibly shaken, she silently slipped out of the room and into the hallway's dark shadows.

Early the next morning, the courtyard gently stirred from its slumber, awakening the surrounding world with its bustle of activity. Roused by conversation, the disciples struggled to escape their nocturnal cocoons neatly encircling the burned-out ash heaps of extinguished campfires. Logan and Patel, on the other hand, were sleeping soundly, their avalanche of cacophony long since relegated to the group's outer fringes.

Imperceptibly at first and then with more effect, several small drops of water began dribbling down Logan's cheek tracing their way down his neckline. Initially the irritant went unnoticed, until finally the sleeping chrononaut groused from his slumber. Agitated, Logan sat up suddenly emitting a noise somewhat resembling a cross between a bear and a lion. Strife appeared close beside him, and using a finger beside her smirking lips, she slapped the other hand over his open mouth. Gritting his teeth, the soggy chrononaut silently rose from his bed. Carefully, he picked his way past obstacles leaving a rattling Patel behind and following dutifully to the stable behind Martha's house. Draped over Strife's shoulder was a half full skin commonly used to carry wine. The prospect of being alone with Strife and a bottle of wine created in Logan an unanticipated rise in heart rate prompting the seasoned warrior to check his surroundings before continuing 'the pursuit'. Noting the 'coast to be clear' he followed unassumingly taking the opportunity to protest.

"Thank you, your highness, for almost drowning me."

"Think nothing of it, she said handing him a rag, "You would have done the same for me." Then holding the wine flask high she turned.

"Now shut up and come over here. I've got something to show you and we're going to celebrate."

"This better be good."

"It is. I shot this last night, while the others were distracted. Remember, when he went to the room in the back? You are going to wet your pants."

"What, twice in one morning?" Logan flashed her a quick grin.

Strife crouched in the softly lit stable exposing her right forearm as she accessed the controls allowing her biometer to interface with Logan's. Facing one another in the tiny stall of the straw-littered shack, Strife passed the wine skin as she set up the display apparatus.

A moment later and the tiny holographic projector flickered to life with the familiar greenish glow. The shimmering images, outlined with the eerie halo of the night vision effect, began as Strife dodged silently out of sight within the shadows of the narrow hallway. Watching carefully until Jesus was left alone in the room, she silently slipped in through the curtained doorway, surprised to discover Jesus curled in a semi-fetal position lying on the floor.

"You found him like that, on the floor?"

"Yes, Shhh!"

There wrapped in a woolen blanket he lay silently except for barely audible sobbing. Strife moved stealthily, unnoticed by the object of her attention. Like a poor documentary, the image shifted angle abruptly until it finally stabilized on a robed hand reaching out from the blanket. Sifting through the debris of the mud and tile floor, the trembling fingers probed the roughhewn stones stopping at one familiar projection and lifting the cracked tile. Reaching into the shadows, the hand retrieved a glowing cylindrically shaped object wrapped in a small velvet blanket. Un-wrapping the object and aligning the capsule's electrodes to a similarly shaped metallic electrode embedded in the tunic's sleeve, the two devices connected. As the scene panned back, Jesus could be seen to relax, his tunic radiating a luminescent glow which filled the room. The floating image dissolved leaving a stunned Logan in its wake.

"So that is how he does it. A quick trip to his battery pack and Zippo! He's his old self again. Just like a junkie getting a fix," Strife mused with a nod of her head and a self-satisfied smile. Logan sat there silently, gazing intently through the virtual images floating before him; at the raven-haired scientist before him. It was several seconds before he choked out a mildly tepid response.

"Where did you get these images?"

Taken aback by Logan's tone, Strife stared back before hesitantly responding with her own sarcasm.

"I bought them online, of course. I just trotted down to the local wireless coffee shop and downloaded them from the 22nd century. What do you mean where did I get these? I was there."

"You were in the room with him when this occurred? Was Patel there too?"

"I was there alone. Patel was with you. You know that," Strife retorted, her tone growing steadily angrier.

"And he didn't see you?" Logan asked pointing to the man in the floating image. Strife shifted her position popping an entire fig into her mouth as Logan observed the subtle stiffening of her posture. Smiling she continued eating while she talked and crossing her legs she shifted her gaze from Logan's eyes.

"He's pretty incapacitated when his battery cells run low. It must be some type of biogenic interface that not only is controlled by him but affects his physiology too. He was a basket case, never even knew I was there." She smiled weakly, obviously attempting to control her irritation. At this point Logan relaxed attempting to change his tone and body language to keep her talking.

"And this battery pack interfaced with his tunic?" he said pointing to the fading image.

"You got it, fly boy. Or maybe I should say we've got it - all right here on biometry. He's a 100% megalomaniac fraud. All we've got to do now is get home."

Logan having risen from where he was sitting restrained the impulse to confront her head-on choosing instead to continue probing verbally with his back to her.

"Are you sure that was the same tunic he always wears? Could he have a spare? What does Patel think?"

"Patel, he's an idiot! That Einstein still hasn't figured out why you keep calling him Albert. As for a spare, don't you think I've watched every move of that man? He sleeps, eats and goes to the bathroom in that tunic. It never leaves his highness' backside and for good reason too! Now, drop the inquisition and let's decide how we're going to get home. Ok? What do you say?"

A moment passed before Logan turned and looking her in the eye, calmly responded.

"If you're sure, then there's only one thing I can say."

Strife stared back, arms crossed and a confident smile on her face.

"Go ahead. Say it. I'm a genius? I want to hear you say it."

Logan slid over to the one rickety chair covered in dust and propped carelessly against the nearby wall. Leaning back in the chair, his arms folded behind his head and feet propped up on the table - he quipped.

"Oh, you're gifted alright. You do have a gift. You're probably the most convincing liar I've ever met." Suddenly he sat the chair down and looked her straight in the eye, "and that is saying a lot."

The look on Strife face's contained a strange mixture of rage, confusion and surprise.

"What! What are you talking about?"

"Just what I said, you're a liar, on the level of a 'Mata Hari' if I had to surmise. My bet is that when you were helping Patel upgrade our telemetry units you slipped in your own corrupted boards. I removed the jury rigging you installed. What I can't figure out is, who helped you design all this, and why?"

"Patel was right about you. You're insane."

Logan rocked back on the wobbly chair, his gaze dropping to the floor as he considered the accusation.

"Yes, I thought so at first, too. What I was asking myself to believe, I thought was impossible, but then I found the evidence and was forced to conclude that you're the one who's one brick short of a full load."

"I'm a scientist."

"And a corrupt one at that. You contaminated the samples and skewed the data. I'd say that also makes you a traitor."

"Prove it!"

"I have all the proof I need right here," pointing to his knapsack.

"What, your dirty laundry?" Strife laughed as she viewed the rough woolen bag hanging from Logan's shoulder.

"No…." Logan pronounced, "***His***!" he said opening the sack so she could see the Nazarene's tunic. Pulling the tunic from inside his knapsack, he held it in the air.

"You see, there's nothing incredible about Jesus' tunic, because he's not wearing his tunic. He's wearing mine! He's been wearing it for weeks now."

Logan turned as he stood up and was suddenly sent crashing towards the wall by a glancing blow to the head. Stunned, he turned to defend himself but not before he received another crashing blow, this time to the ribcage. Strife stood there, a steely eyed glare emblazoned across her face, as she wielded a stout wooden pole with martial arts precision. Logan steadied himself, his survival suit having activated automatically after the first blow. Its protective properties, having shielded his torso, could do nothing for the fireworks display going on inside his head now.

"I told them not to choose you. I told them you were an outsider. I knew you couldn't be trusted. But, oh no, they had to have a hero. They said we need someone the public trusts, an American military hero," she declared spitefully as she swung at him again. This time he reacted but Strife was still faster. Another crashing blow glanced off his back, its force sending him tumbling across the floor.

"They went to all that trouble, just to make you available. What a disappointment you are," she continued slamming him again to the floor. Logan rolled to a sitting position attempting to get his bearings while dusting himself.

"What trouble?" he replied.

"What trouble?" she yelled back, "The trouble that's in my head now! The trouble that's killing me! All so we could free you up, separating you from your tender earthly ties. Who could have known you actually loved them?"

"What are you saying Strife? What earthly ties?" Logan demanded, "What have you done?"

"Wouldn't you like to know, Daddy dear?" she curdled her words pointing a twisted finger at the guardian. "Help me! Help me," she shrieked her face suddenly red with rage. Logan's felt his blood rush to his feet as his heart began pounding. "Cute little boy and girl, too bad they had die so painfully. Now it's your turn."

Suddenly the door opened, startling Strife. In that split second, Logan leaped up slamming his nemesis with an old fashioned body block against the back wall, knocking her head against one of the roughly hewn wooden support beams. Dazed, she collapsed unable to resist as Logan quickly removed the storage cylinder from her suit and stored it in his own. A bewildered Patel entered, wide eyed, looking around at the disheveled room.

"What in Sam Hill is going on here?" Patel exclaimed, distracting Logan just long enough for a groggy Strife to act. With a sweeping motion of her legs, she knocked Logan to the floor, and leaping vanished through the open window and down the alleyway. Logan sat on the floor catching his breath while Patel just stood there, hands on his head, looking down at the empty wine bottle and his comrade in the dirt.

"I knew it would come to this," he proclaimed wagging his finger in the air at Logan; "never force a girl who wears leather to wait on you hand and foot!"

Logan looked up at his annoying friend as he rubbed the burgeoning lump just above his occipital protuberance. Then staring into space he proclaimed.

"Houston, we have a problem."

CHAPTER NINETEEN
A Scandalous Conclusion

Night had fallen over Capernaum and the small group of faithful disciples that still followed Jesus prepared for another evening by the fireside. Strife's disappearance two weeks previously was taken in passing by the group as just one of many defections that had occurred recently. Many of the faithful had fallen away. Jesus was well known by now to have the equivalent of a price upon his head. Having insulted the Pharisees, 'desecrated' the temple, offended Herod by rejecting royal invitations and 'harbored' individuals suspected of planning an insurrection against Rome, Jesus had succeeded in offending just about everyone in society. Thus the threat of violence and the seemingly erratic behavior on the part of Jesus had taken its toll. At one point in the caravan, more than two dozen followers left the group when Jesus appeared to condone the practice of cannibalism. While Logan and Patel were shocked they persisted, deciding to accept Barnabas' explanation that Jesus was speaking metaphorically.

As the faithful prepared to bed down for the night, Patel and Logan met secretly outside of Martha's courtyard. In the tiny stable behind the stone building, Logan and Patel began another night of painstakingly reanalyzing the past six month’s biometry. Methodically, each event was reviewed and recorded with uncorrupted algorithms installed by Patel’s own hand.

One of the many events was the healing of Peter's mother-in-law from her extreme fever. Hunkered down on a layer of clean straw, the two explorers watched as the three-dimensional display began its methodical replay. Alternating between images of Jesus bending over the woman and changing biological data, their nano-lenses displayed the dying woman’s changing DNA structure.

“Now hang on a minute here. No, no, this, this must be wrong. This is impossible. The instruments indicate no measurable energy of any wavelength on any channel,” Patel anxiously observed as he repeatedly rechecked the system’s calibration.

“That’s not possible. Perhaps the instruments are still not working correctly?”

Logan watched intently as Patel checked and rechecked the system’s calibration.

“I’ve checked the circuitry three times. Everything checks out. Your scans show your disease, mine show my disease. Yet these other readings record no measurable electromagnetic radiation at all being employed. As a matter of fact there is no measurable transference of any kind. So, how is this happening?” Patel’s wild gestures were enough to amuse Logan who smiled calmly, while struggling to stifle his own growing sense of wonder.

“You're the expert. You tell me.”

Patel looked at him momentarily before deciding the statement wasn’t an insult.

“Look at this. That’s darn peculiar. The scanners now report Peter's mother-in-law as suffering from terminal stage three disseminated lung cancer, not an infection.” Patel’s voice had climbed another octave.

“Fascinating!”

Silence fell over the room as the two watched. Slowly, as if alive, the damaged DNA uncoiled itself like a snake. Whipping back and forth violently the structure flexed for a few moments before slowly recoiling and reassembling itself. As each peptide fell into perfect order, the cellular organelles regenerated right before the two explorer’s eyes.

“No, that can't be! There must be some sort of error.

I tell you *this is not possible*. No technology in the universe could do that. Every nucleotide on her DNA is being rebuilt from the ground up. And there is no energy acting on the cell at all. It's doing it all by itself, like a pet obeying a command!" Patel was almost squeaking now, as he desperately tried to remain calm.

"Ok, don't blow a fuse, just calm down. So, some force, or someone is reprogramming her cells back to their healthy condition."

"Don't you understand? Whatever *'force'* is acting on these cells is not measurable by any device known to man. If it was a naturally occurring element or energy, we would be seeing it now. There are only two options here."

"And those would be?

"Either we are encountering a natural force not previously witnessed by any branch of science in history or…"

"Or what?"

"Or the changes we are seeing here are being wrought by forces outside of our universe, stabbing down like lightning into time and space, and if such an amazing thing were occurring, the only question is why would anyone try to suppress knowledge of it?"

"So these 'other' natural or 'arch-natural' forces are a threat to someone," Logan mused, "Somebody obviously has a stake in what we bring back, and that would include Strife who has her own opinions, regardless of what the facts may be."

Patel listened intently before replying. "How could she have doctored all these files is what I want to know?"

"She couldn't have, at least not on her own. She must have had help, but who?" Logan pondered.

"They must have planned this from the start. Those algorithms are so technologically convincing that I even believed them. And I designed the original system. So what's so important that they would cover the truth and risk prison? And why would they attempt to deceive millions, possibly billions of people? Not to mention threaten the existence of our nation."

"She said she didn't want them to choose me. She said 'they' said I was a hero and they needed me so people would believe. Who is 'they'?"

Patel simply stared into the images forming before his eyes.

"All my life I've hated Christians. I thought they were stupid hypocrites, believing in fairy tales, pie-in-the-sky dreams. Now, here I am, looking at my life's work telling me the impossible is real! I mean I know it's real! I built these instruments with my own two hands. They were right, all along. How could I have missed that?"

Patel stared trancelike, his voice trailing off into a whispering repetition of "How could I have missed that?" as Logan stood nearby storing his data for the night. Reaching over in an uncharacteristic display of compassion, he rested his hand on Patel's shoulder.

"You're not alone, my friend. A lot of people have missed it. Too many. Now, it's time to go home, before any more do. That is, of course, if we still can."

The evening sun was settling over Capernaum as twelve Roman soldiers on horseback rode into town with Strife in the lead. Swords drawn they entered the disciples' camp furiously, roughly shoving their way past the followers, searching through each of the tents. At the edge of the group a worried Barnabas observed the intrusion. Making his way through the crowd, intent on reasoning with Strife, he was suddenly and roughly thrown to the ground. Struggling to rise, he quickly came face to face with the business end of a sword. Wide eyed he stared at the gleaming metal Gladius hanging only inches from his nose.

"Centurion, do you actually mean to do my followers harm?"

The startled commander whirled about roughly to face the voice. His sweat stained brow dripped with fear as he croaked his reply.

"Now listen Nazarene," his voice quavered as he spoke, "we're not here for you. We're here for the two Egyptians who carry diamonds. King Herod insists they be brought to Jerusalem at once."

"Herod, that sly fox. Go back and tell him they have left us; you will not find them here."

The slightly balding centurion's unkempt beard of thorns, twigs and feathers fascinated Barnabas who rose to stare as the man drew near to the carpenter. Peter started to step forward when Jesus, deftly waving him off, gazed back into the soldier's steely eyes. The gritty officer let out a tiny inexplicable whimper and then composing himself, stepped back sheathing his sword.

"We will look anyway."

"By all means, look," Jesus replied as Barnabas gingerly reached up lifting the edge of the soldier's beard.

"What the devil is your problem?" the crusty man spewed pulling away from Cyprian.

"Oh, nothing. Just searching that nest for eggs," the burly man quipped to an outburst of boisterous laughter from the crowd.

Jesus smiled yet remained unmoved until the crusty soldier had backed away and resumed ransacking the camp. Coughing quietly, he tried to clear his throat. Innocent in nature, the act had the unintended effect of immediately drawing laughter again from both the disciples and several soldiers who were glued to the teacher's every word. Unamused, the centurion spun quickly back around to an abrupt silence and an equally abrupt resumption of duties, albeit with less vigor and the slightest of smirks.

In the meantime, Logan and Patel, aware of their unwelcome guests, had cautiously maneuvered around the city to a stable where several large camels were being groomed. Entering the stable, they approached the owner, a stocky, very muscular man with a bald head. He was bent low to the ground, intently working on a camel's back foot pad. Looking up from his work to observe Patel and Logan's entry, he attempted to shield the glare of the early morning sun coming through the open door.

"Shalom, my little friend, how are you this fine day?" Logan greeted, reaching down with an outstretched hand. Looking up, the man met Logan's smile with a glower. Then, slowly rising to his feet, the little man grew and grew before Logan's eyes until he towered a foot above Logan's head. Patel swallowed hard, his eyes now as big as saucers. The man, whose scowl was only made colder by the hammer he held precariously in one hand, silently crossed his arms staring aggressively towards the two men.

"I'd like to buy two of your camels," Logan said hesitatingly as his own grin faded.

"They're not for sale," the big man groused turning to resume his work. Logan cast Patel the briefest of perplexed looks before proceeding to press his case. Pulling a small money bag brimming with gold coins from his cloak, he dangled them in the air.

"Look friend, if its money you want, we've got plenty of it. We can afford to be generous," Logan announced. The stable owner turned back and walking closer eyed the money bag, before repeating his message more slowly and emphatically.

"Perhaps you are hard of hearing or just slow of wit. I said they're not - for - sale, now beat it!" he repeated gruffly accentuating his resolve with the slow tap of the hammer in his opposing palm.

Wide eyed Patel pulled Logan aside for a quick conference. Logan seeing the fear in Patel's eyes, spoke quietly, as the owner tending his stable was clearing the stall of dirty hay.

"It doesn't sound like they're for sale!" Patel whispered adamantly.

"We can't ride donkeys. That centurion and his soldiers are on horseback. They'd catch us in a heartbeat," Logan insisted quietly. Then stepping back from Patel he spoke loudly.

"I don't think our friend here understood me. I'll just rephrase it."

Logan approached the stable owner again, as the big man turned to face the chrononaut, revealing for the first time the rather large wooden pitch-fork he now bore in his hand.

"Look friend….."

"I'm not your friend. Now beat it!"

Logan hung his head shaking it in disappointment.

"I just wish you would reconsider. We really are reasonable men," Logan continued fascinated by the huge man's ruddy countenance cycling through multiple crimson shades before settling to a steady beet red.

Patel watched with horror at the chain of events proceeding to unfold as Logan ducked, anticipating the pitchfork's inevitable first swing. Like mighty Casey up to bat, the goliath sliced through the air easily missing Logan's retracted crown just glancing the wooden handle off Patel's protruding chin. Predictably, the fragile scientist went down for the count while Logan rewarded the huge man's groin with a right upper cut of his own. The strength enhanced kick from Logan's right foot made an immediate impression, leaving the titan wide eyed, doubled in pain and clutching his injured masculinity. Still partially hobbled, the inflamed giant flailed the air stabbing vainly at the elusive guardian.

The huge man was easily Logan's physical superior, but the swifter Logan easily dodged the man's swing. Grabbing a burlap sack, as the man stabbed at him again, Logan whipped the sack snagging the end of the fork. In one sweeping motion Logan flipped the end of the fork backwards towards the man and over again. The implement, held in a death grip by the titan, performed stunningly well flipping the big man backwards like an oversized lever. Stunned, the assailant gathered himself from the dust and slowly rose to his feet. Logan, now possessing the pitchfork, was bent over beginning to gasp. The months of travel over dusty roads and the relentless progression of his vasculitis had drained his usual stamina.

Despite the awareness of his waning strength, Logan was not yet at a lack for confidence. Instead he was plagued for the first time with an uncharacteristic twinge of concern at possibly hurting his adversary. Never had such a thought in combat previously crossed his mind, and he wondered if his disease might be affecting his ability to reason. Almost as quickly as the thought entered his mind Logan was quick to dismiss it and press the battle. Yet, he found for the first time that he was giving his opponent another opportunity.

"Now, as I was saying, we're happy to pay a comfortable price. How's 200 denarii in gold sound?"

The hairy man charged at the explorer, his dark dung and soot covered tunic giving him the uncanny resemblance of a stooping, snorting bull. Entertained by the battle and acutely aware of his adversary's disorientation, Logan played the part of the matador. Holding the pitchfork forward and waving it like a red cape, he taunted his adversary. This of course inflamed the man even more, causing him to act even more rashly, and allowing Logan to trip his assailant, sending him crashing into various corners of the room. Each pass left the man progressively more and more disheveled, while Logan remained untouched.

Patel meanwhile, who had partially recovered, stood cowering in a distant corner stall both enjoying the show and marveling at how Logan handled such a large combatant. After several passes the stable owner, bloodied and swaggering, finally collapsed after careening into a large stone wall at the far end of the stable. Logan stood there staring alternately at the man on the floor and the pitch fork.

"I see your point," he quipped looking at the end of the implement before tossing its handle harmlessly across the unconscious man's chest.

"Ok, you drive a hard bargain. 250 gold denarii it is, and not a shilling more," he mused in his best English drawl, smiling as he dumped the tiny sack of coins on to the big man's belly.

"Pleasure doing business, you keep the change."

A few minutes later, Logan had both camels saddled while a stunned Patel stood hovering over the still motionless giant. One wrenching tug on his tunic and he was on the crouching back of a snorting desert hack, slipping out from the stable, through the city gate and into the night. Watching the two men disappear into the night stood two shadowy figures and nearby, sporting a handful of horse reins, one cheeky grinning Barnabas.

Two hours later in the torch lit streets of Capernaum,

a lovely traitor and her entourage gathered outside the ransacked stable. A small band of soldiers scoured the nearby buildings as Strife and the Roman centurion interrogated the disheveled titan. His head covered with bruises and still bleeding from a small cut on his temple, the proprietor was furious, gesturing wildly, swinging his arms and hands aimlessly. Strife was mildly amused and without her characteristic aplomb, she failed to stifle even the smallest of a wry smile. This infuriated the victim even more as he seemed to fixate on her expression, unfamiliar with being questioned by a woman. Finally, Strife had enough and pulling the Centurion aside, she left the big man to a lieutenant.

"Tell your men to get moving. Every moment we delay here they slip further and further from our grasp".

The Centurion's response to female authority was as quick and pointed as the finger now angrily stabbed in Strife's face.

"You are a woman! You will not speak to me in such a manner. Your friends will not escape us, and if it is true, as you say, that your friends and the Nazarene intend to overthrow the empire, we will crush them. No amount of wizardry can defeat the combined might of the Roman legions," he barked before turning to walk away.

"Look, Tin-head, if they make it back to their base, they will have in their hands enough power to wipe out all of your legions in a day. What will be left of your glorious empire then? Will they call you Octavius the coward?"

The seasoned soldier turned and raised his hand to slap his female antagonist. His intentions, anticipated by both Strife and her survival suit, were met with the quick reflexes of a well-trained martial artisan. In two easy moves, she easily disarmed her attacker and flipped the two-hundred-pound warrior backward into the air and onto his rear. His landing, loud enough to be heard by all his subordinates, sent up a billowing cloud of dust encapsulating the stunned warrior. When it had cleared, there sat Octavius windless, more stunned than injured, his defeat having been witnessed by more than a dozen of his subordinates. Strife stooped near the silent centurion as she whispered in his ear.

"Now, if a mere woman can sit the powerful Octavius on his tin can with the flip of her wrist, don't you think you should rethink you position on this '*wizardry*'?"

Wide-eyed the centurion slowly rose to his feet.

"We will pursue them," he seethed, brushing the dust from his tunic, "but first we will place you in irons, now!" He motioned as a soldier emerged from the edge of the crowd slowly surrounding them. Strife's eyes remained locked with her adversary's, her pupils dilating and constricting rhythmically in response to the Nano-lens tracking the peripheral threat. Then deliberately, almost instinctively, she raised her left arm pointing it directly at the approaching threat.

"I think not," she announced, her gaze never leaving the commander's as the first faint blue burst of neon glow encapsulated the approaching man as well as two others beside him. The glow shimmered in the morning air for only a moment, leaving those immersed frozen on the ground.

"They're not dead," she said, "but they just as well could have been, had I wanted them to be. Now, are we going to work together or apart?"

Octavius approached Strife, their eyes locked in a battle of wills as he closed within inches of her facc. Strife stared back, her countenance cold and unflinching as the vapor from their breaths mixed in the morning air. The cold war lasted only a moment, its détente initiated by the hint of a smirk and echoed by a sleazy smile of mutual appreciation. Backing away he nodded his head and turned for his horse, calling back to her. "They are headed south. Mount Up!" Then pointing to his troops, he instructed them to give Strife one of the fallen soldiers' horses. The two former adversaries, now allies exited the city gate.

"They must be headed to Jerusalem," Strife asserted.

"Are you insane? They would be walking into such a hornet's nest. Herod has soldiers on every corner looking everywhere for these men."

"Which is exactly why Logan will go there, He will think it's the last place we would look for him. Besides they have friends there who can help them. They will need provisions and that is where they will get them. Let's go," she commanded riding off in the direction of Jerusalem with Octavius on her heels.

CHAPTER TWENTY
Unlikely Allies

Initially it was Logan's intention to ride all night leaving their pursuers choking on the literal dust of Palestine. Unfortunately, after only two hours of riding, he was forced to leave the southern route to Jerusalem and find a safe haven to overnight. Patel, whose general health had been in a continual decline for the preceding two months, was now unable to maintain the pace of escaping a pursuit. His medication almost depleted, he had given himself over to utilizing half dosages or skipping days to finish the mission. Now pale and exhausted he was an impediment to their safe return and incapable of defending himself. To enhance his mobility, Patel had taken to utilizing the defend strength enhancement capabilities of his survival suit at all times. This supplement allowed him to move with minimal effort, but drained the suit of its critical energy reserves.

To avoid detection by Strife and her new found friends, Logan and Patel left the main route, and ascending to a nearby plateau, made camp for the night. Unable to light a fire for fear of detection, the two weary travelers laid out their bedrolls. As they did so, the distant sound of approaching hoof beats became obvious.

Logan, never one to ignore a threat, crawled on his hands and knees to the edge of the plateau. Looking over the edge, he saw Strife and the company of troops commanded by Octavius riding in the distant hollow of the northern valley. Logan and Patel mused at the confusion of the small band as all but Strife appeared to travel in a serpentine if not circuitous route stumbling over and around obstacles littering the desert floor.

The explanation for such bumbling was apparent. Strife, the sole woman in the pack, had been rejected as the leader even though she could see perfectly with the aid of her Nano-lens. The others followed Octavius who carried one of the two remaining torches but appeared to possess the worst vision of the entire pack. Logan and Patel could hear Strife yelling something from her position at the tail end of the train, but it was thankfully indiscernible.

This commotion was fortunate as was the silence of the camels crouching on the plateau behind Logan. The pursuers, riding by at midnight, were oblivious to the fact they were being watched.

The next morning Logan and Patel resumed their trek towards Jerusalem over a somewhat circuitous route.

After a fresh meal of figs and melon, and a full dose of medication, the two men were able to proceed again at a steady clip. Navigating over the dusty and seldom used southern route proved an unwelcome challenge that neither had anticipated. The trail, more pothole than flat surface, left a clinging Patel drained of his earlier ruddiness. A scattering of islands of blue and green bruises dotted his chest, arms and head. The look enhanced by the expression of nausea was profound, both effects being the result of his pummeling from the camel's undulating hump.

"I think I'm going to be sick." Patel moaned, "How did you talk me into riding this overgrown desert rat, anyway?

Patel's customary whine was interrupted now by an almost constant choking noise, making it harder and harder for Logan to ignore.

"That's "desert hack" doofus. Great aren't they? The reason you're riding one is that they're a lot faster, and man the view you can get from up here!"

Logan scanned the horizon before him, his right hand held high over his brow to shield out the sun.

"View, what view? There's nothing but sand!" Patel complained. "We're surrounded by sand and more sand everywhere! Every now and then there's a shrub or a rock! Oh yeah," and then there's that big fireball in the sky roasting my skull. I almost forgot about that, but my brain is so mushy from the heat, that it's a miracle I can remember anything at all!" Then feigning stupefaction he continued.

"By the way where in Sam Hill did you say we were headed?"

Logan peered at the anemic scientist, momentarily concerned that he might really not remember, while at the same time suppressing the very real urge to slap him.

"Jer-u-sal-em," Logan chided.

"Jerusalem! Are you out of your cotton-pickin' mind? Herod is just waiting to hand us our heads on a platter the minute we step foot in that city. We need to head home," Patel rattled again, his two index fingers on opposite hands stabbing the air in two very different and unrecognizable directions.

"Precisely, it will be the last place they'll ever look for us," Logan beamed, "Plus, with the Passover starting soon, we'll be lost in the crowds." Logan darted his eyes away from his friend's gaze, fearful his expression might prompt his comrade to ask why Strife was also headed south the night before.

"Besides, we need provisions to get to the ship. We'll never make it on these camels. We need fresh ones, a place to rest and supplies to navigate the Negev."

There was a long moment of silence before Patel, reflecting on Logan's plan, responded. This time his tone was much more subdued.

"I'm becoming quite a weight around your neck, aren't I?"

Another moment of silence ensued.

"Look Nick, we're all in this together. I don't know what Strife's beef with life is, but I do know I can't live in the shadow of that - that - *man*," he protested pointing back towards Capernaum, "for seven months and leave you behind, so let's just not go there. It's not happening."

Both men were speechless for a moment as Patel stared off into space.

"Now it's Nick..... Huh?" Patel smiled emphatically leaning forward in an attempt to see the look on Logan's face. "He really got under your skin, didn't he?"

Logan said nothing.

"You really must think I'm a goner, you're even using my real name. Now don't get me wrong, I appreciate what you're trying to do. But you and I both know I'm in no shape to cross the Negev. I know where this thing is headed, and if it does, - it's ok. Just get the data home! I don't want my life to count for nothing."

Again, Logan was silent before Patel added, "Agreed?"

"If it comes to that," Logan sighed and nodded, refusing to meet his shipmate's gaze.

Patel sat back now seemingly more relaxed by his comrade's acquiescence.

"So, you believe now?"

Logan hung his head and nodded.

"How 'bout you?"

Patel bit his lip as he fought to suppress a brief coughing fit. When it had cleared he spoke softly.

"Never thought I would… not in a million years, if I hadn't come here and seen it for myself. I had so many questions. Never could get past some of those nagging ones. Like how can there be three Gods.

"Yeh, you and the Pharisees, that's what they want to kill him for. I have to admit it doesn't seem natural."

"Natural, ha," Patel laughed, "what's natural? I mean he wasn't claiming there were three gods. He was saying it's sorta' like there were three forms of the same God. But I couldn't see that. I don't know why?"

"Yeh," Logan sighed, "I know what you mean. Science is a funny thing. If you're not careful you can interpret the data to mean what you want it to mean."

"Yeh, that's exactly what I mean. My whole life I've studied nature, marveling at its beauty and complexity, but blind to the artist."

"Or artists?"

"No just one, expressing his complicated nature through his creation's complexity."

"I'm not sure I follow you."

"Well, think about it. I mean there it is in front of us the whole time and we cannot see it. It truly is as if we are both blind and deaf. What are the major dimensions of the known universe?"

"Well, let's see, there's space."

"Expressed as?"

"Length, width and height."

"What else?"

"Uh, there's time."

"Uh, huh… and its forms are?"

"Past, present and… future," Logan said slowly his eyes widening.

"Yes…and?"

"Matter - solid, liquid and… gas."

"These are simplistic examples and I could go on…"

"Please do."

"…. but the most important evidence is the example we know best - ourselves, made as the Hebrew Scriptures say, "In the image of God."

"Fascinating Spock, now granted I'm not surprised to hear that you might be schizo, three personalities and all that, but in here," Logan said tapping on his chest, "there's just one of me?"

"Very funny. Look I'm serious. I've been thinking about this a lot. We don't even know ourselves. What did Jesus tell that lawyer was the most important commandment?"

"You mean the Shema. Love the Lord your God with all your heart, and with all your mind and with all your soul. If we heard him say that once, we heard it a million times. Why?"

"Look -*'Albert',*" Patel proudly pronounced, "that's the key. Don't you see? We - are three in one - body, soul, and spirit. I mean I can't think of myself without thinking of my body, but if I lose an arm, I'm still me. I have a will, a mind and emotions. Yet something in me tells me I am still more than even that. Something in me is eternal. I have a spirit. I am cut from the mold of my creator; my very essence reflects his nature."

Logan thought for a moment before responding. "Wow… you're right professor. I never saw that. We are all so tripped up over His complexity that we can't see our own."

"There are none so blind as those who refuse to see," Patel whispered as he slumped forward asleep in his saddle.

"Amen, brother," Logan whispered as he smiled back at his friend and guided the two 'taxis' over the dusty terrain.

The next evening was unusually cool for Palestine as the two men approached Jerusalem's northern wall. Patel shivered, exhausted by the day of travel over the rough country roads. Shrouded by a curious veil of fog which hung thinly over the entire mount and densely over the Kidron and Hinnom valleys, they paused just outside the gate. Lit by the golden glow of torch and lamp light, the city of David appeared to hover as if descending from the clouds with an 'other earthly radiance'.

Entering through the thinly guarded *Fish Gate* and obscured by the thickening fog, the two hooded explorers passed seemingly oblivious soldiers. As they entered the market area, they dismounted and led their camels by hand, slowly making their way down the ancient cobblestone streets. The city was silent now, except for the occasional shuffle of Romans pushing through damp murky thoroughfares. Carefully, the two men navigated the narrow lanes of the northern quarter. Gingerly they guided their camels dodging both the markers left by other taxis and the postings of sentries scouring the streets.

Finally, they spotted a recognizable alleyway, which winding into a small cul-de-sac, led them to a warmly lit familiar stone house. Logan cautiously approached, looking carefully to ensure that they were unobserved before knocking. The large wooden door creaked open and two large burly arms reached out in a smothering hug to drag in the exhausted travelers.

Inside shadows on the walls performed a chaotic dance as the oil lamps flickered above the two men and their affectionate hosts. There, Barnabas and his wife welcomed the two weary travelers with relieved hugs and words of encouragement. As Sarah helped the two men settle into the small guest room in the back, Barnabas and the servant boy stabled their camels. Exhausted, Patel immediately retired for the night, thanking his hosts before collapsing into a deep sleep on his bed roll.

In a different part of the city, another type of inquisition was about to take place. Adjacent to the Temple of Herod towered the *Fortress of Antonio,* an imposing edifice through whose magnificently chiseled arches strode the steads of Octavius and Strife, bearing their burdens towards the monarch's retreat.

"We can do nothing without Herod's approval. You realize that, don't you?" Octavius commented as they wound their way down the dimly lit narrow streets of Jerusalem.

"I assumed as much, but this is still a waste of time. They may be getting away even as we speak."

"Even so, you will have to appeal to his highness's reason in a practical manner to win his approval. Do you have anything - to - *offer*, anything to satiate his majesty's -appetite?" Octavius' tone dripped with sarcasm as he stared holes in the back of her neck. Strife, who was used to dealing with predictably difficult men, ignored his spurious innuendos.

"How about all the perfect diamonds he can choke down his puny little throat? How does that sound?" Octavius erupted in a loud boisterous laugh that threatened to awaken the entire sleeping city.

"Where are you from? You are certainly no Jewess. No Jewish woman would dare to speak in such a manner. Perhaps you have some Roman blood in you after all?"

"If I told you, you wouldn't believe me."

"Try me," he pressed as they turned by a raised area of the road looking out over the valley below and a starlit sky above.

"Ok," she said bringing her horse to a halt, then pointing with her right index finger to the sky. "See that large light just beside the three clusters?"

"Yes…" the Centurion replied tentatively.

"That's where I'm from," she smiled nudging her mare on down the narrow street before her. The Centurion glanced down at the road before him, a sardonic smile traced the corners of his mouth.

"You Egyptians do have such an unusual sense of humor."

"I told you, you wouldn't believe me," she returned as he let out a little chuckle.

"I certainly hope Herod is as amused. He has his own unusual forms of en-ter-tain-ment," he continued smiling with a devilish delight.

Three oil lamps flickered in the dimly lit family room where the two men sat talking and laughing. As they reclined by the now familiar parade of dancing shadows adorning the back wall, an impossible friendship spanning two millennia cemented between two very different men. In time, the affectionate conversation drifted back to the serious, sharpened by the cool winter breeze that drifted in from the Palestine desert torturing the lamplight's flame. Sarah, who was busy pulling out more blankets for Logan's bedroll and stacking them next to the entryway, joined the men who were discussing the events of the past two days.

"Where is your friend, the woman?"

Logan looked up at Sarah hesitantly before answering her. "If you mean friend, like the kind who would stab me in the back, then my *friend* is right on my heels."

"What do you mean?" the shocked woman said, stooping to examine the explorer's feet. Logan and Barnabas exchanged a silent smile as Logan bent to raise her from the floor.

"No, you don't understand. She is trying to discredit Jesus and turn us over to the Roman guard."

"No! Why would she do such a thing? I thought she sought the Master's help?" the Jewess exclaimed.

She leaned over the empty chair before her.

"To be honest, I'm not really sure. She obviously has her own agenda, plus that of some very powerful friends. I expect she is probably meeting with Herod, even as we speak."

"Well, she will know you came here!"

"Not a chance! This is the last place she'll look." Logan looked Barnabas' way, seeking some male agreement.

"No, she is a lady. The first place she would look is with friends. She will bring them here, I tell you."

"She's *no* lady."

"Still, she will come here, I tell you. You must leave first thing in the morning."

Barnabas interrupted, his hand gently touching Logan's arm.

"I'm afraid she is right, my friend. No one knows the Lord's fairest better than one herself. We don't want to put you in danger." Logan thought for a moment.

"Nor I you. Ok, we will have to work fast, then. We will leave at dawn. Do you have any friends who can resupply us for a trip of several days into the desert? We have money to buy goods."

Sarah walked to her husband's side and gently laying her hand on Barnabas' shoulder began to speak slowly.

"There is one… a Pharisee. Our people believe he sympathizes with the Master. If not for his fear of losing his position, he would openly join us." Her words elicited a sudden interest on Logan's part.

"Will he help us?"

"God alone knows, but there is no one else to turn to. I will go there at dawn. Now you two sleep and I will keep watch."

"You two have been like family to me. I don't know how to thank you."

"There is a friend that sticks closer than a brother and you have found him," she said pointing to Barnabas. "By the way, how is your sickness?"

"I'm afraid it's much worse. I am almost completely consumed by it, with no more than a few weeks, if that. Patel is much worse. If we don't get home soon…" Logan's voice trailed off as Sarah interrupted.

"Please you need your rest. Go, we will keep watch."

Moments later, Logan was slipping into his bed roll and pulling the hand woven blankets up and over his shoulders. He stopped, troubled by the silence of the cold dimly lit room. He sat there listening in the dark, waiting for what he did not know. He only heard the sound of his breath and the quiet noises of the ancient city's night life. It was then that he realized what he was missing, Patel's snoring.

Immediately he activated his suit's accessory light and examined the quiet explorer. He was alive, but not a noise did he make.

"You must be near the end," Logan solemnly mused as he pulled his friend's blanket up over his shoulders.

Then turning back to his bed he paused, and with his light still activated, unzipped his suit, intending to examine his chest and arms. There on his chest and torso were dozens of swollen blue and purple vessels throbbing and writhing over a sea of crimson flesh. The largest of the serpentine vessels, some three centimeters in diameter, coiled up his abdomen and over his chest like an alien intruder. It pulsed with each beat of his heart, threatening to explode at any moment. Horrified, he looked down and discovered that the vessels now covered his entire body, with only his face and hands untouched.

Quickly, he zipped the suit shut and fighting with shaking hands downed two tablets from his medicine pocket. Then collapsing, he fell exhausted into a deep tortured sleep, his moans not unnoticed by Sarah who knelt in prayer by the large open window of her family room, unmoving, watching.

The two exhausted chrononauts slept soundly on the hard dirt floor of Barnabas' modest home. Almost dead to the world, they lay unmoving until Sarah, still awake and praying wrapped in her woolen blanket, slipped silently from her seat heading down the back alleyway. In what seemed like a moment, she was back rousing Barnabas and bursting into the back room where Logan and Patel were sleeping. Boldly she threw open the crude curtain covering the room's only window and proceeded to abruptly awaken its inhabitants.

"Get up! Get up I say! Get your things now and follow me. The roads are clear and if we hurry we can get across the city before the sentries have changed position."

Logan and Patel, still groggy from their abbreviated night's rest, struggled to rise from their bedrolls. Suddenly a very chipper Barnabas burst into the room to welcome in the new day.

"Arise my sleepy companions! This is the day the Lord has made and I believe we will rejoice and be glad in it," Barnabas bellowed before taking stock of his two newly awakened house guests.

"Oh my, you do look like death warmed over, don't you?"

Logan chuckled looking at Patel, who pale and ashen managed the briefest of smiles.

"You have no idea how close to home you're hitting, brother," the commander replied.

Minutes later the two travelers and their brave friends were navigating the back alleyways of Jerusalem's northern quarter. Heavily wrapped in woolen blankets to conceal them and ward off the cold air, the figures stole their way through the early morning market streets and into the upper city, where only the wealthiest lived. They passed dozens of beautiful whitewashed homes separated by surrounding walls. Logan marveled at the simple beauty of the stone architecture and the tiny, yet lush green gardens growing beside each home. Eventually, as they arrived at one grand opening, a servant quickly motioned the quartet in through the gate. Barnabas and Sarah approached the servant, extending arms of affection as the three briefly hugged one another.

"Elias, thank you so much for your help," Sarah began as the three others followed her lead into the rear entrance of the ornate house.

"Don't thank me, Sarah. My master was very anxious to meet your friends and see for himself who it was that Herod sought so earnestly to detain. Follow me please."

The simply clad middle aged man led the four travelers down a narrow hallway to a stone stairway. The steps descended into a large open basement moderately lit by wall-mounted oil lamps and cluttered with mounds of discarded furnishings, pottery and clothing.

"Looks like my bedroom back home," Logan quipped.

"Yeah, but it doesn't smell near as bad," Patel retorted.

"These are the stores of a man who gives from his heart to the poor," Barnabas interjected turning to the creek of the wooden door behind them. There above them a middle aged man clothed in dignified yet simple robes for a Pharisee descended the dimly lit stairs and emerged into the light. Immediately, Logan was impressed by the warmth yet seriousness of this large man whose thick mottled beard mushroomed from beneath his headdress suspended around two of the largest brown eyes that Logan had ever seen.

"Welcome Barnabas. Welcome Sarah. I must apologize for asking you to meet here in my wine cellar, but your friends have created quite a stir. I'm afraid you are in a great danger. If it wasn't for your carpenter friend stirring up the early Passover masses, you would never have made it this far."

"Jesus is here?" Patel exclaimed.

"I'm afraid so. Why? Does that alarm you?"

Logan looked at his friends and then stepped forward.

"He is our friend and if our coming has anything to do with him being here, we must leave at once. We must find provisions and make our escape as hastily as possible."

"Your concern for your fellow man is admirable, I must admit, but if half of what I hear is true, you, are the ones in danger. What is it you fear?"

Logan looked at Patel, hesitating before answering.

"Beloved, he asked you a question," Barnabas nervously reminded.

"Yes, Logan, what is it that troubles you?" Sarah added.

At this, Patel stepped into the discussion.

"What my friend means is that we don't want the authorities to think he is with us."

"I see…you do not wish to incriminate him."

"Correct."

"But haven't you been with him the past few months?"

"Yes."

The middle aged man nodded pacing about the room silently for a few moments. Suddenly he turned back resuming the conversation.

"I assure you, you will not be discovered here. As for your leaving hastily, you shall have to remain if only for a few days. Right now you will never get through that army today. Wait for God's timing, I implore you. The Passover will be here in three days. At that time chaos will be your cloak and confusion shall be your shield.

"What?" Patel objected.

"The soldiers will not see you," Barnabas interjected as their host continued.

"You will slip right through their fingers, my friends. For now you are my guests. Sarah, I will have Elias go with you and return you to your home. Barnabas, I will provide the money so that you and the carpenter's friends may purchase the provisions for these men."

"These men already have camels, Nicodemus." Sarah interrupted. Nicodemus glanced back at Barnabas as if to scold him. Then looking forward at Logan and Patel again he continued.

"Now that we are finished with being interrupted by this woman, we can continue. As I was saying, your camels will be watched and followed. So I will provide you with fresh beasts adept at the desert climate you travel. Barnabas, have your people take them outside the city to a secure location. You two will rendezvous with your friend here at the pool of Gishon on Friday of the Passover. You shall have your provisions."

"Thank you. A thousand times thank you, but my friends have money," Barnabas interjected.

"You mean their diamonds?" he said first to Barnabas, and then nodding to Logan, "Take them with you, for they are worthless here. They are the very thing Herod seeks. If even one were to be passed into this crowd, it would lead your enemies directly to your location in minutes. No, I think we will use my money. I do have one request, however. I wish to ask one or two questions before we part. Do you mind?"

Logan hesitated, responding with silence and a gesture of open hands.

"First of all, where do you call home? It is obvious you are not an Israelite, but you also do not dress or demonstrate the mannerisms of the Romans. Many say Egypt, but to me you are closer to the Greeks in language."

"Is it important?"

A pair of raised bushy eyebrows met Logan's evasive answer.

"Your reluctance proves it is both important and relevant to my next question. So, where is it you call home?"

"Charleston." Logan's immediate response was too blunt to be disbelieved, but too unlikely to be ignored.

"I have traveled widely and studied geography for many years. Why have I never heard of this…? Charleston?"

"Perhaps because it is beyond your seas and your maps do not contain it, I doubt if any map in Palestine will contain it," Patel interjected. Nicodemus pondered this answer for a moment before asking the question truly on his heart.

"And you three, from so… far away, have heard of the Nazarene and ventured here to be healed."

"Yes."

"Is your illness fatal?"

"Yes."

"Were you healed?" Logan shook his head casting his glance aside.

"No."

"So, He is not truly able to heal?" Logan returned his gaze, nodding his head.

"No, no………he is able."

"He is? He is truly able to heal? Then why, my man, for the love of God, are you not healed? Did you not spend months working alongside of Him?"

Again, Logan hesitated, looking down, not wanting to answer. He could feel the piercing stare of those enormous brown eyes digging into the back of his neck.

"Because, Logan sighed a massive sigh, "to be healed, I would have to do the one thing I was not willing to do." Nicodemus stood erect, a look of incredulousness crossing his face.

"What horrible thing did he ask of you?" He asked gently.

"Believe! He asked me to believe!" Logan almost barked his self-disgust as he stood turning from the priest.

"Believe? Believe what?"

Logan hesitated briefly as he stared in the distance.

"That buried in the bottomless abyss of my soul, I have madly hidden my depravity from myself. I desperately needed someone to love me, warts, scars, bruises and all. Yet I was the one blindly pushing it away."

"Love? Whose love?"

"God's. The love that gives us life each day. The love that sustains us silently through every tragedy."

Nicodemus listened intently. After a moment he spoke.

"I too have known this blindness and am also confronted with a choice. So, I will ask you my final question and then I will ask no more… "

"Only one?" Logan smiled.

"Only one now remains. Is He the Christ?"

Logan looked down thoughtfully at the digital display of the recording device beneath his tunic.

"He is."

Like a disembodied spirit he heard his voice ring out clear and strong. It echoed through the stone lined cellar, touching every ear before reflecting back to its owner. Logan stood there amused by the uncanny irony of his first public profession.

"He is?" came the surprising chorus of two familiar voices. Logan glanced over at Patel and Barnabas who were trying to keep from beaming, a hint of a tear forming in the corner of the Cyprian's eye.

"I'm afraid so."

"You're afraid so, why," echoed the gentle priest.

"I'm afraid for him, and what they will do to him. I'm afraid for me and every soul that has refused his tender grace."

"He is coming to Jerusalem for the Passover. I will go and talk to him for you," Nicodemus continued pensively.

"I shall meet with him and warn him. Do you think he will see me?"

"Yes."

"You sound so sure of yourself."

"Pretty sure," Logan nodded knowingly, "but beware."

"Of what?"

"He will not be what you expect. You will come to him with questions and leave with answers you never thought to ask." Nicodemus nodded silently.

"Yes, Jonny is correct," Barnabas chimed in. "He knows the answer to your questions even before you ask it."

Logan smiled resisting the urge to turn to his good friend, instead choosing to look at him out of the corner of his eye.

"When did I tell you that you could call me Jonny?"

Patel interrupted, pushing Barnabas back gently to stick his head in the conversation.

"Oh, pay him no mind. He's been calling me Albert since we got here. Look, we need to get on with the program here. I'm sick and I need to get home."

"He's right. We better get cracking."

"Until Passover then my friends, Shalom," Nicodemus bowed as he and Barnabas made their way upstairs, where receiving the money, Barnabas hurried on his way.

CHAPTER TWENTY-ONE
A Very Narrow Door

Logan and Patel reclined peacefully, propped precariously on a carefully arranged mountain of linens, which they had buttressed below by a foundation of gurney sacks.

"Ahh…." Logan sighed contentedly straining the precious burgundy liquid through his pursed lips, as the two explorers slowly downed a well-aged flask of their guest's best wine.

"This is the life," Patel reflected as he relaxed in the basement of his first century bungalow.

"Wonder what's taking Barnabas so long," Logan quipped.

All the while Barnabas was busy in another part of the city performing the task of acquiring provisions for his friend's journey. This, his first task was almost his last, as when attempting two days later to return home, he all but directly walked into Strife and her Centurion-led legionnaires. Fortunately for everyone, Sarah and Elias spotted him first, and pulling Barnabas into the shadows of an alley at just the right moment, clasped a hand firmly over his cavernous mouth, and spirited the muffled Barnabas quickly away.

Three blocks to the east a great commotion had commenced triggered by the first century equivalent of a modern traffic jam. There at the eastern gate rode a solitary figure on a foal. He passed through the gateway surrounded by a crowd of hundreds blocking the normal flow of pilgrims into the city. The disruption could not have been timelier, as the Passover masses ran to see the procession spreading palm leafs and coats for Jesus' entry. In the meantime, Barnabas and his friends, oblivious to the distraction, darted from shop to shop acquiring the supplies needed for the trip.

Passover had descended, and with it the ancient city normally brimming with people, was overflowing. Roman sentries dotted the thoroughfares, lost in a sea of surging humanity. Haplessly they attempted to keep order. Every squad and battalion was deployed to a street, a marketplace or the temple. All except one.

This squad, led by one very determined Centurion and an even more determined woman, was oblivious to the crowds. Shoving their way through the streets, Strife drug Octavius and his soldiers, a spectacle beheld by many an amused and stunned onlooker. Their mission was to ransack every follower's home turning over baskets, searching wagons and very nearly disrobing a dozen or more citizens. All in search of the mysterious Egyptians.

Safe and sound inside of the home of Nicodemus, Logan and Patel waited impatiently. Sarah, having returned, had dressed the two travelers in robes and turbans resembling travelers from eastern countries. With their disguises now carefully in place, Nicodemus hugged the two men as they exchanged their goodbyes before heading out into the chaos of the city.

"This young lad is John Mark. He will guide you safely to your destination," Nicodemus smiled patting the freckle faced boy standing at his side. Logan looked at the lad with dismay.

"He can't be older than twelve or thirteen."

"'Leave your expectations at the door my friend'. I believe you will find this young man has some talents we can use. Besides he comes from good stock. He is the first son of Barnabas' brother." Nicodemus replied with a smile as the three made their way out the rear cellar door.

The two friends now under the direction of their trusty guide made their way carefully through the mass of humanity crowding Jerusalem's alleyways. The boy led them effortlessly through the sprawling maze of avenues before them. Only once, did an impatient Patel try to take the lead and enter ahead of them into the mainstream of market traffic. Ignoring Logan, he blundered from the alleyway only to be lassoed with a shepherd's hook and drug back like a wild boar. Incensed the explorer considered slugging the kid until two seconds later an armed squad came marching by. Logan's silent gestures towards the boy elicited a reluctant pat on the head from Patel and no further discussions on who would lead. Twenty minutes later and they were within sight of their goal, the southernmost gate.

Unguarded, except for one sentry, the *Essene Gate* lie some ten meters ahead.

"This is it," Logan observed pointing out the gate to Patel, "If we make it through that, we are home free." Patel, already a bit pale from stealthily navigating Jerusalem's alleys eyed the gate with relief.

"Almost seems too easy doesn't it?"

"Piece of cake, all we have to do is get through that one sentry," Logan answered as he rounded the final corner to proceed down the last alley way.

Suddenly he was and rudely introduced to the pitted surface of the adjoining building's stone wall. Struck suddenly from behind, he reacted instinctively, but not before he was leveled with another blow to the body and pinned to the wall. Blood trickled from the abrasion on his forehead as a large man dressed in brightly striped blue and indigo garments held a large curved knife to his neck. Shouting in what seemed a muffled voice to the explorer's clouded mind to be, he was demanding something. Vainly Logan's dialect computer raced to display the translated words on his Nano-lens. On the other side of the alley lie Patel, himself thrown to the ground by the assailant's initial assault. Shaking the cobwebs from his fragile head he struggled to pick himself up.

Tighter and tighter the assailant pressed his victim against the wall, all the while his rants rising an octave each moment. Closer to the carotid the shining blade inched, its edge threatening at any moment to end the pulse of each heart beat felt by Logan. Holding his hands on his assailant's arms in an attempt to push back against the death grip, Logan was amazed to see that even though his defense mode was activated on his survival suit, his attacker was able to overcome the enhanced strength of the suit. Harder and harder the attacker pressed until the knife just nicked Logan's skin. The small nick released the tiniest trickle of blood which ran down the side of Logan's neck and onto his tunic. Frozen on the sight of the blood, the man's face suddenly became red and swollen as Logan looked into the eyes of a man possessed beyond madness.

"What," Logan gasped, choking out each word, "do you want?" The response again was unintelligible.

"What? I can't understand you." Logan choked, "Is it money? Look I have money." Logan attempted to reach for his coin pouch when his attacker suddenly pressed harder.

"Ahhh!" Logan shifted leaning hard into the vice-like grip pinning him to the wall. Desperately he thrust the heel of his foot into the groin of his attacker, who only pressed in tighter, causing Logan to be unable to breathe. Panic now set in as he began to flail his arms in the air struggling frantically to gouge at the assailant's eyes. Then just at the point of loss of consciousness, Logan heard the crack of a board followed by the faint whine of a familiar friend. Engulfed in the electric blue halo of a paralyzing discharge the attacker had momentarily backed away before collapsing. The noise of the electrical discharge, while faint to an almost unconscious victim, was quite alarming to the citizens in the immediate area. Slumping to the ground, Logan grabbed his throat, coughing and gasping for air.

Immediately, Patel was by his side with an injection of a neuro-stimulant quickly reviving the explorer.

"Thanks." Logan croaked, "Come on we better keep moving."

"First, we're going to seal that wound," Patel spoke proceeding to clean and close the wound.

"Did you see that guy? It was like he was on some kind of drug. And what was that gibberish coming out of his mouth? Some kind of crossed up dialect from the Chaldeans and ancient Babylonian?

"What about my suit?"

"What do you mean, 'what about my suit'?"

"My suit was in *defend mode* and he almost strangled me."

"Interesting, was he human?"

"Everything but the eyes, I've only seen such hatred one other time." Patel listened closely as he put the finishing touches on Logan's wound.

"And that would be?"

"*Legion*, he had the same look."

"He was a demon?" came the broken falsetto of the young boy still holding a shattered club in his right hand. Patel pointed down to him.

"You can thank our 'talented' guide here for getting that big zombie off of you long enough for me to zap him."

Logan bent down ruffling the lad's scruffy black mane and handing him three gold coins.

"Thanks kid, now beat it, he said while wagging his large index finger in the kid's face, "and go straight home." With that the wide-eyed boy, grinning ear to ear, grabbed the coins and retreated quickly into the shadows.

"Ok, now that that's behind us, let's get moving again." The two men rose, collecting their gear to depart, when they heard the shuffle of feet behind them.

"I sure hope you've got a bigger vial of that *Derma-Bond*, Patel. You're gonna' need it when the Centurion here runs his sword through your cowardly little hide."

Logan and Patel spun around to see were confronted by Strife and a small group of soldiers at the far end of the alley. Turning the other way to run, they were met with a similar group of soldiers approaching from the other end.

"Oh, and don't bother reaching for your paralyzers. Mine's already set on kill. Huh, funny how Satorsky never created a directive on us taking one another out, and should I miss, Ocky's men here will be glad to put a lance through your head." A sickly smile spread over Strife's face as she finished her last words. Logan looked at her in disbelief.

"Strife, *who are you*?" "Why are you doing this?"

"What do you mean, why? I know your profile, Logan. These Christian fanatics killed your family. And still you're going to go back and tell them all this is true. What's wrong with you? They killed your family, 'for God's sake'." The tiniest of a devilish smirk crossed her face replaced immediately with deep anguish. "Do you think I'm going to let you do that? You're not the only one who lost people you love. I was six years old when my father, good Reverend Strife, raped me!" Strife sobbed her hand shaking as she pointed the paralyzer at an ashen Logan. "They put him in prison and my mother cried every day of her life for the next thirty years for the only man she ever loved. She never held me again! She never kissed me goodnight again. She never told me she loved me ever again. So now all of you, every one of you hypocrites, the good reverend Strife, and that Rabbi imposter, are going to pay. And I don't care if you and I both roast in Hell for it."

"Victoria, I'm sorry about what happened to your mother, but this is not about what happened to you. This is about innocent men, women and children who are going to die. These are families who are getting in the way of your vengence!" Strive and her entourage drew closer.

"Well, in the words of a popular Christian author, "let them do so, and decrease the surplus population!" Logan was well recovered now and walking over, looked straight into her eyes.

"Who made you so cold?"

Strife looked back smugly but silently before answering. "You did, and all those like you."

"Anything else you and Scrooge have in common?"

"Yes, we're both on the path to Hell. Only, I'm taking

you two with me," She retorted pointing to the sentry to bind Logan and Patel's hands.

"Oh, don't make any extra effort on my part," Patel chimed in meekly.

"Oh, it's the least I can do. After all we're all in this together", she quipped, "one big happy family, remember?" As they were being led away Logan turned to Octavius.

"She has a demon, you know. Don't listen to her."

"Yes, I know," he smiled slyly, "so do I. Besides, my orders come from the Prefect. She has a… way with him," he smiled prompting Logan to look with bewilderment at Strife, "Now, come along!" The group moved off, drifting away from the unguarded *Essene gate*, and in the nearby shadows of the narrow alleyway, a young raven-haired boy clutched his three gold coins.

The road to the *Fortress Antonia* was crowded with military patrols, each alternately marching into and out of the garrison as they returned from duty. Logan, fairly confident of breaking his bindings and overcoming his guards, searched for a way of escape. To execute his plan would require Patel's help however, and with his condition deteriorating rapidly, he was in no condition to fight

Roman soldiers. For now, Logan concluded, they would have to bide their time, and look for a less restrictive environment.

Perhaps all Herod sought was more diamonds to add to his already burgeoning treasury. Logan thought to himself he would gladly give Herod all the diamonds he had if he would only grant both men their freedom.

One additional concern added to Logan's willingness to play captive to Strife's whims. He needed to know how much information about the future she had passed on to her new associates. As Satorsky had been adamant to point out, the least piece of information revealed could dramatically affect earth's history. Even if it did not directly benefit him at the time, Logan needed to know what Herod knew.

So, bound by chains of their own making, the two seemingly helpless captives made their way up the cobble stone roadway to the imposing structure ahead. Entering through the heavy gates of the fortress, Logan and Patel were led through a myriad of torch lit hallways and into the heart of the limestone building. With a nod from Octavius, two enormous doors, ornately adorned with golden overlay, and guarded by two of the biggest Roman soldiers Logan had ever seen, swung open to reveal the Great hall of the fortress.

The Great hall, an enormous cavity within the fortress, was some 30 meters long and 20 meters wide. Its raised ceiling was an architectural accomplishment, reaching some fifteen meters towards heaven. Well-lit with dozens of flaming torches mostly arranged at the end of the hallway, the room glowed with reflected light from walls alternately adorned with gold and bronze trimmings. At the far end of the room, an enormous gilded throne rose some four meters off the floor on its own platform. The throne itself was trimmed with ivory, as were the two large staircases juxtaposed to each side of the platform, ascending to the upper chambers of the second floor.

On the throne sat a large heavy-set man with long richly colored robes and a relatively smallish bejeweled crown adorning his portly forehead. The two captives and their entourage were brought before the throne under a heavily-armed guard. As they approached, Logan noticed an unusual wooden device mounted at the edge of the elevated stage. Unique in its design, like a giant crossbow, it was unusual in that it was posted with its own sentry. The sentry moved the device to follow Logan and Patel, aiming it as a weapon. Strife, who moved close to the weapon, smirked, recognizing the look of fascination she recalled when Logan first encountered the TAV.

"Patel, look that's a 'Scorpion'," the Guardian spoke in a half whisper. Patel jumped as Logan spoke the word scorpion, quickly lifting his feet to avoid small multi-legged creatures.

"Where, where, get it off!"

"No, you dimwit, look there on the platform. See that sentry behind the wooden device."

"Oh, that! So," Patel said relieved "what's a scorpion?"

"Don't you remember your history? Julius Caesar used that device to defeat the Gauls and take over half of Europe."

"Big hairy deal, the Gauls were barbarians, so he defeated a few with that old catapult."

"That's no catapult. That thing shoots arrows the size of small missiles, and Caesar was outnumbered six to one!"

"So what'll we do?"

"If we need to run, we take that man out first. That device probably requires someone who knows how to work it."

The two captives and their escort finished crossing the huge expanse of the hallway to stand in the well-lit area just before the platform. Facing them stood a man some forty years of age, wearing ornate robes, his shoulders draped in long black greasy hair. He smelled the distinctive pungent odor of a curious combination of garlic and myrrh.

Warily the rotund ruler approached the captives as if expecting an attack at any moment. Watching, he was careful to ensure that the sentry manning the 'Scorpion' was keeping the weapon precisely trained on his adversaries. Slowly he moved closer, alternately turning to the officer and pointing to make sure the device was still aimed. With the eye of an engineer he methodically examined each prisoner, walking from one side to the other. As Herod approached Logan, a wave of nausea descended on the guardian as he was almost overcome with the stench.

Obviously pleased, the tyrant's wide-eyed expression became exaggerated and distorted, reminding Logan of the expression he had seen on a penal colony inmate as it tore the wings from a common housefly. Eventually he spoke, his voice somewhat effeminate and whiny, this time reminding Logan of an obnoxious classmate that had ratted on him in primary school.

"So, here we all are at last. You know, I sent one Centurion for you months ago. Rumor has it he befriended that Nazarene and so disobeyed my orders. Do you know what became of that man?"

"Let's see. Let me guess. He's now your second in command?" Logan responded as he deftly struggled to loosen the ropes binding his hands behind his back.

"Ha Ha Ha Ha! You do have a singular wit about you, don't you, Mr. Logan? I was not told that quality about you. Surprising, because I was told so many other things about you……" he smiled leering at Strife as he continued. "You are after all the one who single-handedly defeated a battalion of my elite troops? Aren't you?"

"Did you say elite or petite?"

Herod motioned and a foot soldier struck a blow to Logan's jaw, bringing a small trickle of blood to the edge of the explorer's mouth.

"You see we do know a few things about you. For instance, the special armor all three of you wear does have one weakness---It doesn't cover your head. So let's just say that will be quite enough of your mouth. Your friend here, the enchantress, I believe you call her Strife, has been ever so informative about who you are and where you've come from." Logan shot a look at Strife who remained stone faced.

"I'm afraid several of Octavius' best soldiers will never be quite the same, for she put up quite the fight at first. Let's not go into the particulars, let bygones be bygones. Suffice it to say the Romans are quite adept at physical coercion. It didn't take much to get her to talk, once she was… 'subdued'."

Logan felt a lump in the pit of his stomach as he realized what Herod was so gleefully proclaiming to him. He couldn't fault Strife for talking after what they had evidently done, but he feared the damage done to history.

"Now, as I was saying," Herod continued, "you too will have the opportunity to contribute to my cause."

"And just what cause would that be?"

"Why to take over the empire of course," Herod said with a lackadaisical attitude. Logan hesitated before probing further.

"And if we refuse?"

Herod immediately fell into a veritable fit of uncontrollable laughter, which lasting an inordinate period of time left Herod dabbing the tears from his eyes with the hem of his robe.

"Ahem, yes, If you refuse then I shall have to introduce you to my pet, her name is *Jezebel*. Perhaps you know her by her more common name, 'the cat of nine tails'." Herod's attitude suddenly became aggressive as he drew from underneath a nearby table a two meter long leather whip with metallic barbs on the end. Cradling and stroking the weapon like a cherished family pet, Herod continued, "Your friend the Centurion died under the weight of her claws, and even now, as we speak, your friend, the Carpenter who walks on water; is being prepared to whet her appetite. Ferocious little beast she is, quite the appetite for human flesh. Now, are you going to tell me what I want to know or shall we strip your skin from your body? What is your mission? Who are you spying for and at what port is your ship anchored?"

Logan relaxed, relieved that Strife obviously had concocted a story.

"ANSWER ME!" Herod screamed as he brandished the whip and paced back and forth before his two captives.

"You wouldn't believe me if I told you."

Herod became enraged, handing the whip to Octavius and immediately pointing to Logan. The commanding officer positioned himself behind Logan and cracked the whip smartly down the spine of the chrononaut. Logan instinctively flinched as sparks flew from the metallic barbs dancing off the surface of the contracted survival suit. The woolen tunic, now shredded, fell to the ground in a heap revealing the black and blue garment protecting him. Another blow fell upon the midsection, again with no result. Each successive blow allowed Logan to expose more and more of the rope bindings around his wrist to the tearing action of the barbed whip.

"Amazing, truly amazing armor," Herod said mesmerized.

"Oh, this little thing, it's just something I threw on," Logan quipped.

"Oh, really? Guards, strip them!" With that the guards roughly stripped Patel down to his survival-suit.

"Now remove their armor!" Herod commanded.

This time Logan was ready. Quickly he snapped the remaining strands of his wrist bindings as the first of two sentries pounced. Logan grabbed the largest of the pair and pushed them both backwards into Patel. The timing was uncannily precise, as the loud crack of wood against wood announced the launch of the three-foot iron spike. The lance sizzled as it sliced the air and ripped through the abdomen of the first sentry and into second's. With two of Herod's most trusted guards now firmly impaled, Logan yanked Patel from under the mass of the two fallen soldiers. Lifting him like a child, he gathered the lance and shuttled both behind one of the dozens of colonnades lining the walls of the massive hallway.

"Kill them and I will show you the power of the suits. We can rule together." Strife demanded.

"She's as crazy as he is," Logan said as he holstered the lance from behind the colonnade.

Frantically Herod nodded his head towards the sentry manning the 'scorpion', but not before the shimmering neon glow of a paralyzing beam lanced across the floor felling the soldier. Logan quickly picked up a nearby sword.

"So how do we kill them now?" Herod yelled to Strife as he stumbled up the platform to cower behind his throne.

The answer never came, interrupted instead by the loud noise of brass clanging as Logan disabled another armored ruffian. The next soldier's encounter with the Guardian cast him nearly airborne into His Majesties' royal buffet. Brass dishes, brimming with their culinary contents, flung like Frisbees around the royal throne splattering everything including the inflamed despot who frantically attempted to rescue any remaining morsel.

"Kill them!" he shrieked still cramming delicacies into the gaping hole between his red hot cheeks.

Strife struggled desperately to activate her paralyzer which had become damaged in her previous scuffles with Herod's men.

"Quick, use your paralyzer, get back to the ship!" he yelled at Patel as the remaining three guards converged on him.

Patel turned running for the hallway's large double doors, his anemic speed enabled by the survival suit's capabilities. As he approached the hall's entrance both doors swung open as four large sentries entered quickly to block his exit. Immediately they were illuminated by the blue arc of a paralyzing beam from Logan across the room. With Patel's exit now unimpeded, he raced for the open doorway just as the warning light inside his Nano-lens flashed. The brilliance of the ruby-red light was the last thing he saw as the hardened tip of the scorpion's iron lance penetrated his occipital cortex, severing his brain and pinning him to the hallway door.

Logan stood there stunned, paralyzed by the image of the impaled scientist's bloody form reflexively flinching, his cranium crushed beyond recognition.

With Patel's death, Logan's rage took control. Like a mad man, he inched his way towards the throne, slicing and dicing anyone who stood in his way. Fighting instinctively, his eyes raced to locate the 'scorpion' at the other end of the platform. There sat Strife, perched upon the device as she finished reloading and quickly swung the weapon in his direction intent on releasing yet another 'missile'.

Suddenly, Patel's survival suit exploded in a violent eruption of heat and flame. The force, so powerful that it collapsed the entrance beams to the doorway, totally destroyed all traces of Patel's body and the technology adorning him. The resulting shockwave allowed Logan to swing his current adversary into the path of the oncoming missile, impaling him to a nearby column. With her opportunity passed, Strife screamed at the remaining two guards.

"Kill him!"

"Ahhhhh!" Logan screamed in rage as the remaining two sentries converged on him at full speed, swords drawn. As each man came within range he was met by a flurry of blows from Logan's sword. Deftly sweeping the first guard off his feet, he caused the other to trip over the first, temporarily disabling both.

It was then that Logan noticed the commotion coming from the hallway entrance behind him. Soldiers outside the Great hallway hearing the disturbance within began erecting battering rams to rapidly clear the debris and bodies from the doorway.

"That looks like my exit cue."

Bolting, Logan headed for the large semicircular staircase leading to the hallway's second floor. Half way up the stairway, Logan was intercepted by a grinning Octavius, his sword drawn and held high above his head.

"Going somewhere?"

"I was hoping for a room with a view."

The first blow shattered Logan's sword causing him to default to his iron lance. Spear against foil, the two dueled, each vicious blow further shortening Logan's weapon. One misplaced swing by the Centurion allowed Logan to seize the opportunity. Catching his opponent's arm, he flipped him to the floor, stripping him of his weapon. Logan ascended the staircase with his newly acquired sword while Strife and numerous guards followed in hot pursuit. Despite his enhanced fleet footedness, Logan realized he had no idea where he was going, nor could he forever outrun a determined suit-enhanced Strife. He needed a diversion and he needed one fast.

There, hanging over the staircase, was an enormous tapestry hung by a single ornate rope threaded through two edge flaps. In a single swinging motion, like a shot-putter throwing his disc, Logan launched the short Roman sword towards the wall. It ricocheted off the bricks, just below the large wooden peg which held the supporting ropes, and like a knife slicing butter, the razor-sharp blade severed the cord, sending the enormous tapestry billowing down upon his pursuers. As it engulfed his enemies, Logan gained precious seconds racing down the dimly-lit hallway and into the labyrinth of suites above.

Frantically he searched for an escape route in each of the upper rooms. Strife, who had bolted over the mass of humanity still caught under the tapestry, ascended to the top of the stairway, racing down the hallway searching every room.

Meanwhile, her quarry having entered the last room of the hallway, found himself in the luxurious chamber of the king. Carpeted from wall to wall, beautiful tapestries surrounded the entire perimeter of the paneled room. Magnificent to behold, vaulted ceilings and immensely tall open windows yielded a virtually unimpeded view of the plaza below.

Logan had worked his way around approximately half of the windows of the room when he finally located what he was looking for. Some ten meters below was an innocent enough looking wagon loaded with a large mound of mottle colored hay. With its driver momentarily absent it was an easy target.

Immediately the chrononaut began wrestling to open the grating before him, until he was startled by the clicking noise behind him of an old iron door latch. Turning he ducked just in time to avoid the slash of Strife's sword as she scoured the curtains just above his head. With her first blow unsuccessful, she was not fast enough to anticipate Logan's response- a quick solid suit-enhanced kick to the midriff. The forceful blow, harmless in its effect, was sufficient to propel Strife out of the way. Effortlessly, Logan sailed out the window, breaking his fall by clutching the torn edge of the beautiful drapery. Strife stood helplessly gazing down as Logan smile and waved from the driverless hay wagon now moving away. Some distance behind its owner frantically gave chase. There, covered mostly in the tan and chocolate colored hay of recently cleaned stalls, sat Logan smiling and wiping the droppings from his suit, much like he had in Becky's barn.

Buried up to his neck in clump stained hay, Logan could still have easily viewed the surrounding activity in the fortress' plaza around him. Unfortunately, this was not to be the case as flies swarmed furiously around the dung tainted explorer distracting him from the normal, even mundane activity of the streets moving by him. Slowly the rickety cart made its way towards the end of the courtyard, stopping only for traffic at one section. At this point the driver reached the wagon halting it just outside the prison yard where new detainees were interred. Taking the opportunity to inspect his surroundings Logan noticed some unusual activity as a large group of soldiers had gathered to taunt some poor wretch within their circle. The man wilted under the merciless beating, filthy from the blood-stained mud which coated him like the manure encasing Logan. A large crowd of soldiers and civilians, frenzied almost to the point of exhaustion, gathered around the stone wall enclosing the courtyard.

"Animals," Logan cursed under his breath as he wiped away a fist full of flies. What happened next was not really clear to Logan. Was it the sudden recognition of a man in the crowd that he viewed over the stone wall, or the shadowy edge of the thorny crown on the victim's head that registered first? For there in the crowd, watching the beating was John, Jesus' closest friend. Bitter tears rolled down his flushed cheeks mingled with a torrent of sweat streaming from his brow as he screamed vehemently, begging for the men to stop the carnage.

Logan's pulse quickened as he felt an incredible knot tighten in the pit of his stomach.

"What do I do? What do I do?" he whispered to himself. Why did the cart continue to linger for an eternity?

He looked again only to see the beatings by men twice Jesus' size getting progressively more and more vicious. It was then, for the dust surrounding the Nazarene had changed to mud, that Logan realized the severity of Jesus' blood loss. Turning away for a moment and then back again, Logan saw the carpenter was now down on all fours as a huge man approached. A terrible shriek tore through the air as the titan tore a huge chunk of beard from Jesus' face.

'Why is this happening?' Logan agonized as his head began to spin, the mental and spiritual tug of war of the past few months now coming to bear full force. As he sat there plastered by the surrounding dung, Logan looked back at the blood coating Jesus' skin. Turning, he frantically wiped over and over the refuse from his hands. Desperately he tried to scrub away the dark stains, his mind seeing only the fruit of his own sin stained life. His skull now throbbed with what seemed like a hundred regrets, each threatening at any moment to explode into a chain reaction of irrational acts. Desperately he fought to contain the war within him and remain hidden and silent within the cart.

When he could stand it no more, he decided to act. Powering up his paralyzer, he set it for multiple targets and rose from his position in the cart. His driver who had momentarily stepped down from the cart was nowhere to be seen. Logan's plan, as crazy as it seemed, was to paralyze as many of the soldiers as he could before running to escape with Jesus.

As the paralyzer cycled up to full load, Logan drew a bead from his half-concealed position in the cart. Locking on the three largest guards currently thrashing Jesus, Logan activated the device expecting the usual electric blue discharge. Instead the wrist mounted device emitted a barely discernable high-pitched whine followed by a golden shower of discharge flowing from Logan's left forearm enveloping his entire body. Disabled by his own technology the Guardian immediately collapsed. Slowly he drifted off, dragged down into a suffocating sea of darkness.

Logan's self-induced coma gradually faded, its nothingness replaced by a bone-chilling shroud, penetrating and enveloping him like a massive snow bank in which he lay naked. Death-like in its darkness it cloaked him as if every light in the universe had simultaneously been snuffed out. Gradually these sensations retreated, fading as Logan's mind struggled to rejoin the conscious universe. His brain was still groggy from the effects of the short circuit, when the time-traveler clambered from the safety of his excrement laden cradle.

The cart untouched and parked mysteriously under the shade of a large olive tree, yielded its aromatic cargo back to the dark and dusty streets of Jerusalem. Shaken and weary, Logan drug himself from the roadside and blended into the shadows of the ancient capitol's narrow alleyways. Roman guards patrolled the crowded thoroughfares as Logan, scrubbed 'clean' in a public pool while wearing a 'borrowed' tunic, set himself the task of locating a weakness in the patrols of the southern wall. This task soon proved to be daunting as the meticulous Roman patrols left only seconds in their changing of the guard.

Finally, Logan settled by one particular section of broken-down wall casually patrolled and adjacent to a nearby basket-weaving establishment. Slipping neatly behind a mountain of the woven crocks, Logan drifted in and out of consciousness for hours. His restless sleep was tortured by images of Jesus' bloody beating, Legion's grisly jowls and the flinching corpse of Patel's impaled body. Tainted in between each of these were terrifying reflections of his own final metamorphosis. Terrified, he tore himself from sleep drenched in the cold sweat of fear.

So he sat there, too tired to run and too scared to sleep. For the first time in his life he was forced to be still and contemplate the reason for his life. He began to wonder, 'Why was I born?' and 'What was I meant to accomplish?' and again 'What am I becoming?'. 'What if everything I've ever done and every choice I've ever made, made me?' 'What if each turn led me closer to or further away from what I was intended to be?'

"Huh?" he quietly chuckled, "son of light or son of hell?"

This thought led to its unwelcome progeny crowding forcefully into his mind.

'What if Jesus was right about mankind? What if every wrong he'd ever had 'forced' God to experience it too? If so, at his bidding, God would have been locked in a nightmare, an unwilling passenger of sorts, who providing us the gas, the car and the keys, was made to ride along to every cat house, every drug deal, every porn site, and every bar we'd ever visited. He would truly be the One silently wounded with every sin, and we would be the ones ultimately responsible.

Physically and emotionally exhausted, Logan's mind drifted in and out of consciousness, until suddenly the mountain of baskets he hid under inexplicably trembled and collapsed in a mudslide of wicker. As Logan crawled out from underneath the splintered heap, he looked around him surprised to see no one there. Ahead two guards were locked in a heated argument allowing Logan to slip behind them, up the narrow staircase, and over the wall.

It was noon on Friday when Logan reached the ground outside of Jerusalem's walls. Mingling with the swelling crowds, Logan noticed dozens of people talking heatedly and pointing to a crowded column of people winding up a narrow road off in the distance. Hundreds of people lined this road to the hill called Golgotha, many of them pushing, shoving and jockeying for position in line. Shrieks and wails rang out from the hillside above as two men were raised high upon large wooden structures crudely resembling crosses.

Logan's mind raced, retracing the time with Jesus just before the cleansing of the temple. His recognition of the hillside brought the realization that this was the final waypoint in the most difficult mission of his life. As he struggled with the overwhelming desire to find

Barnabas and head for home, he suddenly heard the unmistakable 'clink' of metal striking metal. Then another blow and another as more wailing echoed down the hillside. Then, nothing for a long time, followed slowly by the sound of creaking wood as a third man, his face shadowed by the sun, was raised between the two already there.

He did not need to see the face to recognize the form, and then he knew he could not leave. There was too much at stake. So girding his loins and shaking the cobwebs from his head, Logan rounded the dusty streets and proceeded to traverse the road to the top. Lost in the ascending and descending multitudes, he smiled knowingly as he went easily undetected by the overwhelmed Roman guards.

Some three hours later, he reached the hillside's apex and cleared the last natural barrier obstructing his view. There hung Jesus, his motionless body unceremoniously displayed between two rugged looking men likewise scourged and exposed for all humanity to see.

What Logan's childhood stories had never told him was how much a man scourged, beaten and crucified could change in the few hours between the beginning of his torture and the time of his demise. As Logan stared at the corpse hanging before him, he realized that he would not have recognized him had it not been for the presence of his mourning disciples. Mary, his mother, the other Mary and John formed a small portion of the inner circle that had stood patiently waiting for the end to finally come. Logan moved in closer towards his friends in an effort to scan the body.

His first impression of the form he saw before him was one of skepticism. The masklike face was drained of all blood and withered from dehydration. Huge areas of raw skin on the cheek and jaw bones had bled into the beard matting it to the neck and face. Logan was shocked at the almost ghostlike skull that stared back at him. It seemed impossible that this twisted shape before him was the same gentle man who weeks earlier Logan had come to esteem and now revere.

As he moved closer, he noticed the large hands, remembering the day they had mercifully "given him the shirt off his back." Quickly he scanned the ground before him locating the neatly folded tunic gathered with a soldier's daily possessions. Kneeling beside the small stack of belongings, he located the identification tag tearing it neatly from the hidden edge within the fabric's bottom fold.

Rising, he returned to study the mask-like face of the corpse before him. The eyes now sunken far back into the head were locked into an open position. Their appearance was unnerving to Logan, so accustomed was he to their deeply piercing gaze.

Jesus' body was also profoundly altered, the extreme dehydration resulting in an ugly contrast between the protruding belly of pleural edema and the other flesh shrunken into what seemed to be the very crevices of the underlying bones.

Circling the cross to see all angles, he scanned the body remembering the gentle moments of laughter Jesus had shared with his disciples as they traded barbs over evening meals. The crowd gasped as the Romans rotated the body preparing to remove it. As they did so, Logan nearly stumbled when the Nazarene's back came into view. The tissue, shredded to ribbons by the 'cat of nine tails', exposed the very sinews, muscles and bones composing Jesus's back. Large sections of his rib cage were flayed open exposing portions completely stripped of all flesh.

The detailed cruelty which the Romans had inflicted impressed Logan as that of a madman seeking to extract the very last ounce of pain he could wring from his victim.

"They hated you without cause," Logan mused silently remembering a line Jesus had once uttered.

The crucifixion itself while cruel, with its large iron spikes driven well into the ankle and wrist regions of the body, seemed to be an almost afterthought to the trauma from Jesus' scourging.

Logan marveled at how anyone could survive such a beating, and later would hear of how the soldiers were punished by Pilate for their unusual brutality. The commander of the guard assembled his soldiers, intending to break the legs of those crucified and hasten their deaths before the Passover officially began. Logan scanned Jesus' lifeless body as the soldiers approached. In only a few moments, the two other men expired by asphyxiation once their legs were broken, but when the soldiers came to Jesus corpse he was spared. Logan's scan revealed what he already knew, death by cardiovascular collapse secondary to ventricular rupture, blood loss and extreme dehydration.

Suddenly the body lurched forward as if to attack the explorer. Logan's heart leapt, as both horrified and startled, he jumped backwards. It was only from this new angle that he saw the soldier with the lance. Blood and water seeped from the newly formed laceration before the soldiers finished their task of lowering the cross to the ground. Logan slid closer to John who wept and spoke silently.

"From the day I first met you, my friend, your heart was ready to burst. '*Eloi, Eloi lama sabachthani.*' Logan nodded his head solemnly in agreement and then whispered as he helped him place the burial napkin over Jesus' face.

"New wine, unfit for an old broken vessel, was poured for us. '*Eloi, Eloi lama sabachthani.*' John hung his head and wept silently as Logan vainly felt for a pulse, himself fighting back the tears. In a few moments the burial sheet was in place, as the two men stood looking down at line of hundreds still waiting to ascend.

"They say you can measure the life of a man lived, by the number of friends at his funeral," the voice behind Logan whispered. With this the guardsman turned to see Nicodemus, braving the ire of both Romans and Pharisees, stepping through the line to help lift the body.

"He is unclean," Logan reminded the Pharisee.

"Aren't we all?" came the reply as Logan smiled stepping away from the body.

Logan nodded.

"You have no idea, Rabbi, how many take their stand with you here today." Nicodemus was silent as he stared at the draped corpse before him.

"If you don't leave now, 'Charlestonian', they may never hear," The Pharisee replied smiling extending both his hands in a hearty grip with Logan's. At once the explorer was gone, heading down the hill towards the rendezvous point with Barnabas.

CHAPTER TWENTY-TWO
The Beginning of the End

A cool damp breeze sent a chill down Logan's spine as he descended the crowded trail to meet Barnabas. The weather was changing, and Logan hoped it wasn't an indication of his fortunes. Above him, looming like an immense tsunami, he beheld shadowy cumulus pillars billowing towards Jerusalem from a northeastern direction. The commander of the guard on Golgotha had been the first to notice the almost unheard-of direction of weather flow, lending credence along with the manner in which Jesus had died, to his statement, "He truly was a son of god."

Down below in the marketplace of Jerusalem, a dozen of Octavius' best soldiers were converging. There in the midst stood Strife conversing with the squad's commander.

"He has eluded us. We've searched everywhere and he is nowhere in the city," the Roman commander complained bitterly.

"He's here. Did you try Barnabas and the Nazarene's friends?"

"They are all out of the city," the commander pronounced with hand gestures of frustration in the direction of Golgotha.

"Out of the city, what do you mean out of the city?" Strife shot back incredulously.

"Pilate has ordered the Nazarene to die. They have all gone to watch, fools, every one of them!"

"Of course, Golgotha! Commander, follow me. Bring your men. I know exactly where we will find him." Strife exclaimed excitedly as the Centurion motioned for his squad. They raced out through the *Gennath gate*, pausing only momentarily to get their bearings and gawk at the panorama of darkening skies.

"That's darn unusual," Strife remarked noting the direction of the approaching wall of swirling darkness.

On the opposite side of the Hinnom valley, powerful winds and dust had begun their dramatic dance announcing the arrival of the season's first winter sand storm. Cloaked in its mist, running and tumbling down the steep hillside from Golgotha, Logan rolled to the bottom and out of sight. Just outside of the *Gennath gate*, somewhere near the *Serpent's pool*, stood the last of his anxious friends and two very large camels loaded with provisions.

Oblivious to the approaching squad of soldiers behind him, Barnabas carefully scanned the horizon for Logan. As he strained, tracing the shadows and outline of Golgotha, the squad led by Strife and Octavius emerged from a local merchant's tent. The small man was a trader in grain and caravan supplies and only too eager to rid himself of his inquisitors. Grasping the arm of Octavius he turned the centurion, motioning in the direction of Barnabas. Fortunately their vantage point was some three hundred meters away and thus the only things visible to the pursuers were the hind sides of several very large camels. Across from these, behind some very large boulders and a small cluster of acacia trees, Barnabas and his trusty mounts waited faithfully.

To say that Strife and her companions were skeptical by this point would be an understatement. The fatigued squad had tracked, tailed, shadowed and dogged more than three dozen wild goose chases. Each step now involved questioning more and more bewildered bystanders while simultaneously inspecting dozens of nomadic tents pitched along the road side. Slowly they grew closer.

On the other side of the boulders, and behind the camels, stood a very concerned Barnabas pacing impatiently as he awaited Logan's arrival. Suddenly, from behind, a strong arm pulled him back into the shadows, its hand clenched over his mouth.

"Quiet! Do you want to wake the entire legion?" Logan whispered before releasing his grip of the large disciple's mouth. The two men turned to face one another, Barnabas' grinned widely.

"Jonny, my good friend, we heard you and Patel were dead. Oh heaven be praised above, at least you have survived. I'm so sorry about your friend. But, oh my, your neck Jonny, what have they done to you? Those barbarians…" Barnabas gasped, his hand reaching to examine the left side of Logan's neck. After a moment of looking closely, he spoke again, his face saddened "We were too late, I'm sorry Jonny".

"What, what do you mean?" Logan said irritated, "What's wrong with my neck?" Concerned, he pulled a small pocket mirror from the sleeve of his survival suit. There in the partial light he saw what he had feared for months. Loosening the collar before Barnabas' ever widening eyes, Logan gasped to see the vasculitis which had spread rapidly, covering eighty five percent of his neck. The normal tan skin tone of his throat was now almost completely obscured by the purple-red hue of a network of inflamed and swollen vessels. Spidery tentacles bulged with their dreaded port wine fluid pulsating like some amoeboid creature growing up the carotid line just below the jaw line. Logan stared at his body momentarily before speaking.

"You are right, my ancient friend," Logan echoed to a wide-eyed and speechless Barnabas, "It is too late for me, but not my people. I haven't much time left. Soon this will consume me," he said pointing to his neck, "and I will become more animal than man. I must get home, now!" Logan straightened his tunic again.

"Beloved, you don't know that. It is too soon to tell. Perhaps you will choose a nice Jewish girl next time. Not as many social diseases to regard," Barnabas quipped as they mounted their camels and headed away from the approaching squad. Logan smiled rolling his eyes appreciative of his good friend's attempt to make light of his condition.

"Trust me, this is no social disease and there's *not* going to be a next time."

"Never fear, the Lord can still work through even this."

"Yeh, how?" Logan laughed incredulously.

"I don't know, we shall see, that is the adventure of the life of faith," Barnabas responded enthusiastically as the two men rode quickly into the partially obscured sun of the approaching Negev.

Unbeknownst to them, they were in the crosshairs of a Nano-lens. Seven hundred meters away, stood Strife, Octavius and their company at the point where Barnabas and Logan had met. Ahead the darkening clouds grew more ominous as the two disciples headed directly into the approaching storm. Strife turned to Octavius.

"Have the men saddle camels for all of us. We will be heading into the desert."

Octavius snapped his fingers and immediately the sentinels rushed to the task.

"You think you know where they are headed?" he responded. Strife nodded her head as she continued to follow the outline of the men fading in the distance.

"He's headed for Idumea, and home."

Twenty-four hours later, Logan and Barnabas had stopped on a rocky ledge overlooking the main road into the Negev. Above them a sea of towering clouds spread out in all directions casting a dark and ominous ambience onto the desert landscape.

Behind them, to the north, Jerusalem was blanketed by its own dark veil refusing to yield to the penetrating rays of the noonday sun. All around scenes of violent winds, hail and intermittent lightning painted the topography as an ever-changing parade of frolicking dust devils danced over the horizon. Silently they finished the last vestiges of a lamb and fig dinner, watching the astonishing scenery transform before them, each deep in thought over the events that had transpired in the last twenty-four hours.

Concurrently, Jerusalem was having its own problems with weather. The dark overcast sky which had dampened the Passover celebration for thousands of pilgrims continued to hang over the royal city. Swirling dust storms terrorized the population as gusts in excess of seventy kilometers per hour tore through the city. Many were fearful as word spread of the unlawful crucifixion of the Nazarene who claimed to be the messiah.

As evening approached, the winds increased, howling through the ancient city's alleys and marketplace. Peppered with blasts, some powerful enough to damage common wooden structures, the mysterious winds raced through the ancient graveyards dotting the city's northwestern section. Marble tombs, shaken from their ancient foundations, cracked open yielding forth their depositories of dead.

In this night of the numinous, many strange and wonderful apparitions appeared to city's troubled souls. Friends and relatives, long since dead, were seen standing in darkened doorways, warning loved ones of the crime committed on Golgotha. The news spread like wildfire as Jerusalem became a city under conviction.

Back on the deserted bluff overlooking the road to the Negev, Logan and Barnabas reclined finishing the last of their meal, both exhausted from their all night trek. Logan alternated, popping figs one second while adjusting the circuitry of the 3-D projector the next.

"What are you doing?" Barnabas enquired fascinated by the tiny device's intricacies.

"Just preparing a little fireworks display," Logan smiled snapping the lid back on to the casing.

Barnabas frowned before beginning again. "Jonny, are you certain it is necessary to proceed at this pace. You are very sick, my friend. I fear the journey may be too much for you." Logan smiled popping another fig into his mouth, chewing slowly before answering.

"I'm fine, and if you'll look below, you'll see why we have been pressing on so diligently." There below on the desert plains rode two advanced scouts from Strife's search party, the trail of the two men they sought scoured forever clean by the cleansing winds of the howling desert. They stopped, momentarily circling, and then proceeded to travel again in a southerly direction.

"This is as far as you go, my friend," Logan informed Barnabas.

"Listen, tender-footed one, the desert goes on for miles. You will not survive! Our enemy is near," Barnabas protested pointing in the direction the scouts had followed.

"Thanks a lot, 'Mister *Son of encouragement'*," Logan smiled responding sarcastically. "That is exactly why you must turn back now. Barney, God has some great things in store for you and I'm not going to be responsible for stopping that. Look, all I have to do is stay ahead of them. Plus, if you head back now you may be able to help your friends bury Jesus." Logan looked down momentarily to calibrate his wrist guidance system. Reaffixing his gaze he met the ashen expression like that of a man who had just seen a ghost.

"Oh no…, Aaah…, you… didn't… know?" Logan stuttered, stunned at his own ineptitude. Slowly, with his hands over his mouth, Barnabas sank to his knees as Logan rushed to break his fall.

"I'm sorry, I'm so sorry. I thought you knew!"

There on the ground, head in his hands, Barnabas began to sob silently. Logan kneeled there, not quite sure what to do, his arm wrapped around the enormous trembling shoulders of the gentle disciple.

"But why? He is God's Son!" Barnabas sobbed loudly. "For *which* act of kindness did they kill him?"

Logan hesitated before answering, content just to rub his big friend's back.

"For the greatest, my friend, for *the* greatest," Logan answered sadly rubbing his dusty friend's shoulder.

"We had been waiting for so long for the Messiah to deliver us."

Logan moved around to sit in front of his crouching friend.

"That's just it, Barney. He has!" Then looking his friend in his tear stained eyes, he continued, "But not the way you or I expected him to. The way we needed him to."

Barnabas grew silent, wiping away his tears as he looked intently at Logan, listening, trying hard to understand.

"I was wrong about Him."

"Beloved, we all make mistakes."

"Yeh, but this one cost me my life, and likely the lives of millions of my people. I just couldn't hear it." Barnabas nodded his head in agreement.

"Because you listened with your ears and not your heart," the big man softly said patting his huge chest.

Logan hung his head, nodding in agreement.

"I didn't want to hear what He was saying."

"Yes, beloved, it is as you say. You are a rebel."

"Now just a minute."

"It's alright Jonny, we all are. You, me, all God's children. We are all rebels. It is the risk He took to free us."

Logan smiled letting the words sink in. "Then he must have thought it a risk worth taking, and we will not debate his profound wisdom."

"Indeed, my friend and now He calls all rebels to be strong and do what's right, to surrender, to lay down our arms, even if it means we have to give up the things we want most."

"And that's why they needed Him to die?" Logan asked.

The burly Levite nodded his head, speaking slowly and sadly.

"The thing each man needs most is the thing he is least able to do, to surrender, to submit, to die to himself. The worse a man is, the more he needs it, and the less he is able to do it."

Logan hesitated, thinking deeply of Jesus.

"Only a perfect man could repent perfectly and he would not need to."

"Exactly, my purple friend, because he was the Christ."

"God had never walked this road, had He?" Logan asked.

"You mean to surrender, to submit, and to die?" Barnabas shook his head. "No. He is above all things and all life flows through and from Him. He is life, it is impossible for him to fail and he can never die."

"So, this one road, where we needed Him to lead us the most, He was helpless?" Logan continued, "God helpless?"

"Yes, He can only give from in His own nature, this He had not," Barnabas nodded.

"But suppose our human nature could be fused with God's divine nature. Then that person could surrender, could suffer and die, because he was a man… and he could do it perfectly because he was God."

"Yes beloved," the Cyprian's eyes began to mist again.

"You and I can go through this only if God leads us through it; but God can only die if He becomes a man[1]."

---

[1] Lewis, CS, Mere Christianity, Chapter 4 the perfect penitent. 1952. Originally published by Geoffrey Bles. C.S. Lewis, *Mere Christianity* (1952; Harper Collins: 2001) 56, 57-58. I borrowed so heavily here that credit must be given to the original genius of CS Lewis.

Barnabas was silent for a moment as the words settled in. Then in a hushed, somber tone he spoke.

"That is why he kept saying, '*for this I have come into the world*'. This, beloved, is the terrible price he has paid for us."

Logan nodded staring at him.

"*For whoever wants to save his life will lose it, but whoever loses his life for my sake will find it,*" Barnabas nodded. "Then you, my brother, must go."

"And you, my friend, must go back. Your friends need you. I can find my way from here, but you must double back. If you stay, you will slow me down and you endanger us both. Stay off the trail and take this." Logan handed him a small black and silver cylinder.

"What is this, Jonny?" Barnabas asked wiping the last tear away and holding up the small device.

"This is a toy, yes, a toy. It makes pretty lights in the sky. After you have seen our enemies and they are well past you, set this on the ground and point it towards the sky. Push this button, and then ride like the wind towards Jerusalem. That way, I will know you are safe and how far behind me they are. Will you do this for me?"

"Yes Jonny, but how will you get home. Even now your sickness spreads?"

"Look, Barney, I'll be fine. I'll get home, but first I need to know you are safe, or I cannot go." Barnabas stood, beginning to slowly walk towards his camel.

"Just one more question, Logan continued."

Barnabas turned agreeing with a smile.

"What does '*Eloi, Eloi lama sabachthani*' mean?" Logan finished.

At this his huge friend's countenance again fell.

"Why must you ask this my friend?"

"Something I heard recently." Logan's words trailed off as the concerned voice of the big Cypriote interrupted."

"It is the Jewish cry of betrayal. It is only uttered by criminals and those abandoned by God," Barnabas continued slowly, "Now, I will go and I will do as you have requested my friend. Only one thing I ask in return."

"Anything," Logan said, sincerely looking Barnabas in the eye.

"Promise me you will believe. You will believe and you will not give up believing, and when it seems impossible, you will yet still believe," Barnabas insisted peering deeply into Logan's hesitant eyes.

"That's a tough order," Logan smiled as he spoke, "but as you wish. I agree. I promise to believe, even when it looks impossible. Now go, my brother. Go quickly."

Barnabas hugged Logan again before running and jumping on his camel. As he did, Logan laughed thinking how he resembled a cowboy from the Old West riding off into the sunset. Stopping only once, he waved and shouted to his friend.

"God's speed be with you!"

"And with you, *Son of Encouragement*," Logan whispered as he returned the wave.

Separating, the two men rode in opposite directions. Logan turned only once to watch the big Cyprian disappear over the horizon and into the dust before him. Then following his wrist beacon, he turned racing headlong through the barren wilderness and into the approaching storm. Hours later as midnight approached, a distant flare exploded, partially shrouded. Its scarlet glow spiraled its way through the towering clouds, climbing them like a stairway to heaven. Logan stopped to look for only a moment as he quickened his pace.

CHAPTER TWENTY-THREE
A Timely Retribution

Two o'clock in the morning arrived quickly as an exhausted Logan spread out his bedroll on the sandy beach of *Ein Avdat*. Here he had planned a short break to water and feed himself and his camel. Four hours later, the sojourner woke to an enormous bolt of lightning and a deafening clap of thunder that caused him to leap from the desert floor. Struggling to calm his pounding heart, he stooped to fill his canteen and splash a little on his face.

Perhaps it was the rippled surface distorting his reflected image that first startled the man. What he saw reflected in the pool's morning light was only partially man, the lower third of his face covered in a ghastly swathe of quivering entrails. Stunned, Logan could do nothing but stare at the mottled gaze looking back at him. Wine and indigo colored vessels throbbed weaving their hideous tapestry encapsulating his entire neck while winding their tentacles up and over his mandible ending just below his lower lip.

Suddenly, a man's scream startled him. First one and then another piercing the morning air. The voice, while very familiar, was difficult for Logan to place. The cry echoed within the canyon its tortured tenor seemingly coming from all sides. Logan traced the upper edge of the jagged cliffs partially surrounding the pool.

"Ahhhhh! Ohhhhhhh! Ahhhhh!", again came the cries. Logan turned to see several shadows on the plateau just above him and to the right. Immediately the Nano-lens adjusted its night vision capabilities allowing the magnified image of the shadows to come more clearly into view. There on the rocky plateau knelt Barnabas caught between two Roman guards with each man twisting one of the huge man's arms. As Logan scanned the big man's face more closely he could see multiple contusions including a left eye so swollen that it was completely shut. There at Barnabas' side stood Strife. Slowly she moved into view.

"Hey flyboy, look who we found yesterday. Hah! We never would have known he was there if not for that little flare you gave him. What would Satorsky say about that, big guy? A little violation of the prime directive, huh, just between friends?" Strife chided in a childish voice.

"Don't worry, we cleaned up your mess." Then holding her hand to her forehead to screen out the glare from the early morning rays she continued.

"Oooh, and speaking of messes, either my *Nano-lens* needs cleaning or you're looking a little purple around the gills, big guy," Strife hissed, her taunts producing the intended grimace from Logan.

"What's wrong? Vasculitis gone to your head?" she laughed. "I guess we can chalk this last slip up to unstable cerebral vascular flow. Too bad your hero 'the water walker' isn't around to clear that rash up for you. I guess you'll just have to die. What a shame."

"Hey, before you go, can I ask your opinion? You always were so opinionated. How do you think I should kill our friend here? I thought a slow painful death like his carpenter friend's would be appropriate. Of course, if I do, Paul is going to be awful lonely on his first missionary journey. Then again… we could work a trade. Say, him for you and the cylinder?"

Logan tried to think quickly, but his mind was becoming more and more clouded by the vasculitis' effects and his extreme fatigue.

"How do I know you'll let him go?"

"You don't. I guess you'll just have to trust me, because you simply have no choice."

Logan moved over to his camel retrieving a small black pouch from the saddlebags. Opening the case he retrieved the small 3D projector he had adjusted earlier. Deftly, he slipped a tiny sliver of a computer chip into the activation port of the device and tucked the entire unit into his suit pocket.

"Commander, what are you doing?" Strife shouted straining to see his movements.

"Just getting the cylinder. I'm coming up. You win."

Logan circled the spring and began his ascent up the sloping edge of the banks to the cliff side. His climb was slow and deliberate, mostly hiding him from view for several minutes at a time. As he ascended Strife turned to Octavius and his subordinates.

"When he gets up here, tie him up immediately. Then have your men set up camp and get some rest. Tell them we will leave at sunrise," Strife commanded bluntly. Octavius, offended at being commanded by a woman, appeared as if he were ready to strike his female subordinate. Raising his arm to backhand her, he was suddenly restrained by his second in command, who pointed to the contusions covering his own face. Reluctantly, Octavius relented, casting an angry glare at Strife, before briskly pushing through his men to apprehend the chrononaut. Quickly he grabbed Logan as he appeared over the edge of the bluff. Too exhausted to resist, Logan was bound and shoved roughly to the ground.

The small black pouch containing the precious cylinder was immediately ripped from his hands and taken to Strife. She opened it instantly, removing the eight-inch glass cylinder filled with transparent blue fluid. Inside the central chamber and suspended by its encompassing magnetic field, the brightly luminescent crystal shone.

Strife's eyes widened at the shimmering glow of the diamond crystal. Its faint aqua hue indicated that the molecular storage was now permanent.

"You're a dying fool, Logan! I would have never surrendered this. Without the crystal you have no proof of anything. You've wasted the final months of your pitiful life and now you have nothing to show for it. Look at you; you're more monster than man now," she seethed jerking his head sideways to see the throbbing vessels now coiling their way up toward his forehead, "You should thank me, because in just a few moments you and your sniveling friend here will both be dead. I'll spare you that horrid transformation you've been dreading. Then I will snuff out the tiny band of disciples Jesus has left and the world will be rid of those miserable Jesus freaks forever. Mankind can be free to progress without the tyranny of religion."

"Sounds like the ranting of a madman to me. Have you been off your medication again?" Logan quipped.

"You're the one who needs medication, you freak. Look at you," she said tersely wrenching the guardsman's head backwards, "What has becoming one of them done for you? Has the Jew cured you? No! You're dying Logan, its over! Nothing can save you now. Not Satorsky and certainly not that dead Jew. That's the kind of insanity religion causes. I'm going to stop it, here and now, before it spreads."

"Oh, so I guess you're going to kill Mohammed too? And what about Buddha and the Dali Lama, or does your little game only apply to Christians?"

"They are the worst!"

"In what way?"

"They talk of unconditional love and commitment and then they rape six-year-old little girls and tell them not to tell anyone or God will punish them, hypocrites."

Logan grimaced as his head was released and snapped forward, his eyes narrowing in focus on Strife's form.

"Strife, I'm sorry for what happened to you. I know how it feels to betrayed at the hands of a monster."

"Betrayed by a monster? Did you say betrayed by a monster? Still don't get it do you? I wasn't betrayed by a monster. I was betrayed by God!"

"What?"

"Yes! That's right I was a true believer. A kid in love with God, until His servant took everything from me. God could have stopped it, but he didn't. You know why? Because He doesn't exist. You're all hypocrites."

"Look, Strife, I didn't know, but if you're going to kill all the hypocrites in the world you're gonna' need a bigger gun, and in the end you're going to be all alone."

"Like you, flyboy? How does it feel to die alone? Or more importantly, how does it feel to die alone at the hands of your monster?" she hissed through clenched teeth faintly veiled by a tepid grin.

"What do you mean 'my monster'?" Logan's eyes narrowed as he spoke through clinched teeth. "You're not dying from cancer, are you? You never were."

"Very astute," she hesitated, "No, you're right. I'm not. How did you know that?"

"Increasing agitation, progressively disjointed thinking, delusions of grandeur and tactless physical relations, I'd say you have progressive traumatic brain injury. We saw it all the time in collision survivors in space. How'd you get it?" This time it was Logan who hesitated. "In the…. explosion?" Strife turned to face Logan, the subtle grin suddenly breaking into a shriek of laughter.

"Why yes….. so you've figured it out?" she choked continuing her hideous laughter.

Logan remained silent.

"They call it multiple micro-aneurysm disorder, it's essentially a slow spreading hematoma. You see, I was injured when we killed your family."

"We?" Logan's eyes narrowed to slits as he spoke tersely.

"Why we, as in the *Remnant*, of course. I thought you had figured that out?"

"I thought you hated Christians?"

"We do! What better way to destroy them than to pretend to be one and then burn their little children alive?" she smiled weakly, stifling a chuckle as her head turned engaging Logan's steely gaze.

"You should have heard their little screams as the fire burned them alive," she whispered. Logan's jaw tightened as stiff- lipped, he fought to keep the tears from falling from the corners of his eyes.

"Daddy help me! Daddy help me!" she shrieked loudly her twisted finger stabbing towards his anguished face. Then suddenly she grew quiet again, "and then your poor wife, desperately in agony, she tried to shield them from the flames with her own body. But daddy was nowhere to be found. He was too busy jumping planets a million miles away saving other families' children. I guess yours just weren't good enough for you, were they Daddy?" she smirked bending low.

Suddenly Logan lunged at her, throwing himself at her as if to bodily impale her. Instead, his left cheek was met firmly by the suit enhanced backhand of his hovering assailant. The blow sent him flailing face first back to the ground. Blood flowed freely from one of the larger vessels that had ruptured on his upper cheek, the large drops mixing in the sand as they drug him along the ground beside Barnabas.

Logan grimaced, face contorted by both pain and rage, and fought back tears as Strife opened the transparent case retrieving the glowing crystal. Holding the almond shaped crystal upwards, she admired the cascade of sunlight dancing off its intricately etched surfaces.

"Beautiful, isn't it? And worth a fortune, too bad it has to be destroyed. Fortunately, I know the only way," she smiled wryly before placing the precious stone carefully into her biometer.

"Tear open his tunic!"

The sentry approached Logan and grasping his collar with two hands roughly ripped open the coarse fabric revealing the survival suit beneath.

"In his upper chest pocket on the right side is a small metallic device. Bring it to me," she said as the soldier retrieved the 3-D device.

Projector in hand, Strife extended its tripod and activated the device by connecting the leads to her biometric wrist unit. Then, summoning the entire Roman guard closely around her to watch, she engaged the wrist port and began to display the video. Familiar scenes of Jesus and His miracles flashed by briefly, mesmerizing the soldiers, who froze like statues watching until Strife paused the floating video.

"This is it, all right. No need for you two anymore," she seethed grabbing a Roman soldier's lance, as she marched over to where Logan and Barnabas sat. Logan watched incredulously as the woman approached his Cyprian friend.

"What are you doing? You promised to let him go!"

At this, Strife squatted by Logan's side. With a cock of her head she smiled and then with almost a whisper.

"So I did."

Logan immediately felt a chill run down his spine as he realized what Strife was about to do.

"Jonathan!" Barnabas exclaimed, his eyes widening as he too realized Strife's intentions.

"Leave him alone, he's done nothing to you," Logan screamed, "I'm responsible for his actions. Take out your blood thirst on me if you want someone to hurt".

"Truer words were never spoken, you are responsible," she agreed spitefully as she suddenly drove the iron tipped lance through Barnabas' upper right chest, pinning him to the rock. Barnabas screamed as the weapon found its mark.

"NO!" Logan shouted.

"And I do want to hurt someone, you," Strife declared angrily stabbing her finger towards Logan's face, "So you just watch him die, knowing that you're responsible. All you Christians are responsible. Responsible for what you've done through the ages and responsible for what your God did to me!"

She turned away from Logan and pointing the sentry towards Barnabas commanded, "Untie him".

As he did Barnabas slumped over on his side, the bloody tip of the lance protruding through his severed tunic. Logan sat there in a state of shock, trying desperately to grasp the situation. He strained close to his fallen friend bending forward to discern if he was still breathing.

"There, I'm as good as my word. He's free," she said sarcastically as the bonds were loosened.

"You devil! What have I ever done to you? What has he done?" Logan replied through clinched teeth as he slid forward attempting to support his wounded friend. His efforts were greeted by the lance of another guard who, well aware of Logan's potential for violence, held the tip close to his blood-soaked temple.

"Oh, you are all guilty. Your pardoners robbed the peasants blind. Your capitalists ravaged the environment and your priests raped six-year-old boys and girls," she shrieked, "So, just sit there, and watch while he dies and I destroy this crystal. Then you're next. Oh, and don't try to break the ropes or you'll find a lance through your head. They know about our armor and Romans learn quickly how to compensate," she smiled holding up the crystal, waving it in Logan's direction. For a moment she pretended to drop the stone before catching it in midair and returning it to her biometer.

"Six years old," the Guardian mused. "So that's it? Wow! That's terrible." Sweat beaded on his forehead rolling down his furrowed brow. "Now you're on a vendetta to even the score. Wipe out Christianity now and maybe two thousand years from now your trash heap of a dad won't hurt you. Is that the plan?"

"Shut up!" she screamed again. "Do you hear me? Shut up or I'll kill you right now. You think you've got it all figured out. Well you just sit there. I'm going to enjoy watching you as what's left of your little world goes up in flames."

Logan sat still, helpless to aid his friend or to stop the desecration of history about to occur. Strife walked over to the tiny projection unit and reinserting its power cable into her wrist unit, displayed the holographic file in 3-D space. There along the lower edge of the interface flashed the blinking skull shaped icon labeled 'DELETE'.

"In its transition cylinder the crystal is almost impervious to all natural and manmade forms of destruction. But now, exposed" she said as the fluid drained to the storage chamber, "this beautiful diamond is vulnerable. A flick of this tiny switch," she said flicking her index finger back and forth, "and everything you've worked for goes up in smoke, flyboy. What's wrong Jonny, that big bloody vessel on the side of your temple looks like it could just pop," Strife smiled continuing to taunt by waving her index finger over her wrist keypad.

"Say goodbye to your hero, Freak'," she announced as she activated the delete function with her wrist-pad.

The screen read in large letters, "DELETION COMMENCING".

As the software initiated, she looked up at Logan who was staring at her intensely.

"See you in Hell," he declared as suddenly the flickering 3-D image changed from

"DELETE" to "PROGRAM DOWNLOADED" to

"HI STRIFE",

then displayed a florid rainbow of colors and designs which drew the entire squad closer. Suddenly, the display ended as quickly as it had begun, replaced now by a floating display that read

"CODE: 1-2-6-0"

"SUIT DESTRUCT SEQUENCE ACTIVATED"

"**SEE YOU IN HELL**".

As Strife's epitaph flashed across the screen, Logan lunged, simultaneously twisting and kicking the guard beside him towards the main group. Rolling over and in front of Barnabas, he shielded him, as his survival suit automatically switched to defend mode.

"What the…………………………..?" were the last words Strife uttered on this earth as a solitary golden spark jumped from her wrist-pad to her adjacent paralyzer setting off a cascade of events. Stunned, she froze as an all-encompassing flood of gold and blue electrical discharge erupted. The resulting fireworks emanated from and consumed her entire survival suit flowing through the power cables and into the holographic projector. Like a spark set to a fireworks display yields an ever-expanding cascade of destruction, so each expanding electrical wave begat another. The resulting shock wave of repetitive discharges filled the air striking anyone possessing any conductive material. As the surrounding guards, heavily armored in their protective iron plating, crumpled to the ground, Logan's suit shielded him and Barnabas. Moments later and it was over with the electromagnetic pulse leaving no one conscious but Logan.

Slowly, the guardian rose to a sitting position to scan the smoldering plateau that surrounded him. His survival suit had protected him, but its energy cells now nearly depleted, prevented him from breaking the ropes. To free himself, he crawled to the nearest fallen soldier and using the sharp edge of his sword cut the bindings.

Rising he walked over to Strife. For a moment he hovered over her body before stooping to lift her charred wrist. Gently he laid the arm across her chest, crossing it with the other and brushed her scorched hair from her once beautiful face, his head bowed in despair.

"Where there is jealousy and selfishness there is Strife and every evil work." Logan's voice trailed off, "Sorry, I guess I forgot to tell you about that virus in the projector. Guess now, you can finally see the big picture."

Carefully he lifted the luminescent crystal from her shattered biometer, taking a moment to determine that there was no damage, before placing it back into the transition cylinder. Fluid filled the protective chamber at once as he proceeded to check each soldier's pulse before returning to Barnabas.

"Huh? She's the only one dead," he said amazed at the turn of events.

Slowly he lifted and turned his wounded friend into a sitting position on the large boulder behind him. Then, with deliberate and gentle pressure, he extracted the lance from the Cyprian's shoulder. Only once did Barnabas stir at the tugging of the lance. Logan knew from past experience of battle wounds that this was a bad sign and that most likely his friend was near death.

A quick check of Barnabas' pulse and respirations confirmed this as Logan waited for the energy cells on his survival suit to regenerate. Even without access to his biometry unit, Logan could tell the large man's breathing was steadily growing more labored by the minute. His only option was the emergency cardio-stimulant cartridge that each traveler carried in his suit. Crossing over to Strife's partially blackened corpse, he opened her pocket and extracted the still intact cartridge. Locating the antecubital vein on Barnabas' right arm, he injected the drug, watching for a reaction. Immediately the large man stirred as his vital signs improved.

Logan whispered a prayer as he tried to reposition the big man. "If only I knew I could move you." It was then, as if having a life of its own, that the tiny green light on his wrist's energy cell flickered and began faintly to glow. Scarcely able to believe what he was seeing, Logan checked his battery level again. To his amazement the indicators now showed partial battery power returning.

"Heaven be praised," Logan whispered surprising even himself as he began to scan the gentle giant's vital signs. In a moment Logan was informed that the Cyprian's heart and major arteries were undamaged, but that he was losing blood rapidly. Logan felt the tears coming back. Choking them down, he spoke gently to his silent friend.

"Sorry, my friend, but I will have to take you with me if we have any chance to save you," he whispered as the tears, now dripping, threatened to cloud his vision. Working quickly, Logan removed the emergency roll of gauze from his own survival suit, using it to fashion a sterile patch to compact the open wound. Then, designing a leather binding from an unconscious soldier's uniform, he wrapped the patch tightly against the shoulder temporarily slowing the flow of life-giving fluid.

"Just one more item to complete," he whispered as again he rose and crossed over to Strife's lifeless body.

"Such a waste," he spoke sadly as he extracted a small cylindrical device from another pocket of her survival suit placing it firmly on her upper torso. Pressing a small red switch on the surface of the device resulted in a faint whine and the illumination of a tiny red flashing light. The ensuing rapid retreat from her body was barely sufficient as Logan was thrown to the ground by a violent flaming explosion. Shaken, he rose from the dust to see her corpse engulfed in a brilliant fire consuming body, suit and equipment. As he stood brushing the debris from his tattered tunic, he couldn't help but reflect on the tragedy that was her life. Watching her corpse burn on the plateau above *Ein Avdat* was not how he had imagined this mission to end.

From the edge of the rocky plateau came a weak groan reminding him to rush back to his fallen friend's side. Carefully he lifted and re-examined the patch, finding the blood beginning to flow freely again. Lifting the big man, left arm over his shoulder and with the assistance of his now functioning survival suit, Logan attempted to navigate the steep trail down the bluff to the lake below.

The descent was steep, so steep that Logan spent most of his time stumbling down the hill. As he struggled to remain upright, his effort was impeded by Barnabas' blood, which flowing across his cheek, mixed with his own and into his eyes.

"I guess this makes us blood brothers," he gasped as he wiped away the lifeblood of his unconscious comrade.

"I always wanted a little brother," he choked as dragging the huge man he tripped and dodged past the next group of boulders.

"Hope you're not offended but you're not exactly what I'd call little." Red faced, he strained continuing to move down the steep path.

By the time he reached the bottom of the hill, Logan could do nothing but drag his friend's body down the sandy trail towards his camel. Near the end of his descent, Logan, exhausted and despondent, stumbled rolling head over heels down on to the lake's rocky landing.

When at last he could rise, he sat there unmoving and disoriented. Slowly the cobwebs cleared from Logan's mind making him once again cognizant of his surroundings. It was then that he noticed the small campfire and the lone figure by the lake filling water skins and carefully placing them in the storage bags on Logan's camel. The man's back was to Logan, who approaching slowly, assumed that the other was intent on stealing his beast. As he came closer, though, Logan felt a strange sense of familiarity with the man. Exhausted and desperate for help, he decided to appeal.

"Please!" he gasped barely able to speak, "Please! You've got to help me. My friend is hurt. If I can only get him to my ship, I just need some help lifting him," Logan pleaded as he gestured towards his fallen friend and the desert before him.

"A ship? In the desert? What a strange place for a boat," Jesus smiled, turning to face Logan.

Leaping backwards, the explorer frantically back-peddled over his own feet, landing soundly on his pride. There he lay in the sand, unable to move, pointing up with shaking hand at the apparent apparition hovering over him. Amazed as much at the trembling of his own hand, as by the specter before him, Logan stuttered.

"No, it's, it's not possible. You're dead!"

Jesus smiled as he gently grasped the pointed finger and its tremulous gripper pulling the explorer from the ground. Logan released the carpenter's hand slowly, unable to stop staring at his own still tingling from the fading sensation of living flesh.

"Blessed are those who have not seen and yet still believe," Jesus smiled. The all too familiar phrase came reverberating with Julie's voice inside Logan's skull. How many times had she quoted this simple verse? Images of arguments scattered throughout the history of their marriage flashed briefly as the words dug in deeply. Like a man frozen in time, he stood there, just staring. His world and the reality of so many of the reckless choices he'd made slammed down on him like the collapsing walls of a burning house. He struggled, trying hard to analyze what his senses were absorbing. Suddenly, Jesus stepped closer. The movement, while slight, startled Logan, almost causing him to fall a second time.

As he steadied himself, Logan studied the risen Jesus for the first time. The rough facial features had softened and were now perfectly balanced. Jesus' complexion once scarred now seemed to glow, a mild elevation of one eye was even, a slight crook in his nose from a childhood injury was straight and his slightly bowed stature had straightened such that he appeared one to two inches taller than Logan remembered.

For a moment Logan doubted. Then it struck Logan that this was the same man, only without physical defect. As the ramifications of this realization began to sink in, Jesus again interrupted Logan's thoughts. Extending his hands, Jesus' wrists showed the deep depressions where the iron spikes had been driven.

"You remind me of another of my disciples, perhaps you remember him. He had a rational mind like yours, pessimistic, almost bordering on cynical. We called him Thomas. There is an uncanny resemblance, perhaps he is an ancestor of yours." Jesus smiled as he spoke.

Not quite sure how to respond, Logan's mind suddenly recalled his fallen friend. Turning he pointed in the direction of the trail.

"My friend, I've got to get him some help."

Even as Logan spoke Jesus was already making his way to the fallen disciple. Slowly he turned Barnabas from the side position to his back, supporting his head with his forearm. Looking up at Logan, Jesus smiled as he spoke.

"I hope you don't mind; my followers bought back your tunic," he said pointing to the still blood-stained garb he wore, "I'm afraid it's a little worse for the wear. We never did trade back again."

Logan looked at the tunic Jesus wore, streaked with the dried tributaries of a scourging.

"No, I don't mind… Help him if you can, please," Logan stuttered slightly as he spoke.

"If I can?" Jesus smiled softly looking up as he gently lifted Barnabas to a sitting position and tore open the Cyprian's tunic. Logan smiled back weakly, his expression nearly on the brink of tears. Jesus stared at him briefly, as if he saw something he had not seen before. Then, turning, he breathed directly into the silent man's wound, causing the laceration to close right before Logan's bewildered eyes. As the tissue sealed upon itself, leaving only a subtle scar, Barnabas began to stir and cough violently.

"Where am I?" he croaked weakly, attempting to sit upright. Logan dropped quickly to his knees trying to support his friend as Jesus rose.

"You are with friends, my child. You are safe. You have always been safe," Jesus spoke softly stepping away from the big man.

"Oh, praise God! I am in heaven with the Lord, and my prayers are answered, for you are here too, Jonny. But Jonny… you still look so… bad," Barnabas spoke as sitting upright able to support himself he grimaced at the chrononaut's face. Logan smiled, hugging his friend gently before rising from the man's side.

"You are not in my Father's house yet, my friend, but soon….. in the wink of an eye, - in the wink of an eye. Now rest," Jesus spoke, handing him a water skin to drink from and laying a folded blanket under his head. Slowly the big man reclined as Jesus covered him, tenderly tucking in the disciple much like a parent would a young child. Smiling, Logan watched the Nazarene with amazement.

"He will rest now. When he awakens, he will be strong enough to travel, but what of you, my friend?"

Logan hesitated, his head down turning away before answering.

"I must go home."

The two men walked slowly towards Logan's camel.

"I must tell them what I've seen".

"What have you seen?" Jesus asked. At this there was a moment's hesitation as Logan tightened the leather strap attaching the saddle to his camel. Logan looked up as a small break in the clouds revealed the approaching sunrise.

"The God who loves me through my pain," he spoke nearly choking on the huge lump in his throat.

"Many will refuse to believe. And you have such a short time to tell them."

Logan thought about this, his demeanor becoming more determined. "I've got to try, if even for just a single day. Those who won't believe are like me. Ignoring a heart desperate to believe, they listen instead to the voices in their heads."

"So Rebecca was right?"

"About what?" Logan nodded.

"Once you've seen truth, you can't "un-see" it."

"I'm a 'new creation'," Logan smiled weakly.

"*You've evolved,*" Jesus grinned as he pronounced the last word helping Logan with his saddle adjustments.

Logan laughed sadly nodding his head. The two stood there silent for what to Logan seemed an eternity. Head down, he stared at his sandals, wanting to speak, but not knowing quite what to say.

"You must take them a message for me."

"Anything," Logan whispered.

Reaching out he grasped Logan's left hand with both of his. Turning the traveler's wrist upright and sliding the tunic up his arm, Jesus exposed the extensive network of spidery veins covering the lower portion of his forearm.

"Logan, my son, I forgive you for ignoring me most of your life," Jesus spoke gently as Logan unable to meet his gaze stared silently at the ground. "Your sins are forgiven."

Slowly the distorted and twisted veins faded before Logan's eyes. Through tear clouded eyes, Logan frantically tore his suit open, checking his arms and torso, where clear, healthy skin appeared in place of dead swollen tissue. The tears now fell steadily, as Logan fought the desperate urge to sob.

Jesus paused a moment, allowing His friend to regain composure. This time he spoke much more deliberately, with a sadness Logan had never heard in his voice before.

"Logan, tell them there are some things that even God cannot do. He is - '*self-constrained*'. He cannot make a square, round, or the color yellow, red." Jesus paused to clear His throat before continuing, "And he can't stop loving mankind."

"Then show yourself, why don't you intervene?" Logan interrupted, his enthusiasm replacing his tears.

"Each one must be truly free to choose, my friend," Jesus' calmly replied, "All creation is for you, even these earthly temples you reside in." Jesus walked over to the small fire that he had built earlier, throwing on a few small limbs to keep it burning. Logan followed, remaining close, waiting for Jesus to finish. Jesus crouched before the glowing embers.

"The icy hand of fear makes a very poor substitute for the embrace of love's flame," he said staring deep into the blaze before him. "So, out of love for man, the Father must remain unseen. Even this is done for your good, not for His."

"And in return?"

"I have only one remaining mission for you Commander Jon of Logan, it is your most important." Jesus quipped rising to look Logan in the eye.

"Love others as I have loved you."

Logan hesitated looking intently back at Jesus.

"I didn't even love my own family enough to protect them. How can I love as you do?"

"Greater love has no one than this that he lay down his life for a friend." Jesus smiled.

"And how do I do that?"

"You already have," Jesus continued nodding towards Barnabas, "as he and others will one day attest."

Logan's eyes shifted downward in amenability.

"One more message needs to go to your generation. Ask them why they stopped loving me?"

"They blame God for everything bad in life," Logan replied."

"Yet refuse to acknowledge me for any of its beauty."

"There's that pesky evolution again," Logan quipped. Jesus' smile echoed the one on Logan's face.

"They need me."

"And you need them?" Logan reflected, "You've allowed yourself to love them and so now, in your own way, you need them, don't you?"

Jesus nodded.

"Not like you need, but in my own way."

"Humanity's selfless gray-haired mother, watching and waiting for her soldier boy to come home?" Logan sighed.

Jesus hung his head nodding silently. Then, briefly he looked up through glistening eyes, and he whispered through an anguished smile, "The prodigal's dad."

Logan remained silent a moment longer.

"But why the cross?"

"It was the instrument for the final union with you."

"Why? What did you experience on the cross that makes you one with us, man's brutality," Logan asked shaking his head incredulously?

"Betrayal," Jesus whispered.

"But you knew what Judas was doing."

"Not man's," Jesus looked intently at Logan. The sorrow etched deep in his face. Logan paused thinking deeply before muttering.

"God's?"

"Jesus nodded silently."

"*Eloi, Eloi lama sabachthani*," Logan whispered.

"You mean you died believing you'd been discarded by God?"

Jesus nodded again. "The essence of humanity's despair." Logan paused again trying to take that in.

"What was that like?"

Jesus sighed.

"Like drowning, all alone, in an ocean of sorrow."

"I know that feeling."

"I know you do, now so do I."

"Divine empathy, 'It is finished', huh?"

Jesus nodded stiffly.

"But you're here?" Logan reflected.

"Even this, has been redeemed. No one will lose anything for my sake."

"All things will be made right?" Logan asked. Jesus smiled.

"Now go, for there are still many who wish to see you fail. They will be coming for you soon, but do not fear them, for I will be with you, even to the end of the age. Oh, and one other thing, *WE* - will be waiting for you when you are finished." Jesus smiled as he nodded across the narrow beach to a small clearing on the other side of the lake.

"None of mine, have I lost."

There in the dim morning light of the first Easter's sunrise stood a beautiful woman with auburn hair and two oh so very familiar children. Hand in hand they stood by a spindly acacia tree, their smiles beaming as they met Logan's eyes. This time Logan was helpless to contain the tears.

"Julie!" he called out desperately.

"Hi Jonny," she called back, "we miss you, so very much, and we love you. We will see you very soon. For now, do what only you can." Logan had never seen three such beautiful faces in his entire life as he looked at his family.

"We love you daddy," called out the children, "We are very proud of you. Please listen to Jesus."

"Give Beci and Tommy a hug for me. They're getting a great dad. See you on the other side." Julie smiled with a nod.

Logan turned and began to run to his family when suddenly they vanished. He turned, ready to beg that Jesus bring them back, but He and Barnabas too were gone. Tears still in his eyes, Logan walked slowly to his camel and stepped up into the saddle. As he activated his wrist mounted homing beacon, Logan realized for the first time in his life he feared nothing, not even being alone. What a strange sensation, this experience of total peace, he thought to himself.

Turning his camel to the south and following the direction of the ship's beacon, Logan looked back only once at the clearing where Julie and the children stood only minutes before. His bitterness completely erased, there was only one thing left to do. He must get home with the truth before his enemies could stop him.

CHAPTER TWENTY-FOUR
The Final Battle

The howling winds of the northern Negev swept downward over the sandy plains laid out before Logan. Plunging in a terrible descent, each blast lacerated the wasteland spewing translucent curtains of dust into the morning air. At moments, Logan would pause, straining to catch just a passing glimpse of the northern sun peeking between the encircling ripples. For hours now, man and beast had battled the swirling clouds of sand that intermittently obscured the landscape before them. Still, the camel seemed instinctively able to elude the obstacles littering their path, as Logan followed the signal emanating from TAV-1.

To protect himself, Logan was forced to wrap his head with the spare turban Barnabas had instinctively packed with the food stores. The ends of the turban effectively shielded his cheeks, forehead and eyes, allowing Logan to press deeper into the suffocating darkness settling on the terrain.

Lulled to sleep by the camel's methodical undulations, Logan was rudely awakened as his exhausted ride collapsed beneath him, throwing him face down in the sand. The flustered guardian surfaced spewing a mouthful of foul tasting silt and emptying a hat full of sand from his turban. This experience convinced the explorer to pace himself, not wishing to travel the last twenty kilometers on foot.

Several agonizing hours later, Logan arrived climbing the foothills of the Negev Mountains to the plateau overlooking the Arava valley. Here, man and beast stopped to rest, taking advantage of an unexpected break in the turbulent weather. Kneeling side by side, the two devoured the last of their provisions. Mesmerized, they surveyed the valley's gleaming hillsides, set ablaze by the filtered rays of the golden hour.

A quick check of the beacon, and a pleasantly surprised Logan quickly located his 'ship' less than three kilometers away.

"We've got it made now, ole' boy," Logan quipped as he patted the camel's head, feeding it figs to reward its herculean effort. The beast, letting off an appreciative snort, struggled to its feet again as Logan remounted, driving towards an ominous wall of blackness ahead.

Unencumbered by inclement weather, Logan and the camel broke into a gallop through the sundrenched western bluffs surrounding them. Stark and lifeless, the range was a welcome sight to the guardian who recalled its broken hills from the team's ascent some nine months earlier.

His beast now rested and refreshed; Logan could not resist the urge to race headlong across the desert. With each passing minute he became more and more obsessed to arrive at his destination and escape from the unknown adversaries Jesus had spoken of. Descending the largest of the sloping bluffs and heading into the vast open plains remaining between him and the ship, Logan hastily pushed the camel to its limit.

Keen to head Jesus' warning, he constantly checked behind for pursuers, almost totally ignoring the tremendous cliff of billowing sandstorm threatening to collapse down upon him. By the time he realized what the dark cloud ahead was, he was both unable and unwilling to change direction, instead plunging full speed into the enveloping whirlwind. Immersed in a murky sea of violent wind and blinding sand, man and beast stumbled recklessly forward following the homing beacon.

At times the air, congested as it was with sand, was barely breathable. The camel's face, mouth and eyes quickly became caked with saliva-sodden clay causing the animal to collapse once more into the dust with its rider.

Realizing the beast could not continue, Logan dismounted, washed the animal's face and loosely tucked a thin protective cloth over its head. Hands out-stretched with near zero visibility, Logan proceeded alone, following the glow of his wrist beacon.

Gradually, he inched forward under a steady barrage of sand and wind, ever careful to guard closely the precious transition cylinder. The device, stored securely in his survival suit, was protected by a specially designed vertically shaped pocket in his right chest region. Despite the compartment's advanced locking mechanism and reinforced armor, Logan found himself nervously checking and rechecking the receptacle to insure the device's safety.

As he did so, he stumbled to his knees over one of the dimly lit rocks littering the desert floor. Rising he instinctively became aware of something moving off in the distance to his right.

"Hello! Hello! Is someone there," his shouts hopelessly lost in the cacophony of wails rising up in the desert winds.

"Nothing," he muttered noticing the descending blanket of angry clouds above. The landscape was growing darker now, and Logan felt the tingle of a silent chill run down his spine.

Moving forward again, he suddenly noticed a fleeting ripple at the edge of his night vision scanner. Pausing, he searched vainly, peeking through the protective face wrap at a shadowy horizon before him.

At first, there was nothing, nothing but the mournful wail of the desert winds haunting Logan's mind. Darkness surrounded Logan, cold black darkness. Nervously he rescanned the area for signs of life. "Dead zone" came back the analysis, meaning there was no form of life anywhere within two kilometers of Logan.

"That's impossible, there's no such thing as dead zones on earth," he muttered tapping on his wrist control.

"This thing's busted, stupid sand-based implement."

Logan moved forward again unable to shake the feeling that he was being watched.

"Come on Logan, hold it together," he whispered to himself, "Last time you felt this way was on - was on - the deck of Empress." His voiced trailed away as another shadow darted out of his left side vision.

"Who's there?" he called out louder, turning quickly back to his left. Once again he was greeted with the constantly changing pitch of the wind as it rapidly swirled around him. Like an unearthly choir, blending the wails of souls caught between this world and the next, the eddies harmonized into a symphony of death. Logan paused, as another tiny pinprick of a shiver slithered down his spine.

Hostile as the environment was, it was beginning to pale in comparison to the pounding of his own heart. Years of military training took over as he instinctively made attempts to control his breathing and pulse rate. Each of his attempts proved futile, as the slate gray clouds above broke out into a thunderous explosion of sound sending giant arcs of lightning across the sky. He quickened his pace, although at this point he had difficulty seeing well enough to move without falling.

Then something moved.

The shadows were back.

"Who's there?" he shouted.

This time the shadows were unmistakable and numerous. First to the right and then to the left Logan turned. Each time, there was nothing. Alarmed, he looked at his homing beacon and quickened his pace to outrace the apparitions. Seven meters more and they were back, this time approaching from the opposite direction. Their appearance lacked definition, merely a formless ripple in the swirling sand filling the air around him.

Perhaps it was this very lack of definition that contributed to Logan's incredulity at the first attack. The blow was like a body block from behind, both forceful and indefensible, undeniably deliberate in nature. Logan lay in the sand, stunned and shaken, thrown some three meters from where he had originally been standing. His survival suit, now covered in sand, had provided only limited protection from the sudden collision with his lower ribcage. Struggling to his feet, Logan remembered the last time he had felt a blow like that during a college football game. His back had ached for a week after he played punching bag, instead of quarterback, against an overwhelming defense. Now, not only could he not see his enemy, he felt sure he was unable to defend against it.

"Who's there?" Logan shouted again, the desperation now becoming evident in his voice. Nothing but wind was his answer as he rose halfway only to stubbornly sit again.

"No, that's just what you want me to do, run," He whispered to himself.

His mind raced attempting to devise a plan of escape. As he did so, he noted that the atmosphere around him was changing. 'How odd', he thought as he watched the clouds growing darker, hovering progressively closer and closer to the ground. At this his skin began to tingle, irritated by static electricity discharging from the low hanging clouds. While this was distracting, the charged atmosphere somehow enhanced Logan's ability to view the apparitions. Using the night vision capabilities of his *Nano-lens*, Logan could now see the rough outline of their bipedal shape through the swirling sand. The shadows quickly appeared every few seconds, numbering anywhere from six to eight apparitions at any one time.

Able to appear and disappear at will, his adversaries waited patiently to close in on Logan. And so he sat there, like a hunted animal, unwilling to move.

Finally, the shadows moved away, allowing Logan the opportunity to attempt an escape. Heading again in the direction indicated by the homing beacon, Logan utilized his suit's strength enhancement to quicken his pace and race toward the ridge overlooking the landing plain where the ship lay buried.

He paused momentarily for the final beacon reading when suddenly he was struck by two shadows racing at him from opposite directions. The first apparition leveled him with a blow to the upper chest, while simultaneously the other struck from behind flipping Logan backwards head over heels into the sand. It was a moment before Logan could lift his head again and shake the sand from his hair. The sky above him had changed once more, but this time it was not the eerie atmosphere that concerned Logan. There, some twenty meters above him, in the intermittent shadows of heavenly flashes, circled a dozen shadow-like 'sharks' ready to devour their prey. Each of the shadows darted feverishly down through the ghostly clouds seemingly energized by the dancing tentacles of electricity tracing their winged profiles. Instinctively, he knew now was not the time to play dead.

Shaking away the cobwebs, he rose again, franticly trying to run towards the ship. As he did so, immediately a swarm of encircling shadows set upon him. This time he attempted to defend himself against the impending onslaught.

"Oh, man…." Logan whispered to himself as he assumed a crouching position taught in martial arts. His only thought at this point was to get his adversaries to break ranks long enough for him to escape. From a military standpoint a diversion was what he needed, but what kind? Logan didn't even know what he was fighting, much less how to distract them.

As these thoughts raced through his mind the first shadow struck from behind. Whirling in an arc-like motion, Logan attempted to roll with the punch, striking back at his attacker. The blow landed solidly yet scattered only a fistful of sand. Unfortunately, the fruitless result of Logan's successful blow left him open to attack from the opposite side. It was at this point that Logan was struck viciously by two additional shadows attacking the chest and head area. Logan's brain spun as he felt the blood draining to his feet. He lifted his arms attempting to shield his head from the pummeling now being rained down upon his body. Each blow seemed to tear through the defensive shielding of his survival suit, the last breaking a rib in his lower thorax. In vain Logan attempted to kick or punch anything within arm's reach. The resulting blows again tore through nothing but wind and sand.

Then, as quickly as they had begun, the beatings stopped. Logan kneeled there in the sand, barely able to breathe, his throbbing head in his hands, as every nerve ending in his body cried out in pain. A few more moments and still nothing, nothing but the wind and the sand swirling in fanciful patterns over the ethereal landscape in front of him. With the pain subsiding and Logan's head clearing, he fought to recover his bearings. Logan was now able to refocus as he scanned the landscape around him.

"Why don't you just kill me and get it over with?" he muttered to himself. And then a new thought occurred to him.

"You want something. That's why you don't finish it," he mused looking down at the blue flask. "You want this."

As he did so, he noticed a new ripple in the air ahead approaching him. This new shadow, much larger than any of the previous ones, was different in nature. In addition to Logan being able to physically hear this creature's approach, he could smell it. Never in his life had he ever smelled anything so bad, so rancid, like an animal carcass decaying in its own avulsed fluids. Like *Legion* it reeked, only much worse. As it approached, the sand beneath it crackled and crunched as if crushed in a giant vise.

"Uh…This can't be good," Logan said rising to his feet. As he ran the shadow swept down upon him, snaring him in a choking death grip. Locking his arms between himself and the invisible apparition, Logan pushed with all of his remaining strength against the crushing weight. The overwhelming stench of the creature's breath was now firmly in Logan's face. Never in his life had he ever even imagined something smelling so bad, like the smell of a hundred decaying corpses abruptly exhaled into his mouth. Hopelessly trapped, he began to gag reflexively and vomit making it progressively harder and harder for him to breathe. As he struggled images exploded into his mind. Images of horror and near-death events he had experienced in life. He fought against them, forcing his mind to focus on the battle before him, but each time the images returned, stronger and darker. At first, they were images of ghastly deaths he had witnessed in space, but now as he fought them they changed. Now, before him was a car, burning with screams emanating from within. The screams, he recognized at once, were those of his wife Julie and his two small children. Vainly he struggled against the car door, wrestling desperately to pry the fixed barrier open.

"Julie, Julie," he screamed out as he pushed against the apparition.

Immediately came a tiny whisper from behind, "We're with Jesus……."

Logan stopped, his mind clearing.

Suffocating under the crushing weight, Logan knew he had but one chance left. Pulling his right hand free from the creature, he reached the small red switch on his left wrist activating the suit's paralyzer. The electric blue discharge erupted, illuminating both man and foe in a fiery arc that lit up the sky and excited the surrounding static energy incasing them. Logan exploded free, thrown solidly to the ground and momentarily paralyzed.

To his credit, he calculated that his survival suit would protect him from most of the paralyzer's discharge. He was right. What he didn't calculate was the overwhelming effect of static discharge. There on his Nano-lens, in large green letters flashed the message "System failure", telling Logan he was now on his own.

This was the last blow. Exhausted and vulnerable, the guardian made one last ditch effort. Launching himself from his crouching position, Logan gathered all of his strength into one full scale race to the ship.

Immediately, as he set out, three shadows like projectiles shot through the desert air leveling him. This time the retribution was even swifter and more violent. The blows came heavy to Logan's head and thorax, as he instinctively coiled himself into a fetal position shielding the precious capsule. Blood oozed from the lacerations now peppering his face. It flowed down his cheeks mixing with the sweat and saliva tainting his lips. The foul flavor hung in his mouth like drunken vomit, its taste a visceral reminder that once again he was helplessly and hopelessly alone. After several moments the beatings paused.

Logan's head pounded and his sides were riddled with contusions. By now he had come to recognize this cat and mouse pattern his tormentors delighted in. His right eye swollen shut and blood pouring from above his left eye, lip and nose, Logan strained to see through the swirling sand with just one blood tainted eye. His survival suit, now useless to protect him, was itself ripped in several places. The largest of the tears, located at the right shoulder, extended into the adjacent pocket.

"Who are you?" he yelled this time desperately hoping for an answer to buy more time.

"What do you want?"

Again, only silence echoed back.

Logan knew from the pattern that he had only precious seconds before the attacks would begin again. With his head spinning and nausea from the pain in his ribs overtaking him, Logan realized the cylinder was gone. He panicked, desperately searching the sand around him.

Scarcely able to move and distracted by the search, Logan ignored the warning flashing before his eyes. The heads-up-display of his system's Nano-lens flashed.

CARDIO FAILURE IMMINENT: SHOCK ALERT

What this meant Logan realized when he vainly attempted to move.

"There," he choked hoarsely as straining his half swollen left eye, he spied the partially buried cylinder. Some half meter ahead its faint glow was just barely perceptible. As the shadows began their approach from the rear, Logan strained, twisting his torso just far enough to catch his fingers on the edge of the device. Flipping the cylinder backward, he clutched it just in time before being struck again. This last attack landed him solidly, face down, planted between a large boulder and its newly formed sand dune. Slowly, he rolled on to his back.

At this point, Logan could neither feel nor move any of his extremities. A cold shiver began to run uncontrollably through his body as the indicator in his *NanoLens* showed his pulse racing to one hundred and fifty-two beats per minute. Desperately clinging to consciousness, he was just able to make out the once more dislodged cylinder. It was lying well out of his reach just ahead of him in the adjacent dune. Any attempt to retrieve the lost device was now impossible. Helpless, Logan lay motionless in the deepening sand, his hands and feet drawn inward, aware of the effects of shock settling in. Quietly, the explorer drifted into a shadowy state of unconsciousness, his body sinking into a gradual burial of sand.

Defeated and dying, Logan watched through closed eyes as his Nano-lens imaged the shadows' final approach. Unable to raise even his head, he could feel the carotid pulse in his neck slowing gradually. Little by little the flashing warning dimmed as the pulse indicator gradually faded from view.

CARDIO FAILURE
PULSE: WEAK, THREADY
WARNING! MODERATE SHOCK

Like vultures circling their prey, dozens of winged shadows glided earthward surrounding their partially buried adversary. The harder he struggled to move the weaker he became until, finally, he could move nothing at all, except his mouth.

Barely able to mouth the words, much less speak them, he began to beg.

"God, forgive me, I've failed," he prayed for the first time in his life.

He choked as each word which fell from his lips was accompanied by a tear from his eyes. The sky was now thick with shadows as they continued their terrible descent, the horrid smell of death returning. Powerless, Logan watched as the largest specter approached gingerly, and then ever so slowly, bent over the fallen guardian and reached out one long talon like arm for the cylinder.

"God help me! God please!" Logan felt the icy chill as the apparition brushed up beside him and its crypt-like breath crept down upon him.

Frantically, Logan cried out in heartbreak, his cry reaching out with a desperate faith he had never known before.

"Jesus…dear Jesus, please help me," he sobbed into the sand beneath him.

The exact chain of events that unfolded next was unclear to the explorer. What Logan did remember was a sudden brilliant flash of pure white light followed by a tremendous rainbow-colored shock wave reverberating through the atmosphere and crushing everything in its path.

As the force of the shockwave rolled through the clouds above and down over the landscape around the explorer, every shadow in its wake shattered like glass. Logan marveled through nearly closed eyes as the groundswell rose, and then like a massive tidal wave expanding and crashing down, flattened everything in its path.

The shadows now cleared from his immediate vicinity, Logan felt enough of his strength return to raise his head and roll to his side. There, on the sand dune next to him, rose the distinct outline of a partially buried sandaled foot. The massive shoe, covered with the thinnest veneer of sand, resembled the leather strapped design worn by a Roman centurion. Dust and sand particles, clinging like iron filings to a magnet, outlined its ornate design. Beside the shoe lay the sandy outline of a partially buried glowing cylinder. Still in the smoldering clutches of a severed talon, the precious device lay unharmed. The appendage, which resembled more claw than hand, had been cleanly separated at the elbow.

Logan believed he might be hallucinating, until he recognized one subtle detail. There on the forward and side arches of the partially buried foot hung two oval medallions intricately designed with raised initials.

GB

At first, he almost dismissed the design, until he recalled where he had previously seen an exact replica - on his rear end.

"'GB'…Gabe? - Gabriel!?" he choked on the words. Immediately, Tommy's questions replayed in his mind like a phonograph stuck on the scratch of an old LP. A picture puzzle assembled at warp speed, the details of the last year of his life rushed in together. Now he understood, as his pulse strengthened and he turned to see the nearly invisible outline of the warrior angel towering over him. This apparition, like the smaller shadows before him, could barely be discerned from the swirling sand which danced over and clung to the creature like new fallen snow.

Suddenly, the apparition moved colliding with another smaller shadow in the fiery blue arc of electrical discharges that outlined their semi-transparent forms. Locked in immortal combat, the two sword welding specters exchanged a series of blows raining down a torrent of electrical sparks over the barren landscape. Arch speed met dark power as the giant angel sliced through one apparition after another in a blur of colored swings and thrusts. Singly or sometimes in pairs, Logan's tormentors attempted to engage the heavenly apparition only to be dispensed into eternity in a show of superior skill and remarkable agility.

Intimidated, the smaller shadows momentarily retreated, leaving an open plain of swirling sand around Logan and the apparition. Grasping the fallen cylinder, Logan suddenly felt himself heaved upright by the nape of his suit, as his advocate urged him to walk towards the buried ship.

"Move!" The apparition's deep voice demanded. "We haven't much time."

Logan, stupefied at the sound of something he could not see but could definitely feel and hear, struggled to stand. Replacing the cylinder into the torn pocket from which it fell, he attempted to walk. This ended as he suspected in a dismal failure as he collapsed to his hands and knees, unable to rise.

Logan realized his body was still suffering from the effects of shock from the beatings he had taken. With the apparition now once again engaged in a battle that illuminated the landscape around him, Logan reached into his suit pocket, removing the tiny unused syringe marked "cardio stimulant". Carefully he unzipped his suit's left sleeve, locating a gratefully normal looking antecubital vein, and injected the precious transparent fluid.

The effect was dramatic as Logan felt his strength return despite the pain enveloping him. He was now awake and able to focus on the mission at hand. With his adversaries being thrashed in a fiery display of heavenly fireworks, Logan quickly replaced the crushed nano circuit that communicated with his buried ride home. Depressing the activated wrist control, the miniature display illuminated flashing its warning.

EMERGENCY LAUNCH SEQUENCE ACTIVATED

Some two hundred meters away a whine from another century filled the air as Negev sand was slung rapidly from the TAV's rotating upper hull. Slowly the vessel began the process of resurrection from its fiery grave of almost ten months. Logan's wrist display confirmed the successful initiation of the launch sequence, warning of the precious few minutes he had to liftoff.

Still two hundred meters away from the life-craft, Logan had arisen and was slowly stumbling his way along the ridge overlooking the partially buried vessel. He staggered, righting himself each step of the way, while close, but at a safe distance the apparition followed guarding the chrononaut's back.

Clashes continued all around Logan as he blundered forward through the sand, rolling down a large dune to the edge of the ridge. Looking over the edge, Logan smiled as he spotted the emerging TAV some seventy-five meters away. The northern edge of the semicircular ridge descended rapidly to the plains where the TAV had landed. Logan's intent was to quickly move along this one-hundred-meter perimeter slope to the rising craft. If he hurried, he could just make it with two minutes to spare.

Sound though the plan might seem, it was not to be as Logan was suddenly and viciously struck from behind.

The blow, though weaker than before, was sufficient to propel him over the edge of the rocky cliff. It was then that Logan saw, out of the corner of his eye, the smaller apparition that had escaped Gabriel's defenses, plunging him towards the rapidly approaching desert floor below. Quickly he covered his head with his arms, attempting to minimize the damage, when he felt a jolt heralded by an other-worldly baritone.

"His angels will guard your feet from falling", came the proclamation as Logan was suddenly jerked upward only inches from the ground and dumped unceremoniously in a nearby dune. This relief was only momentary as he turned to see his timely guardian plunging to a thunderous crash before him. In his rush to snag Logan, the angel lowered his defenses allowing two of the smaller shadows to send him careening to the ground. Logan watched with fascination as before him, in the large crater formed from the archangel's impact, a shower of electrical discharges erupted skyward as the apparitions battled yet again.

The crater was some twenty to thirty meters from the ship and lay directly between Logan and his destination. As he navigated his way around the sloping depression, marveling at the battle within, Logan noticed the shadow of an enormous winged apparition gliding over the desert floor.

He paused, his mind struggling to comprehend and avoid an invisible creature capable of casting a shadow. It was then, as he watched, that he realized the new entity's intent. For as the winged creature descended on the valley, its flight path changed radically bringing it directly in line with the Arch angel still battling within the crater. Logan, who was now running at the edge of the small crater, noted that Gabriel was dispensing with the previously observed smaller apparitions. With their fate now sealed, the angel turned towards Logan unaware of the approaching adversary.

"Twelve O'clock!"

Logan shouted at his companion while pointing skyward as the glow from the last shower of sparks faded. The words were barely off his lips when Gabriel's sword met the intruder's, just in time to barely deflect a tremendous blow. The deflection, though successful, sent the angelic warrior flailing uncontrollably against the crater wall.

Logan, figuring the conflict between the two shadowy Goliaths too risky to observe, redirected his path towards the gradually rising vessel. The subsequent battle that followed was terrifying even to Logan. As the two combatants clashed, the ground beneath them trembled. Their outlines, only roughly discerned in the blowing sand, intermittently became clear as each warrior's lunges were deflected. Huge electrical discharges arced between the entangled apparitions yielding fleeting glimpses of their appearance.

As Logan closed within five meters of the now hovering vessel, he couldn't resist the urge to turn back and record the two titans. There on the desert tundra, locked in a fiery duel, the apparitions stood. Logan's mouth hung open as his scanner began to record the two apparitions. Both warriors were enormous, some four meters in height with large flowing wings that more closely resembled lacy streaks of misshapen lightning bolts than the feathery images of childhood fantasies. Gabriel's form, while difficult to discern, vaguely resembled the outline of a man's completely composed of energy. The archangel's torso appeared to be draped in a tight fitting robe of light. Protecting his head was a helmet of light, sweepingly shaped like that of a bird of prey, enveloping all but his facial features. His arms and legs were all draped in light such that they blended with one another obscuring any specific detail to their structure.

The giant angel's adversary was, surprisingly to Logan, similarly shaped. Again, composed of energy, most closely resembling an abstract painting of light, the enemy stood like a man. Its countenance and form were partially obscured by Gabriel who stood between Logan and the beast. Despite this, brief glimpses of the apparition gave its upper torso and head the vague appearance of a dragon. Its chest and upper arms resembling a man's, the creature's head and forearms had mutated to a hybrid reptilian-human appearance.

The two celestial swordsmen, trapped in a stalemate of thundering lunges, completely ignored Logan until his recordings began. Instinctively, the heavenly warrior turned at the biometer's activation. Intent on discouraging the recording the Arch angel turned to reveal a frighteningly crystal-clear scowl just long enough to lower his guard. The result was a devastating blow to the head partially deflected by the helmet, but sufficient to send the giant crashing to the ground a mere five meters in front of Logan.

Logan watched horrified as the huge depression in the sand demarcating the angel's position remained unchanged. With the heavenly protector lying silent and unmoving, the adversary, intent on Logan's destruction, turned his way.

Now Logan knew he was in trouble. With the cylinder in his breast pocket, he made a desperate dash for the glowing ship's ladder. The welcome sight of the cascading red, white and blue running lights and the scorched American flag pressed Logan faster. The once proud American plaque which had read,

"USSA, Kind Goodness We Can Trust",

had been damaged by the reckless inferno of reentry. The cryptic message now adorning the ship miraculously read

"US A in Go d We Trust".

Perhaps it was the sensation of an icy chill that ran down Logan's back or perhaps it was the sudden appearance of a large winged shadow on the ship's hull that terrified Logan. Whatever the cause, Logan felt the sudden impulse to duck, and that is just what he did. This resulted in the apparition careening headlong into the heavily reinforced nacelle of the TAV-1 as Logan artfully dodged back the other way.

Stunned, but not injured, the apparition turned to attack again. With Gabriel lying helpless in the sand, the enraged creature determined to destroy Logan. It rose from the ship erect, with its wings and talons fully outstretched, and dove for the chrononaut. As it did, Logan noticed a faint elevation in the sand. Running towards the distension, Logan recognized the subtle outline to be of an enormous sword covered by a thin layer of sand. As he dove for the sword, the enormous shadow of the winged apparition closed on the sand before him. In one motion Logan rolled from the earth, clutched the sword's handle and spun the blade upward to meet the demon.

As the sword swung upward impaling the shadowy creature in a fiery thrust, Logan wrenched the weapon upward, slicing the creature's midsection open and sending it crashing to the earth. The resulting torrent of electrical discharge threw both man and creature in two opposite directions.

Logan lay there for what seemed like an hour as the revolving sky above began to gradually clear. Wakened by the familiar whine of the TAV's scramjet engines as they began the final launch sequence, Logan rolled over onto his knees. Unable to rise, he was suddenly collared by an unseen force and set on his feet. This time he did not have to ask who.

"Alright, alright, I'm going. What's your hurry?"

Logan quipped through swollen lips while limping to the ladder and gradually beginning the climb. Slowly the ship rose with Logan still half hanging in and half out of the hatch. Clinging to the guardrail, he caught a fleeting glimpse of an all too familiar ripple out of his remaining good eye. Suddenly a swift kick collided with the left side of Logan's 'lower cheek' propelling him through the hatch and into the ship. Logan lay still as the hatch slowly closed. Just before the seal engaged, the chrononaut heard a familiar deep voice.

"I told you, I'd be glad to," the voice echoed off the metallic walls as the ship lifted slowly towards the clearing sky. Unseen by Logan, as the vessel accelerated upward, was an extra passenger clinging to the outer scaffolding. With each swing of his radiant sword the heavenly apparition swatted a path through the cloud of swarming shadows pursuing the tiny vessel. Gleaming metal met brilliant sunlight as the ship cleared the brunescent carpet of cumulus covering the peninsula below. In moments it had cleared the atmosphere, parting its way through an enormous cloud of golden celestial well-wishers. Its two passengers hurdled heavenward on a mission of mercy destined to unite them for eternity.

CHAPTER TWENTY-FIVE
The Prodigal's Return

Gradually, as the TAV-1 hurdled through space in route to its rendezvous with the black star, the sojourner began to heal. Despite the vicious beatings, his physical ailments were miraculously limited to three broken ribs, severe bruising of the liver and spleen with a mild hematoma, as well as a mild cerebral contusion and a dozen mild to moderate skin lacerations. Twenty-four hours after launch and a self-administered bottle of IV fluid and Logan was alive and semi-lucid. The medical facilities aboard his craft, while limited, were sufficient to ensure that Logan was in no danger of dying. In addition, Logan was aware of a marked improvement in his symptoms the moment the angel first appeared by his side. His mental status, on the other hand, was a somewhat different issue. The days that followed found Logan unable to escape from the reality of his experiences.

Trapped within the three by two-meter confines of his tiny ship's cabin, Logan faced the un-amiable task of reviewing his life. Compounding the clearing mental confusion was the fact that his entire view of reality had been overturned. Logan had seen both the impossible and the unbelievable played out right before his eyes and he was still having difficulty assimilating it.

At times He would lay awake at 'night' playing over and over in his mind the details of the past 11 months. The miracles he had seen and dismissed, and the missed opportunities to talk with Jesus, now haunted him. He spent hours reviewing each word recorded of each day spent with the disciples. At times, when he would 'trip' over an accidental recording of his big burly friend Barnabas, a tear would come to his eye. What man could better illustrate to Logan what it meant to be a man of God? Always cheerful, always glad to be alive, always encouraging others and willing to lay down his life for a friend. Logan felt humiliated when he thought of his own life compared to this man.

And what of Jesus, had anyone ever felt so totally rejected? Did Logan really know pain? When he thought deeply, he knew his pain was only a drop out of an ocean that spread to eternity.

The difference now was that where there was only pain before, now there was hope. Logan's regret, while still very real, now finally lost its rule as his task master. Now free to reflect on the memories of the past, Logan could see the hand that guided each step of his life. As he filtered through his memories in light of the past few months in Palestine, it suddenly dawned on him that his life had a profound purpose. He alone had been chosen to make this voyage and survive, and he alone must take this message home.

Even more profound than that was the realization that he would soon be the world's only living twenty second century apostle. The enormity of this responsibility slowly began to gel in Logan's mind as he crossed through the wormhole and approached home.

"I can't do this. I'm no saint!"

Despite his fear, he could not refute the obvious. There was no one else. If he didn't do it, it wouldn't get done, and Jesus had sent the message with him.

The second concern to cross his mind was that there would be those who would oppose him. They would be men in very powerful positions in life, in politics, the media, in business and even in religion. With this in mind, he resolved that to succeed he would have to circumvent the system. Only this would insure his message was dispersed to the masses. To do this, he would have to outrun the Lexington.

The massive viewing screen occupying the unadorned wall of Professor Satorsky's internal boardroom glowed from the images dancing across it. There in the heart of the giant research vessel Satorsky reclined, watching the events of the day unfold. His mammoth vessel in hot pursuit was far too slow to catch the tiny TAV which had escaped his grasp only seventy-two hours earlier.

The craft, either unable to respond, or unwilling, had transitioned out of the black star some three hundred and twenty-eight days after leaving. Its communication tower destroyed; the Lexington had been unable to transmit digital signals commanding the TAV to dock. Now the vessel careened seemingly out of control at near light speed velocity toward earth. Nothing known to man could travel fast enough to catch the craft powered by the gravitational strength of a black star. As he pondered the fate of the crew, one fact was known. Only Logan had survived. The Lexington's sensors caught a brief glimpse of the life signs on board the vessel as it sped through her defenses toward home.

In addition, a surface scan of the TAV's contaminated hull allowed the researchers to determine that the vessel had been on earth and buried for some eleven months. So despite Satorsky's concerns over Logan's mindset aboard the craft, he determined they would be short lived.

"Excuse me Professor Satorsky, but we have a priority one message from the President coming in on channel one. He insists on speaking with you, NOW," the communication chief's voice broke in over the researcher's news channel. Reaching the comm. switch on his desk, Satorsky flipped it to the on position. The voice on the other end sounded tense and angry.

"Satorsky, what's the meaning of this. You told me they would be debriefed before returning to earth. Who or what is in that ship?" the President's voice demanded.

"Now, John, calm down, calm down. I told you that you have nothing to worry about. We've scanned that ship and it's been in Palestine for over eleven months. Believe me, the man in that ship is more dead than alive. If, and mind me I said - IF - he can land that beast, when he opens that hatch what will emerge will be hideous, more monster than man. No one will listen to the ravings of a lunatic, much less a dead man. And that's exactly what he is, John, a dead man," Satorsky stressed.

"I know what the CDC says, Satorsky, but if Logan comes out of that ship spouting religious verbiage about a dead Jew, lots of people are going to listen."

"Look John, **no one** is going to listen to him. I've made sure of that. We have the world's leading researchers on radiation disease talking to the media on what they can expect. They've made simulations on the spread of the vascular disease now encasing his entire body and those images will be making their way on the air at any minute. **If** anyone watches his landing, it will be for a circus show, because that is all they will see. Our people will strap him to gurney and wheel him off just after the cameras snap his hideous picture for the entire world to see," Satorsky reiterated reclining once more in his easy chair.

"I don't have to tell you what this means if you are wrong Satorsky. You better hope your researchers know their science."

"Lighten up John; it is *impossible* for that man to be anything other than a hideous grotesque monster. Do you hear me, **im-poss-i-ble**? Don't worry. I'll see you at the inauguration ball in January. Good day!" and with that the conversation ended.

Back on earth word spread rapidly that the *'GOYIM'* mission had been successful in sending, and returning, a manned vessel on the first trans-temporal exploration trip. News reports across the globe were frantically interviewing any and every expert available. Scientists from disciplines as diverse as Middle Eastern archeology to medical researchers in the field of radiation poisoning filled the digital media. Other experts versed in the fields of critical thinking prepared the masses for acceptance of the all but inevitable secular conclusion.

In a modest hotel room, just outside of Cape Canaveral Florida, one family was especially intent on the interview before them. There on the edge of their bed Tommy and Rebecca sat glued to the interview, while Becki stared sadly at the near mile long runway located in the distance. From the twentieth floor of their hotel, Beci could just see the famed Kennedy facility, over one hundred years old, still used to launch the nation's most historic explorations. It was here that Logan would land, if he still could.

The "Daily Briefing", one of the nation's most popular news talk shows, was featuring two familiar faces as its lead interview. Drs. Livingston and Mahdia sat across a very modern looking table separated by a rotating holographic image of Logan from the chest up. The interviewer, an attractive woman in her late thirties resumed the conversation.

"Welcome back! If you've just joined us, my two guests are Dr. David Livingston from the National Aeronautics Division of Medical Research on Radiation Poison, and Dr. Ravi Mahdia from the National Space Guard Medical Division stationed aboard the rescue vessel Potomac. Our two distinguished guests are the first two medical experts assigned to assist Commander Jonathan Logan's disembark should he successfully land his TAV-1 re-entry module today. That landing is tentatively scheduled for three o'clock eastern standard time on runway one at Cape Canaveral." Pausing the interviewer turned to face her guests before asking the first question.

"So, Doctor Mahdia, if I understand you correctly, you are verifying all of Doctor Livingston's findings on astronaut Logan?" the interviewer continued.

"That is correct. I was there when Commander Logan received his initial exposure to the gamma radiation. What Dr. Livingston has observed regarding his physical condition is accurate," Mahdia stated, his face grimacing with the pronouncement.

"So, there's no chance that Commander Logan could survive this trip long enough to tell us coherently what he experienced?"

As Livingston replied, he referenced the holographic simulation rotating in three dimensions between the two physicians. The image transformed slowly. Back in the hotel room the children now on either side of Rebecca watched in horror. Gradually, dark red and purple vessels swollen from the vasculitis branched out climbing up the image's neck to encompass the entire face. As the vessels coalesced over the last healthy tissue of the face, the head became inflamed swelling into an edematous mass of distorted tissue. First to be affected was the left side of the face, with vessels protruding forward over the frontal region and obscuring the left eye. The image before them transitioned gradually transforming until it bore no resemblance to the handsome figure shown just moments before.

"Commander Logan is suffering from late stage inflammatory vasculitis secondary to gamma radiation poisoning. By now the disease has spread so diffusely to all of his organ systems as to impair his ability to breathe, much less think. I'm afraid that Commander Logan's condition will have progressed to the point that he will be no more than a vegetable at worst and a monster at best," Livingston stated grimly.

"So, this is what we will see step off of the TAV today, doctor?" the interviewer asked hesitantly as the swollen image rotated before the viewers.

"**If he walks at all**, this is undeniably what he will look like. Most likely we will carry him off in a stretcher," he emphatically reiterated. Mahdia looked down nodding his head in agreement.

"Then there is no chance for Commander Logan?" she asked, almost pleading.

"None."

"Without the auto-pilot he won't even be able to land, much less initiate re-entry," his voice trailed off in a tone of dismay. Thirty-five kilometers away in the modest hotel suite Rebecca clung to her two children as they silently wept.

In another part of the country, the same interview was watched and greeted by a very different response. Perched anxiously around the enormous table occupying the situation room sat the President and his twelve cabinet members. The President rose smiling and patted each of his closest advisors on the back as the men stepped out of the room with the display playing. On the screen behind them a reporter spoke from Cape Canaveral.

"And here, Jackie, is the day that all of America has waited for, the return of the crew of the TAV-1 vehicle. NASA tells us that the TAV-1, short for Temporal Asynchronous Vehicle, should appear in the western hemisphere sometime around 12:05 pm Pacific time. The small conical-shaped craft emerged at just under light speed from the black star Gamma X1A yesterday but was unable to ignite its nuclear engines to slow until late last night.

Communication with the craft has been limited to navigational telemetry due to speed and suspected damage to the craft's external reception disc."

The first reporter spoke from an elevated platform overlooking the main runway on a beautiful sunny summer day. The screen quickly shifted back to the anchor desk at the main channel. A beautiful blond-haired woman sat behind the desk speaking emphatically at the audience.

"Sharon, is it true that NASA still does not have any knowledge of the outcome of the mission, nor of the fate of America's first chrononauts?"

"That's true, Jackie. NASA did anticipate, however, that the extreme gravitational and radiation effects might damage the communication system. They therefore devised a unique method of revealing to the American people and the world the outcome of this historic mission." An animated reentry simulation appeared on the screen. "If Commander Logan is still able to pilot the re-entry vehicle, or if the autopilot is still functioning, TAV-1 will enter our atmosphere flanked by military scramjets. The vehicle's trajectory will eventually carry it in an arc over the United States on its way to a landing at Cape Canaveral, Florida this afternoon," the reporter spoke as the simulation demonstrated the semicircular path of the TAV. "Observers should watch for a red, white and blue exhaust pattern if the historical Jesus of the Bible is verified.

If proven a hoax, a white exhaust only will be seen. Major population centers that might be able to see the historic re-entry include San Francisco, Los Angeles, St. Louis, Chicago, and the entire eastern seaboard." The screen switched back to Sharon again.

"And of course, Jackie what we all fear the most is that Commander Logan, disoriented by the last stages of his radiation exposure, might override the auto-pilot misaligning the ship's re-entry and burning up in the atmosphere." The seriousness of her words reflected by her countenance.

As she spoke, somewhere above the Pacific Ocean, TAV-1's heat shield began to glow as the small craft entered the outer atmosphere. Dozens of kilometers below, a dozen silver fighter jets popped through one sound barrier after another on their way to their historic escort.

Suddenly, with low orbiting satellites following the descent of the spaceship, there was an incredible explosion. Broadcasters panicked attempting to focus in on the tiny craft just entering the atmosphere. Debris and smoke clouded the imagery as the cameras finally came into focus on the familiar conical radiation shield which had erupted into a fireball of flames. As it gradually split into two halves it disintegrated in the atmosphere right before their eyes. A collective gasp from billions of viewers was then mercifully relieved as the tiny re-entry module of the TAV emerged from the resulting flames appearing in the western sky. The entire world, now glued to their monitors, watched anxiously as suddenly a new voice was heard broadcasting over the NASA channel.

"TAV-1 to NASA control, TAV-1 to NASA control, Communication restored, request permission for landing approach vector." Logan spoke loud and clear to a stunned world and one very hesitant air traffic controller.

There was a moment's silence as the tower's controller collected his wits and then responded with quavering voice.

"NASA control to TAV-1, is that you Commander Logan?"

"Uh, that would be an affirmative NASA. You were expecting someone else? Now may I have that vector?"

"Yes, I mean no! You uh, you are cleared to land at the Cape on runway one. Approach vector 112.3 East … and Commander, a very grateful and relieved America welcomes you home. You're on international television. Do you have anything to say?

"Only it's good to be home, NASA. Mission accomplished. I bring 'Good News'."

Logan's response echoed across a mesmerized nation as the gleaming ship streaked above the Golden Gate Bridge.

From its nacelles streamed brilliant red white and blue billows of color chasing behind. The tiny ship, gleaming in the afternoon sun, streaked overhead escorted by fighters on each side. The colored tracers now echoed by Logan's escorts created a display visible for hundreds of miles. As the ship arced over a half dozen major cities, thousands ran from their homes and businesses looking skyward at the 'trains up in the sky'.

Farmers in their fields, passengers in their cars and workmen on construction sites stopped to look at the armada of rainbows passing overhead. And in Florida, one small family waited patiently on the tarmac, hoping against hope for a new day as the tiny ship turned towards home.

Epilogue

To say that the world was a little surprised when the hatch of Logan's ship popped open would be an understatement. Perched aside the sleek white cruiser as it sat on the steaming tarmac of NASA's Runway One were Livingston and Mahdia. Behind them stood a team of medical experts towing a gurney in hand. Every available emergency medical instrument known to man was at their fingertips as an emergency evacuation car hovered nearby.

The teary-eyed expression of Logan's two friends as they removed the chrononaut's helmet would become infamous and the recorded images discussed for years. As surprised as they were by the time traveler's countenance, it paled to their reaction when he removed his jacket, wearing a NASA t-shirt, and revealing a completely normal and impressive physique. The headlines which accompanied the photos of these initial images included such pronouncements as "Miracle Man" and "Time Traveler Healed".

As stunned as the rest of the world was, there was at least one family with quite a different set of emotions on display. Descending from the elevated platform adjacent to the motionless ship, Logan approached an almost hysterical Rebecca and two young children filled with a strange mixture of joy and disbelief. Logan's first embrace was a deeply romantic kiss that became the cover of many national publications and a standard to shame the majority of the male population.

His next encounter came from the loving arms of two small children still too young to truly understand the miracle they embraced. Clutching the teary-eyed fan club that threatened to smother him with kisses, Logan completely missed the four-legged family member preparing to pounce on his long departed master. This third encounter from an old 'Lab' named *Trigger* laid him flat on his back with national media recording as the canine wonder lapped Logan's face. Thousands on hand who witnessed this miracle of rebirth and celebration of reunion responded with tear-filled jubilation.

In the days and weeks to follow, the President and his cabinet became the subject of a congressional investigation leading to the first impeachment of the twenty second century and the socialist party's fall from power. Attempts at suppressing the crystal's priceless data had been squashed early on, by Logan's pre-landing release of the recordings over the worldwide net. Even more important, with discussion of secession now no longer at the forefront of political strife, America once again consented to consider the Savior's claims.

Logan, once one to never darken the door of a church, became the center of a dynamic international evangelistic ministry appropriately named 'GOYIM'. His marriage to Rebecca took place only three months after returning from space healing six broken lives as he became husband, daddy and 'master'. A proud and adoring nation attended the wedding.

The medical community was notable for several prominent conversions, the most famous ones being lead investigator Dr. David Livingston and chief medical officer, Dr. Ravi Mahdia. Dr. Livingston authored three journal articles detailing the pre-mission status versus post-mission status of Logan's physical condition. His articles and lectures were alone responsible for the conversion of over one thousand physicians and researchers in the following ten years.

Finally, the transition cylinder, whose contents were freely displayed for the world to review, brought about a worldwide resurgence of the Christian faith not seen since the early church. Commander Jonathan Logan became known to the world as the *'fourteenth apostle'*, arguing strongly for the faith and committing his life to evangelism and international mission work. To this day his ministry maintains and affectionately displays the original tunic worn by Jesus. The ministry's message was simple.

'The One who loves you through your pain, who knows you best, seeks to be with you for eternity'.

The choice is yours. He is, as He has always been, waiting for you to come home.

Epi-Prologue

A dear and trusted friend suggested the novel approach of placing this prologue at the end of the book, so as not to bias the reader.

I thank you Kirk for this advice as for the dozens of other words of wisdom you have poured into Goyim. May you receive a jewel for your crown.

The writing of Goyim has been one of the most enjoyable activities of my life. Combining my Christian faith with my love for science and apologetics has been a perfect exercise for venting the desires of my soul. Of course, overarching this exercise is the goal of glorifying God and lifting up "the young Prince of this Universe" for all to see. His word promises us that if He be lifted up He will draw all men and this is GOYIM's underlying current.

To accomplish my goal, I have admittedly taken some liberties with my story. Suffice it to say that I, above all others, am the first to proclaim that this work is first and foremost a work of fiction inspired by fact. That our Lord's word is inerrant, to a true believer, goes without saying. That it is fact, should be, but will obviously will not by all be embraced.

GOYIM seeks to engage the reader's imagination in the realm of filling in the missing details and wondering what Jesus of Nazareth was really like. Scripture plainly says that if all His works were made known, the details would not be able to be contained. With this in mind, let the reader always remember that scripture takes precedence over any interpretative work, not the least this one.

Included within the story line is the struggle of one man's coming to faith and his encounter with many of the strongholds and obstacles the enemy puts in the way. To have woven apologetics within the text was my only defense against these attacks, and thus I have leaned heavily upon the writings and teachings of such historical greats as Augustine, Aquinas, G.K. Chesterton and C.S. Lewis. Contemporary thinkers such as Ravi Zacharias, Michael Ramsden, William Lane Craig and Steve Brown have also contributed. I am greatly indebted to these stalwarts of the faith.

In regard to potential critics who might accuse me of advocating violence or a successionist philosophy, let me take this opportunity to refute such a ridiculous claim. Christianity teaches a belief in peaceful resolution of conflict at all costs. Jesus instructed us to go to our enemy and try to resolve conflict. We might have a sword to defend our families, but not an armory. Logan fights to defend the innocent and save humanity, not the other way around.

Finally, as to strongholds, I have included pages from my own spiritual pilgrimage and lessons from the fiery trials of my own stubborn rebelliousness. In it all, the Lover of my soul has been faithfully at my side guiding me, demonstrating His steadfast love. Sometimes gently and sometimes forcefully, He has been completing his work in me and countless others, making tender this stony heart. He wishes to do the same for you.

Resources to help you on your way:

1) Answers to difficult questions concerning does God exist and the problem of evil

William lane Craig, PhD https://www.reasonablefaith.org/

https://www.reasonablefaith.org/writings/question-answer/submit-question#faqs

2) Answers to cultural issues and man's moral responsibility to man

Ravi Zacharias https://www.rzim.org/listen/ask-away

https://www.rzim.org/listen/vital-signs

3) Answers to families that are hurting and in crisis

James Dobson https://www.drjamesdobson.org/home-2

4) Answers to those hurting and seeking answers from God

Charles Stanley https://www.intouch.org/watch

Steve brown https://www.keylife.org/

Tony Evans https://tonyevans.org/

5) Answers to families in Financial crisis

Dave Ramsey https://www.daveramsey.com/

6) Scientific answers to beginning of the Universe

Hugh Ross https://www.reasons.org/home

Ken Hamm https://answersingenesis.org/

7) Authors to read

Jesus Christ The Gospel of John

Augustine Confessions

CS Lewis, GK Chesterton, Lee Strobel, Timothy Keller, all the above authors and their staff

69727688R00217

Made in the USA
Columbia, SC
17 August 2019